SNAKE-BITE

ROBERT HICHENS

SNAKE-BITE

AND OTHER STORIES

BY

ROBERT HICHENS

AUTHOR OF "THE GREEN CARNATION," "THE GARDEN
OF ALLAH," "BELLA DONNA," "THE CALL
OF THE BLOOD," ETC.

NEW YORK

GEORGE H. DORAN COMPANY

CONTENTS

♥

SNAKE-BITE
AND OTHER STORIES

ONE: SNAKE-BITE

I

THE SPIRIT OF ADVENTURE

In the market place of Beni Mora rumour was busy with the name of the American, Horace Pierpont, who had already been staying for six weeks at the Hotel Excelsior. Mr. Pierpont was unmarried, enormously rich, and neither young nor old. He looked a man of about forty, was lean, strong, tall, and very striking in appearance. Some people thought him remarkably handsome; others considered him almost ugly. But there was no one who overlooked him, who forgot to see him when he was present.

His face was long, clean-shaven, with powerful features. The nose was hooked and arbitrary, the chin prominent and determined, the mouth very mobile and well-shaped, neither large nor small. The eyes were narrow, steady and fearless, in colour grey; often they seemed to be full of a delicate and almost lazy irony under the thin sweep of mouse-coloured brows. Pierpont's hands and feet were large and strong. He was a bony man with a great frame. He looked like a careless aristocrat, who had seen the world and men, who had sat at many feasts and known many experiences, and who was gifted with a keen, though never boisterous, sense of humour, and with an unfailing self-possession.

9

Pierpont's hugeness half frightened, half disgusted some people. Others were impressed and attracted by it. These called him "a glorious-looking man." The Arabs of Beni Mora admired him, and thought him one of the most kingly travellers who had ever penetrated to their oasis. They respected him, too, because he had an immense fortune.

This fortune had not been gained for himself by Pierpont. He was no hustling captain of industry, and he knew very little of Wall Street. His father, now dead, Carrington Pierpont, had bequeathed to him his millions, and he had never worked hard for a living. For a few years he had been in the diplomatic service, and had lived in Paris, London, Rome, and Madrid. Then he had retired and had travelled widely. He had a taste for ornithology, was an intellectual man, an unwearied student of his kind, and a good, though not untiring, sportsman.

Certainly he enjoyed life. By nature he was, or believed himself to be, exceptionally independent. He liked travelling alone, and had seldom, if ever, felt the need of a "circle" or of a "home."

This was his second visit to Beni Mora.

During his first visit, a couple of years ago, he had lounged in the sun, had read books in the Count's garden, had ridden on horseback to the various oases of the Zibans, and had studied Arabic in a mild way with Ali ben Hilmi, who read aloud in one òf the cafés every evening to a serious crowd of dark-eyed listeners squatting pell-mell upon the floor.

But this time it seemed he had a very special purpose in visiting Beni Mora, and it was this supposed purpose of his which was now being discussed throughout the village wherever the Arabs congregated together. In Beni Mora, now attached to the Bureau Arabe, there was an Arab called Saad ben Youssef. He was *un homme sérieux*, reputed extraordinarily honest and faithful, a man of his word, and diligent in any task to which he put his hand. And he had given his proofs several years ago in a very great undertaking.

A small party of Americans, four in number, had come out to Algeria to undertake a tremendous pilgrimage. They were resolved to travel by caravan from Beni Mora to Tombouctou. Well, they had carried out their project, and Saad ben Youssef had been in charge of the caravan. He alone of the Arabs in Beni Mora had travelled the whole distance. For three times on the way the caravan had been changed, and new men and fresh animals had been requisitioned. So Saad ben Youssef was noted in Beni Mora as a man who had seen great wonders, who had traversed the whole region of the Touaregs, and who had received a large sum of money from the Roumis, whom he had efficiently aided in the carrying out of a remarkable enterprise. In the bazaars many and many a time had he related the marvels of that prodigious journey, told of the land of the ostriches, of the wild beasts which abound near Tombouctou, and of moonlit evenings about the Touaregs when the unveiled women of that strange and almost legendary tribe assembled about the tents to make sweet music for the travellers, while the men, shrouded in their veils, remained at a little distance, watchful, enigmatic, their weapons in their hands.

Of late Horace Pierpont had been seen continually in the company of Saad ben Youssef. The owner of the Excelsior Hotel, a French doctor, had sent one day to the Bureau Arabe asking the Arab to come that evening to the hotel to make acquaintance with the millionaire. Saad had obeyed the summons, and, since then, he had been with Mr. Pierpont every evening after his work at the Bureau Arabe was finished. They had strolled together, had sat in the garden of the Gazelles together, had taken coffee and played dominoes together in the street of the dancers. What did it all mean? Saad as yet had said nothing, but every Arab in Beni Mora had made up his mind on the matter. The American millionaire

was going to make the journey from Beni Mora to Tombouctou, and Saad ben Youssef was once more in luck.
Again would he see the marvels of that prodigious journey. Again would gold pour through his fingers, or stay
deliciously in his big brown palms. All the greedy and
the adventurous had clustered about Saad with eager
smiles and parasitic gestures. But hitherto Saad ben
Youssef had been mum. He knew how to keep his
counsel and was a master of long unsmiling silences.

It was a hot and cloudless day, and Fay Mortimer had
gone out with Ali, the small boy, half Arab, half negro,
who had become her devoted attendant, to sit under a
group of three palm trees by a rivulet of water at the
edge of the oasis. She had with her in a hanging bag a
bit of embroidery, a book, and two packs of cards. Sometimes, especially when her mind was disquieted, she
soothed herself—or strove to believe that she soothed
herself—with a game of "patience." Her husband,
young Doctor Mortimer, had gone out with Dr.
Bucheron, their host of the Hotel Excelsior, to visit in
consultation a French officer of Spahis at the barracks,
who was dangerously ill with a fever caught in the ex-
treme South of Algeria, whither he had recently been
on some mission. All the morning was Fay's to do what
she liked with. But this was no completely novel experience. For the Mortimers had already been in Beni
Mora for nearly two months.

Nevertheless, Fay had not yet become thoroughly accustomed to the startingly new life into which she and her
husband had recently been thrust. That was the word
she used in speaking to herself of this desert life. They
had by marvellous circumstances been "thrust" into it,
she and Alan.

Three months ago they had been living in Margate,
and she had never travelled farther than Paris and Zermatt. She had been partly educated in Paris, and had
been to Zermatt for her honeymoon. That had been

when she was only nineteen. Now she was nearly twenty-two.

She hadn't at all revelled in the life at Margate. In fact, she had disliked part of it very much indeed, though she had honestly made the best of things for Alan's sake. It was not his fault that he wasn't rich enough to put a plate with his name on a door in Harley Street, or Queen Anne Street in London, and to sit down and to wait for patients. Fay's father had stuck to his word. He had told her that if she married in a hurry a penniless young doctor he would not give her any allowance. Swept on the waves of tempestuous emotion she had done just what he had wished her not to do. Sir Henry Kennion was very well off, but, unfortunately, he practically always meant what he said. So she, Fay, had had to put up with Margate, in which town of fine airs and graceless trippers her husband had picked up a practice cheap.

A cheap practice in Margate, and now here she was in Beni Mora!

Alan had caught a severe chill one bitter night when he had been called out to visit a patient. Bad symptoms had declared themselves. A winter abroad had been urgently advised. They had thought about a locum tenens in Margate and Davos for themselves. And then, out of the blue, the Beni Mora temptation had come to them. Quite by chance—if there be such a thing as chance—Alan had been called to the Cliftonville Hotel to see Monsieur Maurice Darbley, who had an interest in one of the great London hotels and who "ran" the Imperial Hotel at Beni Mora during the winter season. They had become good friends, and Monsieur Darbley, hearing of the young doctor's misfortune, had offered to lodge him and his wife rent free, and to give them their pension at the Imperial during the winter, on condition that he was allowed to advertise "a resident English doctor" as attached to his hotel for the season. Alan Mortimer had jumped at the opportunity. So now Fay

was sitting under the three palm trees at the edge of
the oasis. In a couple of weeks the big hotel would be
opened. Meanwhile she and Alan were at the small
and quiet Excelsior having a holiday. Certainly just
now Alan was away at a consultation. But that was a
rare event out here.

When she had quarrelled with her father about Alan
he had said something to her which she had not been
able to forget. He had said, "Fay, you don't know your
own mind yet, and you don't understand your own heart.
You are a bit of a volcano. You think young Mortimer
is the only man in the world for you. That's great
nonsense. You've been in love before, and, if I know
anything of you, you'll be in love again. If you were
thirty instead of only nineteen, I might consent. For
life isn't merely a question of money or of the position
one holds in the world. But you are betrayed by a
surface emotion, and you think that your deeps are
calling. Wait!"

And, of course, being a bit of a volcano, she hadn't
waited.

She recalled those words of her father now as she
looked out over the sunlit waste and listened to the song
of the water behind her. Had he been right?

She had certainly been what is called "in love" more
than once before she had met Alan, in love sufficiently
to feel desperate, to lie awake in the night, to weep and
to long. And—since she had met Alan? Why did such
an abominable question come to her? It had only come
to her quite lately, never at Margate in spite of the cold
winds, the asphalt promenade, their very banal house in
Cliftonville, and the extraordinary trippers, who bur-
rowed into the sand even when they were dresssed in
black cotton velvet and bugles, and who lay on their
backs before the whole world presenting their greasy and
shining faces, open-mouthed, to the astonished heavens.

Little Ali was squatting at a short distance from her
in the eye of the sun, staring under his tarbush, with his

naked feet sticking out on either side of him, and his almost black hands, with much lighter-coloured palms, resting on the warm earth. For a moment she envied him. Then she opened her bag and took out the cards. A "patience" might possibly soothe her.

Slowly she began to lay out the cards in lines on the hard ground, bending her lovely little head and puckering her white forehead. Three knaves in a row and then seven spades in succession. How oddly the cards were coming out!

Little Ali cleared his throat noisily, and then did something which Fay particularly disliked. She looked up from her game, and was just going to rebuke him gently, when something made her forget all about Ali and his unfortunate lapse.

At perhaps a hundred yards from her she saw two figures moving slowly over the brown bareness which edged the stones of the dry river bed, dividing it from the first palm trees of the oasis. One was a huge, gaunt man clad in white drill and wearing a Panama hat, the other an almost equally tall Arab in turban and burnous. Thin smoke wreaths curled about them. So still was the atmosphere and so clear that Fay could see, even from that distance, the delicate spirals against the glitter. She flushed slightly as she recognised Horace Pierpont. The other she did not recognise, but Ali was quick to inform her.

"L'Américain avec Saad," he remarked, in his thick childish voice.

"Saad ben Youssef?" inquired Fay.

Ali nodded his head, and the tassel on his tarbush sprang to and fro. Again he cleared his throat.

"Ali!" cried Fay imperatively, holding up her right hand and fixing her large golden brown eyes on him. Ali twisted his broad negroid nose, and with difficulty refrained. But though he refrained he was moved to a demonstration of some sort, and unexpectedly he uttered a loud cry, which startled Fay and caused the two figures at the edge of the desert to pause and turn round.

"You—i—you!" yelled Ali again, pleased with the success of his effort.

"Ali, be quiet!" exclaimed Fay, almost angrily. "How dare you make such a noise?"

"*V'la ton ami qui vient!*" returned Ali, smiling.

The huge figure in white drill, with a loose-jointed nonchalant gait, was advancing towards them accompanied by the Arab.

Fay reddened again.

"Ali, I'm very angry with you," she said. "If you can't behave yourself I shall have to get another little servant."

"*V'la ton ami!*" repeated Ali, quite undisturbed, and now smiling from ear to ear.

"Hallo, Mrs. Mortimer, playing patience! How delightfully idle of you. May I join you?"

The rather harsh and grating but very individual voice, which seemed somehow to belong inevitably to the big-boned, lean body that stood before her, dropped down to Fay as she looked up very gravely.

"Ali's manners are abominable."

"I'm thankful they are. *Allez!*"

A flung coin accompanied the command. Ali leaped, grasped, looked into Horace Pierpont's eyes, and went off towards the negro village.

"You know Saad ben Youssef?"

"*Bon jour,* Saad."

"*Bon jour,* madame," returned Saad in a grave, deep voice, which sounded lazily sad.

He lit a cigarette, his long hands with henna-tinted nails moving with a delicate precision. Then he walked a short distance, sat down beside the stream and gazed tranquilly towards the Aures mountains.

Pierpont stretched his great length on the ground by Fay's side and looked at her with steady eyes from under the shade of his tilted hat.

"I wanted to get you alone," he said.

"Why?" asked Fay, banishing curiosity from her face and voice.

"I've got something in my mind. It has to do with your husband. If I presently speak to him about it, and he comes to tell you, you will not let him know I mentioned it first to you?"

He was always looking straight at her with his narrow, very intelligent grey eyes.

"Why should you tell me first?"

"I wish to."

"I suppose there would be no harm in my——"

"Oh, not the least in the world."

"Very well," said Fay.

She believed that she had meant to say something quite different. But the two words just happened out of her mouth.

"Of course I know Mortimer is out here because of his health. But physically he's strong, isn't he?"

"Oh, yes. But his chest was affected. It's only a question of a few months in the right climate. At least that's what the doctors say."

"Exactly. And in the right climate he could do what most men could do."

"What do you want him to do?" asked Fay, with sudden energy.

With a long sweep of one great arm Pierpont indicated the desert.

"Look at that motionless sea. I'm going to set sail upon it, to take ship, and go out on a long voyage. Do you know where Saad has been?"

The sensitive blood rushed to Fay's temples. A strange song seemed to drum in her ears, barbaric, provocative and tremendous. Suddenly she felt violently excited and desolate; she knew.

"You are going to make the journey to Tombouctou," she said.

"I am."

"And——" She was silent, staring at him.

"Why not dare to say it?"

"You want my husband to go with you?"

"Women understand everything," he returned quietly. "Saad reckons the journey at four months and a half to five months, by camel of course. The camel is the only ship for that sea."

Again he waved his long arm.

"When he covered the route before not a soul was ill from start to finish—really ill. Now and then there was a touch of something, as there is everywhere, in Margate —anywhere."

Margate!

Fay was inundated by a flood of jealousy, jealousy of men. Margate for women and the journey to Tombouctou for men! The scales were too uneven. She felt almost in a passion and she wanted to cry angrily. So she sat very still and said in a cold voice:

"Alan is pledged to Monsieur Darbley for the winter."

"And if I can settle things with Darbley? D'you think your husband would come? The fact is I want a doctor with me. It's safer. I'm fond of life. I haven't the slightest desire to go before my time. And there are moments when a doctor, a skilled surgeon as Mortimer is, comes in very handy."

Fay looked into Pierpont's long, irregular face, and though she did not know it, her eyes flashed anger at him.

"Even if you arranged with Monsieur Darbley I don't see how Alan could go," she said.

"Why not?" said Pierpont, knocking out his pipe.

How she hated him at that moment!

"Well, Alan is stupid enough to be rather fond of me."

And her lips trembled in spite of herself.

"What has that to do with it?"

"What has——" she paused. "What do you mean?" she said, in a different voice.

"Would you be afraid of the journey?"

"You—you meant—you wish me to go too?"

He said nothing, but looked at her steadily. She felt that she became suddenly white.

'I—I didn't understand," she murmured, and there was a helpless note in her voice.

"But now you understand why I spoke to you first," he said, pressing some tobacco into the red-brown bowl of his pipe. "If you say you'll come J'll ask Mortimer. If you don't I shall probably not feel justified in asking him. It would perhaps be hardly fair to you."

Fay said nothing, and looked out over the desert. Her face was still very white. . . .

That evening the Mortimers and Horace Pierpont dined at the same small table in the *salle-à-manger* of the Excelsior Hotel. They had fallen into the habit of dining together since they had come to know each other casually as fellow-guests in the pleasant white guest-house which stood facing due south. Pierpont was a sociable man and delighted in good talk, and he had evidently taken a fancy to the young doctor, and enjoyed discussion with him. So they "pooled" the table, and Pierpont was not bored with his own company.

When that evening's dinner was over Pierpont asked Mortimer to stroll with him to the street of the dancers.

"Of course," said Alan, in his quick, warm tenor voice, which nearly always sounded eager and vital. "Shall I run up and get you a wrap, Fay?"

"No; I think I'll stay at home. I've got an interesting book by Metchnikoff. You'll find me on the balcony of our room when you come in. Good night, Mr. Pierpont."

That evening Pierpont did an unusual thing. In returning her good night he held out his big hand with long fingers and enormous prominent knuckles. After an instant's hesitation Fay put her hand in it, and when he pressed her hand she felt like something being swallowed.

She ran up to her room, and from the balcony saw

the two men walk slowly away down the white garden
road between the dwarf palms and mimosa trees. A
yellow dog of nondescript breed cheerfully accompanied
them. Alan was quite a good height, over five feet ten,
and well built, but she noticed that he looked a small
man beside Horace Pierpont. Was not such bigness
really almost a sort of deformity? It seemed to Fay
that she strove to think so, but failed. The physical
bigness of the American really exercised upon her imagination a sort of almost overpowering fascination.
She did not know exactly why. His fortune was vast.
So everyone said. And he was about to go upon a vast
journey through the vastness of the desert. The man
himself, that is the soul of him, must surely be tremendous, too, compared with the average soul of man. Was
not its bulk shadowed forth to her, and to others, by his
careless and unfailing self-possession? Never, even for
a moment, did he give the impression that he was sensitive to opinion, sensitive, that is, in the sense of shrinking ever so slightly from an opinion that might be ad-
verse, even hostile, to him. Never did he seem to be
on the defensive. Since she had known him, Fay had
become acutely aware how often most people are secretly
or openly on the defensive.

He was surely a big man.

And now he was going to tell Alan what he had told
her by the stream in the morning.

In the white-walled, rather bare, and exquisitely clean
bedroom which she shared with Alan there were two
small beds, side by side, each enclosed by its mosquito-
net. A balcony, just big enough for two, projected beyond the French window above the paved terrace below. Fay wound a gauzy white wisp of a thing round
her long white neck, which somebody (of course a man)
had once said was like the throat of a deer, put the lamp
on the table behind her long straw chair, lay down on it,
pushed up a big pink cushion to the level of her golden-
brown head and opened the Metchnikoff book.

But she did not read one word of it. She was in the street of the dancers assisting at a debate. What issues hung on it! And yet—did they? Were not all the issues in her own hands? She was absurd enough to look down at her narrow, long-fingered hands. The wedding ring and the emerald ring Alan had given her glittered now as she held up her left hand. If she had obeyed her father's advice they wouldn't be there. And where would she have been now if a certain native obstinacy had not formed part of what Americans would call her "make-up"?

What stars they were! And how the dogs were barking! It was surely a night for the deciding of a fate, ominous with prophecy.

She lay very still, and she was conscious that her nerves gnawed at her, as they had gnawed at her when, as a child, she had waited to be called in to the ugly room of the dentist. She wished she could rush upon her fate. Lying there under the stars, and hearing the dogs bark on the house-tops and by the tents of the Nomads, was almost intolerable. Yet she did not move.

About half-past ten she heard steps, and then sounds of voices.

A quick tenor voice spoke at some length; then a rather harsh, rugged voice briefly replied.

Fay quickly slipped sideways out of her chair and into the bedroom.

A minute later the door opened and Alan came in, looking excited, his honest, intelligent and very clear hazel eyes shining, and his chestnut hair rather disordered by the cap he had just pulled off.

"Oh, Fay, not gone to bed yet! That's right. Why not come down for a minute?"

"Down! To the terrace, d'you mean?"

"Yes."

"But I've said good night——"

"To Pierpont—never mind. We've got an Arab with

us, Saad ben Youssef. I think you'd like him. He's an extraordinarily interesting fellow."

"Very well, I'll—no, it's late. I think I won't."

He held the door open, looking at her.

"No, really, I think I won't."

And with resolution she unwound the scarf from her throat.

"I've seen Saad already," she added.

"I know. But I should like you to hear him talk."

"It's—it's really too late."

And turning her back she went towards the wardrobe.

"All right. I'll tell Pierpont, and be with you directly."

The door shut and she heard him in the uncarpeted passage hurrying away. She began to undress with a sort of trembling deliberation. She laid her white gown away in a trunk carefully. Then she looked in the glass. She saw a slim, girlish figure, very delicate in line. The arms were thin, and the skin which covered them had a polished and almost transparent look. The waist was naturally small and the bust but slightly rounded. The hips were narrow and the limbs were long in proportion to the body. In the face, with its small features, straight, short nose, curved lips and little determined chin, there was a kind of pale expectancy. It was the sort of intensely feminine face which makes very male men feel the glory of the contrast between the sexes and understand their manhood. It seemed to ask instinctively without knowing that it asked, and half-broodingly to dream over its own tenuous mystery. Perhaps the volcano was asleep.

Steps sounded again in the passage, and Fay turned round as Alan came in.

"Saad has gone," he exclaimed.

His voice was rather louder than usual. He threw down his cap on the chest of drawers, where some flowers stood in the midst of books.

"Oh, are you beginning to go to bed already?"

"Do you want to talk?"

She slipped on a white dressing-gown.

"Fay, you always look delicate, but you are strong, aren't you?"

"Yes; stronger than you are now."

"This out-of-door life is doing wonders for me, and the air. D'you know what I believe I need to get absolutely well?"

"What?"

"Just to rough it, and keep nearly always out of doors; in this climate, of course."

She pushed the mosquito-curtain and sat down on the edge of her bed.

"I don't know about the roughing it," she murmured, looking down.

"I do. I say, will you hate it if I smoke? The window's wide open."

"No; do smoke."

He lit a cigar which Pierpont had just given him, sat down by the window, leaned an arm on the table by the lamp, and looked at his wife with a sort of intensely eager and searching scrutiny, which was totally unsuspicious.

"I wonder if you have the spirit of adventure in you, Fay."

"What has made you think about such a thing?"

"I wonder whether you ever long to have some extraordinary experience, to get right out of the ordinary, to keep out of it, to forget it."

"When it rained at Margate, Alan, really sometimes I did."

"You darling!" he said, in a different voice.

He moved, as if about to come to her, then stopped with the exclamation:

"Oh, my smoke!"

"Well?" said Fay.

"Now don't be frightened; I've had a most startling proposition made to me to-night by Pierpont."

"Mr. Pierpont! What does he want?"

"He's going to do a tremendously interesting thing. He's going to travel through the desert from here to——" Alan paused.

"Where?" asked Fay. "To Tunis."

"Tunis!" Alan laughed and jerked up his head.

"Why do you laugh?"

"It sounds so absurdly near, like going from Margate to Birchington. No; Pierpont is going on camel back to Timbuctoo, or as they call it here, Tombouctou."

"Good gracious!" said Fay.

She moved from the bed, letting the net slip softly, and sat down on a chair.

"Not ordinary, is it?"

"No, but Mr. Pierpont isn't ordinary."

"You like him, don't you?"

"Oh, yes. He's interesting and very agreeable."

"Powerful too—somehow."

"Is he?"

"I seem to feel that he is."

"Perhaps. Well, and what is his proposition?"

"Don't scream! It's simply this. He wants a doctor to go with him, and he's asked me."

"You!"

"Me."

"To go to Tombouctou!"

"Yes."

"But you have promised Monsieur Darbley."

"Of course I should have to get him to let me off—if I went."

"And if he refused to release you?"

"I wouldn't go then, though I've no contract. I'll deal squarely with him, of course."

"Then you do want to go?"

"Pierpont offers me all expenses till I get back to England, and a thousand pounds every six months I'm with him. The trip would probably last six to eight months, or so."

Fay sat looking down. Then, still looking down, she said:

"And what should I do all the time you were away?"

"Now for it!" said Alan, getting up.

Fay glanced at him across the table, and saw that the excitement in his eyes had become stronger. They had shone. Now· they burned. By that she realised how much he wanted to go.

"Of course I could never leave you for six months. You must know that."

"Then what is the good of talking about Tombouctou?"

"Couldn't you brace yourself, steel yourself, call up the spirit of adventure in yourself, and say you'd come too?"

"My dear Alan!"

She, too, got up. She was feeling horribly insincere and hated herself—in a way. But about her, as if in the air, she felt Pierpont, felt as if he were directing her, impelling her. And that seemed partially to excuse her to herself.

·'My dear Alan!" she repeated. "How could a woman do such a thing?"

"Isabella Bird——" he began.

And he spoke of famous women travellers, quoted Mary Kingsley and others, then broke into a laugh as he looked at the slim form in the white robe on the other side of the table.

"They weren't like you," he had to confess. Then he added:

"But they didn't have two men to look after them all the time, as you would have. And Saad too! Saad is going to manage the whole thing. That's why I wanted you to have a talk with him. I thought he would impress you."

"But Mr. Pierpont! He—he can't really be willing to saddle himself with a woman on such a journey."

There was now a faint red in her cheeks.

"He'd—surely he'd get utterly sick of it?"

"He says not. You see, he's rich enough to do the whole thing as well as it can be done. Now let me just tell you!"

He came round the table, forgetting his "smoke," sat in the armchair, and made Fay sit on his knee, holding her round the waist. Then he talked—talked till the night grew late. And Fay listened with the faint red still in her cheeks, and carried on simultaneously an intensely active life in her brain which her husband knew nothing of.

"I must sleep on it," she said at last. "It's the most extraordinary proposition I ever heard of. No doubt it would be wonderfully interesting, an experience never to be forgotten. It would almost make me famous, wouldn't it?"

"I should think so! The girl who'd travelled from Beni Mora on a camel to Tombouctou!"

"Let me go, Alan. Don't talk to me any more."

He let her go. Presently she slipped under the mosquito-curtain without bidding him good-night. And then till morning she—lay awake on it. She had, in a way, promised Pierpont by the stream that she would go if Alan consented. When Pierpont was actually beside her it had seemed impossible to do otherwise. But now he was not beside her. And since Alan knew things seemed different.

A thousand pounds every six months.

Her cheeks burned in the dark. What was Pierpont really? What was he to himself? She didn't know. He was to her an enigma. Women don't always know what men are. Fay didn't know what Pierpont was. But one thing about him she did know. He had within him the spirit of adventure. It was not his project of travelling by camel to Tombouctou that proved this to Fay; it was his invitation to—well, to a doctor to go with him.

* * * * * *

"If the idea worries you, Fay, of course we'll give it up," said Alan, three days later.

Fay was looking worried. She was pale, and had sleepless eyes with a very faint blueness beneath them. She was restless, and even a little irritable, and seemed unable to settle to anything. And she had come to no decision about the great matter, or, if indeed she had, had said nothing about it.

"I suppose we must decide one way or the other," she said, rather crossly.

"Yes; I really think I must give Pierpont a definite answer. And Darbley arrives by the train from Constantine this afternoon. I'm going to meet him at half-past two."

"I'll tell you to-morrow morning."

As she said the words Pierpont came round the corner into the small oval space surrounded by trees where they were sitting in the Count's garden.

"Will you ride with me at two to-day? It isn't very hot, and I've got hold of a horse that's a weight-carrier."

With a quiet smile he glanced down at himself.

"To-day? I was just saying to Fay that I'd promised to meet Darbley at the station," said Alan.

"A pity! Will you come, Mrs. Mortimer?"

Fay looked at him and knew he had overheard her last words. She opened her lips to say some polite form of "No," and said:

"Yes, if you like, and if I can get that grey mare from Coreau's stables."

"I'll see to that," said Pierpont. "I'll go about it now." And his giant form disappeared among the trees.

"We must give him his answer to-morrow," said Alan, passing a brown hand over his chestnut hair and lifting his eyebrows rather anxiously.

Fay did not tell him that she knew Pierpont meant to have it that day.

Pierpont got the grey mare from Coreau's, and they rode into the desert, going out through the village towards the north-west.

"We'll leave the dunes on our right," said Pierpont,

"and get a fine gallop over the great flats between them and the road to Amara. And we'll come home by Sidi Zerzour."

He did not ask Fay if she was up to such a long ride. He knew she was a good horsewoman and wiry in the saddle. She glanced at him half submissively, half with defiance as he finished. Her lips were mutinous, and her lower jaw and chin obstinate. But her eyes—were they not the eyes of a slave? And her figure in its thinness looked almost fluid.

They came to the dunes. On the left were the shining flats. Here and there, far off, the dull green stain of a distant oasis showed on the tawny waste. The horizon was lost in a dream of indigo blue more wonderful than the indigo blue of a tropical sea. An eagle hung in the near lighter blue above their heads. A little wind came and went, savouring its freedom and telling them with its whispering voices tales of the magic of emptiness.

Pierpont had chosen well the place for her decision.

"To the left!" he said, in his harsh voice, pressing his knee against his horse's flank. "Good-bye to the dunes."

He looked at Fay and they were off, and the little wind with them, whispering more loudly as they raced towards the dull green stains that were palms, and the indigo blue that was the call to women and men to go onward.

"Now, after that, can you hesitate?"

They were beyond the track to Amara, and the ground was broken and tufted with dusty halfa grass. The horses picked their way at a foot's pace.

"I don't mean to go," said Fay, looking at her horse's thin neck.

"Why not?"

"Why do you want us to go? It's a mad idea."

"Mad ideas keep me a live man."

"You would get sick of us. It's just a whim, and you would repent of it."

"Do you really mean that you're afraid you would?"

"I shall not risk that."

"Then I shall ask your husband to come alone with me."

Fay grew scarlet.

"You told me you wouldn't do that."

"You told me you would come if he would."

"I hadn't had time to think over it then. Alan wouldn't go without me."

"He wants terribly to go. I must have a doctor. I know he is poor. I would offer him great bribes. I would fight hard against your influence. And I generally get my way—even with men."

"Why is that?" she said, with a sort of sombre bitterness.

"My intentions are very strong, stronger even than my limbs."

She glanced at his great frame and thought of centaurs.

"Alan wouldn't leave me," she said.

"Very well; we'll fight it out."

A slow defiance of this man smouldered within her. Yet she felt doubtful of her own powers. Suppose he did prevail upon Alan to go without her? How much did Alan love her? Till this moment she had never bothered about that question. She had assumed that Alan would sacrifice anything for her sake.

"I don't know why you are so determined to take Alan," she said. "You could easily get a French doctor to go with you. Most people would jump at such an offer."

"But you don't."

"I'm not a man."

Pierpont pulled up his horse and turned its head to the south.

"Look!" he said.

Fay turned her horse too.

And they looked out over the desert.

"Are men to have all the adventures?" he said. "Is all the real glory of living to be exclusively theirs? Some women haven't thought that. What about Isabella Eberhardt? You've been reading her books, I know. Haven't they said anything to you? Don't you remember your Kinglake, and the strange lady of the Lebanon? Isn't the spirit of unrest in every human being who's worth anything? I know you better than you know yourself. You are longing to go. If you don't go, all your life you'll regret it. You'll lie awake in the night many a time, and you'll clench your hands and think, 'What a fool I was! I was the greatest of all cowards for I was afraid to be happy. I was afraid to make my life interesting!'"

The harsh voice seemed just then to be telling Fay her own innermost truth, to be prophesying what she knew must inevitably come to pass if——

If!

But there was always her secret obstinacy to be dealt with. And it persisted now. She looked towards the far horizon, she looked towards Tombouctou. But she would not give in.

"We must fight it out," she said. "Now, I'm tired. Let us go home, please."

That evening Alan told her that Monsieur Darbley wouldn't stand in the way of his going.

"He's been awfully decent about it. He says it's the opportunity of a lifetime, and I'm not to think of him at all. So now it depends entirely on you, Fay."

"Alan, I think a woman would be horribly in the way on such an expedition."

"Tell me the truth," he said, looking at her with his eager bright eyes. "Are you afraid to go?"

After a pause she answered:

"Yes, I am."

Alan sat still for a moment staring at her. She saw by his face, and even by his attitude, that he was tremendously disappointed.

"Well, Fay," he said at length, in a voice that was definitely cheerful. "We'll give it up. I expect you are right. It's probably too great an undertaking for a woman."

"Yes," she said faintly.

Alan got up, came to her, and gave her a rather boyish kiss.

"And now——" he said.

"Why, where are you going?"

"I'm going to tell Pierpont. He ought to know at once."

And he went out of the room quickly.

They had been talking in the salon of the hotel. Dinner was just over, and Pierpont had gone off, probably into the garden to smoke. Fay sat alone and looked at the room. Just opposite to her hung on the white wall a marvellous photograph. It showed an ocean of sand waves in the track of a setting sun. On the crest of one wave were the footprints of a camel. Just beyond an Arab, with his face to the sunset, lifted his bronze-coloured arms, from which his white burnous fell back, in a gesture of fanatical worship. Liberty and silence lived in the photograph. Fay looked at it for a long time, and tears came into her eyes. Alan was horribly disappointed, but she felt sure that his disappointment was as nothing compared with hers.

Presently she got up, and went out to the terrace. She had seen from the open French window that no one was there. Pierpont and Alan were fighting it out somewhere else.

She walked slowly up and down for a long time under the stars in the warm night air. What was Pierpont saying to Alan? How would he try to persuade him? And if Alan were to give in—what then? She would certainly say nothing. She would accept the situation and they could go away together. Pierpont would no doubt have punished her. But how about himself? Surely it was not possible that she had misread him, had failed to understand his real desire.

What a long time they were away! She was getting quite weary of walking. The waiter came out and stared.

"Do you want to shut up the house?" she asked him.

"No, madame—no. The gentlemen are still out. I cannot shut up till they come in."

He sighed and went in slowly.

Alan must certainly be arguing the matter. He couldn't have refused point blank in such a way that Pierpont had had to drop the subject. She looked at her watch by a light from a window. It was past eleven.

Just then she heard voices on the high road close to the railing of the garden. Pierpont was speaking. She stood very still by the window. Now she heard Alan. He and Pierpont had stopped and were talking by the garden gate. She wondered why till she was aware of a grave voice interrupting them. Saad ben Youssef was with them. Now she caught the words, *"C'est la saison. On doit partir maintenant."* Then she missed something, and then she heard distinctly "Tombouctou."

They were still talking about that journey; they were even discussing the right moment for departure. Then Pierpont had had the audacity and the cruelty to do what he had threatened to do, and it seemed that actually he had prevailed. It must be so. Otherwise, why should they be with Saad talking about the departure?

"Alan!" Fay called sharply.

To herself her voice sounded horribly loud in the night. But he did not hear it. She waited, and still they were talking by the gate.

"Alan!" she cried out again.

"Fay! Is that you? Where are you?"

"On the terrace. Do come in. It's very late, and they want to shut up the house."

In a moment she heard his step and saw the darkness of his form among the little trees.

"It's not much after eleven," he said, as he came nearer. He ran lightly up the few steps to the terrace. "What's the matter?" he added, as he came up to her.

"Nothing. Why should there be?"

"Your voice sounded so—so unusual."

"I don't know why. Let us go to bed."

"Pierpont's just coming. He's at the gate."

"Surely we needn't wait for him."

With a quick gesture Alan put his hand on her arm.

"Fay, tell me, do you dislike Pierpont?"

"Why should I dislike him? He's quite an agreeable man."

"But you don't like him! Oh—here he is!"

Pierpont sauntered up the narrow road. He was smoking his pipe, and he took off his hat when he saw Fay.

"Still up, Mrs. Mortimer! You're wise. It's divinely beautiful, more beautiful than daytime."

He stepped on to the terrace.

"The waiter doesn't think so," said Fay prosaically.

"The waiter?"

"He wants to shut up."

"I'll send him to bed, and lock up myself."

He called in a loud voice:

"Louis!"

The waiter appeared, looking obsequious in the dim light.

"I'll lock the door. Don't bother to sit up."

"Thank you, sir."

"Here, Louis!"

He gave the man something. Louis looked more obsequious and went in. When he was close to the door he stared at what he held in his hand.

"Good night," said Fay to Pierpont.

"We can't let you go yet."

He drew forward a straw chair.

"Stay another ten minutes."

Fay opened her lips to say no, and sat down in the

chair. Alan and Pierpont sat on a bench which was close against the wall.

"I heard you talking at the gate," Fay said abruptly. "You were still discussing Tombouctou. When do you start, Mr. Pierpont?"

"It ought to be very soon. All the preparations are well forward, including a tent for you."

She grew scarlet in the darkness.

"But we aren't coming. Didn't Alan tell you?"

Alan shifted on the bench, crossed his legs, held his right knee with his clasped hands, and answered for Pierpont.

"I've just been telling Pierpont what you said to-night, Fay."

"Yes," said Pierpont, "and I've just been talking to Saad about the furniture for your tent, Mrs. Mortimer."

There was a sound of humour in his voice, but it was an arbitrary voice. A sudden desire to bring matters to a crisis overcame Fay and she said, with an elaborate carelessness:

"Why don't you go with Mr. Pierpont, Alan? It's a splendid opportunity for you. I can go back to England and stay with father. He's all alone, and he'll be glad to have me."

"But we both want you to come, Fay. We'll take good care of you, never fear. Saad says you will be quite reasonably comfortable and perfectly safe. Of course, if you really hate the idea we'll give it up."

Hate the idea! Fay had great difficulty in keeping back a shriek of laughter which seemed trying to fight its way out between her lips. There was something terribly ironic in being loved so much by a man who knew so little about you. Her conception of her husband's abysmal ignorance made her feel reckless, but Pierpont's narrow grey eyes held her silent.

"Tell your wife what Doctor Bucheron says," Pierpont exclaimed, in a rasping voice.

"Doctor Bucheron! What has he to do with it?"

asked Fay, looking quickly from Pierpont to her husband.

"Now, Pierpont," said Alan, with vexation, "I didn't wish——"

"I think your wife ought to know."

"Tell me, Alan!"

"No, really——"

"Then I will," said Pierpont, leaning forward and thrusting out his chin. "Your husband consulted Bucheron about his health the other day, when I first asked him to come with me. And Bucheron strongly advised it, even urged it."

"Probably Doctor Bucheron doesn't wish to have an English doctor here all the season interfering with his practice."

"Oh, Bucheron makes plenty of money with his hotel. Beni Mora can be very cold in January and February. I'm going south. The open air existence is the ideal existence for your husband just now. We can travel by easy stages. But that sort of life makes everyone hardy. Come now, Mrs. Mortimer, will you set yourself up against a doctor?"

"It seems there's a conspiracy to force me to go to Tombouctou. You will be saying next that if I refuse again I may be the cause of Alan's death."

"Of course I should do very well here for the winter," Alan interposed anxiously. "I never meant you to know about Bucheron."

"But now I do know, and it puts me into an awkward situation."

"I hope so," said Pierpont, with smiling malice.

Fay got up from her straw chair.

"Do you absolutely refuse to go without me, Alan?" she asked, standing in front of the bench and looking down at him.

She noted an instant—only an instant—of hesitation before he answered.

"Of course I do."

He got up with Pierpont.

"Either you go or the thing's given up, Fay."

"Very well. We won't argue any more about it."

She paused, keeping them on the sharp edge of expectation; then coldly and decisively she added:

"I will go with you. I will go to Tombouctou."

"But, Fay——"

"Don't say another word, Alan! I am going. Understand that! I have made up my mind. The matter's settled. No doubt it is written in the stars."

An almost fanatical look came into her face.

"You think," she said, gazing at Pierpont, "that you have managed the whole thing. And I dare say Alan supposes that a sense of wifely duty has driven me into submission. But you are both wrong. I have always wanted to go."

"Fay!" exclaimed her husband.

She turned on him almost fiercely.

"Who wouldn't want to make such a wonderful journey? Why the mere thought of it sets my blood on fire!"

"But then why on earth——"

"Do we always think we ought to do what we want most to do?"

"But when we both——"

A contemptuous smile curved her lips for a moment.

"Perhaps I thought I should be a burden on the way," she interrupted. "Perhaps I thought you'd both end in secretly cursing me for being with you. Yes, yes, you might—you may! But now I don't mind whether I'm a burden or not. I've given in to you both. Take care I don't rule you with a rod of iron when I have you both at my mercy in the desert. Take care!"

She began to laugh, but there was something almost sinister in the sound of her low laughter.

"Good night, Mr. Pierpont," she added, suddenly checking herself, and looking at him with deep, almost threatening gravity. "I may as well let you know something about women."

"What is it?" he asked, returning her look steadily.

"They are never more dangerous than in the moment of giving in. A prudent man doesn't force things on a woman."

She turned, walked quickly down the terrace and disappeared into the house.

"We shall have our work cut out for us, Mortimer!" said Pierpont, with a laugh.

"Oh, of course, she was only joking," returned Alan, rather uncomfortably. "Anyhow, I'm glad she really wants to go."

"She's a woman of spirit. I always knew that."

"Well, if she is she'll have plenty of chances for showing it on the journey, I expect."

"No doubt."

"Good night, Pierpont."

"Good night."

Directly Alan came into their bedroom that night Fay said:

"Alan, I wish you to tell me something."

"Of course, I will. What is it, darling?"

"Did Mr. Pierpont try to persuade you to leave me here and go with him alone to Tombouctou after you had told him I didn't mean to go?"

"Yes, he did, but only when I said you were afraid to go."

"Afraid! You told him I was afraid?"

"I repeated just what you said to me. There was no harm in it. Any woman on earth——"

"Perhaps. But there's one woman who is not afraid of anything. And I'm that woman."

"I'm sure Pierpont must understand that now. Fay, tell me, do you secretly dislike Pierpont?"

"What makes you think so?"

"Was that your real reason for refusing to come at first?"

"I don't actually dislike him. No. But, perhaps because he's so rich, he is inclined to suppose that he must always have exactly what he wants. I resent that."

"I don't think he means to——"

"Did he try to bribe you to-night to go with him?"

Alan looked uncomfortable.

"Bribe is hardly the word."

"Use another then. Did he offer you money?"

"He said he must take a doctor with him, that he'd far rather have me than anyone else, that money was no difficulty, and that I could name my own terms."

"And you? What did you say?"

"That it wasn't a question of money, but of your feelings about the matter."

"But you could have gone without me."

"Oh, no."

She remembered that instant of hesitation on his part.

"Alan," she said, coming close to him, and holding his two arms with her long-fingered hands, "do you love me very much?"

"Don't you know it?"

She looked into his eyes with a piercing intentness.

"Some women need a great deal of love, more love than the average woman needs. I do. I wonder how much love you have to give me. Some men have more than others. Some men have a great store. They are the dangerous men to women like me."

There was something sombre in her voice, something almost menacing in her eyes. Her hands were still on his arms when he put them round her.

"I don't know exactly what my love-capacity is, you strange girl. But you would know if——" he paused, staring into her face.

"If what?"

"If a great test came."

"What sort of test?"

"Haven't you enough imagination to think of one for yourself?"

"Have you?"

"Yes. For instance, if you were very ill, if you were dying, you would know how much I loved you."

She slipped out of his arms.

"You have a professional imagination," she said, as she went towards the dressing-table.

Putting up her hands she began to take the earrings out of her ears.

"When shall we be able to start?" she asked.

"Very soon, I believe. Oh, Fay, I'm so thankful you've consented to come."

"Are you?"

"It's an opportunity in a thousand."

"Yes, it is that."

"And if you have the spirit of adventure——"

"I think I have a good deal more of that spirit than you have."

Again there was an almost menacing look in her eyes as they regarded him in the mirror.

"Perhaps. But, anyhow, I have enough to feel most awfully keen and excited about the journey. I shan't sleep, I know I shan't."

"Don't be ridiculous."

"Isn't it natural to feel excited under the circumstances?"

He moved about the room, then stepped out upon the balcony and was silent for a moment.

"Pierpont's still out," he said presently in a low voice, putting his head into the room.

"Well, don't begin talking to him, because I'm going to bed."

"He's really a splendid chap. I'm certain of that."

"Yes, because you are the one doctor he wants to take with him to Tombouctou."

"Hang it, Fay, isn't it natural to be gratified when one's powers are trusted?"

"Of course. Now do come in and shut the Persiennes."

Alan obeyed reluctantly.

"I almost hate to shut out such a night."

"And to shut out the great millionaire."

He looked at her doubtfully with his hands thrust deep into his pockets. His eyes looked feverish, and his thin body, which had rather obviously been ill, leaned a little to the left side.

"I say, you won't be horrid to Pierpont when we get right away from everyone, will you?"

"No; he will be our master."

"What rubbish!"

"At any rate, he will have the right to call the tune."

"Pierpont's a gentleman, Fay."

"And a man too."

"Isn't that in his favour?"

"Of course. But it's men who are men that call all the tunes worth the playing. You see, they don't care how much they give the piper. Now please be quiet, Alan, I'm going to say a prayer."

She knelt down by the side of her bed and hid her face in her hands. Her bending figure seemed to him to express *abandon*. He couldn't help wondering very much what she was praying about.

But she never told him.

From that night Fay lived in a condition of hidden excitement, hidden emotion, which often gave her a curious sensation of living a double life in some strange and feverish dream. Outwardly she was self-possessed, energetic, and practical. Really she was tormented by doubts, fears, expectations, hopes. Yes, even her hopes tormented her. For the shapes of them all seemed to her monstrous. They passed through her soul like great bellying clouds at sunset, shot with colours that were vivid, or ominous and dark with the presage of storm. Sometimes their vastness was linked in her mind with the bigness of Pierpont, who had called them all into being, and she felt a terror of the immensities which included a terror of the desert. But the spirit of adventure within her was a doughty combatant of fear. Often it had the upper hand. Then she rejoiced at the prospect before her, she exulted at the working of Fate. And always, at every moment during this period of preparation, she was strongly alive. Life had a keen edge like the edge of a sharpened sword. If it drew blood presently, what of that? Better to suffer by living than to suffer by not really living; better to be cut in pieces quickly by a bright blade than to be suffocated slowly under a mass of soft pillows.

Alan was surprised by the tireless energy of his wife. The prospect of the journey, the effort of decision, had wonderfully changed her. More eager than he had ever seen her before, she was surely harder too. Once when he commented on this gently, she said:

"Soft women can't do such things as I'm going to do."

"You are a heroine in Beni Mora," he said. "The Arabs are amazed at your courage. But I don't want you to turn into one of those lean, sunbaked women who look as if they had been born in the saddle, or with a gun in their hands. I don't want you——"

She interrupted him decisively.

"My dear Alan, remember that if this great journey changes me very much that will be your fault. You persuaded me to undertake it."

"Or was it Pierpont?"

She remembered an instant's hesitation, and answered:

"No, it was you. I am going because of you."

"Let's hope you will never repent of it."

"*I* don't intend to," she said, smiling. "Repentance is often a sign of weakness. If you are going to repent of a thing, you shouldn't do it."

He looked at her almost anxiously.

"Sometimes I scarcely understand you, Fay," he said gravely.

"Perhaps we shall all come to a fuller understanding of each other and ourselves on the journey. We may even know too much by the time we arrive at Tombouctou, if we ever get there."

"Saad swears he will bring us there safely."

"Then that's settled. Now I'm going into the market with Mr. Pierpont. I've got one or two things to buy."

She left him alone. He stared after her, and presently saw her slight form going down the sunny white road towards the village with Pierpont's huge frame striding beside it. Saad ben Youssef followed them at a short distance. As Alan watched the three moving figures he thought of the words of his wife. It seemed to him at that moment that he knew too little. He felt that he was wrapped in faint mists of ignorance. But those figures and he were soon going out into the glaring lands, where colours were strong and outlines were hard and clear, where the light of the sun was fierce, and the shadows lay like living things on the burning gold of the sands.

Which was better for a man, to know too little or too much? *"Qui odit veritatem, odit Lucem."* Well, he loved the light, so surely he would love any truth discovered in the light.

Yet something in Fay's manner, or something perhaps in her eyes, had troubled his spirit for a moment.

The three moving figures disappeared on the white road. The hot stillness of noon was about him. He leaned his arms on the balcony railing, and he seemed actually to hear the great silence into which he was going; the silence of the wastes where there seems to be nothing, and where there is a nakedness that is akin to the nakedness of truth.

For the first time he felt a creeping dread of the journey.

II

THE HORNED VIPER

For two days the Saharan sirocco had prevailed. The wind from the north-east, perhaps born in the sand hills of the great Erg, had driven across the desert for hundreds of miles carrying the sand grains with it. Now at last the wind had died away, leaving a fiery heat that was intense as the heat from a furnace, and a silence that was startling almost as a great outcry.

During the sand-storm Pierpont's caravan, under the direction of Saad ben Youssef, had lain at Insalah, an oasis containing three native villages lost in the bosom of the central Sahara. Long ago our travellers had been made free of the Sahara, but they had not fully understood its menace, its power for evil, until this sirocco came upon them, whispering to them with its hot and insidious voice: "Give rein! give rein! Civilisation has no meaning here. The voice of conscience tells nothing but lies. Here men and women may do as they will, and they must will according to my behests. Give rein! give rein!" And the wind died; and the hot and insidious voice grew faint; and the sand grains settled down once more on the vast enigmatic wilderness. But the storm had left its mark on temper and soul; it had affected Fay and her husband and Horace Pierpont more even than they understood.

So far the great journey had seemed to be a success. Having carried his point at Beni Mora, Pierpont had shown none of the vulgar conceit of triumph. He had been considerate and charming in every possible way, in moments of difficulty serene and courageous, in long hours of monotony patient and philosophic, strong always, and yet easy to live with. And hitherto he had never too obviously called the tune, although the size of the caravan and the comparative comfort in which they lived, showed how liberally he had paid the piper.

Alan, who had always liked him, had become enthu-
siastically devoted to him, and made no secret of the fact,
being always an open-hearted and unselfconscious fellow.

And Fay?

She was more reticent than Alan.

Long before the caravan reached Insalah Alan had
marked a change, a development in his wife. During
the journey she had shown a resisting power, and indifference to physical discomfort, that were extraordinary. Perched on her Mehariste camel she rode day after
day without complaint over the burning sands, the dry,
stony water-courses, the hard-baked earth broken up into
mounds innumerable tufted with halfa grass, the rocky
hillocks that here and there rose grotesquely·in the midst
of the great desolation. She never called a halt because
she was more weary than others. Wrapped in the dream
of the desert she seemed pertinacious, filled with a strange
longing to go onward and ever onward. She had become bronzed by the sun without losing the almost
ethereal look that Alan delighted in. Her eyes glittered
with fires caught surely from the fires of the sun. There
was a sort of robust delicacy in her appearance, a fine
drawn energy in her movements and postures which Alan
wondered at sometimes and admired always. The only
woman in the caravan, she seemed worthy to be there
taking part in an enterprise of men. And she seemed
aware of her own worthiness. Although not usually
capricious, she subtly made her will-power felt as she
had never made it felt in the ways of civilisation. A certain inflexibility was often manifest in her. It was not
ugly though it was sometimes not free from obstinacy.
It went naturally enough with her physical strength, her
readiness to endure. In the bracing of herself for this
unusual effort she had, perhaps unconsciously, acquired
a mental robustness which marched, as it were, along-
side of her bodily powers.

She certainly ruled in the caravan. And now and then

she showed that she knew this, that there was intention
in her ruling. Then Alan remembered her words on the
terrace at Beni Mora, and wondered if Pierpont remembered them too. Hidden in her wand there was surely
the rod of iron she had spoken of. Alan did not find
it irksome upon his shoulders. But occasionally he wondered whether Pierpont felt otherwise. He had never
found out exactly what his wife thought about Pierpont.
She revelled in their adventure. That he knew. It had
shed a new life all through her. Yet he sometimes believed that she resented that very insistence of Pierpont
which had—so Alan supposed—brought her into it, that
she had a secret intention of repayment. Nevertheless,
they got on marvellously well together in the terrific intimacy of their situation. And Pierpont never showed
the least regret for what he had done. So no doubt it
was "all right." At any rate, it was all right till the
sirocco came.

When the wind died into fire and the dead silence fell
over the plain Saad ben Youssef arose, uncovered his
mouth and went to the Travellers' House in which the
Mortimers and Pierpont had been lodged for greater
safety against the storm. He suggested that they should
leave Insalah that night. There would be a bright moon.
They could travel in the cool. Everything was ready
and there was nothing to wait for now that the storm
was over. While he spoke from a room close by there
came sounds of coughing.

Pierpont, who looked thinner and more big-boned and
angular than even at Beni Mora, and who was burnt to
a deep brown by the sun, said he was ready to be off that
evening, but must consult the Mortimers before deciding
and, followed by Saad, he went to their room and knocked
on the palm-wood door. It was opened by Fay. Looking
beyond her they saw the doctor lying stretched on a pile
of gaudy rugs on the uncarpeted floor. Till now he had
borne the long journey splendidly, but during the sirocco
he had suffered. The sand grains, which penetrated

everywhere, had irritated his throat and chest, and brought on a hacking cough; his cheeks showed a strong flush through their freckled brown, and his eyes looked unnaturally bright and almost fiercely observant. It was evident to Pierpont that sirocco had played the devil with his friend. He had never seen Mortimer look at all like this before. Mrs. Mortimer, too, looked strung up and as if she were on the edge of her nerves.

"Let's go! Let's go!" exclaimed Alan directly the proposition was made. "I've taken a hatred for this place. Let's get away from houses out into the desert again."

"Is he fit to start?" asked Pierpont of Fay.

"Of course I am," cried Alan, raising himself on his arm. "It's only the cursed sand that's made me like this."

He glanced quickly from his wife to the American, and the hard cough broke out in his throat.

"Then if it suits you, Mrs. Mortimer, we'll be off at nine to-night after dinner and travel till dawn."

"I shall be thankful to go," she replied.

There was something unrestrained, almost reckless in her manner.

"Why?" he asked.

"Why? Oh—I hate being under a roof. I—I——"

She twisted her hands together.

"I want to get on," she added.

"Come out. It's as still as death now. Let him rest till evening," Pierpont whispered to her while Alan was coughing. "Come, Saad. We'll be off at nine, Mortimer."

"Right!"

Again the loud cough broke out. Pierpont shut the rough wooden door. Fay had said nothing, but he knew by her eyes she was coming, and he waited for her outside in the shadow cast by the house-wall, with his feet planted in the sand. Saad had slowly drifted away to the camp which was pitched in the oasis a little to the south of the village.

The silence that prevailed seemed unnatural, almost sinister, after the uneasy uproar of the wind. The masses of palm trees were motionless. But the water in the small trenches which led from the wells glided happily on its way. The sun blazed implacably over the sand plain and the low sand-hills in the distance surmounted by palm leaf barricades. As Pierpont stood there he felt that in this strange lost place, in this dead peace after the storm, Fate was at work dealing with him almost as the potter deals with the clay inexorably. Till the sirocco came he had felt that he was not only his own master but the master of others, despite the light tyranny of Fay. Now there was within him a feeling of being governed. It had come with the sirocco. He disliked, almost hated it, but he could not get rid of it. He heard the sound of a step, the creak of a door, and Fay stood beside him in the sand.

"We'll go into the oasis," Pierpont said.

"Yes. How horribly still it is!"

"Horribly?"

"Yes; I can hear Alan's cough in it. I hated the wind, but now I almost want it back."

"You're ultra-sensitive. The sirocco has affected you."

"And Alan too."

"Alan! How?"

They had been walking over the deep sand. Now he stopped, and stood looking at her.

"How? You don't mean physically, do you?"

"No. Let us get to the palm trees. Then I'll tell you."

She spoke quickly, unevenly, like one preoccupied and secretly impatient. They came into the shade of the oasis. Behind them, in the distance, the red clay walls of the officers' quarters gleamed in the sunshine with a sort of moody brilliance. The dull yellow water was at their feet. Over their heads the tufted trees spread an unwavering protection against the burning blue of the heavens. Among the wrinkled trunks shadow and light were mingled in the breathless hush of nature.

"Sit here against this palm trunk," said Pierpont brusquely. "What's the matter with Mortimer?"

He stretched his great body beside her.

"Of course I know he isn't so well as usual, not nearly so well," he added.

"I wonder how ill he is," said Fay, in a low, almost surreptitious voice.

"How ill?"

"Yes; last night, when the storm was raging, I thought, 'Suppose he were to be very ill. Suppose he were to— to die! What would happen then?' I seemed to be asking the sirocco."

"Well—what was the answer?" said Pierpont harshly.

"There was no answer."

"Because you asked the sirocco. You should have asked me."

He paused, staring at her, devouring her with his narrow grey eyes. She did not look at him, and said nothing.

"You haven't told me what is the matter with Mortimer," he added, after a moment.

"He seems to have suddenly changed towards me."

"In what way?"

"If it wasn't so absurd I should say he suspected me of something. His eyes are suspicious."

"Because he is unwell. The same thought that came into your mind may have come into his. He may have said to himself, 'If I were to become very ill, if I were to die, she would be left with—him.' And then, not being well and being under the hideous influence of sirocco, he may have felt the touch of jealousy!"

A slow flush crept upon Fay's cheeks as he spoke. He watched it with a sort of hunger.

"He's been horrid to me the last two days. All the time we've been married he's never been like that till now."

Tears came into her eyes. The deep melancholy of
sirocco possessed her. Pierpont thrust out a great bony
hand and took hold of hers.

"It's illness. He can't know."

Fay's hand started in his. He held it fast.

"Know what?" she said uncontrollably.

"What you and I know, what we knew before we left
Beni Mora. We have never spoken of it but we have
always known it. The devil that kept us back from being frank about it has been driven away by that wind
from hell. It went on the wings of sirocco."

She left her hand lying quite still in his, and, looking
into his face almost defiantly, she said:

"I am tired of pretending too. In such a region as this
it seems so horribly unnatural to pretend anything. In
these last days I have sometimes felt desperately reckless. More than once, when he was horrid to me, I nearly told him."

Now she tried to draw away her hand, and he let her
do it.

"What would you have told Mortimer if you had
spoken?" said Pierpont.

Fay got up and stood by the palm tree under which
he was lying. Just then she felt a need to look down upon
him.

"Oh, just why I came on this journey. He doesn't
know why, and neither do you. You're surprised! But
men scarcely ever know a woman's reason for what she
does. I came because once in Beni Mora I asked Alan
a question and he hesitated—only for a second—before
answering it. That second's hesitation of his was my
reason for coming. You didn't persuade me though
perhaps you thought you did."

"What was the question?"

"This: 'Do you absolutely refuse to go without me,
Alan?'"

"I remember. You said it on the terrace."

"Yes. Alan could have left me to go with you. When

I knew that I felt I could come. I was changed that night. I—it was almost as if I became suddenly wicked."

"Now I understand why you were menacing that night."

"Some of my softness went out of me for ever," she said, with a sort of strange, almost weary, bitterness.

"Do you repent of what you have done?"

"No. But I'm suffering."

"So am I."

"What did you mean when you tried to force me to come? What do you mean now?"

"I had found a girl who knew how to make me love when I thought I had lost the power. I meant to make certain of being always inevitably with her, far away from all the infernal interruptions of ordinary life."

"And then?"

"Perhaps I meant to try to pour my influence upon her always when I was with her."

"And—then?"

"I let the future keep its secret."

"But Alan would always be there."

"I was ready to chance that."

She gazed at him in silence. At that moment something inside of her surely turned pale. Yet she did not feel irresolute.

"Did you—did you think he was very ill?" she murmured.

"I let the future keep its secret," he repeated.

"Why did the sirocco come?"

When she said that Pierpont knew that till the storm he had been able to endure without too great misery the bizarre and even horrible situation which in Beni Mora he had striven to bring about. Now, abruptly, he felt that it was unendurable.

"To put an edge to our human misery," he answered moodily. "To light up our madness so that we could see it plainly and know it for what it is."

He felt the silence; he looked at the dead stillness;

everything seemed to have stopped except the energy in their two souls.

"What are we going to do?" he said at last, looking again at her.

"What can we do?"

"Do you really think he suspects?"

"I don't know. But he's horribly uneasy. It's almost as if the sirocco had made him clairvoyant. And at this moment I don't think I mind. I could almost go now and tell him."

"That's the vile influence of the wind. It will pass away from us, and then we shall be desperately sorry, we shall curse ourselves, if we do anything irreparable now."

He clenched his great hands into fists.

"I won't be the sport of nature," he exclaimed. "I'll be my own master."

"I've always felt that you are tremendously strong."

"You, who rule me!"

He got up.

"No, don't!" she said. Don't!"

He thrust his hands into the pockets of his riding breeches and stood still.

"Can Saad have spoken to Mortimer?" he said after a minute, during which he had kept his eyes fixed on the ground.

"Saad! How could he know?" said Fay in a startled voice.

"He knows because he's an Arab. Arabs know everything."

"But if he did know, surely he would never speak of it to a Roumi."

"I never can tell what an Arab will do, or not do. I don't understand the breed."

"I must be mad to-day," she said. "I'm sick of pretence. Something in me wants Alan to know. But if he did know, this isolated life of us three, from which we

can't escape, would be impossible. For how could we
go on travelling together if he knew?"

"How could we do anything else? We can't well break
up the caravan. We can't divide Saad in two. And he's
indispensable to us all. If Mortimer says anything—
I don't believe he will, but if he should—you must laugh
at him. Don't yield if you have an impulse to speak
the truth. Choke the words down. Fay, do you love
me?"

"Yes. You seem to enclose me."

He moved.

"Then let me——"

"No; I love you, but I don't mind your suffering. I
want you to suffer. I meant what I said on the terrace
at Beni Mora. I yielded to Alan and you, but I always
meant to punish you. Why will men never let women
alone?"

"Wouldn't women curse them if they did?"

"There is Saad!" she whispered.

The tall figure of the Arab was visible in the glaring
sunshine coming towards them across the sands.

That night they left Insalah by the light of the moon,
journeying due south across the shining silver of the
sands. Alan was warmly wrapped up, for when the night
grows late it is chilly in the Sahara. His cough still
troubled him. As the long line of laden camels moved
on noiselessly at a regular pace, Fay and Pierpont heard
it, and it seemed to Fay to strike on her heart like a
little hammer as well as upon her ears. And, looking out
from her moving height upon the radiant immensity
spread around her, she said to herself, "Will he die?"
and "If he should die!" And she felt almost like one
struggling with difficulties in a dream. She did not want
Alan to die, and yet she knew that life could never be to
her the gift she desired while he lived. If Alan could
cease from her life and leave her legitimately free, without dying, she could give herself to the happiness every

woman wishes for. Yet even then a regret would haunt her. For she was fond of Alan and she knew that. She was fond of him, but he did not encompass her. She felt equal to, or even superior to him. She had the habit of him and he had always been good to her. But he was not impressive to her. She looked upon him as quite an ordinary man. Pierpont, on the other hand, impressed her, made her often secretly wonder, even secretly fear. And of one thing she was absolutely certain, as women can be certain of things never brought to the test of experience; she was absolutely convinced that if she ever belonged to Pierpont she would worship him. And never, not even when she had believed herself to be violently in love with him, had she felt just like that about Alan.

The shadows of the camels and of their riders moved over the radiance of the sands furtively. The great stars glittered in the firmament. Now and then a camel driver broke into a melancholy song. And those three, who knew each other so well, and so little, pursued their double journey, of the body and of the soul, through the night of nature and the twilight of human life, specks in immensity, yet each one of them a world. The chill of the midnight touched them, and, presently, the different chill of the dying night. And the spell of sirocco went with them.

In the blazing heat of noon on the following day they were encamped far away from any oasis or native village, in the midst of a vast plateau of dried earth mingled with chalk, with sand-hills billowing in the distance like waves of a sea dyed orange by the flames of the sun.

And here, in this desolation, unknown to them, it was ordained that the drama in which they were involved should come to a sudden crisis.

They intended to rest all day, and to continue their journey by night. During the morning, weary with much riding, they slept. At midday they met in the shadow of an awning stretched before the Mortimers' tent to have their lunch, followed by coffee, pipes for the men, and a cigarette for Fay.

Alan still looked ill and strangely self-conscious, but he professed to be much better already, now that they were away from the village. He wore a forced air of unnatural cheerfulness, and his whole demeanour was that of a man filled with uneasiness which he was trying to hide. Warned by Fay, Pierpont was on the alert for a change in his friend, but it was more marked than he had expected. Before the short meal was over he felt convinced that something which as yet neither Fay nor he knew of had occurred to startle Mortimer out of his normal contentment. Mortimer's physical condition was certainly worse than usual, and mentally no doubt he was still unfavourably influenced by sirocco. Pierpont knew by his own experience that people sometimes take several days to shake off entirely its evil spell. But— there was something else. He wished to think other- wise; he even tried to force himself to think otherwise; but his effort was vain. There was a new politeness, a creeping formality in Mortimer's manner towards him, which put intimacy at a distance. He found himself "making" conversation, wondering what to say next, looking over to Fay for help. Something horrible, like a fetid breath from civilised life, poisoned the air they were breathing. Pierpont's tremendous self-possession seemed to tremble on its throne. He damned him- self for a sirocco-victim, and in that he was justified. But no amount of self-damning could do away with his conviction that Mortimer had somehow got on the track of his and Fay's long hidden secret. And suddenly he realised, sitting there by the tiny camp-table on which they took their meals, and eating the sardines, the cous- cous, the bits of stewed mutton, the peculiar impossibility of the situation which would be created by Mortimer's discovery of the truth. That a man should love another man's wife—there was no novelty in that! But that a husband of Mortimer's type, as Pierpont knew by instinct totally incapable of playing the rôle of a *mari complaisant,* should be forced by circumstances to live in day and night intimacy with his wife and the man she loved and by whom she was loved, realising exactly how matters were between them—there would be a diabolical novelty in such a situation. And such a situation no innocence of body could save. Pierpont tried hard to trick himself into the conviction that his anxiety was groundless, was born of sirocco, but as the meal progressed a sort of desperation overcame him. The change in Mortimer's demeanour was too marked to be misunderstood. Here was a usually natural man, a man still like an honest, well-meaning boy, a man, moreover, hitherto openly devoted to him, Pierpont, obviously playing a part. And Mortimer did not act well. He was too unaccustomed to acting to play any rôle cleverly.

The uneasy conversation presently languished and died. They sat in a sombre silence.

At last the meal was over, and Saad set the coffee before them. The men lit their pipes, and Fay began to smoke her cigarette. The heat of the noontide was heavy upon them. The stones with which the plateau on which they were camping was strewn glittered in the tremendous sunshine. The heavens above them were as brass. The stillness about them was like a living thing waiting for some great action. And the immense nakedness of the land for the first time seemed to utter to Pierpont's soul an implacable condemnation of the deception he had practised, of the lie he had lived so long. All through a life made easy by his vast fortune and by his powerful personality, by the self-possession which had never yet failed him, and by the will of iron which had upheld him and brought people in obedience to do what he wanted, he had never been tormented by the thing men call conscience, and he had seldom indeed failed to possess himself of any pleasure, or any passion, which had tempted him. Now he suddenly felt small, mean, even almost fearful. Yes, in the midst of this fierce heat, this blazing world, he felt the intimately cold touch of fear. He sat staring into the distance and wondering about the future.

Presently he heard Fay and Alan talking together. They were speaking about Arabic. On the journey they had all been studying Arabic, and had amused themselves by comparing each other's progress. It had been agreed that Alan showed the most marked aptitude as a pupil of Saad's. He really had what is sometimes called a knack for picking up a language almost without knowing how he did it. Pierpont now heard Fay speaking. She said:

"I don't know how it is, but though I can talk a little I can't ever properly understand when Arabs talk together."

"I can understand," said Alan.

There was nothing remarkable in the words, but the way in which they were uttered struck forcibly on Pierpont. It seemed to him that Mortimer spoke them with a sort of biting significance, and he looked sharply across the table and met the young doctor's eyes. They were fixed upon him in a stare, and seemed full of hostility.

"Eh? What is it?" he said, jerking out the words almost unconsciously, forced, he felt, to ask those eyes why they looked at him like that.

Mortimer looked away at once, smiling.

"You were in a brown study, Pierpont."

"Yes. I feel the heat more than I generally do to-day. I think I'll be off to my tent for a bit. Perhaps I'll lie down again."

Without looking at Fay he got up and strode off.

His tent was pitched perhaps a hundred feet away. He went to it, and sat down inside it on his folding-chair. What had Mortimer meant by those words which had sounded just like a threat? He lit a fresh pipe and pondered over the matter. Why should Mortimer's understanding of Arabic, when spoken among themselves by the Arabs of the caravan, have any dangerous significance for himself and Fay?

After a time he felt the small enclosed space in the tent to be insupportable to him. He longed to get away for a little, to lose sight of the encampment, to hear no longer the occasional voices of his men, the trickle of music from a vagrant pipe, the snatch of a nasal song, the grunt of a camel. The smallest sound or movement was hateful to him just then, seemed to paralyse his power of thought. He got up, pulled off his riding breeches and the thin drawers of silk he wore beneath them, put on a pair of loose white trousers and a huge straw hat with a pugaree, took his sun umbrella and smoked spectacles and stepped out of the tent. And as he did so he looked towards the Mortimer's tent. They were no longer sitting under the awning. No doubt they were lying down inside the tent. Walking softly, he went away from the encampment, going towards the west. Almost immediately he saw Saad following him. He stopped. The Arab came up.

"I don't want you, Saad," he said. "I'm only going a little way. Leave me alone."

"You will not go very far, Sidi?"

"No, no. Only a few yards. I'm going to have a smoke and look out over the desert. Tell the Arabs no one is to come and disturb me."

"Very well, Sidi."

Pierpont went on. Saad stood where he was looking after him.

In the region where they were now the plain here and there was broken up by shallow gullies, almost like fissures in the earth. Pierpont presently came to one of these. He looked back, saw the camp in the distance, the white-robed figure of Saad at gaze, smoke curling up from a fire. He waved a hand to Saad and went down into the gully. On the side opposed to the camp he found a meagre mimosa shrub growing. He stretched himself at its foot, adjusted the sun umbrella, and fell into meditation.

After Pierpont had left them Fay and Alan sat for a minute in silence. Then Alan knocked out his pipe rather violently against the edge of the table, glanced sideways at Fay and said:

"What are you going to do, Fay?"

"What can one do but rest here, or in the tent?" she said.

"You won't go with Pierpont? I'll bet you he doesn't lie down, but goes out for a stroll in the desert."

"In this heat? It would be madness."

"Well, isn't Pierpont a bit mad at times?"

"I've never noticed it."

She paused. Then something within her drove her to add:

"What do you mean? In what way is Mr. Pierpont mad or even eccentric?"

"It isn't everyone who'd ask a woman to come on such a journey as this."

"Why, *you* begged me to come when I refused to."

"I don't claim to be any saner than Pierpont."

"It's not very polite to me to say that. Here's Mahmoud coming to clear away."

As she spoke she threw away the end of her cigarette, got up and went into their tent, Alan lingered a moment by the table. Fay heard him speaking in Arabic to Mahmoud. He was certainly becoming quite fluent in that angry language. She began slowly to take off her frock. What else could she do but lie down? She might sit in a chair, but in such heat it was surely best to let the whole body repose. She slipped on a thin loose robe, white and yellow, and looked at the bed. And as she looked at it she saw the bedroom at Beni Mora; she was again with Alan there on the night when he came to tell her of Pierpont's offer; she remembered her sleepless night. And then, presently, she remembered how she had

prayed on that other night when she had consented to
make the great journey. She shut her eyes and tried to
feel herself back in Beni Mora. But in her whole body,
as well as in her brain, she was conscious of the central
depths of the Sahara, of the irrevocable distances that
must be traversed slowly, painfully, before that body and
soul of hers could be either again in Beni Mora or in
Tombouctou. Innumerable days or nights on camel back
must be endured before she could be free from the Sahara, could escape from these human beings who were
with her, fellow prisoners in the great freedom, chained
together in immensity.

She heard Alan whistling outside. He was trying to
whistle an Arab melody, and, of course, failing in the
effort. He broke off and tried again. Fay went to her
bed and lay down. And the sirocco seemed to lie down
on the bed with her, as if it had crept after her from
Insalah without her knowing it. Waves of sirocco
seemed to flow over her, hot, heavy waves, carrying her
blindly somewhere as a great flood carries a corpse.
Alan's ugly whistling drew a little nearer and stopped at
the tent door. She looked. As she looked he stepped in,
turned with his back to her, and seemed to be peeping at
something. For his thin body was bent for a moment,
and his head was thrust forward.

"What are you looking at?" she asked.

Putting one hand behind him he made a gesture which
seemed to mean "Hush!" She was silent. Presently he
turned round.

"It's as I thought. Pierpont has gone off alone into
the desert."

"Why shouldn't he? There's nothing very odd in
that," she said, with nervous irritation.

"No. But it's odd that I knew he was going to do
it."

He pulled off his coat, threw it on the ground and
rolled up his shirt-sleeves. His arms were red-brown.
He had no waistcoat on and the thinness of his body was

very apparent. He was as lean as a panther. He caught hold of a chair, pulled it to the side of Fay's bed, and sat down facing her. She felt half afraid of him. She did not know what he was going to do or say, but she knew he was going to do or say something exceptional. She also felt afraid of herself. She knew quite well that she was not normal, that she was swayed by an influence of nature. She might have the sense to struggle against this influence, since she was almost sharply aware of it. But on the other hand she might find herself powerless to do so.

"I told you just now I can understand Arabic when the Arabs talk it among themselves," Alan said slowly.

"I wish I could. That's the only way to get to know the Arabs," said Fay.

"Yes. They're a bad-tongued race."

"I've always heard that. Mr. Pierpont thinks so too."

"They're tremendous gossips."

"I suppose they are."

"Just before the sirocco came I heard two of them gossiping, Saad and Mahmoud. It was quite by chance. It was the night before we got to Insalah, when we were at the oasis of Foggaret el Zoua."

He leaned forward and laid one of his red-brown hands on the bed. Fay noticed that the fingers of it were clenched.

"I got up that night when you were asleep. I had insomnia."

"You never told me of it."

"No. The tent seemed a prison. I put on a burnous and went out. I went a little way and sat down on the ground. I happened to sit close to the tent where Saad and Mahmoud were sleeping. At least not sleeping—they were talking, and I smelt keef. What do you think they were talking about?"

His eyes were fixed upon her and looked quite unlike Alan's.

"What?" she asked unwillingly.

"You."

Fay lay still for a minute. One of her hands had lain near Alan's. She drew it softly away and covered it with a fold of her gown. Then, slightly sticking out her chin and with her obstinate look, she asked:

"What did they say about me?"

Alan's hand quivered on the bed.

"They said, that is Saad said—they talked about us all, not only you—that Pierpont had only asked me to make this journey because he wanted you to go."

"Silly!" Fay formed with her lips.

"Saad ben Youssef was telling Mahmoud, evidently for the first time. I should think he was under the influence of keef. He coughed several times, as keef smokers do."

"Keef-mad!" Fay formed with her lips.

She longed to push the sirocco from her. It lay so close to her; it embraced her; she felt in its arms.

"He said several very odd things—odd to be invented, I mean. He said to Mahmoud that Pierpont told you about the journey before he told me, that he asked you to go before he asked me."

Fay shrugged her shoulders against the big pillow. They made a dry little noise.

"He declared that all your hesitation about going was a piece of acting, that you had promised to go from the beginning and had always meant to go."

"What liars Arabs are!" Fay managed to whisper.

"He said"—Alan's voice went up a little—"you and Pierpont loved one another—loved one another! Just imagine! He said that I knew it, but that Pierpont had offered me such a huge sum of money to come, that, of course, I couldn't refuse it. He actually said that of me."

And Alan's body shook in the chair, as if with suppressed laughter.

"I take Pierpont's money—I take—for such a reason!

By God, Fay, how is one to help laughing at these devils?"

And his body shook more violently, though his lips were not even smiling.

"What it must be to have such filthy imaginations!"

Fay lay quite still and said nothing. She felt oddly vague. It had come—the blow. Whether Alan believed what the Arab had said or not, she felt sure that he would never again be with Pierpont as he had been, open-hearted, admiring, an enthusiastic friend; whether he believed or not he would always have moments of doubt-fulness about Pierpont and her. She knew that by the look in her husband's eyes. And yet, for the moment, she only felt vague. She stretched her thin body slightly and sighed.

"Well?" said Alan.

He was always staring at her, was devouring her with his eyes.

"Well?" she said.

He leaned forward, pressing his clenched hand on the bed. The veins stood out on his bare arm and looked violent.

"Isn't it pretty bad to have such a thing said of you as that, and not to be able to do anything? I couldn't go into the tent and thrash Saad. He's Pierpont's servant, and, besides, we depend absolutely on him for every-thing. If anything were to happen—if he were to leave us we should be in great difficulties."

"What does it matter what an Arab says? You and I know it's a lie. Isn't that enough?"

"Why d'you speak like that?"

"What do you mean?"

"In—in such a——it scarcely sounded like your voice."

She turned uneasily on the bed.

"It's so hot, and so terribly still. I don't feel like my-self to-day."

"I hate the desert!" he exclaimed, with sudden bitter

violence. "I wish to God we had never come on this journey. Whatever happens, it will be months before we get to the end of it. Even if we turned back now it would be weeks before we could reach Beni Mora."

"Turned back?"

"Yes, you and I."

"How could we possibly do such a thing without a reason?"

"D'you think I can enjoy travelling on for months, in the midst of a crowd of beasts who think—think——"

"Arabs!" she said.

"Fay!"

"Yes."

"When I told you you didn't seem surprised."

"Nothing they could say could surprise me."

"But don't you mind its being said?"

"It's disagreeable, of course."

She was trying to struggle against a growing morbid desire to give in to circumstances, to put her two hands in the hands of Fate and let herself be taken unresisting even to perdition. Just then the one thing which she felt she could not do was to go on acting, lying, dodging things, being subtle, trying for self-preservation. She was possessed of a desire, almost voluptuous, to go with the tide, like a twig borne along on a wave of the ocean. She remembered, of course, Pierpont's warning. No doubt he was right. These moods of sirocco would pass. But what did it matter? Since Pierpont had spoken of this love of theirs it seemed to her to have a different character, to demand different conduct on her part and his. Their deception seemed to her far greater, far more deplorable even, in this region, far more ridiculous and useless, now that they had been frank with each other.

She raised herself on one arm with a hand under her cheek and looked steadily at her husband.

"Shall I tell you exactly why I came on this journey?" she said, in a louder, harder voice.

"Yes," he said. "Tell me."

"It wasn't because Mr. Pierpont was determined we should go with him."

"Why was he so determined?"

She ignored his question.

"It wasn't because you wanted so much to go and tried so hard to persuade me."

"I did try. But you said afterwards you had been longing to go all the time."

"Alan, it was because you could have gone without me."

"I!"

He straightened himself up abruptly.

"How can you say that?"

"I say it because it's true."

"But I absolutely refused——"

"You could have gone. Don't let us discuss it. I know it. I knew it when I asked you on the terrace at Beni Mora that night, 'Do you absolutely refuse to go without me?' You hesitated before you answered. A hesitation like that tells a woman everything—everything. From that moment I decided I would make this journey."

Alan was silent for a minute. His face looked drawn, and his eyes were fierce, and seemed to be gazing inward, as if he were searching himself. At last he said:

"Why did you refuse to come before?"

"I had a reason."

"What was it?"

She hesitated, trying to struggle with sirocco.

"Never mind what it was."

"You shall tell me. You always wanted to come. I asked you to come. Then why did you try to avoid it?"

"I thought it would be unwise for me to travel so far."

"You—you——"

In spite of the marvellous dryness of the heat which
enclosed them sweat burst out on his face.

"Did Pierpont speak to you about making the journey
before he spoke to me?"

Fay twisted her lips into a sort of smile.

"Do you believe Arabs then?"

"I didn't believe them till we were at Insalah and
sirocco came."

"Ah!" she said, on a long breath. "The sirocco came."

"Then I began to think things over. I felt horribly
ill. I thought, 'Suppose I were to die on this journey
and what Saad told Mahmoud about Fay and Pierpont
were true.' Is it true? Is it true?"

An almost fierce desire came to Fay to cry out, "It is
true!" But she resisted it with all her remaining force.
She let her arm drop and her head fall on the pillow.
Still twisting her lips in the little smile, she said:

"If you believe what Arabs say you will believe anything. You might even believe me if I said it is true."

She shut her eyes.

"Now do let me rest," she murmured. "It's so terribly hot."

There was a silence. Then she heard him say:

"I'm going to Pierpont."

And she heard him go out of the tent.

When Alan was outside the tent and had walked a
few steps he stood for a moment motionless. He was
still bathed in sweat. All his body was damp. He had
a strange dual sensation: he felt both dull and violent.
Saad ben Youssef was no longer standing at gaze. He
had gone into the cook's tent, and was squatting there
with the Arabs, engaged in one of those violent and
interminable conversations which alternate with the long
and profound silences of the men of the East. The
hobbled camels were resting and eating their fodder with
sideways moving mouths. The desert stretched around
empty under the blaze of the sun. Nothing moved in

the vast expanse, no figure of man, no body of animal or of bird. Where was Pierpont?

Alan had seen him start and knew in what direction he had gone. After his pause, almost mechanically Alan followed in that direction and presently came to the edge of the shallow gully in which Pierpont was lying. He struck the gully at some distance from Pierpont, who was turned from him and looking in the opposite direction from that by which he approached. Pierpont was now stretched out at full length by the mimosa shrub. His trousers had got rucked up and Alan could see some of the bare brown skin of his great legs exposed to the sun as he lay. His socks had fallen down nearly to his ankles. There was a look of disorder in his presence which was unusual, for, as a rule, without being at all a dandy, he was particular about his clothes and was always perfectly neat. Walking in the bottom of the gully Alan approached him slowly. The heat seemed even greater in this depression of the ground. The earth seemed to shimmer with heat. Far off those mysterious vapours out of which the mirage arises lifted themselves like smoke from the tawny waste, and the orange-coloured crests of the sand-hills gleamed under the flames of the sun.

When Alan was quite near to Pierpont his foot shifted on a loose stone; the latter heard the noise, lifted himself and looked round.

"Hullo, Mortimer," he said, in his harsh, very individual voice. "Come to sit with me?"

"Yes."

"How did you find me?"

"I saw you start from our tent."

"The tent was hot and I felt a bit restless."

"The sirocco seems to have waked us all up."

"Waked us up! Did we need that?"

"I can only answer for myself."

He sat down near to Pierpont, but not close to him, and a little above him. In his hand he had a rough stick such as the Arabs often carry. He never felt at ease when walking unless he carried something. He held this stick across his knees now as he sat, bending a little forward.

"Perhaps I did need waking up," he added.

"I can't say I'd noticed any peculiar sluggishness in you."

"I've been having a talk with my wife."

"She's lying down?"

"Yes."

"I think we're all rather done up to-day, in spite of what you say. A sirocco like that at Insalah really plays the devil both with body and mind. We shall want a few days to recover our balance, to get back our usual spirits. I noticed at lunch that we were all rather flattened out. But in a journey like this there must be such moments I suppose."

"Why have you come out here?"

"For something to do."

"But why come away from the camp to a place where you see nothing? As you're lying you can see nothing except the gully."

"This mimosa attracted me. Even a shrub like this means a lot in the midst of such a desert as we're in just now."

"What were you thinking about when I came up?"

"I believe I was half asleep."

"Oh, no, you weren't."

"Then you know more about me than I do about myself?"

"I know more than I did a very few minutes ago."

Instantly it flashed into Pierpont's mind that Fay had madly yielded to the sirocco-impulse of which she had spoken to him in the oasis at Insalah. He remembered her words, "I could almost go now and tell him." He lay very still, and his long determined face did not change.

"Friendship ought to be based on knowledge," he said carelessly.

Alan pulled his broad-brimmed panama hat down on his wet forehead.

"I want to know something. I want to know why you asked my wife if she would come on this journey before you asked me if I would come."

"I didn't."

"I've heard that you did."

"She has told him," thought Pierpont.

"The fact remains. I didn't."

As he reiterated the lie he had a sensation of fighting with the woman he loved.

"I did not tell your wife first."

His voice was imperative and ugly in its harshness.

"Every Arab in the camp knows you did!" said Alan violently.

And he broke into a desperate fit of coughing.

Pierpont was conscious of an immense feeling of relief. He realised that he had nearly fallen into a trap.

"Ah!" he exclaimed, with contempt. "So you've actually been taking vile Arab gossip for truth! You've overheard some camp slander and you've believed it. If you hadn't told me yourself——"

"I haven't told you!" Alan interrupted.

"But it is as I say. If not, deny it! Who else could have said such a thing?"

"My wife might have said it."

"Your wife! Are you crazy, Mortimer?"

Pierpont was lying on his right side leaning on his right arm. He had not changed his position during their conversation. Just behind him in the hard earth of the gully there was a large crack or rent, which Alan looked down on but which was invisible to Pierpont. At this moment, while Pierpont was in the act of saying his last words, something attracted Alan's eyes to this rent in the ground. He looked. Surely he had half seen something move for an instant. He was just beginning to

wonder what it had been when he perceived the head
of a grey snake pushed out of the crack not far from
Pierpont's left leg. On the head, above a broad snout
and a pair of small eyes with vertical pupils, were two
straight horns. This head remained out as if the snake
were watching or listening to something. It looked surreptitious, intent, and strangely mental. Alan was fas-
cinated by it.

Before coming on this great journey he had naturally
made certain medical preparations. He was engaged to
accompany the expedition as a doctor, and it was his
business to be ready to deal with any medical or surgical
emergency which was likely to arise. He had made inquiries as to the special dangers of the region they were
about to traverse. Among them one of the first which
had been mentioned to him had been the danger of snake-
bite. He knew that the *cerastes cornutus,* or horned
viper, was one of the deadliest snakes in existence, and
that certain regions of the Sahara were infested by it.
He had in his medicine-chest, safely locked away, a certain serum, first produced by Calmette, which was anti-
venomous, and which, if injected at once into the body
of one bitten by the horned viper, in combination with
injections of permanganate of potash, would almost certainly save the sufferer from death. Now for the first
time he looked upon this enemy of the desert, and was
surprised by the smallness of a reptile which contained the
power to slay a man. And he looked, too, upon the man
whom he had thought of as his friend, but whom he
now thought of as his deadliest enemy.

"Are you crazy, Mortimer?" repeated Pierpont, with
a sort of almost fierce defiance. "Has your ill-health
shaken your mind?"

The horned viper shifted very surreptitiously a little
nearer to Pierpont, upon whom it seemed to have concentrated its attention. Alan's hands closed mechanically
upon the long stick which he had been holding lightly
across his knees.

"My ill-health!" he said. "Who says I'm ill?"

The horned viper paused, then crept on its white belly an inch or two closer to Pierpont. The whole of it had now emerged from the rent, and Alan could see that the tip of its tail was black. Behind its staring, vertical eyes were two streaks, dark and oblique. Its little straight horns were like two menaces and suggested a mind wary and acute, a soul implacable in its evil. The whole of the reptile looked intense. In intensity at that moment Alan was own brother to it.

"Are you counting on my ill-health?" he continued slowly, and with a sinister emphasis. "But what would you do in the desert without a doctor? You were so determined to have a doctor."

"You aren't well, you aren't yourself, or you couldn't possibly talk like this. If I didn't see what your condition is, do you think I would put up with such an abominable insinuation as you have just made? You ought to know me too well——"

"But if all this time I haven't known you at all!" Alan interrupted quietly.

He was able to bridle his violence now because he had suddenly been filled with a sense of immense, almost of exuberant power.

"And what could you do out here, whatever I said, or did? How could you get rid of me? How can we separate? We are tied up beyond hope of getting loose from one another. Besides that you depend on me."

A sudden red rose in Pierpont's lean cheeks.

"Depend on you! What the devil d'you mean by that?"

"Simply that there's no other doctor within a good many miles."

And Alan laughed; but his eyes were intent. For the viper had moved noiselessly along the hot earth and was now close to Pierpont's leg.

"And you made such a point in Beni Mora of the absolute necessity of having a doctor always with you.

Both my wife and I remarked that you were—shall we say exceedingly careful in regard to your health?"

"D'you mean to imply that I'm a physical coward?"

"No; only that you take great care of yourself."

"You're offensive, Mortimer."

The viper crept forward and rested its head on a rucked-up fold of Pierpont's trousers, just above his bare leg. He noticed nothing, but Alan held his breath and his two hands strained themselves round his stick. The natural impulse to kill a noxious reptile was strong in the doctor, but a stronger, overpowering impulse held him back. The desire to know dominated him. His wife had evaded him. Pierpont had probably, indeed almost certainly, lied to him. There was something concealed from him by them both. Of that he felt positive. Fate had, perhaps, brought to him out of the bowels of the desert a means to force the exact truth from these human beings who possessed the devilish power to withhold it from him—for ever if they would. Could he be such a fool as to destroy the weapon given to his hand before it had struck?

"You're damnably offensive. But I put it down to your condition."

"There you make a big mistake. I feel ever so much better already than I did at Insalah. I shall be quite fit to look after my wife till this journey is ended, never fear."

The viper raised its head, slipped forward and poised itself above Pierpont's bare leg, slightly quivering.

"Strike!" something in Alan said. "Strike, you foul thing! Strike!"

As if it had heard the injunction the reptile again slipped forward and dropped upon Pierpont's bare leg.

"What the devil——" he exclaimed in a loud, startled voice.

He made an abrupt and violent movement.

"Ah!" he cried out.

The horned viper had bitten him.

Alan sprang to his feet, gripped his stick, and in an instant had killed the snake. He turned it over with his foot, looked at it for a moment with an indescribable expression, then kicked it violently away from him.

"It's a *cerastes cornutus,*" he said to Pierpont.

The two men were now standing close together at the bottom of the gully. Pierpont looked hard into the doctor's eyes.

"You knew it was there!" he said. "You knew when you said that I depended on you."

Alan faced him in silence. Pierpont thrust his hand into his pocket, pulled out a silk handkerchief, bent down and tied it tightly round his leg just above the bite.

"I must get to the camp," he said, lifting himself up.

He did not show any sign of pain.

"Of course you've brought anti-venomous serum with you," he added.

Alan made no reply. Without another word Pierpont set out for the camp. Alan followed him up the side of the gully. In the distance the camp was visible, the tents, the hobbled beasts, smoke curling up to the blaze of the sun, and one figure, a woman's, standing at the opening of a tent motionless, gazing out over the desert. When he saw that figure Pierpont stopped.

"You can save me, can't you?" he said to the doctor.

"I suppose I could."

"Are you going to save me?"

"That depends on you. You've lied to me. Now you must tell me the truth."

After a pause, Pierpont said:

"I have told you the truth."

"If you don't tell me," said Alan, pointing to the distant figure by the tent, "she shall."

"She can only say what I have said. You must be mad to believe Arabs."

"I feel that she and you are trying to deceive me. I know it."

"You mean the sirocco has told you a lie."

"We'll soon prove that. When we get to camp go to your tent without a word to her. If you say a word of all this I swear I'll let you die."

Pierpont looked at him in silence. Then he walked slowly onward. He began to limp slightly and leaned on his stick. Alan kept beside him and did not speak again till they were close to the camp. Then Alan said:

"Remember; not a word of what has happened, or of what we've said, to her, or I'll let you die. If it's murder, I don't care. I've got to know the truth."

"You do know it."

"If she backs you up, after I've done with her, perhaps I'll believe what you've said. Go to your tent and lie down. Don't say a word to the Arabs. I'll come to you very soon."

As they reached the camp Pierpont was limping no longer. Fay, who was still at the tent door, looked at them with a curious, almost sullen expression. Pierpont took off his hat with a smile.

"The heat out there was too great. I'm going in to lie down for a little," he said.

He turned and walked into his tent, still without limping.

"Whatever he is he's a sportsman!"

That thought went through Alan's mind almost against his will. Then he turned to Fay.

"Come into the tent, will you, Fay?" he said. "There's something I want to tell you, something I want you to tell me. And we haven't much time."

"Not much time! What do you mean? Surely we've almost unlimited time at our disposal out here."

"No, we haven't. Come in."

She looked at him, then followed him into the tent.

"Sit down on the bed, Fay," he said.

She sat on the side of her camp bed. He sat down on his with his hands thrust deep into his pockets. They were clenched, but Fay could not see that, and his face was much calmer in expression than when he had left her to follow Pierpont.

"Now listen to me, and whatever I say don't cry out."

"Cry out!" she said, startled.

"Yes. We've got to keep this from the Arabs."

"Go on!" she whispered.

He crossed one leg over the other and stared out through the tent door.

"If I choose it," he said, "in a very few hours Pierpont will be a dead man. Sit down!"

She sat down again. She was trembling slightly.

"Why d'you say such—such a cruel thing? It's horribly unmanly to try to frighten a woman."

"It's the truth. Just now in the gully Pierpont was bitten in the leg by a horned viper."

"Ah!" she cried, again starting up. "And you, a doctor, sit here!"

She caught hold of him by the shoulder, and her hand seemed made of iron.

"Go and save him. You have the power, haven't you? You've got something against snake-bite!"

"Whether I save him or let him die depends on you."

She gripped him more fiercely.

"Then you'll save him!"

"Do you love him?"

She gazed at him, trying to read in his eyes what she had to say for the saving of Pierpont's life.

"He's our friend. You are here as his doctor. If you let him die you are a murderer."

"Do you love him, Fay?"

She was silent, still holding his shoulder.

"He's waiting!" said Alan.

"As a friend I think I do love him."

"Do you love him as a woman loves a man? Do you love him as you once thought you loved me?"

She said nothing.

"Was that the reason why you refused for so long to come on this journey?"

Gazing at him and holding him fast she made—so it seemed to her—a supreme effort to read what was in his soul. Never before had she so longed to speak the plain truth to a human being. But Pierpont's life hung on her action. How could she dare to speak it?

At last she said: "Mr. Pierpont doesn't love me. I'm quite sure of that, though I think he does care for me, and I know he respects me. I'm fond of him as a friend. I acknowledge it. But if I hated him, and he died by your wilful neglect of him, when I saw him dead I should hate you much more. I should hate you as I never thought I could hate any human being."

Her grasp of him relaxed. In the sudden softness of her hand he seemed to feel hatred.

"Now go and save him!" she said.

She took away her hand. Alan got up.

"I'll get the remedies," he said in a husky voice.

And he turned to go out to the place where their luggage was heaped beside the lying camels. As Fay watched him moving she knew he would do what he said; she knew he was going to save the life of Pierpont. And as that knowledge came to her there came to her with it an overwhelming sense of moral degradation. Alan hadn't loved her quite enough. Otherwise she would not have come on the great journey. But in his way, the way that was possible to him, Alan had loved her. Suddenly she felt a stern necessity to rise up to the best that was possible to her, and she felt also a stern necessity to see Alan rise up to the best that was possible to him.

"Alan!" she called out. "Come here! There's something more I must say."

He came and stood in the tent door.

"Alan, I have told you a lie. I do love Horace Pierpont, and he loves me. We both knew it at Beni Mora. We never spoke of it there. But he did tell me about the journey before he told you, and I realised he would ask you to make it not because you were a doctor, but because he cared for me and wished to have me near him. I was insincere with you in concealing that. I felt I couldn't tell you after I had refused to go. When I understood that you could go without me—that night on the terrace—somehow my sense of chivalry, of honour towards you, seemed to die in me all in a moment. Women are made like that, Alan. They can't help it. If it's anyone's fault it's the Creator's. So then I said I would go. But Horace Pierpont and I never spoke of our love for each other till the other day at Insalah. Then we spoke together. He has never taken me in his arms. He has never kissed me. Once I asked you how much love you had to give to me. And I said that some men had more to give to a woman than others had, and that they were the dangerous men to women like me. I was thinking of Horace Pierpont when I said that. I feel he's a big man and that he loves in a big way. Now you know all the truth. Go and save him now, Alan, knowing it. Somehow I feel you can. You are a generous man. I have always known that in my heart. Save him and then let us part from him. We must go back to Beni Mora, Alan. You will have done a great thing, though it is such a simple thing to do, and, of course, just your plain duty. But to be able to do it in this moment will be great, I think, and I shall always love you for having been able to do it."

Then she turned away from him, knelt down by her little camp bed and laid her face in her hands.

At that moment she was conscious of a wonderful sense of peace. A great burden seemed to have slipped from her shoulders. In a moment she heard Alan's voice say:

"Thank you, Fay. I'll go and look after him."

And then she was alone.

Pierpont, who had stripped to his shirt, and was lying down on his bed, heard a step and looked at the tent door.

The doctor came in carrying a leather case in his hand.

"How are you feeling?" he asked.

"Pretty well. There's beginning to be a faint sensation of nausea."

"That'll increase, I expect. And you may be cold presently."

"Cold!" exclaimed Pierpont incredulously.

"Yes. We shall have to remain here and keep you quiet for several days, in all probability. I'm going to inject Calmette's anti-venomous serum, and, close to the bite, permanganate of potash."

He began to open the leather case. His manner was quiet. His voice, to Pierpont, sounded professional. Pierpont lay and watched his preparations for a moment. Then he said:

"What did she say?"

"Oh, she backed you up. Evidently I've been a fool. The sirocco has got into my veins and poisoned me, body and mind, for the time. I ought to apologise to you, I suppose. Now then!"

"Wait!" said Pierpont.

"There's no time to lose."

"No, no—wait! I do love your wife. I loved her at Beni Mora, but I never told her so. I never said a word to her. But I loved her and I love her still. That's why I asked you to come with me."

Alan stood by the bed with the needle in his hand.

"Does she love you?" he asked.

"Not a bit. She knows nothing about it. But I couldn't let you cure me without telling you. I thought I could in the gully, but now—damn it!—I can't."

"Pierpont, you're a tremendous liar. But I don't think you'd lie except for a woman. She's different. She's —she's"—his mouth twitched for a moment—"she's given you away, Pierpont. She backed you up at first. But when she saw I was getting the serum she couldn't keep it up. And now I've something to tell you, and then we shall be clear. I let the snake bite you. I wished it to bite you. But I can't let it kill you, Pierpont."

He bent down over Pierpont and injected the serum into him.

Fifteen days later, after a brief but sharp illness, Pierpont stood in front of the officers' quarters at Insalah and watched a caravan start for the north. Fay Mortimer had found the fatigues of desert travelling too great for her endurance, and had been forced to abandon the journey to Tombouctou. Her husband had, therefore, resigned his position as doctor to the American, and was on the way back with her to Beni Mora. The almost impossible had been accomplished. The caravan had been broken up. Two French officers with an escort had happened to pass Insalah on their way to Ouargla just when the Mortimers and Pierpont were debating what to do. And at the instance of Colonel Laperine, the commandant of Insalah, they had agreed to look after the Mortimers as far as Ouargla. From there it would be quite easy to reach Amara and Beni Mora. Saad ben Youssef remained with his master.

As the moving caravan crawled, a long darkness, over the sunlit sands, Colonel Laperine, who was standing beside Pierpont, remarked in French:

"That was a very charming woman."

"Mrs. Mortimer; yes, she is charming."

"Much too charming to go to Tombouctou. And yet I think she was very unhappy at giving up the journey."

"D'you think so? She went off quite gaily."

"Oh, yes. She went off quite gaily."

"Well, then!" said Pierpont lightly.

"Are they happy together, those two?" asked the Colonel, still following the caravan with his keen eyes.

"Surely! Don't they seem so?"

"He looks very ill, I think."

"He doesn't look well, poor chap."

"If—— I wonder whether she would break her heart?"

"I think she has a great opinion of her husband," said Pierpont firmly. "He's a fine fellow. The trouble he took with me was quite wonderful."

"Then you certainly have cause to think well of him."

"I have, indeed."

"There's something about Madame Mortimer that intrigues me very much," said the Colonel, "and—the devil—I don't know what is. She looks to me like a woman who has travelled even farther than Tombouctou. She looks—but speculations are useless. With a woman one never knows."

"No," returned Pierpont. "With a woman one never knows."

With a sigh Colonel Laperine turned away and went into his quarters.

But Pierpont stood where he was till the moving darkness of the caravan faded into the golden bosom of the sands.

TWO: THE LOST FAITH

I

WHEN Lord Sandring returned from America he was in high spirits. His visit had been more interesting, more delightful, even than he had anticipated. He had been warmly welcomed in various centres of culture, had met many fascinating personalities, and to crown his satisfaction, which, indeed, almost amounted to complacency, had brought off a *coup;* yes, really a coup. He had persuaded, induced, got—he finally settled on that strong, virile little word *got*—Olivia Traill, the most remarkable woman in New York (if he knew anything of women), to promise that she would cross the ocean in February and pay a visit to London to show them all how well-founded his theories were. His peers might call him a crank, a fellow with a bee in his bonnet, a victim of charlatans, even a bit of a charlatan himself. Pioneers, the hewers of new paths through the forest of ignorance towards the clear light of true understanding, were always girded at, sneered at. Olivia—it had already come to that, merely Olivia— Olivia would show them! Lord Sandring went about almost chuckling under his bristling brown moustache, as he repeated to himself again and again that Olivia would show them!

Lord Sandring was unmarried, rich, and just at the right age. He was thirty-eight; old enough to know, young enough to exult. The follies of youth lay behind him, the dreary regrets of old age perhaps before, but far ahead in the distance. Meanwhile, there he was —mature, like an excellent bottle of wine. And he had *got* Olivia to do it. He was indeed a happy man when he walked into the Bureau of Psychic Healing, which he had established at his own expense in a quiet street not far from Piccadilly. He was going to make Harley Street "sit up," by Jove, he was. The doctors laughed at his pretensions, but wait till Olivia arrived!

She came by the Yellow Star Liner, the *Hiawatha,* and Lord Sandring and his ardent coadjutor, Miss Averil Jones, met her on the quay at Liverpool. It was a day such as might have been described in the *Inferno,* but Lord Sandring was in a state of properly controlled ecstasy, and Miss Jones, in a coat and skirt of heather mixture, boots the shape of the foot, and a hat that would have looked well on the head of a statesman of sporting tendencies, beamed over her pince-nez as who should say "Hallelujah!"

"Are you quite alone?" said Lord Sandring, as he grasped Olivia's firm hand and looked into her steady, unworldly grey eyes.

"Oh, yes," she said, in a strong mezzo soprano voice.

"No maid?"

"I don't need a maid on a journey. Do you?" she turned her cordial eyes on Averil Jones.

"No, of course not," said Averil. "But then, I never wear anything that fastens behind!"

"Now you're treading on the verge of the mysteries," laughed Lord Sandring. "Hullo!"

At this moment a tall, well-dressed young man, apparently almost a boy, with light, straight hair, a short upper lip, and ardent, indeed almost fanatical, blue eyes, suddenly interposed his athletic figure between Olivia and her welcomers.

"I've got all your luggage together," he said to Olivia. "Your porter's number is fifty-three, a short man with a nose—well, I mean, with an unusually large nose. Shall I——?"

"Let me introduce you to Lord Sandring," interrupted Olivia.

The young man swung round with an eager, searching look.

"Lord Sandring, this is a friend of mine, Fernol West. Fernol, this is Miss Averil Jones."

"Glad to meet you," said the young man. "You may possibly have heard of me. Not that I am famous! But she cured me. I'm just one of her marvellous cures. My father is Garstin Allerton West, the financier. I had a bad accident in Central Park, fell from my horse. She pulled me out of hell."

Lord Sandring glowed.

"Of course I've heard of you. I was hoping to meet you in New York, but you were in Chicago with your father when I was there. You are one of the greatest proofs of our dear friend's powers. Miss Jones, you remember my telling you——"

"The case is tabulated at the Bureau," said Averil. She gazed at the young man with profound interest. "You're tabulated," she assured him.

"Sounds cosy!" he rejoined. "Seems to give me a sort of niche over here, makes one feel at home. I shall think of that at the Savoy to-night. I owe it to her. I owe everything to her."

There was something striking in the tone of his manly voice, something that suggested worship, a hidden thing absorbed, living by, and in, some atmosphere, deprived of which it must fail and fall away and be as nothing. Lord Sandring's thin, eager face suddenly became grave, intense. A piercing curiosity shone in his small, dark eyes. He lowered his head and gazed at Olivia.

"I was enabled to do him good," she said simply, without the least trace of conceit or egoism. "He had faith in me and that made it inevitable. Now, good-bye, Fernol. I'll remember—number fifty-three, with a nose. I'll write to you when I'm settled."

The young man took off his soft hat. But Lord

Sandring had a word to say to him, more than a word.

"You'll be at the Savoy!" he said. "I shall be certain to find you there if I call?"

"Oh, yes. It's good of you to say——"

"Good! I'm deeply interested in your case. You are a living wonder, Mr. West."

"That's what my people over there say."

"You are a great proof that my theories are founded on the impregnable rock of truth. Lunch with me to-morrow in the restaurant at half-past one, will you? We must be friends."

"So—you didn't come alone!" said Lord Sandring to Olivia, as they went towards the customs, jostled by the crowd in the gathering darkness of winter. "You brought one of your 'cures' with you. A very sensible thing to do. It will help us greatly with London."

"But I didn't bring Fernol," she said. "He turned up on the boat. I knew nothing of his intention. But I'm very glad he came over. I love him."

Miss Jones jumped in her heather mixture under the statesman's hat.

"One loves those whom one has healed," said Olivia. "They are witnesses to the Divine Power, and one can't look at them without joy. And joy and love are twins, I think."

"Oh, in that way! I quite understand!" said Miss Jones, with a little air of evaporation.

"I know! I know!" said Lord Sandring.

She took a long and very feminine survey of the Faith healer, and then added: "I think you are very universal, Miss Traill."

"But very personal, too," said Lord Sandring. "Intensely personal."

"There's the nose!" exclaimed Olivia. "I'm certain that's number fifty-three."

"How quick you are!" said Lord Sandring. "Nothing escapes you! You are really wonderful!"

And he made for her porter.

Within half an hour they were all in the London express, rushing through the darkness towards the great city.

They had agreed not to talk at the request of Olivia. She had said very simply that she wanted to "get ready" for London. She had never yet been there. She was going there not as the ordinary person goes on business, or pleasure, or family affairs, but to bring to London her great power of healing, a new force, almost a new gospel. Although absolutely free from pose, Olivia took herself and her powers seriously. She could not do otherwise, for she believed herself to be the repository of a noble force, and she had to be careful of it, to guard it, to cherish it, lest it might diminish or die out altogether. So she "gathered herself together" while the train ran on, while Lord Sandring read "the Hibbert Journal," and Miss Averil Jones turned the pages of "Country Life" and meditated on the respective beauties of Tudor and Georgian homesteads.

Olivia was only just twenty-eight, but she had had already a remarkable career. The daughter of a Boston bookseller, she had been an unusually earnest and meditative child, though crammed full of vitality, and not without the saving grace of a robust sense of humour. She had worked hard at college and had done well. But her teachers, and even many of her school-mates, had felt rather than noticed in her something that set her apart from the typical "bright" student, who is good at passing examinations and carrying off prizes. Sometimes she had seemed to fall into walking dreams, to become abruptly remote, and at these moments there was about her, as if emanating from her, an atmosphere heavy, indeed almost sullen, which suggested a caged power softly struggling to spread itself over large spaces. Many were disturbed by this atmosphere, and asked Olivia why she was so "odd" at times. She had no satisfactory answer to give them. For it was no satisfac-

tory answer to tell them that she felt "odd" in these moments.   She herself did not know why she was seized
with a strange sensation as if someone were thwarting
her, as if she possessed something—some power—which
she ought to give out, to exercise, but which she was
obliged to keep shut up within herself, useless, till it lay
like a burden upon both her body and soul.   Sometimes,
giving herself up to introspection, she asked herself what
this power was.   But she could not identify it.   She did
not feel that she was superior to her college mates in
intellect.   She had fairly good brains, but there were
many others who had brains as good as hers, or much
better.   Her imagination was not remarkable.   She was
not conscious of possessing the peculiar gifts of one des-
tined to be creative.   Nevertheless, she often felt that she
possessed some hidden force which set her apart from
all those about her, and at times it seemed almost to rend
her.   Then she became melancholy, brooding, perhaps
sullen, and was beset by a numbing misery half spiritual,
half physical.   This continued till she was seventeen.
    Then enlightenment came.
    A young and pretty girl who was afflicted with St.
Vitus's dance arrived at the school.   At times she was
like the other girls, but in moments of excitement, or
if she were startled by any unexpected happening, she
would twitch, jump, turn her poor head awry, jerk her
hands and arms, almost rattle in the throes of her piteous
complaint.   Some of the girls laughed at her till they
were rebuked by the mistresses; others were afraid of
her.   Nearly all the pupils wondered at and finally pitied
her.   And the poor child pitied herself, and was deeply
ashamed of the exhibitions she gave.
    Olivia, who had a great deal of stillness and calm,
despite her abounding vitality, had never before wit-
nessed such a nervous complaint, and at first she looked
on it with an amazement which she tried to conceal.   Her
amazement was succeeded by a shrinking of disgust for
which she blamed herself severely.   But her blame of

herself did not drive the disgust away until the appointed time.

One day when Olivia had fallen into one of her "moods," as her college mates called her peculiar fits of depression and uneasiness, Lily happened to be in the room with her reading. Lily was deeply interested in her book, and was sitting quite still, immersed, self forgetful and happy. Olivia was brooding in a corner. A dog outside gave vent to a piercing and prolonged howl.

Instantly Lily fell into a sort of convulsion. The hand which was holding the book shot up from her lap, hurling the book into the air. Her head jerked frantically. Her whole body was in violent movement. Even her teeth snapped. Olivia sat watching for a moment. Then, as if ordered, she got up, came over to the child, stood in front of her, gazed steadily at her, and said in a firm, rather loud voice:

"Lily, you need not do that."

"I—can't—help—it!" gasped the child.

Olivia stretched out her hands.

"Yes, you can. Take hold of me."

The child mechanically snatched at Olivia's hands and clutched them.

"That's right. Now believe that I can stop you from shaking like that and I shall be able to stop you."

There was authority in her voice, authority in her whole bearing, and in her steady and shining eyes. Lily looked at her, and was quieter.

"Now lift your hands with mine and press them against your forehead."

Lily did so, and in a few minutes was perfectly calm.

"I can cure you of your trouble," said Olivia.

"But the doctors can't."

"That's no matter. Just tell me—do you believe that I can cure you?"

After a pause, and a long look, the child replied simply:

"Yes."

That was the beginning of Olivia's career. She had discovered what the power was which she had long suspected she possessed, which she had long sought for. She was a natural "healer."

An extraordinary feeling of relief, of emancipation, came to her. She seemed to float into peace. Strength thrilled in her, tingled all through her. A great oppression was removed. The burden dropped from her—the burden of ignorance. She had not known what she was, now she knew. And she was wonderfully happy, and worshipped. She worshipped what was within her, and Him who had put it there. But she did not worship herself. For, even in that first moment of illumination, she regarded herself as a vessel into which something precious had been poured, and she was humble in spirit.

She was humble, but she was exalted with faith. Faith made her feel strong like a lion and prodigiously independent, as if the world belonged to her, was suddenly enclosed in her hand.

So—Olivia began her career, a career which was to bring her into extraordinary prominence, even into fame.

She cured Lily of St. Vitus's dance—not immediately, but within a few months. The nervous excesses became less violent; less prolonged; the intervals between them widened; finally they yielded instantaneously to treatment by Olivia, and at last ceased altogether.

Lily's parents were enraptured, and Lily herself regarded Olivia as a giver of life. The cure, having been made in a big school, was carried abroad by many tongues of mistresses and pupils.

Olivia was soon on the way.

At first her parents were inclined to be alarmed by the new and startling development in the family circle, but they quickly "came round" when they realised Olivia's quiet determination, and noticed the respect in which she began to be held by many of their neighbours. Mr. Traill had an important and prosperous bookseller's business, and as his daughter's fame spread abroad he found that it did him no harm. Certainly the doctors showed a strongly antagonistic spirit, and were contemptuous of his daughter's cure, but, on the other hand, the newspaper men took her up. She was written about, interviewed. People thronged to his store to inquire about her, and often bought books when their curiosity was partially satisfied. Olivia's peculiar gift, if gift it were, certainly made things hum in the store. And then Olivia herself was greatly improved since that first strange episode with Lily. A sunny cheerfulness radiated from her. Her vitality of mind and her vigour of body were strengthened. It was impossible not to feel the power which emanated from her, difficult not to believe that it was wholly beneficent.

Her parents would never submit themselves to Olivia when they were unwell, which happened now and then. They stuck to the family doctor, who, by the way, was a good customer to the store. But they soon began to be rather proud of her "cures" in the town, and acknowledged that there was "something in it all." America is the home of strange "cults." By degrees a sort of "cult" for Olivia grew up. She took it all very quietly and reasonably. Her head was never in any danger of being turned by the noise made about her. She was full of robust common sense, and never encouraged folly in others. But side by side with the strain of common sense in her there was another strain. When she had discovered her power of healing she had discovered the source from which it flowed. That source was faith. When she stood before her convulsed school-mate she had felt that she was resting on a rock, the rock of a great faith; faith in her power to heal, faith in Him who had given it to her. At that moment she had realised a mighty truth, that faith can move the mountains. And she knew that she had moved her first mountain on the day when Lily was cured.

From that day onward she strove to live by faith. She boldly called herself a faith healer, and declared that though no doubt she possessed some peculiar physical gift, without faith she would be powerless to employ it beneficially.

She spoke quite frankly to those who cared to listen about the necessity of this strange and mysterious aid, and demanded co-operation from those who consulted her.

"I don't believe I can bring about a complete cure of any malady if I fail to convey my own faith in myself to the patient," she said. "I need reciprocal faith."

And often she would say to the sick:

"I believe that I can cure you, and you must believe it too. Then we shall work together, and all must go well."

Very seldom she failed to pour faith into those who came to her. The mere sight of her often swept away scepticism.

Olivia was not beautiful. She was fairly tall, with a rather large frame and robust shoulders. Her features were blunt and rough hewn, lacking in fineness and delicacy, but powerful and indicative of will. Her brow was broad and intellectual, and her grey eyes were large and lustrous. She had splendid brown hair, full of life and warm colour, which she wore parted in the middle and gathered into a big roll behind. Her whole appearance suggested honesty, fixity of purpose, energy and kindliness. There was never a trace of self-consciousness in her look or manner. Her bearing was fearless and simple. She always dressed plainly, with extraordinary neatness, and never wore anything that was eccentric or likely to draw attention to her. Most people were instinctively attracted to her at first sight. There were some who declared that she possessed hypnotic powers and used them without acknowledging them.

Her fame gradually spread from her native city to distant parts of America. She was discussed, written about, praised and abused. The Christian Scientists soon heard of her, and tried hard to persuade her to declare

herself one of their body. But she told them plainly
that she found grave errors in their teaching. She
thought the denial of disease either insincere or ridiculous. She considered that to tell people that disease
exists only in mortal mind was to tell them a flat lie.
She held that disease does exist, that it ravages the tis-
sues of the body, that it causes often agonies of pain,
that it may devour the organs by which men live, and
bring about the cessation of life, but that it may be ar-
rested and finally expelled by the mysterious curative influence of another body helped by the mind and soul
within it.

"I have such a body," she would boldly declare, "and
by it, using it as a vehicle, I convey the healing force
which is mysteriously connected with the soul." She
never tried to cure people without touching them. "I
don't believe I could do it," she said. "I have no faith in
what the Christian Scientists call 'absent treatment.' Perhaps I am wrong in my scepticism. I can't help that.
My beliefs and my disbeliefs are given to me, I suppose,
like my hands and feet. I find myself unable to change
them. I think it honest to acknowledge them. Christ
used the body in healing, and I cannot do less than He
did."

She firmly believed, and always upheld, that all the
so-called miracles of Christ were performed within the
natural Law, were not arbitrary violations of it. (Perhaps she forgot the raising of Lazarus.)

The incident which made Olivia famous throughout
the whole of the States was her cure of Fernol West.
. . .

Fernol West was the only child of one of the greatest
financiers in America, and was adored by both his
parents. He was a particularly strong, healthy and joy-
ous boy, very athletic and devoted to sports and games,
crammed full of life and hope and promise. When he
was eighteen he was the victim of a terrible accident.
While out riding in Central Park his horse, a very diffi-

cult one, bolted and dashed the rider against a tree. He was picked up senseless, and remained unconscious for three days. Then he opened his eyes, moved, spoke, took nourishment readily. His delighted parents thought that all danger was over. There was a wound in the head, but it gradually healed. No limbs were broken. The boy was soon able to sit up, to walk. He remembered his accident clearly. He knew what was going on around him. The doctors, the most famous in New York, said that he would soon be all right. He had had a tremendous shock, but boys as strong as he was got over such things, got over almost anything.

"It will be all right with him soon."

That was the verdict. And presently there was the rider—"He is all right."

But time passed and it wasn't all right with Fernol.

His accident had left him mysteriously and horribly changed.

He regained all the former strength of his body, but he had lost all his zest for life. He was haunted day and night by the black dog of an intense nervous misery. He tried to take up his old occupations, to study, to play games, to ride and shoot. His old companions sought him out. His devoted parents did everything they could think of to make existence bright and cheery for him. Love surrounded him. Money was lavished upon him. But it was all in vain. He got up in the morning dreading the day that lay before him. He went to bed at night secretly fearing the dark hours. Nobody was able to be of any real good to him. No amusements really distracted him. Formerly he had been devoted to music. Now the sound of music deepened, put an edge to his wretchedness, drove him lower down in his nightmare. Sometimes, carried by his malady beyond the restraining sense of shame, he would put his head down on his mother's knees and cry till he was exhausted. As he said himself, he felt "damned." It was inconceivable by him that he had once enjoyed almost every moment

of life, had enjoyed getting up, bathing, eating, studying, talking, playing games, shooting, dancing, reading
a book over the fire, meeting other fellows and knocking
about with them, sitting in a corner with a pretty girl.
He moved as one encompassed by a hideous black cloud
dreading everything, above all dreading himself.

Nerve doctors were called in to him. They said he
was the victim of acute neurasthenia, no doubt brought
on by his accident. They prescribed all sorts of things:
massage, physical exercises, tonics, sleeping in the open
air, rest cures, moving about, hypnotism, cold douches,
travel, hard mental work, no work at all, gaieties, complete solitude. Their followed advice did Fernol no
good. Even the hypnotists failed entirely with him. He
was not mad; he was just profoundly and unalterably
miserable. The brain specialists said that there must be
some obscure pressure on the brain. An operation was
suggested, but as the surgeons evidently did not know
exactly what they would operate for, Fernol's parents
would not allow it.

The boy began to be haunted by a longing for suicide.
But as he was sane he fought against it. Nevertheless
he wished with all his might that he could die painlessly
and have done with his misery, which was almost unbearable.

At last his parents tried a Christian Science healer,
who treated their son for a long period with absolutely
no result. This had seemed to them the last chance for
Fernol. Its failure left them and him in despair. The
boy said to his mother:

"Mum, I shan't be able to stick it out very much
longer. You don't know what it is. Nobody who hasn't
had this sort of thing can know what it is. I tell you
it's like going about and knowing you are damned for
all eternity. I'm sane, though you mightn't think it.
I swear I'm sane. But I can't stick it out much longer.
When I hear anyone laugh or see a happy face it just
——"

He broke off, and again had one of his dreadful fits of weeping.

That night the mother said to his father:

"Garstin, what are we to do?"

"There's nothing more we can do," said her husband.

"But if Fernol should——"

She did not dare to finish the sentence. They looked into each other's faces for an instant in silence.

Then Mrs. West said:

"There's only one more thing I can think of—that woman in Boston."

"What woman?"

"Olivia Traill."

"Another doctor! But——"

"No; she's a healer."

"That's what the doctors call themselves," said Mr. West bitterly.

"She lays her hands on people."

"Much good that'll do! No; we've tried everything. The boy'll never be right again."

"Let us try that Miss Traill," said Mrs. West. "It will be useless, of course, but—she has made wonderful cures, they say."

"Who say?"

"Well, the newspapers."

"The papers! Good God—if that's all!"

"I can't help it. I shall take Fernol to Boston."

"But we've tried the Christian Scientists."

"She isn't one. She doesn't believe in their theories."

"Then what does she believe in?"

"Herself, I suppose. She contends that it's done partly by faith."

"Money-making humbug."

"Do you mean that you would grudge any money ——"

"No, no! Take Fernol to Boston, my dear, if you can get him to go."

"I think he would try anything, poor child. It's—it's heartrending, and one feels so impotent."

"One feels what one is," said Mr. West drearily.

At first Fernol refused to go to Boston.

"It's no good, Mum," he said. "It's no good. I thought that hypnotist fellow might put me right. I believed in him. Even after sixteen goes of it I still hoped. But——"

"Come, for my sake."

"No, Mum! Don't ask me any more. Faith healing! And I've no more faith in any damned thing! Don't drag me to Boston."

"Go by yourself then!"

"No, Mum. Don't ask me."

She gave it up. But, to her great surprise, after a few days, Fernol said to her desperately:

"I am going to Boston. I can't stand another week of this. What's that woman's name?"

"Olivia Traill."

"Where does she live?"

"I don't know. But her father's a well-known bookseller. Ask for——"

"I'll find her."

There was an almost frantic look on his grey face; a frantic light shone in his sunken blue eyes.

"She'll be no earthly good, but I'll find her." . . .

Afterwards Fernol often told the story of that visit to Boston, told it as a man might tell how out of darkness he was caught up into Heaven.

He sought out the bookseller's store, and went in among the stacks of books and asked for the address of the bookseller's daughter.

A clerk looked at him curiously and gave it.

"When does she see people?" asked Fernol.

"Any time, I believe," said the clerk. "If she's in."

"I'll go now."

And he was out of the store in an instant. Not many minutes later he stood at the door of a modest apartment on the western outskirts of the city. A maid-servant answered his ring. He asked for Miss Traill.

"She's out at a meeting," was the reply.

Fernol felt a sickness run all over him till it seemed to find its way to his soul and make its home there.

"When will she be back?" he said.

"I couldn't quite say."

"May I wait? Please let me wait. I don't care how long she is. I'll just sit till she comes."

"You need her, I can see," said the girl. "You can come right in. She'd wish it."

"Would she?" said Fernol.

"She'd wish it."

He often said afterwards that something in those last words of the girl, and in the way they were said, gave him "a sort of lift."

"She'd wish it."

He stepped in, put his hat down, and was shown into a plain little living room, without any pictures or orna-ments. On the wall hung a scroll showing the words: *"Thy Faith hath saved thee."* A few books were lying about. They were all by the great optimists of the world: Emerson, Browning, etc. Fernol sat down in a small, but very comfortable easy chair, rested his head on the back and looked at the scroll. Presently he shut his eyes. He didn't feel sleepy, but he did feel in-clined to be passive. As he sat there life somehow seemed just bearable. For many months, though he had borne it, it had seemed unbearable. He laid his hands on his knees and let his muscles relax.

"There seemed to be something in the room," he af-terwards said, "that quieted a fellow down."

He sat like this for over an hour without taking count of time. Then he heard steps in the passage, the open-ing and shutting of a door and a voice speaking. It said:

"I'm rather late, Annie. Has anyone called for me?"

Another voice—the girl's—answered in a long and careful murmur. Then the first voice said:

"That's quite right. Never turn anyone away who seems really to need me. I'm here for that. Just take my hat and cloak and I'll go right in to him."

Fernol sat up. His misery was still upon him, that almost unbearable misery, at the same time vague and terrific. But he felt a sense of expectation which was new to him since his accident. Then the door opened and Olivia came into the room. He got up. She looked straight at him with a smile, held out her strong hand cordially, and said:

"Good evening. I'm sorry I've kept you waiting. I've been out to a lecture. What's your trouble?"

"Don't you—don't you want to know my name?" Fernol stammered.

"If you'd like me to know it."

"Fernol West."

Olivia sat down very near to him.

"Thank you. Now sit right down and I'll try to help you."

He obeyed.

"I've come from New York. My mother heard of you. She wished—I thought I would come."

"I'm glad. You're all wrong. I can see that. You're just choke full of what Metchnikoff calls 'disharmonies.' You know what I mean by that, don't you? You keep striking discords inside, and they make life hideous to you."

"Yes, that's just it. Life is hideous. How did you know?"

"Your face shows it. You want to get back to the harmonies."

"I do, oh, I do! It seems so unmanly—but I can't help it."

"Of course you can't. It isn't your fault. How did it begin?"

He told her the story of his accident and of his apparent recovery from it. Olivia listened with concentrated attention without interrupting him by a word.

"The doctors said I was all right," he concluded at last. "Until I had to go to the nerve men."

"And what did they say and do?"

"Well, some of them said I was all right, too, if I would only use my will and look on the bright side of things."

"In your condition that's easier said than done. Tell me everything they tried on you. Don't miss anything."

He told her about everything, including the suggested operation, the efforts of the hypnotists, and of the Christian Scientist.

"He told me there was no such thing as disease, that my trouble only existed in mortal mind."

"I sometimes wish it was so," said Olivia. "But, you see, the trouble is that it isn't."

"Then you think I am really ill?"

"You're very bad," said Olivia. "You're right down in Hell, and you've got to be pulled out. I know how you feel."

"Yes?" he said. "I—I thought I would come to you."

"Very well. Now, then, the first thing is to get quite clear between ourselves. I'm not a doctor, I'm a healer."

She spoke without the least trace of irony.

"I can heal," she said, quietly in her full voice. "I can heal you. That's as sure as that we're sitting here. But you've got to help me. Let's have a little talk about faith. Goethe says some fine things about Faith."

She paused, seemed quietly to collect herself, and then, leaning forward, quoted:

"In Faith everything depends on the fact of believing. Faith is a profound sense of security. The strength of this confidence is the main thing. Faith is a holy vessel, into which every man may pour his feelings, his understanding, and his imagination, as entirely as he can."

Again she paused.

"That's what Goethe says about Faith. And someone greater than Goethe said, 'If thou canst believe, all things are possible to him that believeth.'"

"Yes—I remember that," said Fernol.

"And I daresay it seemed to you just an improbable assertion, as it does to a great many people. Now, when you set out for Boston, had you any hope at all that I might cure you?"

"I don't think I had," said Fernol.

"Well, you took a ticket all the same. And when you got right here where I live?"

"I don't think I had any real hope."

"And when you sat in this room?"

"I—I seemed to feel something in this room."

"What?"

"I could hardly say. I felt quiet here, in a way."

"Did you hear me outside?"

"Yes."

"I meant you to. Get anything from my voice?"

"I—I don't know. But—yes—perhaps I did. I do believe I did."

"And then I came in, and here I am. D'you get anything from me?"

Her large grey eyes were fixed upon him, but tranquilly. There was no effort in their gaze. They just rested upon him, like the eyes of a good friend.

"Yes, I do," Fernol said at last, after a long silence.

"What do you get?"

"I feel more of a man with you than I have felt since I had the accident."

"You'd given up all hope of being cured, hadn't you?"

"Yes."

"And what do you say now?"

"I feel that if anyone on earth could put me right it would be you."

She smiled, almost tenderly and quite happily.

"That's just what I want you to feel. You're coming my way. And I'm just all faith; I haven't a doubt in me about my power to put you right. But I've got to fill you right up with faith too. Reach out your hands."

Fernol obeyed, and Olivia took hold of them, and kept them in hers resting on her knees while she went on talking about faith, and quoting what great men had written and said about it. She filled the little room with faith, till it almost seemed to the boy that he could see faith hovering there about the two of them like something tangible. Then at last she was silent and just sat holding his hands. Perhaps ten minutes went by; then she released his hands.

"You're better," she said.

Fernol started. Suddenly, when she spoke, he realised that for ten minutes he had been feeling contented —interested for the first time since his accident. That was very wonderful.

"You—you want me to go now?" he said.

He did not want to go; he dreaded to leave that room.

"I don't want you to go at all," said Olivia; "but I've got to get some tea, and then I have one or two others to see."

Fernol got up.

"Shall I see you again?" he asked.

A horrible anxiety pulled at his heart.

"Why, of course! I may have to see you a good few times. I can't tell yet how long it will take. But it's going to be quite all right. Where are you putting up?"

He told her the name of his hotel.

"Go there and keep quiet. Don't see a lot of people. Keep yourself for me. Read——" she went over to a table and selected a book—"Read some Walt Whitman. I love old Walt. And come here again to-morrow at the same hour. I feel very happy about you."

Her strong face lighted up with a splendid smile.

"There's a lot of faith in you already. But I want it to fill you right up. Faith makes men, and women too."

Fernol stood for a moment gazing at her. Then, with a slight awkwardness and with a flush on his face, he said:

"May I—will you please tell me what the fee is?"

"Oh, I never charge anything. See here, this is how it is. My father's a bookseller——"

"I know. I went to his store to get your address."

"Well, he's a good father to me. He knows how I feel, that to sell what comes out of the spirit into the body and goes out to those who need it badly wouldn't help me any in what I am trying to do. I never could hold with that, somehow. It would seem to get in the way. So he just keeps me going like this. It's good of him, but he's a good man though he runs a prosperous business. There's nothing to pay. And now before you go, just lay hold of this. You're not cured yet. So don't think it. Maybe before you get back to where you're staying, you'll feel almost as bad as ever, perhaps quite as bad. If you do, just say to yourself: 'But I was well for ten minutes. And to-morrow I shall be well for half an hour.' I tell you that. Do you believe it?"

"Yes," said Fernol.

"That means you're on the way to be perfectly well. You've got your two feet on the path that's to lead you right into the blessed sunshine. I do feel happy about you. Come again to-morrow at the same hour, and write to your mother to-night that you're better. I guess that will ease her mind."

"Thank you," he said. "She will be glad; my father, too. But you give me all this and I——"

"I like giving out. That's how I get in strength."

"That's funny."

"You'll try it some day and find it answers."

And she went with him to the door. As she opened it she said:

"Don't forget that letter to your mother."

"No, I won't."

"And if you feel very bad to-night, you'll write it just the same? You'll tell her you're better?"

"Yes."

"And you'll mean it, won't you? Then just put a good thick line under the words. Score them under. What time will you write?"

"Any time."

"No, that won't do. Tell me the time."

"Just before I go to bed—ten o'clock."

"At ten o'clock I'll sit and think of you scoring a line under 'I'm better.' "

She shook his hand and let him out. . . .

Just before ten o'clock that same night Fernol sat in his room in the hotel and felt terribly miserable. The influence of Olivia Traill seemed to him to be operative only for so long as he was with her, to be limited to her close neighbourhood. It was great. He knew that. He had felt it like something one can grasp and lean on. But when her door had shut her out from him, when he was alone, could no longer see her steady eyes and hear her reliant voice, he had fallen again into the blackness. And awful doubts had assailed him. If she could only act upon him when he sat with her, felt the clasp of her hands, he could never be healed by her. For he could not live always in her presence. Was she like a doctor whose treatment was only efficacious while he was sitting by the patient's bedside? Fernol was almost terrified. For he had mounted, and now felt like one fallen from a height and lying bruised and bleeding in some hideous ravine. Nevertheless, as the hour of ten drew near he remembered his promise, went to the writing-table and sat down. He did not like to break his promise. That would be dishonourable. And yet how could he write to his mother a lie? It would make her happy, fill her with hope, and then, when she saw him again, her old distress would return upon her intensified. Had he the right thus to deceive her, to lay up for her such a burden of grief?

Yet he took paper and pen. He began to write. The clock struck ten. He thought of Olivia. He knew she was doing what she had said she would do. She was sitting in her little room thinking of him. She would take nothing from him. She was a splendid woman any-how. A sense of pure chivalry came to the boy, guided his pen in the words: *"I am better."* Then he hesitated. Could he score a line under them? "Yes, damn it, I will!" he said to himself with a sort of defiance. And he drew a thick line. As he did so the cloud lifted from him—for just a moment, and he thought Olivia was smil-ing in her room. . . .

Three weeks later he wrote to his mother:

"I am cured. Olivia Traill is the greatest woman I have ever met. I am happy. I enjoy everything I do. And it is all owing to her."

He returned to New York a changed being. His parents saw once more the gay energetic youth, full of the zest for life, whom they had rejoiced in and mourned almost as we mourn for the dead. They could not con-tain their delight. Their gratitude to the woman who had wrought the marvel was unbounded. Her abso-lute disinterestedness in the matter astonished them al-most as much as her extraordinary powers. Mr. West, especially, who was one of the shrewdest and hardest men of business in the States, found it almost impossible to believe that Olivia wanted no reward for all the time she had given up to his son.

"But no one does anything for nothing!" he said. "You must have made a mistake, boy. She'll send in the bill to me."

"I tell you, Father, she never takes money for her cures."

"Then she must take something else."

"She doesn't!" asserted Fernol, almost indignantly. "She works for the sake of humanity. There's no other woman like her. If you could only see her you'd understand."

"Does she know who I am?" said Mr. West.

"Of course she does."

"Then she's certainly a right down extraordinary woman."

When he was alone with his wife Mr. West said:

"I feel like going over to Boston to see this Miss Traill. I can't quite understand things."

"How d'you mean, dear?" asked his wife.

"Doesn't it strike you that Fernol may be in love with her?"

"I had thought of that," Mrs. West said, reflectively.

"Fernol will have big money some day."

He glanced at his wife.

"She might be playing for the big money, eh?"

"If she were I'd forgive her. I'd forgive her anything for what she has done."

"Well, Kate, I think I'll just run over to Boston and have a look at her. I can judge women as well as most men, I guess. That's why I married you."

Mrs. West found it difficult to combat this proof of her husband's astuteness. Moreover, she was intensely anxious about the Faith healer. So she encouraged him to go. He returned from Boston almost as enthusiastic as his son.

"The boy's right!" he said. "There's no other woman like Olivia Traill. And she's no more designs on Fernol than I have on the Presidency. What's more she won't take a cent. She's a grand woman. I only hope Fernol isn't in love with her. For she'd never look at the boy. I'm certain of that as I am that I shall carry through the amalgamation of Chicago Automatics with—but you take no stock in such facts, though you don't mind playing with the interest. A woman like Olivia Traill wouldn't fall in love easily, and if she ever did she'd choose a man among men. She's strong, she's bully strong, she'd look for strength."

"But our boy is strong, Garstin!" said Mrs. West, with a slight sound of huffiness in her gentle voice.

"Not in the way such a woman would want. Besides, she's seen him very sick, remember."

"And what has that to do with it?"

"You'd jump to it if you knew her. Watch it, Kate, for the boy."

And Mrs. West watched it, with that gentle, terrible cleverness of the adoring mother, and came to a not too unhappy conclusion.

Fernol adored Olivia Traill, but not in the way of a hopeful or even a longing lover. He looked up to her as a lover never quite looks up. There was a peculiar moral admiration in his worship which somehow excluded the possibility of physical passion. Mrs. West soon found that out, and was perfectly at ease in the matter.

"Fernol could no more imagine Miss Traill belonging to him than I could imagine belonging to Mercury," she said. "He sees her with wings, Garstin."

"So you've figured it out that I haven't got any wings."

She stroked his hand.

"I should never have fallen in love with Mercury. We needn't worry."

And they didn't. But they made a tremendous propaganda for Olivia. And the papers were full of her marvellous cure of the millionaire's son. Fernol had no sort of shyness in alluding to his former condition of misery and contrasting it with the glory and wonder of his now abounding health. He tried to pay part of his great debt to Olivia by singing her praises. He interested himself in the progress of her fame. He was furious with those who attacked her, resented all criticism of her almost fanatically. There was indeed a hint of fanaticism in him since his return to health which had been absent from, or at any rate had lain dormant in, him before his accident. This marked a slight, but definite, change in the boy. But few people noticed it as anything strange.

And his father and mother thought it quite natural, and even fine, a proof that their boy had in him chivalrous feeling and an almost fierce sense of gratitude. Fernol's great desire was to persuade Olivia to come to New York, and, at last, with the help of his parents, he achieved it.

She stayed with them for a week in Fifth Avenue.

From the first moment of her arrival she conquered Fernol's mother. And she conquered many others in New York. She wished to have a quiet visit and the Wests wished her to have it, but it was impossible to keep everyone out. There were many who were anxious for her to try their healing powers on them, and who clamoured to be received by her. She was firm in refusal of these, however, and saw only the Wests' most intimate friends. She had come to have a little holiday because she needed it. She knew when rest was necessary for her, and she was resolved to have it. So she went about with Fernol and his mother to see beautiful things, pictures, statues, antiquities, and she let them take her to hear fine music.

"I'll come here again some day to work," she said. "There's a new field for me here, and I feel like tilling it and putting in some seed. But not just now."

It was when they were at a concert one afternoon that Fernol realised, with a sort of almost cutting sharpness, what Olivia had done for him. Music, once his delight, had been a torture to him when he was ill. Now, once more, it led him into those pure regions of joy to which no other art gives the soul of man entrance.

"When I hear music I know what you have done for me," he whispered to Olivia, during a pause. "And music makes me almost ache to do something tremendous for you. Why can't I? It hurts."

"You do all I want by being healthy in body and mind and soul," she said. "By being clean and bright right through."

After the concert he returned to this "ache," as he called it.

"That's the worst of music," he said. "It makes one feel one ought to do wonderful things, that one might do them if—something. But what is the 'something'? Music never seems to tell me."

"Perhaps some day you'll find some wonderful thing to do lying close to your hand, Fernol," said Olivia. "And then you'll do it, without music. I believe in doing things without anything from outside helping. All that is necessary to prompt us to the finest actions we are capable of lies in ourselves. I'm certain of that."

"You must be right. You always are," he said. "I hope if I ever can do anything wonderful I shall do it for you."

Olivia carried out her intention of putting in some seed in New York later on. She left Boston, rented a modest apartment which the Wests found for her in a quiet street not far from them, and settled down there to carry on her strange profession. She still refused to take fees, and continued to live on the very moderate allowance she received from her father. And people of all classes thronged to the little room where she saw patients, and read, as they came in at the door, the words Fernol had seen on the scroll at Boston, "Thy faith hath saved thee."

It was there that Lord Sandring found her when she had been in New York for over three years.

II

Lord Sandring was an enthusiast about what he called "Psychic Healing," and proclaimed his enthusiasm in season and out of season. He was an amiable man, with a good deal of energy and some cleverness, but he was easily carried away, and on more than one occasion had been taken in by charlatans. Society was inclined to laugh at him, and the medical profession sniffed in a

superior manner when his name was mentioned. But
he was delightfully imperturbable and revelled in con-
troversy. He was always keen to have "a slash at the
doctors," and frequently appeared on the platform in
support of his bureau. He possessed large estates in
Northamptonshire and Wiltshire, and, when they would
allow it, tried his powers of psychic healing on his ten-
ants and villagers. He asserted that he had made several "cures," and had published a beautifully-bound
volume dealing with them in detail. His claims and as-
sertions had been received, alas, with polite incredulity
by a sceptical world, but opposition only nerved him to
renewed efforts. He was of those who doubt the value
of any new theory unless it is attacked, and often said:
"If the doctors didn't go for me I should be afraid I
was on the wrong road." Such a man is difficult to
knock out, and hitherto, even after the most violent bouts,
Lord Sandring had always gone smiling out of the
ring. But, as his "Psychic Healing Bureau" did not
make much headway, he had gone to America to seek
for "new blood." Olivia Traill's arrival in London was
a triumph for him. He had persuaded her to come over
for a short time merely in order to show people that he
had preached a true gospel, that the healing power, backed
by faith, could accomplish marvels, that spirit could
sometimes do for the body something that medicine could
not do. His psychic healers had not been altogether lucky
in their well-meant endeavours to get the better of physical troubles. His instinct told him that the time had
arrived to "make a big splash." He meant to make this
big splash with Olivia.

She had come to London simply to put some seed in
new ground. She had accepted from Lord Sandring
the money for her passage over, not a penny more. He
had prepared for her a room at the Psychic Healing Bureau, where she would receive patients, and he had given
it out that the famous Miss Traill would not make any
money out of her visit to England, but came to put her

extraordinary powers gratuitously at the service of suffering humanity. He had also arranged for her to deliver a short course of lectures on "Faith," "The Power of Spirit over Matter," and kindred subjects.

Olivia's first lecture at the small Queen's Hall was not largely attended, but several well-known people were present. Among them, to the great surprise of Lord Sandring, was the celebrated soldier, General Sir Hector Burnington.

What Sir Hector was doing in that *galère* Lord Sandring could not imagine. He came in two or three minutes late alone, sat down at the back of the room, stayed till the end of Olivia's speech, and then got up and went out. Lord Sandring saw the General's towering figure on its way to the door as he rose to "say a few words" of comment on the lecture and of thanks to the lecturer. He was almost stupefied, but recovered his aplomb in a moment, and spoke with his usual energy and effectiveness. Afterwards he said to Olivia:

"I wish the audience had been larger, but you had one of our greatest men to hear you."

Fernol West, who was with them, said eagerly,

"Who was that? Was it the immensely tall fellow who sat at the back?"

"To be sure it was," said Lord Sandring.

"I saw him," said Olivia. "Who is he?"

"Sir Hector Burnington, the only man we've got with a genius for organisation and a supreme power of managing men."

"Burnington!" exclaimed Fernol. "You don't say!"

He flushed with pride for Olivia.

"We must get that in the Press."

"I shouldn't," said Lord Sandring, with unusual self-restraint. "Burnington's a wonderful fellow, but he's an odd fellow, and wants careful handling, if he can be handled at all. Some of the politicians say he can't. As to women—well, Miss Traill, I daresay you know his reputed views about them!"

"They say in the States that he thinks we are not helps but hindrances to any big man who's got big work to do in the world. Is it true?"

"True as gospel. Burnington has no use for women, but they worship him from afar."

"I wonder why he came to hear a woman speak," Olivia said thoughtfully.

"That beats me!" said Lord Sandring. "You spoke grandly to-night. I wonder what he thought of you."

Olivia did not show any anxiety to know the great man's verdict, but even she, who was almost entirely free from personal vanity, was secretly impressed by the fact that Burnington had sat and listened to her—a woman—for over an hour.

A few days later she received the following note:

> *2a, Cadogan Square, S.W.*
> *Feb'y. 17th.*
>
> *Madam,—I have not the honour of knowing you, but I heard your first lecture the other night at the small Queen's Hall. You are evidently a genuine believer in the power you claim to possess. I should like to have a few words with you if you have no objection. As I prefer not to set foot in the Psychic Healing Bureau— not that I have anything against it—I should be glad to know whether you could appoint a time to see me somewhere else. I should not detain you for more than a few moments.*
>
> *Believe me, Madam, yours faithfully,*
> HECTOR BURNINGTON.

Olivia laid down this letter, after she had read it carefully twice, and sat wondering for a moment. She felt both surprised and interested; she also felt flattered. The General's reputation was enormous. He was regarded by his countrymen as their supreme efficient, a man who had the strength and the intelligence to pull whole countries out of messes, to quiet rebellions by his mere presence on the scene of them, to set staggering protectorates firmly on their feet. He had transformed a war. What had he not done? But Olivia's peculiar interest in him sprang from report of his personality and from her remembrance of his many adventures, which had been recounted in the newspapers of the world. The mysteries of the East hung about him like heavy odours. Far away he had built up his reputation in regions whose mere names suggested romance. He had ruled over peoples whose wild eyes had never looked on our complicated civilisations, and had inspired them with reverence and awe. He spoke strange dialects of the East, and, a master of travesty, had travelled as a blood comrade with men who would have slain him had they known who he was. And he was reputed to be strangely selfless and heroic, and threaded through with a strain of fatalistic mysticism. He stood out from his nation as something portentously invulnerable; a soul of bronze in a body of bronze; supremely successful but cold and indifferent in his success, alive not to love, not to pity, not to fear, not to enjoy, but to get things done.

"Why does this man want to see me?" Olivia asked herself.

And the quiet firmness of her was slightly shaken. A hidden string vibrated for just a moment. She sat down and answered the letter, suggesting that the General should come to the little furnished flat which she had taken in Buckingham Palace Mansions on the following evening at six o'clock. She was usually at the Bureau till after five. In reply to her note she received on the following day a telephone message, taken by the porter of the mansions when she was out. The message was:

"The gentleman Miss Olivia Traill kindly wrote to will call on her at six o'clock."

When she had read it—she only did so at a quarter to six—she sent down a message asking the porter to bring up anyone who called at six. She was not expecting any visitor but Sir Hector. After her day's work she usually rested, unless she had to deliver a lecture. Lord Sandring would have gladly "run" her in his social circle, but she had resisted his kind importunities.

At five minutes to six when she was in her small sitting-room awaiting Sir Hector there was a ring at the bell. She went to answer the door, and found Fernol West with some flowers for her, and a new book by Rabindranath Tagore, which he knew she wanted to read.

"I didn't wait for the lift. I just ran up," he said. "May I sit with you for a bit?"

He saw that she hesitated.

"You're busy."

"No; come in, Fernol."

She shut the door.

"I'm waiting for someone who is coming to see me at six. It is Sir Hector Burnington."

"Burnington coming here!" exclaimed Fernol. "Do you know him?"

"No. He wrote to me."

"Is he ill?"

His eyes shone.

"If he's ill and you cure him the whole of England will believe in you. It will silence even those beastly doctors. They've begun to attack you furiously already. Have you seen to-night's *Messenger?*"

"No."

"There's an article by Sir Mervyn Butler called "Human Credulity and the Charlatans," warning people against you. Oh, it's made me so mad. These wretched fellows who can't——"

"Don't abuse people. That only does you harm."

"I know. But it's difficult when I know what you are, when I'm a breathing proof of your powers. Is he ill? Is Burnington ill?"

"Not that I know of."

"It may seem inhuman, but I would give anything

for him to be downright sick, real bad, so that you might cure him. Ah, it would go all over the world in a moment—such a cure as that!"

"Fernol," Olivia said, looking at him steadily. "I hope you will never be fanatical about me. I don't like fanaticism at all. I think it is unhealthy. And I want to feel that there's nothing unhealthy in you."

Before he could answer the front door bell rang.

"There he is!" said the boy, with an eager start. "Oh, I oughtn't to be here."

"You need not speak of his coming. I should be sorry to have a great name used. Now you might let him in."

As Fernol turned to go down the little hall, he whispered, with a sort of laughing worship,

"I can't help it. I want him to be ill, desperately ill!"

A minute later he opened the sitting-room door, showed a strongly flushed, excited face, and said,

"Miss Traill, Sir Hector Burnington has come to see you."

Then he stood against the wall, rather like a soldier at attention, and gave room for the famous general to pass.

Seen close in the bright light from electric burners Sir Hector looked almost gigantic in height. As a matter of fact, he was just over six foot three. His face was unusually dark in complexion for an Englishman; his dark brown smooth hair was parted in the middle above a very broad and very low forehead; his nose was straight and short, his chin firm but not aggressive, his mouth determined with tightly closed full lips. His ears were large, were set close to his head and indicated power. His figure was lean, and his tread was firm and striding. But in that first moment of meeting Olivia looked at his eyes. They were very peculiar eyes, set far apart, long, in colour green and brown—some people called them "greeny brown"—with unusually small pupils. And there was a curious glazed look in them, which suggested not dulness of intellect but secrecy, a remoteness that somehow was watchful. Impossible to look into them! Yet they seemed to look into you as well as beyond you. On his upper lip the general wore a thick brown moustache with a marked curve in it. His eyebrows were almost straight.

He strode in, looking imperturbable, grave and quite un-self-conscious, and held out a long brown hand.

"Good evening, Miss Traill. Very good of you to see me. What's your friend's name?"

"Fernol West," said Olivia.

The general shook hands with Fernol, neither cordially nor coldly.

"I'll be off now," said Fernol to Olivia.

She knew he was simply longing to stay, but she did not like to keep him as an appointment had been made with her visitor, so she said good-bye.

"Good-bye—sir," said Fernol to Sir Hector.

"Good-bye."

Fernol turned to go, took two steps towards the door, hesitated, then abruptly swung round.

"If you'll allow me I should like to tell you that when I was broken to pieces, she put me together again. They attack her. They've attacked her to-day in a paper called the *Messenger*. But I was in hell and she's made life worth living for me. I swear it."

He paused. There was something almost violent in his look and manner. He covered Sir Hector with an eager, searching glance.

"Ah!" said Sir Hector.

And he turned his strange glazed eyes on the lad.

Fernol waited an instant more, then went out, shutting the door rather sharply behind him.

"I did him good, so, as he's a chivalrous lad, he sings up in praise of me," said Olivia simply. "Please sit down."

Sir Hector sat down without any comment.

"Allow me to tell you the reason of my visit," he said. "I heard of you some two years ago. I know the States pretty well and I see American papers. As I happen to be interested in various things which most English people deride, and as I believe in a great deal which untravelled islanders, profoundly ignorant and proud of being so, deny, I attended your first lecture—as I mentioned in my note. I wished rather to obtain an impression of you than to listen to what you had to say. The impression I obtained was that you thoroughly believe in yourself."

"Yes, I do," said Olivia, looking steadily up at him from her chair. "I have absolute faith in my power of healing."

"Without it you could probably not heal even a slight nervous complaint," returned Sir Hector.

"I don't think I could, though I am sure I have some exceptional physical gift. It may be a gift of conveyance, which most people lack."

"Ah!" said the general.

He stared either at her, or beyond her—she was not quite sure which—for a moment, then he continued, in his deep and steady voice,

"I am not married, and I live at present—I'm looking into the condition of our artillery at the moment—with my only near relative, my unmarried sister. She is four years older than I am—sixty. She was, in my opinion, the finest horsewoman in the British Isles, but eight years ago, when I was in Afghanistan, she had an accident in the hunting field. Her horse, a big Irish hunter, fell at a wall and rolled over on her. She was kicked on the back of the head. Since then she has suffered from agonising headaches. They come on about once in ten days. The pain at first is slight, gradually increases— she often keeps about for some hours after the premonitory symptoms—and finally becomes terrific. Then she goes to bed and stays there, usually from twenty-four to thirty-six hours. After that the pain subsides and ceases.

Of course, she has had all the big doctors. And she's got
one—a pleasant fellow, Mervyn Butler by name—who
attends her regularly. He doesn't do her any good and
she knows it. But he does something, and I suppose,
when one's in such a condition, it's a sort of relief to know
something's being done. (I've never been ill in my
life, so I'm no judge.) It isn't pleasant to me to see
my sister under these perpetual attacks. And they'll certainly break her up in time if they aren't stopped. I
should like you to try to stop them."

"I will gladly do so."

"Ah!" said Sir Hector, with his peculiar stare, which
suggested to Olivia that he was looking out over some
vast expanse in the foreground of which she was set,
an almost infinitesimal figure.

"That is very kind of you. Thank you," he answered,
after the pause which was characteristic of him. "But
there's a drawback."

"What is it? Her doctor would——"

"Her doctor doesn't matter. He doesn't cure her and
I shall have no consideration for him. He fails in his
job. And no consideration should be shown to failures;
otherwise you create a sort of forcing house for the culti-
vation of inefficients. My sister is the drawback."

"Why is that?"

"She's the most sceptical woman in England about
anything mysterious. She likes hard facts, things ascer-
tained by science."

"Hard facts. And you?" said Olivia.

"I've travelled widely, and she hasn't," returned the
general. "I judge by results. My sister's doctor knows
a great many medical facts and is totally unable to cure
her headaches. He and his facts are, therefore, quite
useless to my sister. But, as women are remarkably unreasonable, she pays him heavy fees to go on not curing
her. Multitudes of women in England do exactly the
same. My sister will probably be entirely sceptical of
your power to do her any good if you come to her as

a healer . . . because she is ill. And her scepticism might frustrate your attempt to heal, I daresay."

"Perhaps it might," said Olivia. "But, then, what is your plan?"

"How do you know I have a plan?"

"I don't think you would have come here without one."

"Ah!"

Again the stare and the pause—a long pause this time. Then the general said:

"I told you that these headaches return every ten days, or so, with remarkable regularity. One knows when they are due. What I wish to do is this. I intend to arrange for a dinner party at my house on a certain evening. I shall know pretty well when to fix it. Even if my sister's headache has started she'll be down. She never gives in till she's obliged to. I want you, if you will, to come in the evening after dinner. (I hope another time you will honour me by dining.) My sister will meet you socially, will be able to observe you and see what you are, without connecting you with herself. It is possible that you may be able to impress her with confidence in your *bona fides*. If so, the ground will be prepared for the attempt at a cure. Then the cure might be attempted under favourable conditions."

"I am quite ready to come," said Olivia. "But please tell me one thing. Do you believe I can make such a cure?"

"I think it quite possible."

He stared into the distance.

"People are often sceptical from sheer colossal ignorance, or they are afraid of seeming superstitious. Both superstition and scepticism may grow from the same root—the root, by the way, of nearly all evil. I may write to you then?"

"Certainly."

"Do you object to cigarette smoke in your drawing-room?"

"Dear no!"

The general lighted up, after offering Olivia a cigarette, which she refused.

"Now," he said, "I wish to say a word or two in confidence. I shall probably be offered almost immediately one of the highest posts a man of British birth can fill. For years it has been the ambition of my life to get this particular post, because I know I am peculiarly fitted for it. It's a job I could do better than any other man I can think of. But it would be necessary for me to have a woman at my side if I accepted it. My sister is at present far too ill to undertake the position. She must be made sound."

In saying the last sentence the general seemed to be giving an order to someone.

"The doctors can't do it," he added.

"And if I fail in my job?" asked Olivia.

"H'm!" said the general.

A faint smile flickered over his face.

"You'll kick me out of your consideration into the limbo where the charlatans dwell, I suppose?" said Olivia.

"I shall be deeply obliged to you if you succeed," he replied.

He got up.

"The matter's quite clear now, I think."

"Quite clear. But may I ask you something?"

"Please do."

"Why, when I spoke just now about hard facts, did you say, 'I've travelled widely and she hasn't'?"

"I merely meant to convey that in travelling one comes up against many people with peculiar gifts, and that, therefore, one is not so disposed to deny possibilities as those who seldom move out of the region in which they were born. The English have some remarkable gifts as a nation; but their limitations are also remarkable. My sister is very English. She hates humbug. Having only just come over here, you may not know yet that in an English mouth the word humbug often covers just those very things which are most worthy of minute investigation. Ah!"

He stared down at her and, for a moment, there seemed to Olivia to be something piercing in the expression of his strangely detached eyes. He held out his hand. She got up and took it.

"If your friend, Mr. Fernol West, would care to come to my house with you when you come, I should be very glad to see him," said the general. "Good-bye."

He turned and went out of the room, striding with long loose limbs which looked as if they were made to grip a great war horse.

Six days later Olivia received a note from her visitor asking her if she would come to his house the following evening at half-past nine; in a postscript was added:

P.S. "I shall be very glad to see Mr. West, too."

Olivia wrote to say she would come and would give Fernol the message. She believed that she knew why Fernol was invited. Miss Burnington was sceptical; Fernol was an almost fanatical believer. The general knew that. Olivia had already realised that he was a man who usually had a purpose behind what he did.

Fernol was overjoyed when she gave him the invitation, and on the way to Cadogan Square on the following evening he expressed his feelings with animation. His chivalry had been hurt by Olivia's reception in London. So far her visit had not been a great success. Not many people had consulted her, and the attacks upon her, led by Sir Mervyn Butler, had been fierce. In a certain very well-known weekly paper it had been roundly asserted that American charlatans ought not to be allowed to prey upon the gullible English public, and that the powers of the police ought to be extended if they were not already sufficient to deal with such people in a fitting manner. Olivia's name had not been mentioned in the article, but it was obvious at whom the arrows were aimed. And a sentence in which "Pernicious busybodies whose brain power is as low as their rank is high" were gibetted was undoubtedly meant for Lord Sandring.

"I like Lord Sandring," said the boy to Olivia in the taxicab. "And he's worth all these beastly journalists and doctors put together. But I rather wish you hadn't come over under his auspices. I've found out that they laugh at him and the Bureau in London."

"I dare say they do," said Olivia's calm voice.

"Yes, but I mean he's really made some bad mistakes. He's made claims without proving them. He's had some rank failures connected with his Bureau. I can't bear to see all that come back upon you. Besides, it sets up a regular wave of unbelief."

He broke off, then said in an excited voice:

"I count a lot on this evening. If Sandring has done you harm—of course without meaning to—I count on Burnington to set you where you ought to be. I don't ask you to tell me why he called on you, or why he asked us to-night, but, of course, I know it must be something to do with your lecture. You must have made a fine impression on him. And he's a thundering great man. It's grand of him to ask me, and I can't think why he's done it. Can you?"

"He didn't say," was Olivia's quiet answer.

"If only he could fall sick and you could cure him! I would give anything for that."

"I don't like to hear you wish sickness for anyone, Fernol. That's the wrong sort of mind action. Sir Hector Burnington has never been ill in his life. My wish for him is that he never may be."

"I know it's all wrong of me, but don't you see——"

"I never want anyone to wish an unclean thing because of me."

"Unclean!" cried Fernol, as if stung.

"Yes, Fernol. I call it unclean of the mind to wish evil to anyone for any reason.

"I shall never be selfless like you," he said almost sulkily.

And he did not speak again till they reached the general's house.

As a footman opened the door of a large drawing-room on the first floor Olivia heard a murmur of conversation and was conscious of a very unusual feeling. Perhaps she was not quite sincere with herself in mentally calling it "excitement"; perhaps nervousness would have been the right name for it. She knew that it was caused by something in Sir Hector's personality, by the expectation of a great man who had impressed her with the sense of his ruthless bigness. Since she had met him she quite understood why he managed to make the men under him work up to the very limit of their capacity. She felt that she was about to be tested as she had not been tested hitherto. And a slight anxiety crept through her. She did not like it, and instinctively she put her head a little back, sticking forward her chin, as she walked into the room, followed closely by Fernol.

"Miss Olivia Traill—Mr. Fernol West," said the footman.

And immediately there was a silence in the drawing-room.

Sir Hector met them, shook them by the hand, and took them to a tall woman, with thickly waving white hair, who was getting up from a sofa by the fire.

"Let me introduce my sister."

Olivia looked at the pale, lined but handsome face of her hostess, a face marked with the impress of suffering, and at once lost her feeling of anxiety. Miss Burnington said a kind word or two, in a cordial, yet strictly non-committal manner, then turned to make the new-comers known to her other guests, Mrs. Harford, Lady Pangbourne, Colonel Lumley, and Sir Mervyn Butler.

At the mention of the last name Fernol's young face was flooded with indignant blood. This was the famous doctor who had attacked Olivia in the *Messenger*. Of course, the Burningtons were not aware of that or they would never have arranged a meeting between the two.

Making a strong effort at self-control Fernol stared at the enemy, and saw a good-looking, clean-shaven man, with a massive head covered with snow-white hair, deep-set yellow eyes, and a smiling sarcastic mouth. Then he found himself—he scarcely knew how—in a corner near a grand piano, talking with Mrs. Harford, a pretty woman, with a worn-out face, bright, quickly glancing eyes, and a pathetic smile, the wife of a well-known politician. She got him in less than five minutes on to the subject of Olivia.

"The general sprang her on us as a surprise," she said. "Do tell me about her. She's had quite a bad Press over here."

Fernol took up the cudgels. Mrs. Harford listened, at first with indulgence, then with swiftly growing interest.

"It's a great pity she's let Lord Sandring nobble her," she said presently. "He's got so hopelessly wrong with the doctors."

She glanced at Sir Mervyn, who at the moment was sitting with Colonel Lumley, a handsome man of not more than thirty-six, with a sharply intelligent soldier's face, and was taking very deliberate stock of the woman he had so recently thrashed in an article.

"I hate doctors," said Fernol, in a very low, very fierce voice. "Oh, I'm sorry!"

"Millie Pangbourne seems interested," said Mrs. Harford. "But she's interested in everybody who makes a noise."

"A noise?" said Fernol.

"In the world! If you don't she physically can't trouble about you. Her eyes mechanically refuse to see you. She's trained them to it, I suppose."

Lady Pangbourne, a dark, smart, pale and puffy woman, with self-conscious eyes, was engaged in a rattling conversation with Olivia. She did all the rattling. It was plain to see that Sir Hector's "surprise" had given her impetus. The general and his sister were in the group, and Fernol saw that Miss Burnington was watching Olivia with close attention, and that, while doing so, occasionally she winced, as if flicked sharply by whipcord, shut her eyes for an instant, and compressed her pale lips.

"She's got one of her horrible headaches coming on," observed Mrs. Harford. "She oughtn't to be up. But she's almost as iron in resolution as her brother. Fortunately for him he's got iron health too—never been ill in his life."

"Oh, does Miss Burnington suffer from headaches?"

"She's a martyr to them, a real martyr. Sir Mervyn is her doctor."

"Then why doesn't he cure her of them?" said Fernol. She caught his boyish sneer on the wing, as it were, and gave it a faint smile.

"For the best of reasons," she murmured. "Because he doesn't know how to."

"She could!" said Fernol.

"Can that be why she's here?" said Mrs. Harford. "The general always has a purpose——" She broke off. "It would be just like him," she concluded after an instant.

At this moment Miss Burnington shivered, and, losing her self-control for a second, put a thin hand to the back of her head. Sir Mervyn got up.

"Forgive me," he said, in a weighty agreeable voice, "I see you are suffering. Now do forget about us. Go up to bed and just do what I advised you with the——"

Before he had finished she had put her hand down and was smiling.

"No, no! What's that, Lady Pangbourne?"

"But, dear, you really look——"

"What were you saying?"

"I forget—something about Boston. Miss Traill, why don't you show us what you can do with poor Miss Burnington?"

As Lady Pangbourne said this she looked as alert as a weasel, and put her head on one side.

"Sir Mervyn won't mind. Will you, Sir Mervyn?"

The sarcastic lips smiled.

"I should be very much interested to see an exhibition of Miss Traill's healing force."

Olivia sat quite still for a moment looking at Miss Burnington. It seemed to her just then that she was back at her old school. She shut her eyes and saw Lily convulsed. And there came upon her that irresistible feeling of power to heal, of necessity to exercise it, that had long ago revealed to her what she was intended to do in the world. She remembered what Sir Hector had said about the scepticism of his sister, about the importance of preparing the ground. But something within her swept away caution. She felt too strong, too certain of herself just then to be cautious. She opened her eyes, and they rested on the face of Sir Mervyn Butler, who was looking at her with an expression of half amused, half contemptuous satire. No doubt he thought that her silence, her closing of the eyes, were calculated effects, tricks of the Sibyl designed to create an impression on the foolish. His face said so plainly. Sir Hector was watching her, too, with his remote and yet penetrating gaze. She looked at Miss Burnington.

"I never try to heal people in public," she said quietly.

"Very wise of you, Miss Traill," said Sir Mervyn.

"But——" She paused. Then she said to Miss Burnington, whose face was twisted with agony:

"I know I could do you good if you were able to believe in me. Can you believe in me?"

Miss Burnington evidently made a great effort to control herself. Her thin tall body stiffened under the influence of the mind.

"It's very kind of you to care," she said. "I'm sorry I am making such a fool of myself. But I'm really afraid there's nothing to be done for these tiresome headaches."

"I can cure you entirely in time," said Olivia, "if you
will only help me by believing I can."

Miss Burnington forced a smile.

"I should be only too thankful to anyone——" she began.

She broke off and got up from her sofa.

"I'm very sorry, but I must go up to bed," she said.
"The pain's too severe. Do forgive me for making such
a fuss. Hector, I'm quite ashamed of myself."

"Let me take you up," said Sir Mervyn.

"No, no,—I don't want to break up the party. Good
night. Good night."

She went towards the door. The general looked at
Olivia. She rose and followed Miss Burnington.

"Please let me come with you."

"It's too kind of you, but——"

She turned towards Olivia.

"Well," she said. "If you really . . . just to my bedroom door."

They went out together.

"Oh, but I wanted to see it done!" said Lady Pangbourne in a frustrated voice. "I thought they just put
their hands on people and the pain fled away."

"You are mixing Miss Traill up with your recollections
of the New Testament, Lady Pangbourne," said Sir
Mervyn. "These good ladies from the United States
are not all direct descendants of the Apostles."

"May I please tell you what Miss Traill did for me?"
said Fernol.

His cheeks were burning and he clenched his hands.
He came and stood before the doctor. . . .

Meanwhile Olivia had accompanied Miss Burnington
into her bedroom and shut the door. A fire was burning in the grate. Miss Burnington felt vaguely for the
electric light switch.

"No; don't turn it on," said Olivia. "Let us sit by
the fire."

She drew Miss Burnington down gently into a chair
and took both her hands.

"I will make you believe in me."

The firelight flickered over her strong face.   Miss
Burnington looked at her with eyes full of pain.

"I'm a fearful sceptic," she said.   "I can't help it."

"Do you believe Sir Mervyn Butler can cure you?"

"Sir Mervyn—oh, no!"

"Yet you call him in, don't you?"

"Yes.   I suppose I've a faint hope——"

"Have a little hope in me.   That's all I ask of you—
yet."

"Well, I do believe you're a very kind woman."

"I never take any money.   I only wish to do what I
was intended to do when I was sent into the world.
We are only at ease with ourselves when we do that.
Now sit quite still.   Don't say anything and I shall very
soon make you much better."

Miss Burnington leaned back in her chair and shut
her eyes.

"The touch of your hands is certainly very strong and
very soothing," she murmured.

It was half-past eleven when Olivia returned to the
drawing-room.   She found Sir Hector alone with Fernol
West.   He looked at her with, she thought, a sort of
severe enquiry when she came into the room.

"Your sister is asleep," she said.

"That's very unusual.   Did she take a sleeping
draught?"

"No.   I got her to bed.   No one must disturb her.   I
will call and see her to-morrow.   Now, Fernol, we must
be going."

"I'll have a taxicab sent for," said the general, ring-
ing the bell.

While the servant was getting it, they stood by the fire,
and Olivia told them what had happened in the bedroom.

"Your sister was in such acute pain," she said, "that

I think it undermined her scepticism. She clung to me as I suppose she has clung to her doctor. That seemed to be enough—her longing to be helped. Anyhow, I was able to diminish the pain, and finally she fell asleep. That is a step on the way to a cure."

"I am immensely obliged to you," said the general.

"You've done a lot for your country," said Olivia. "I shall be very glad to do something for you."

"If you cure my sister you will have done a great deal."

When he said that Olivia wondered whether he was thinking of his sister or of himself. His words, "She's got to be made sound," were still in her memory.

"I'm sure you are very fond of her," she said, almost appealingly. "She's a very brave woman, I should think."

"It would be odd if she were a coward," he returned.

The footman came in.

"The taxicab is at the door, sir."

"I'll take you down," said the general.

He came out bareheaded on to the pavement and helped Olivia into the cab.

"Good night," he said.

His large hand grasped hers.

"If you get my sister right Sir Mervyn will hate you."

"Isn't he fond of your sister?"

"Very, I believe; but fonder of himself as a sacred repository of medical science. Good night, Mr. West. Sir Mervyn considers you a neurotic, but you are an excellent fighter."

He turned away and disappeared into the house, leaving the footman to shut the door behind him.

"I—a neurotic!" said Fernol indignantly as they drove away. "Sir Mervyn said that because he won't have it that you can cure anyone, and I told him, I told them all, how you had cured me. I'm glad Sir Hector thinks I can fight. He's a glorious fellow. All England looks up to him. He could do anything for you."

"I don't want him to do anything for me," said Olivia.

"No; but others may wish for you more than you wish for yourself."

And then he fell into silence. But in the cab Olivia could feel the excitement of his atmosphere, and the doctor's verdict "neurotic" on Fernol stayed somehow disagreeably in her mind. When Fernol had first come to her in Boston he had certainly been suffering acutely from what the nerve doctors generally call neurosis. Did any trace of that old malady still show in him, perceptible to the trained observer? Or was Sir Mervyn merely malicious? She wondered a little. Surely she had made a complete cure of Fernol? She had never really doubted it till this moment. She was not sure that she doubted it now. But since they had been in London she had noticed once or twice. . . .

The taxicab stopped at the door of Buckingham Palace Mansions, and Olivia said good-bye to Fernol.

After a hard fight, one of the hardest of her career, Olivia conquered Miss Burnington's headaches. Her difficulty in doing this came, she believed, from the peculiar mind of her patient, for Sir Hector's diagnosis of his sister's nature had proved to be right. She found it almost impossible to believe thoroughly in any power which partook of the mysterious, any power to which she could not attach hard facts of which she could make a list for the benefit of herself and those about her. When Olivia had once in the course of argument with her quoted Sir Hector as an example of partially mysterious powers, Miss Burnington had disagreed with her.

"My brother rules men because he knows more about their jobs than they do themselves," she said. "He is a storehouse of knowledge."

Olivia could not gainsay that. But she tried to make Miss Burnington acknowledge that the extraordinary influence which the general exercised over men was partially due to something totally independent of knowledge,

to a force born in him, not acquired by him, a force felt
by everyone but not to be explained by anyone.

"Oh, Hector is no hypnotist," said Miss Burnington,
with a touch of sarcasm. "He is just a wonderfully able
man with a remarkably strong character. He does big
things because he *knows*. There you have the secret of
his power over men."

"Then it isn't a secret," said Olivia, with her pleasant, strong smile.

And she set herself again to the struggle with Miss
Burnington's malady; and she won, almost in despite of
Miss Burnington; almost, but not quite, for Miss Burnington was longing to be cured, and had lost all faith in
the doctors. Perhaps her longing helped Olivia, was the
weapon which put her scepticism out of action. Olivia
believed so, and was thankful. For she had never before
wished so ardently to triumph over any ill-health as over
those headaches of Miss Burnington. Sir Hector's influence was potent upon her, that influence which she felt
to be mysterious. Like the men who worked under him,
and were often afraid of him, she wished, even longed,
to satisfy him, to wring from him a "well done." Hitherto
she had never worked to win the approval of anyone.
Her efforts had been made because they were necessary
to herself. She had healed as an artist creates to satisfy
an imperious need. But now a change had been wrought
in her.

"My sister must be made sound."

As upon the scroll in her room at the Bureau her patients saw "Thy faith hath saved thee," so, during her
fight with Miss Burnington's scepticism and ill-health,
Olivia saw gleaming before her mind's eyes those words
of Sir Hector. She had received her order from this
strange man. She was determined to carry it out. And
at last she did carry it out. The headaches came more
rarely, lasted a shorter time when they did come, became
less and less painful, and finally ceased. Two months
went by without any headache at all. Miss Burnington

looked, as all her friends declared, "a different creature."
The dread which, despite her almost Spartan courage,
had haunted her eyes and been seen of men, faded from
them. A day came when she ventured to say:

"It really seems as if I might consider myself cured."

She was, of course, deeply grateful to Olivia for the
extraordinary kindness and assiduity which had been
shown without any hope of a reward. She had indeed
come almost to love Olivia. Nevertheless, so strong was
her ingrained habit of mind, she could not be fully persuaded that the cure was entirely owing to Olivia's power
of healing. It might be so. The facts seemed to point
that way. And yet—might it not be a mere strange
coincidence that she began to get better only when Olivia
came into her life? Might not some physical change have
been at work which happened to begin manifesting itself
just after she was brought into contact with Olivia?
Miss Burnington did not express these characteristic
doubts of hers to anyone except her brother. But they
prevented her from coming out into the open as a whole-
hearted champion of Olivia's powers. She was a very
sincere woman. Had she been positive that Olivia, and
Olivia only, had cured her, she would certainly not have
hesitated to proclaim the faith that was in her. As it
was she showed, hand in hand with her frank and freely
spoken of gratitude to Olivia, a certain reserve. She
could not help it. She was one of those rare women who
have to be true to themselves. She was not sure, and so
she would not say she was sure.

This slight but definite holding back on her part in-
furiated Fernol West. And he spoke hotly about it to
Olivia.

"After what you've done it's unfair," he said. "I believe it's because you're a woman."

"I'm quite certain it isn't," said Olivia. "Miss
Burnington has been extraordinarily kind about me."

"If Sir Mervyn Butler had done for her what you have

done she would have told everyone in London what a marvellous doctor he was. But women hate to give credit to a woman. I can't think why. Now, if it had been the general he would have said straight out that you had cured him, although they call him a despiser of women. He's great enough to do that."

"I'm quite sufficiently rewarded for what I have been able to do," said Olivia.

"How are you rewarded? People still write against you over here. You have never been accepted as you were in America."

"If I tell you, will you give me your word of honour not to repeat it?"

"Yes."

"Sir Hector has told me that he is convinced his sister's restored health is entirely owing to me. And not only that. He said to me only yesterday that if he were ever ill he would call me in and would not summon a doctor."

Fernol was silent for a moment.

"Did he say that?" he said at last.

There was something so peculiar in the tone of his voice that Olivia wondered.

"Yes," she said. "And I know he meant it. That is reward enough for me."

"Did he give you his word?"

"What do you mean?"

"Did he give you his word he would call you in?"

"I have just told you what he said. Why should he give his word? He never is ill, thank God."

"That's just it!" said Fernol slowly. "He never is ———. So what's the good of such a promise?"

He paused, like one thinking deeply, brooding almost. Then he said,

"The English are fearfully slow in catching on to big things that they're unaccustomed to, aren't they? We are more open-minded in America. Look at the way you've been ignored here, except when you've been libelled. It makes me sick. I should like to give them a lesson."

"Them?" said Olivia. "Whom?"

"The people over here, the doctors and the whole lot of them. They want it badly."

"Oh, I shall soon be going back to America. And it's high time you went. Your father wants you to help him, and you ought to be at work."

As she spoke she looked at him rather narrowly.

"I don't like to see you idle, Fernol."

"Do you want to get rid of me?" he said.

"No. But I want to see you busy and happy in the best way. I don't think you're quite yourself here in London."

"That's because of the way they have treated you."

"I am quite satisfied," said Olivia smiling.

"Because Sir Hector said that?"

"Coming from him it did please me very much."

"Well, I only wish he could have the chance to fulfil his promise," said Fernol. "Then the English would catch on to you at last. For everything Burnington stands for is gospel to them. They say he'll be the next Viceroy of India."

"I shouldn't wonder if he were," said Olivia.

"Would you be glad?" he asked her.

"Yes. I think he would be the very man for such a great post."

"You are wonderfully unselfish, Olivia!" he said.

There was a sort of break in his voice. His expression was oddly emotional. He gazed at her and she saw an affection in his eyes which stirred a faint anxiety in her.

"You do everything for others, and no one does anything for you. Sometimes I hate the world."

"Fernol, dear, if you talk like that——"

"Well?"

"I shall think I didn't really cure you," she said, soberly, almost sadly.

"You did cure me!" he exclaimed passionately. "And I shall never forget it, never."

And he flung out of the room.

When he had gone Olivia sat for a long while quite still. She was more disturbed in mind than she had ever been before, disturbed about Fernol and herself. She was almost sure that Fernol had guessed her secret. How? Had his curious devotion to her made him clairvoyant? or—did perhaps others know? For some time she had been deeply in love with Sir Hector, but hitherto she had believed that she had hidden her love from everyone. She was possessed by it, but she did not wish anyone to suspect that possession. For she felt sure that Sir Hector felt nothing for her. She could not imagine him loving a woman in that way. He seemed to stand entirely aloof from the ordinary human passions, isolated from them by an almost cold intensity, the intensity of the tremendous worker, concentrated on the doing of big things for his country. Perhaps—probably even—he was abnormally ambitious, but she did not feel his ambition as she felt his greed for work, his lust for the job he was fitted to carry through in the world.

Only a great man could be like that; no woman could ever care for accomplishment in just that way. In a woman's life work could never shoulder love out of the path. Did Fernol know her secret? She feared so. He had looked at her strangely when he said, "You are wonderfully unselfish." There had surely been knowledge in his eyes. She was touched by Fernol's devotion to her; she was grateful for it. She knew he was not in love with her, never had been. And yet to-day she felt as if there were something almost dangerous, almost menacing, in his affection; she felt almost afraid of—or was it for—Fernol.

She had known for some time that the post Sir Hector was hoping for was the Viceroyalty of India. That was why he had been so anxious for his sister to be well.

There must be a woman out there to be the handmaid to his glory.

Was he not less, or more, than human?

There was a good deal of disquiet in India. A woman had been active in stirring it up. So rumour said.

He would soon crush it, that man of bronze.

It was tragic to love such a man. Yet she knew that she clung to her love. A word from him meant more to her than all the deeds of others. She had satisfied him, had come up to his expectation of her in what she had tried to do for him. That was enough reward. The attacks, the contempt or indifferences of others, were as nothing to her.

It did not occur to Olivia that, for the first time since she had found out her power as a healer, she had used that power for a partially selfish reason; that, for the first time, she had been instigated to a healing effort by something akin to egoism. Her love had made her think of, act for, her own advantage; and her love now prevented her from being quite sincere with herself.

A week later it became known that the Viceroy of India had sent in his resignation, and Sir Hector's name was mentioned in the *Times* as his probable successor.

Two days after this piece of news had been read by Olivia, Sir Hector telephoned asking if he could see her at a certain hour. She had never received him in her flat since his first visit there, but she had seen him many times in Cadogan Square. She answered saying she would be at home at the hour he mentioned, and, punctually to the moment, he strode into the room.

She thought him looking rather worn, even a little weary. But he smiled as he gripped her hand.

"Is it true what they say in the papers?" she asked. "I hope it is true."

He shrugged his big shoulders.

"We shall know presently. I've got a word or two to say to you about my sister. Let me sit down and light up, may I?"

"Yes, do.

When his cigarette was alight and he had crossed his long legs comfortably, he said:

"Now, tell me. Do you believe that my sister is really cured—finally cured?"

"Yes, I do," said Olivia, without hesitation. "Do you doubt it?"

She looked at him with a sudden keen anxiety which transformed her strong face.

"I wanted to hear your opinion. I know it is an absolutely honest one. I am not given to trusting women, but I trust you thoroughly. I am not speaking of your intellect; anyone can make a bad mistake. I am speaking of your *bona fides.*"

"Thank you," said Olivia. "But I wish you would tell me your opinion."

"I don't know that it would be worth much on a matter of this kind. She certainly seems to me to be cured. Since her accident she has never looked, never seemed, as she looks and seems now. The change is extraordinary."

He pulled his moustache and looked straight before him. After a pause he continued:

"Fernol West is a strange young fellow."

"What made you think of him just then?"

"Well, he's the only 'cure' of yours whom I happen to know. He dined with my sister and me last night. I ran across him in Whitehall and asked him."

"I didn't know," said Olivia. "I haven't seen Fernol to-day."

As the general said nothing she added, after a silence:

"Why do you think Fernol strange?"

"Well, I've had a great deal to do with men of all classes and a good many nationalities, and it strikes me that there's something decidedly unusual about young West. Last night I noticed it."

"Did Fernol do or say——"

"You know my sister. She's abominably truthful, eh?"

"She's thoroughly sincere. I love it in her."

"Like answers to like. Last night you were spoken of. West stuck up for you, as he always does, and was very bitter about the way you've been treated over here. (By the way, that's a good deal Sandring's fault. Between you and me he's more than a bit of a fool.) Finally, he asked my sister if she wouldn't, in some public way, acknowledge that you had cured her of her torturing headaches."

"I am very sorry Fernol did that."

"Then, of course, my sister's drastic sincerity came into play. She said she couldn't do that because she was not positively certain that her cure had been owing to you. She spoke of nervous headaches, of how nerves and the imagination seem to be connected sometimes, implied that, possibly, she had been mentally influenced rather than physically. You know how women run on, messing things all up together. I saw West was getting more and more excited. Finally, my sister said that if she had had some perfectly definite disease, such as cancer, or diabetes, and had been treated by you and recovered, she would have told the whole world what you were. As it was, she could only be tremendously grateful to you, and say that it was quite possible that you had had a great deal to do with getting rid of her headaches. Ah!"

"And then—was that all?"

"Well—no. West just managed to contain himself. But I never saw a pair of eyes look more menacing than his did."

"Menacing!" said Olivia, sitting forward in her chair.

"Yes," returned the general with quiet force. "He turned to me and asked me if I were cured by you of ill health whether I would publicly acknowledge it. I said I would—and let them laugh at me as much as they liked. Then he became calmer. I took my sister upstairs. We'd just finished dinner and I had to go to the telephone. When I came back to the dining-room I found West standing by the window with the curtain pulled back."

"What was he doing?"

"Getting some air. He looked odd—deucedly odd."

"In what way?"

"White. However, we finished our wine together and he seemed to calm down. But all the rest of the evening I felt that he was keeping something under. In India I've seen two or three native soldiers run amuck. H'm!"

He was silent and seemed to be thinking profoundly.

"What did you cure West of exactly?" he asked presently.

Olivia told him.

"It was like acute neurasthenia. Some of the doctors thought there was some pressure on the brain. He was desperately miserable and haunted by a desire to kill himself."

"Ah!"

He lit another cigarette and uncrossed his legs.

"The brain!" he said, as if to himself. "My sister fell from a horse, too," he added, speaking to Olivia.

"Yes, I know."

"There might be something akin in the two cases?"

"I—perhaps there might."

After a minute of silence Olivia said:

"I'm afraid you doubt my cure of your sister."

"Well—no; I don't."

"Not even—after last night?"

"You follow me, I see."

He looked full at her. And this time she did not feel like a tiny figure in the foreground of some vast space over which he was gazing. Her heart began to beat fast.

"My instincts guide me more than you might suppose," he observed. "I believe you have made a cure of my sister. But I wanted to test your mind. I might sacrifice a good many people if I thought their sacrifice would advance things. But I shouldn't care to sacrifice my sister. She is an unselfish woman where I am concerned. I don't wish to take too great advantage of that weakness in her. Well, I must leave you."

He got up. So did Olivia.

"I'm—I'm almost sure now that you wouldn't call me in if you were ill," she said.

Her lips were trembling. She could not keep them still.

"Would you wish me to?" he asked.

"Yes, I should."

"Then I would give you the chance to put me right. It would be my way of paying the debt I owe you. I always settle my debts. Some men have reason to wish I didn't, I believe. Good-bye."

He stood for a moment looking towards her. And again Olivia noticed, this time more definitely, some subtle change in his appearance. She could not have defined it, but she was strongly aware of it.

He shook her hand and went out.

When he had gone Olivia sat for a long while thinking about him, about Miss Burnington, about Fernol, and about herself, and she was conscious that her usually steady and strong mind was troubled. Events seemed to be stealthily grouping themselves together to make an ugliness, some shape that she would not care to look upon. Presently she even began to feel as if that shape were looming over her, although she could not see it yet.

She did not meet Fernol that day. A week went past, and she neither saw him nor heard from him. This surprised her, as he generally looked in on her at the flat three or four times a week. Saturday came. She went as usual to the Bureau. She had been there about an hour when a messenger arrived with a note for her.

It was marked *"Private and urgent."*   **She opened it** and read:

"Strictly private.

"2A, CADOGAN SQUARE.
"*Saturday.*
"MY DEAR MISS TRAILL,
    "Can you possibly come at once? My brother is very unwell and wishes to see you. Please do not say a word to anyone about this. I know I can rely on you to keep the matter a secret.
"*Yours sincerely,*
"HONORIA BURNINGTON."

III

Olivia burnt Miss Burnington's note, had a taxicab called, got into it and was on the way to Cadogan Square within five minutes of the receipt of this message. As the cab moved out into the stream of traffic she leaned back and shut her eyes. The great moment of her life had surely come. She was trying to collect all her forces to meet it. But for the moment she felt frightened, horribly frightened, almost like a child struck for the first time and shuddering not merely in body but in soul. Fernol's desire had been fulfilled. That was strange. She thought of ill-wishing, of the old superstition connected with the burning of a waxen image of your enemy, of the more modern belief that by the force of his thought a man may cause to happen that which he longs for. Was Fernol's thought-power very strong? Could he have set himself to an evil use of it? She saw before her Sir Hector and Fernol, the great man and the excitable boy. It was fantastic to suppose that such a man could be influenced by such a boy. Yet there was force in Fernol. His concentrated devotion to her had proved that to Olivia long ago. And more than once he had almost passionately expressed a wish that

Sir Hector could have the chance of redeeming his promise. And now the chance had come. Sir Hector was going to redeem it. She did not doubt that. Directly she had read Miss Burnington's note she had understood.

She strove to gather her forces together; she called upon her faith as if it were distant and needed a summons.

When the cab stopped she opened her eyes.

She got out and rang the bell. A footman came to the door.

"Can I see Miss Burnington?" she asked.

As she spoke her eyes searched the young man's face and found only a stolid indifference.

"Yes, ma'am," he replied. "Miss Burnington is expecting you."

He shut the door and preceded her up the staircase.

She waited for a moment in the familiar drawing-room which to-day seemed unfamiliar. Then Miss Burnington came in looking anxious and—Olivia thought—almost stern.

"Thank you for coming," she said quickly, holding out her hand. "Had you gone to the Bureau?"

"Yes. I got your message there."

"I sent to your flat too. Miss Traill, you know my real regard for you, don't you?"

"Yes."

"And my great gratitude to you. But I'm afraid you may doubt both when——"

She broke off, then resumed:

"Hector made me send for you. And, of course, his word is law in this house. But I want him to have a doctor at once. I want him to have Sir Mervyn. If you will only refuse to go to him then the road will be clear, and he must give way. Don't you see? It isn't that I doubt you. I know you are thoroughly sincere. But Hector's life is so precious and science——"

"Sir Hector wished for me," said Olivia. "Doesn't that show——"

But Miss Burnington interrupted her.

"He insisted. He said he had a debt to pay and he meant to pay it."

"That was like him!"

"But I know you will feel yourself that it is madness not to send for a doctor. He has never been ill before, so he can't understand. My headaches—they were nothing. Anyone may have—but—I'm asking a great deal, I know. It is almost like an insult, but indeed I don't mean it so."

Suddenly, with an almost violent gesture, she took both Olivia's hands in hers.

"I don't know how to make you understand, but I can't help it. I have no real faith in any healing power outside medical or surgical science. If you will only refuse to go to Hector I can call in a doctor. May I? May I?"

"Your brother trusts me. If I refuse he will think I don't trust myself, that I am a humbug. He has asked for me, and I must go to him. Remember how ill you were."

"And now I'm well. Yes, I know, I know. But I'm nothing."

"You were everything to me when I was treating you. And now he will be everything to me. Dear Miss Burnington, please take me to him."

Miss Burnington's thin figure stiffened.

"Well, if I must," she said, with a beaten intonation. "But just one thing. Hector doesn't wish anyone to know he's ill. He's ashamed of being ill, I believe. At any rate—unless we can't help it—we are not to say a word."

"But the servants?"

"Only Sidney, his valet, knows. The others think he's got a slight chill and is keeping his room."

She stood quite still, then threw back her head.

"Please come up," she said.

But now a strange hesitation seized Olivia. She was afraid to go to that room upstairs, to see the man who was ill.

"Miss Burnington—wait a moment!" she said.

"Yes? What is it?"

"What is the matter?"

"I don't know."

"Is he very ill?"

"You will see for yourself, Miss Traill. Do you believe you can cure anything?"

Her dark eyes looked piercing, as if she would read the soul of her visitor. Olivia did not answer her. There was a moment of silence. Then Miss Burnington said:

"He has never been ill before. I cannot understand it. I can only suppose that he has eaten, or drunk, something which has made him ill. His constitution's marvellous. But no one is safe from a chance of that kind."

"No, of course not. Well, let us go up."

And she followed Miss Burnington out of the room.

Sir Hector lived on the second storey in a set of three rooms at the back of the house—bedroom, bathroom, and writing-room. Olivia had expected to be taken into a bedroom, but when Miss Burnington softly opened a door she saw a small chamber full of books, and containing a large flat writing-table, a settee and some arm-chairs. Sitting with his back to her, close to the fire, towards which he was leaning, was Sir Hector.

So he was up! She felt a strong sense of relief. But it died away as he looked round.

"Here is Miss Traill, Hector," said Miss Burnington. And she went out of the room.

Sir Hector sat with his head turned towards the door and his eyes fixed on Olivia.

"Very good of you to come," he said. "There's something wrong with me."

"Yes."

She came up to the fire.

"What do you feel?"

"As if I were going to be very much worse than I am now. It's been coming on for days—stealthily—creeping on me. I kept about till I was afraid of people noticing it. To-day, when the light came, I knew I couldn't do a thing. So here I am—useless. If you don't stop it I shall soon be pretty bad."

"Yes, I can see that."

She sat down. Now that she was close to him it seemed to her that the pupils of his strange eyes had altered. When she had met him first she had been struck by their abnormal smallness. Now they were larger, or, at any rate, looked larger.

"What are you staring at?" Sir Hector said, with a touch of almost sharp suspicion.

But she did not answer him.

"Just tell me what you feel," she said, in a practical voice.

"Well, I should say it's all very much like the beginning of enteric."

"Enteric fever! That's the same as typhoid fever, isn't it?"

"Yes; intestinal fever. I've never had it, but I've seen chaps sickening for it by the dozen. They were all as useless as I am. I feel tired all the time—without doing anything. It's abominable. The thought of food turns me sick. My head aches like the devil. And it's all getting worse. I'm on the road to something infernally bad, Miss Traill, and the pace is quickening every hour. I'm certain of that."

He lay back with a heavy sigh.

"I thought you didn't look quite as usual the day you called on me," said Olivia.

"The day after young West dined with us. It was just beginning then, I believe."

There was a moment of silence, during which Olivia looked at the man whom she loved, noticing the almost sinister change in him. He was pale, a bad colour. A sort of crust of weariness lay over his strength, like moss on a wall of stone. There was something hopeless, broken, in his whole aspect. Even his great limbs looked hopeless. Near his eyes fever seemed lurking eager to light up her torches. Olivia knew—something that was not medical knowledge told her—that this man who had never been ill in his life was on the verge of a dangerous, perhaps a deadly, illness. And an agony of pity and fear swept through her, pity and fear for him and for herself. At that moment she felt very helpless. The fact that he had sent for her, that he had held to his word, given when probably he had felt, like most healthy and very strong men, that illness could never come to his powerful body, touched her too much, almost unnerved her. Had she really any force within her that could operate on a human being whom she felt to be far above her, on one whom she loved? To believe so seemed to her at that moment to be almost an insolence. Yet if her faith in herself deserted her she must surely be useless. She must believe in herself more strongly than she had ever done before. The supreme chance had been offered to her by fate. She must seize it. She must triumph over her own weakness of a woman who loved, and who, because she loved, feared.

She strove to recover by force the sensation of mysterious power which had filled her when she went up to Lily and said: "I can cure you" . . . She got up and stood before Sir Hector, looking down upon him.

"If you hadn't made me a promise," she said, "would you have sent for me?"

Sir Hector opened his eyes.

"I have sent for you," he replied, with a touch of his old commanding brusqueness. "That's enough. But please keep it quiet. I hate people to kncw I am ill. If you put me right—that's another matter."

"If I do I will ask you to give me another promise—never to tell anyone, either that you were ill or that I was able to help you."

"And—young West?" he said, faintly, but with a strange half smile on his lips.

"Fernol? Why should Fernol ever know? Now, please give me your hands."

That evening Olivia telephoned to the Savoy Hotel and asked for Fernol West. She feared that he might not be in, but almost directly she was put through to him.

"It is Olivia speaking," she said.

"Oh!" said Fernol's voice at the other end. "Are you all right?"

"Yes. Have you anything to do this evening?"

After a perceptible pause Fernol's voice answered: "No."

"Will you come round and have a talk, then? I'm all alone."

Again a pause, then the voice: "All right. I'll come."

Olivia put the receiver up and looked at her watch. It was half-past eight. If Fernol started at once he would be with her in ten minutes. She wondered whether he would start at once. She had received through the telephone an impression of reluctance. But, of course, he would come. She sat down, took up the book of Tagore, which he had given her, and tried to read. It was essential that she should be serene, complete mistress of herself to-night. Any turmoil of spirit must weaken her. She must banish anxiety, suspicion, and, above all, fear. She must control thought.

"He will be better to-morrow," she said to herself. "I know that. He's getting better now. To-night he's going to sleep calmly. He will wake refreshed, free from headache, free from *malaise*. The headache will have left him. He will be much better."

She put down her book and insisted on these strong and hopeful thoughts. Fear disintegrates. Suspicion does harm to her who suspects. Doubt is destructive. Faith can move the mountains. Presently she sent her mind to Palestine, to dwell in imagination by the delicate shores of Galilee. When she had read the Bible, very often she had wondered at the lack of faith shown by many of those among whom Christ wrought His miracles. "If I had been alive then," she had said to herself, "I should have been one of the first to believe, and I should never have wavered in my faith." Now she wished to think herself back into that mood of robust and glorious confidence. She looked into the fire and trod the ways of the Holy Land with Christ. "Only believe!" What is impossible to God? And God works through men and women, sends His spirit—a double portion of it—into those who wait for it, and are eager to receive it. He had helped her to heal, and He would help her to heal again. Through Him she could walk on the waters. But if once she let fear invade her, complete trust desert her, she would sink in them. They would sweep over her. She would drown. . . .

Presently she moved and looked up. She had made a strong effort of mind and will and she felt almost tired. She glanced again at her watch. It was twenty minutes past nine. And Fernol had not come yet. She was beginning to wonder whether he would come, in spite of his "All right!" when the door bell sounded. She got up, but she did not go at once to the door. Something held her back. She waited, looking towards the passage. The door bell sounded again. Then she turned out the electric light with the exception of one lamp in a corner, walked down the passage and opened the door.

Fernol West was standing outside. The night was cold, and he was wrapped up in a big fur coat with the collar raised to his ears.

"Well, Olivia!" he said.

His blue eyes were fixed upon her, and she noticed that instead of moving he stood quite still where he was, almost like a man who doubted whether he would be let in.

"Good evening, Fernol. Come in. How late you are. I'd almost given you up."

"Am I late?" he said.

He stepped in and she shut the door.

"Take off your coat. I've got a good big fire."

"That's splendid. It's horribly cold. I walked."

He went to hang up his coat.

"Why didn't you take a cab?"

"I wanted air."

The words recalled to Olivia Sir Hector's description of Fernol standing by the dining-room window in Cadogan Square with the curtain pulled back.

"Don't you get enough in the day?" she asked.

"Not always."

He had hung up his coat. As he turned round from the hook he shivered.

"It's cold!" he exclaimed. "Let's get to the fire."

"Yes. You'll soon be splendidly warm. . . . Sit down here close to it."

She drew forward an armchair. For the first time with Fernol she felt embarrassed. She knew why, but she did not wish him to notice it. He sank down in the chair with a boyish sort of flop, and stared into the flames. She sat on the sofa and took up a piece of work.

"Smoke if you like."

"No, thank you, Olivia. I'm off smoking."

"Why's that?"

"I don't know."

"Nothing wrong with you, I hope?"

"Wrong!"

He shot a side glance at her.

"Why should there be?"

"I don't know. But you haven't been near me for quite a long time."

"Just over a week."

"Well, that's quite a long time—for us."

"Yes, I suppose it is."

There was a pause. Then Fernol shifted his chair round towards her.

"Since I've seen you I've dined with Sir Hector and his sister," he said.

"I know."

"Oh! You've seen them, then?"

"Sir Hector called here the next day."

"Did he? And he told you, of course? It was good of him to ask me. But I can't stand Miss Burnington."

"I like her very much."

"You like everyone. It's your creed. But I can't. I'd give my life for a friend, but some people——"

He broke off and moved his hands nervously.

"I think I will smoke," he said. "D'you mind a cigar?"

"No; anything you like."

He drew out and lit a cigar. She noticed that his left hand was trembling.

"Are you still cold?" she asked.

"No; why?"

"Your hand is shaking."

He started.

"Give it to me for a moment."

"It's all right. I'll hold it to the fire."

He stretched his right hand out towards the flames.

"It's your other hand," said Olivia.

"Oh," he said brusquely. "Don't bother about me."

"Fernol, what is the matter with you? Why haven't you been near me all these days? What's troubling you?"

"Who's been talking to you about me?" he retorted almost savagely.

"Nobody has mentioned you, except Sir Hector."

"And what did he say?" said Fernol, with an ugly glance at her.

"Don't you like Sir Hector?"

"Yes. He's a real live man."

"Well, you may be sure he has never said anything against you."

"Have you seen him again since he called on you?"

"Yes. I saw him to-day."

Fernol was staring at her. Was it the light of the fire which set two gleams in his eyes?

"To-day! Here?"

"No; I called at Cadogan Square."

Fernol said nothing, but continued to stare at her like one who was fiercely expectant of something. Olivia realised that he was in an acute state of nervous excitement, was quivering with anxiety, or under the lash of some intense desire. Could he have got wind of Sir Hector's illness? That seemed impossible since even the servants in the Burningtons' house did not know the truth. She was not a curious woman, but Fernol's look, his whole manner, woke in her a strong curiosity mingled with an under reluctance which was akin to apprehension. Everything to-day seemed fighting against her, fighting to beat down the strength which had made her what she was, a woman who was of use in the suffering world, one to whom the afflicted came, and from whom they went away renewed. Even Fernol was, perhaps unconsciously, attacking her, Fernol, who had been one of her greatest joys, a piece of her handiwork of which she had been humbly proud. She no longer felt proud of him. To-night something in him forced upon her a knowledge that was a deadly foe to her soul. A voice within her said clearly again and again, "Fernol is not cured. You thought him cured, but you were wrong. Look at him, listen to him, and be sincere with yourself. You know that you have not cured him."

At this moment, while Fernol was staring at her, the voice was louder than before, the silent voice which nothing can drown, not even the roar of Niagara. It drove Olivia to greater frankness. She could not be really frank to-night, because she had to keep the secret of another, but she could surely clear away some of the débris which divided her from Fernol.

"Fernol," she said, in a resolute voice. "You know I believe very much in the force of thought, don't you?"

"Yes."

"I look upon thought as a weapon for good or evil. A wicked thought, I believe, does harm to the thinker. But that's not all. It may harm another too. It often does. I am sure of that. Some of us are much stronger in thinking than others. We can put much more force into a thought than they can. I believe you and I are strong in that way. I know you are. You can concentrate tremendously. I feel it. And I feel it specially to-night."

"I don't know why you should," said Fernol uneasily.

"You and I are good friends. That links our minds together perhaps. It helps me to feel your mind easily. But to-night, though, I feel I· don't know. I wish you would help me to know. I've been afraid for some time."

"Afraid! What of?"

"That you might be led to think in a wrong way."

"What way, then?"

Suddenly Olivia resolved to tell Fernol the secret which perhaps he had divined. An obscure instinct, of which she was scarcely conscious, but to which she yielded without a battle, a woman's instinct, drove her to do this. But her cheeks flushed as she spoke.

"Fernol, I'm going to give you a proof of my friendship for you, and I know I can trust to your honour never to speak of what I am going to tell you."

An expression that was like an expression of fear changed Fernol's face.

"Don't you want me to tell you?" she asked, startled.

Fernol passed his tongue over his lips and clenched his hands together.

"Yes—yes. Go on! Go on!" he said, roughly.

"Perhaps you know it already," she said, seized with hesitation.

His look and manner were so strange that they checked the impulse within her. At her last words the boy's face seemed to her to go white in the light from the fire. But perhaps that was an effect of the flames.

"Know it!" he exclaimed. "How should I know it? Of course I don't. . . . Well, what is it? Tell me—please!"

"I care very much for Sir Hector Burnington."

She stopped. He said nothing, and seemed to be waiting for something else.

"Do you understand what I mean?" she said.

"You love him!" said Fernol.

"Yes. No one knows that but you."

"Is that all?"

"All!"

"Yes, or have you something more to tell me?"

"Isn't that enough?"

"Why do you tell me?"

"I thought I would."

"But why? I know you have a reason. What is it, please?"

He spoke with a sort of dogged obstinacy which surely was the child of apprehension.

"I am not sure."

She stopped and searched her mind.

"It was something—there seemed something to clear away from between us. And I want you to know how anything which affects Sir Hector must affect me, because of my feeling for him. I know very well that you care for my happiness. I don't seek it in any selfish way. Sir Hector only looks on me as a sincere sort of woman trying to do her best with any powers she has. I look for nothing more from him than that. He is made for big work, not to love any woman. I have no illusions about him—none. Such happiness as I can ever have in connection with him must lie in seeing him strong and happy and able to carry forward the great things he is meant to do for his country. Now, Fernol, I have bared my heart to you. It hasn't been easy, but I have done it. Do something for me in return."

"What is it you want me to do, Olivia?" he asked, in a voice that for a moment was husky, as if he were moved by some strong emotion.

"Promise me that you will never—of course, I mean in thought—try to do harm to Sir Hector!"

"Why—why should you suppose——?"

He stopped. He was no longer looking at her.

"We don't know exactly what a concentrated desire may be able to accomplish. Lots of people would probably say nothing, unless it were aided by some definite action. But my own experience tells me it may accomplish a great deal—wonders even—good things—horrible things. What is faith but a great concentration; a sort of gathering together of the best forces of the soul? When you came to me in Boston, and we were together so many times in my little room there, and I saw how dreadfully wretched you were, my one desire was to get you right. It was so strong that it was almost like an enormous physical effort which I made. I felt as if I were standing up and fighting against the powers of darkness for you. And I—I thought I won."

"Thought!" Fernol exclaimed. "You did win!"

"Thank God if I did."

"Do you mean you have ever doubted it?" he said passionately.

His cheeks were flaming, and he looked straight into her eyes.

"I never doubted it in America."

"And here! What do you mean? How can you say that—what is there the matter with me? I'm perfectly well. Anyone can see that."

"Don't be angry, Fernol. But just answer me one question. Two or three times you have said to me that

you wished Sir Hector could have a chance to carry out
his promise to me. You know that could only happen
if he were ill. Have you gone on wishing him to be ill?
Have you concentrated on that?"

"You always come first with me," he said obstinately,
looking down. "That's my idea of gratitude. You
condemn it, I know. But I can't help it. I can't be like
you."

"Then you have concentrated on an evil desire?"

"Why do you go into all this to-night? Is—is there
anything the matter with Sir Hector?"

Something in Fernol's expression as he asked this
question startled Olivia. She felt at that moment almost
certain that Fernol did know something of what had
happened in Cadogan Square. But her promise to Miss
Burnington prevented her from touching on the subject. If she did touch on it, if she allowed Fernol to
pursue it any further, she would be unable to keep Sir
Hector's illness secret from Fernol. She was forced to
be something less than sincere.

"What I wish to say to you, Fernol, is this," she
said, ignoring his question. "If you care for me really
at all, if you wish to show gratitude to me, there is only
one way in which you can do it. Turn your mind from
evil desires. Put good desires in their place. Use your
strength only in a fine way. Wish well to Sir Hector.
I know you will now I have told you what—was very
difficult to tell. I cannot bear that for me you should
become evil. It makes me feel that it would be better,
far better, if you had never seen me. If I produce evil
in you I must be an evil influence. I—I hate to think
that of myself."

She was deeply moved as she spoke. Something that
had been firm seemed to be crumbling beneath her feet.

"Good night, Fernol," she said, after a pause. "I want
to be alone now."

He stood looking at her in silence, but he did not move.

"Please go," she said.

"Yes. But say that you know you did cure me first."

"You could not be fanatical about me if you were thoroughly normal," she answered, looking at him with steady, sad eyes. "The sane mind in the sane body is never fanatical."

"Then you think I am mad?" he cried, bitterly.

"Oh, Fernol, it's no use—perhaps we are both exaggerating things to-night. Don't let us talk any more. Now, good night."

She took his reluctant hand.

"Give yourself to good thoughts and all will be well, dear Fernol. Send good thoughts to me and—to him too. Perhaps we both need them."

"It would be no use," he said, almost in a whisper. "But, anyhow, I would die for you."

He wrung her hand, hurting her. But she did not wince.

"Do you believe it?"

"I don't want you to die. I want you to live and be fine."

"Perhaps some day you'll——"

He did not finish his sentence but left her. She heard him in the passage taking his heavy coat down from the hook. Then there was a long silence. No doubt he was putting his coat on. But the silence lasted till she was surprised at it and wondered what could be happening.

"What are you doing, Fernol?" she called out, without going to the door.

Instantly she heard a movement. Then the outer door was opened and shut. He had gone.

"He's sick—he's sick!" said the voice within her. "The man you love is ill in body and the boy you thought you had healed is ill in mind and soul. You never healed him. You can't heal. You haven't the healing power. Perhaps you had it once, but it's left you. It came to you, it stayed with you a little while, and now it has deserted you. You're an empty vessel. You're worse—

you're a humbug. You know you haven't got what you claim to possess, and so you're a living lie."

As she listened to the voice, the faith within her was shaken. It seemed to grow pale, to be fading away, to be dying. And a sensation of despair seized her. But she fought it. She recalled the many cures she had made—or was it had seemed to make?—in America, the deep confidence she had inspired in women and men, the gratitude which had been showered upon her. And then she recalled the attacks which had been made upon her, the cruel names she had been called, charlatan, humbug, crank, self-deceiver. Self-deceiver! Had she been really that all through her career as a healer? Had she been, as it were, self-hypnotised, and, because of that, had she hypnotised others—Lily first of all, and then many suffering human beings? She saw, as in a vision, a long procession of those who had sought her out, headed by Lily. Presently Fernol went by with his eyes bent down to the ground, as if he dared not let her see what was in them; and long after him Miss Burnington with a sceptical smile on her lips. She had not believed. Perhaps her brains were too strong, too penetrating, to be tricked. And last of all strode Sir Hector, with his mien of bronze, and his strange glazed eyes. And he looked at her, and his motionless lips seemed to be saying: "I am the great test. Cure me and all will believe. But if you fail, death is waiting for me, and you will have been my murderer."

Then, in her fight to bring back red life to the fading faith, she told herself that the reason of this hideous collapse was that she had been less, or more, than a woman, and that now she was just a woman. She had loved, or thought she loved, humanity, the mass of created beings, with their affections, their sorrows, their terrors, their yearning desires; now she loved one man. And he blotted out humanity from her view; he expelled humanity from her heart. She knew the narrowness of a great love. Her widely diffused power of sympathy had shrunk. She saw it as a burning spark, minute but fierce with the terrible fierceness of fire. She would let the world go for one man.

But she would not let him go. She would not fail in the job he had set her, the greatest job a woman who loves can have. Exactly how much he believed in her power she did not know. He was a difficult man to read. He had never been ill before, and perhaps even now, in spite of his assertion that the pace was quickening, could not realise that at the end of the path he was treading death might be waiting. Such a man is apt to have the illusion that he is invulnerable, until old age leads him by almost imperceptible degrees to cessation. He was paying a debt. But if he got worse? If the knowledge were forced on him that he was in the hands of a loud-mouthed impotence? She would give it all up before that moment came. She herself would proclaim herself helpless.

But she shivered when she thought of making such an acknowledgment to such a man. What a contempt he would have for her. If she was not what she claimed to be, she was far less than the unknown millions who had made no claim to be other, or more, than their brethren. She was only an assertive nothingness. Her cheeks burned at the thought of being found out to be that by the man whom she loved. She could not bear it. Women can bear so much, but there is the impossible—the one thing that cannot be endured. And that would be the impossible for her.

Suddenly she wished she had medical knowledge. She could have used it to back up her mysterious power. (She was trying to smother the voice.) Sir Hector's words recurred to her mind. "I should say it's all very much like the beginning of enteric." Possibly, if a doctor—Sir Mervyn—had been summoned he would have diagnosed the case as one of enteric fever. And then he would have done certain things. What things? She wished she had a medical book handy. That would tell her a good deal of what she needed to know. Her eyes fell on a bookcase against the wall of the little room near the door. It was not likely that—— She went over to the bookcase.

"Sir Walter Scott's novels"; "Shakespeare's Works"; "The Mill on the Floss"; "The Sorrows of Satan"; "Shelley's Poems"; "Wuthering Heights"; "The Life of Goethe"——

She read on and on till she came to the bottom shelf, which was larger than any of the others.

"Chambers's Dictionary."

There were many volumes. She sought eagerly for the letter E, found it, and drew out the heavy book.

"Enteric Fever—*see* Typhoid Fever."

She sought again, and found what she wanted.

Presently she laid the book she had been reading down upon her knees. What was the matter with Sir Hector? Was he sickening for typhoid? From what she had just read she judged that possibly, even perhaps probably, he was. Yet the disease was rarely met with after middle life. He was between fifty and sixty, and tremendously strong. It seemed very unlikely that, living as he did in excellent hygienic conditions, he would be stricken by such a disease. Since she had read about typhoid, her former preoccupation about Fernol's state of mind seemed almost absurd to her. Ill-wishing could not produce an illness which science had long ago proved to be caused by an organism. And yet she could not get rid of the feeling that somehow Fernol's peculiar concentration on her was harmful, or might be harmful, to Sir Hector. Whenever she thought of either, the other came up in her mind immediately. The great man and the excitable boy were inexorably linked together. Her instincts were at work in the matter. She knew that, and she had long ago learned that instinct is greater than reason. The fact that Fernol's openly and vehemently proclaimed wish that Sir Hector might fall ill had been so quickly followed by his illness was a very strange coincidence, and Fernol's behaviour troubled her terribly. He was certainly concealing something from her. His eyes were furtive. His whole manner suggested acute uneasiness. All his former frankness and joyousness had left him. What was the matter with him? What did he know about Sir Hector? What was he expecting? He seemed to be quivering with some secret expectation.

She looked down again on the book and her eyes fell on the words: "The pupils are generally somewhat larger than normal." A little lower down she saw the brief statement: "Death may take place by coma, by exhaustion, in consequence of severe hemorrhage of the bowels or of perforation of their coats, or from pneumonia or some other complication; rarely from any cause before the second week."

Perhaps the second week of the illness had begun. Sir Hector had told her that he thought "it" was just beginning the day after Fernol had dined with him.

Suddenly Olivia turned white and cold. A horrible thought had come upon her like an enemy. She hated it. She was indignant with herself for being able to hold it in her mind. Quickly she shut up the dictionary, put it back on the shelf, turned out the lamp, and went to her bedroom. But the horrible thought went with her, poisoning her mind, doing harm surely to her soul. She did not know how to get rid of it. She undressed, wrapped herself in a dressing-gown and knelt down by her bed. She wanted to pray, but though for years she had practised thought-control and had achieved an unusual mastery of the mind, to-night she was like a city invaded by a horde of brutal enemies. It was as if she heard the tramp of their feet in the night, saw the glare of their incendiary fires. She knew the impotence of the conquered. In vain she tried to concentrate on God and her close connection with Him. Fernol rose up before her. She saw a glass of wine set on a white cloth; Fernol standing by a window holding back a curtain; Sir Hector entering the room. But it was impossible.

Such a thing was impossible. She crushed her face down in her hands. How could such a punishment come upon her when she had always exerted herself for good? Always she had aimed at helping people and not at self-advancement. She could not accuse herself of trying to become rich, or of the more subtle endeavour—the attempt to win notoriety or glory. A certain fame had been hers in America; but, honestly, she could say that she had not sought it. She was not conscious of being an egoist. Then, surely, such a fearful punishment as she had just conceived of could not be meted out to her. When she looked around her she certainly saw much apparent injustice in the fates of men and women; nevertheless, she had always believed in the Divine justice, and it would be a refinement of injustice that could bring about, or even allow to be, what she had just thought of, was thinking of now in spite of all her efforts to drive it out of her mind. Something unhealthy in Fernol must have infected her to-night. But her mind was not reading his when it had formed that hideous surmise.

A something disturbed her. She did not know what it was, but she lifted her head from her hands and listened. It was surely some sound in the flat. Presently she felt, rather than heard it again. She wondered what it could be. She had an odd feeling that there was someone near her, either attending to her in some peculiar way, or trying to tell her something. Sir Hector! She sprang up and stood still. Perhaps he had suddenly become worse; was wishing her to be with him. Perhaps Miss Burnington was sending for her. She thought first of dressing quickly, and went to her wardrobe. But just as she was opening its door she was again aware of some muffled and yet near sound. This time she went out into the passage. And immediately she heard distinctly the telephone bell in the drawing-room. It must be that Sir Hector was worse. She ran down the passage, went into the drawing-room, and took down the receiver.

"Yes—yes? What is it? Is he worse? Shall I come?"
she said.

She was so obsessed by the idea that the message
was from Cadogan Square that she did not think of imprudence till she heard Fernol's voice saying:

"It's I—Fernol. What's the matter?"

"Fernol!" she said.

"Yes. Is who worse?"

"What, Fernol?"

"Is who worse?"

"I—I thought it might be someone of those I have
been treating. What is it you want? I was going to
bed."

"Sorry I disturbed you. I just wanted to tell you I
know very well what you were thinking about me to-
night."

She fancied that there was a sinister sound in the
voice that was speaking.

"I—I don't think I understand," she said.

"Oh, yes, you do. You were thinking I was wrong
in the head—mad, in fact. But you're mistaken. I'm as
sane as you are. Good night."

"Fernol," she said. "Fernol!"

But she was cut off.

After this she made no further attempt to pray. She
no longer even tried to control her thoughts. She let
herself go to thought and to emotion as heedlessly as
a terrified girl. There was no longer firm ground beneath her feet. Fernol's reiterated allusion to madness,
his uncalled-for assertion of sanity, drew her on to the
contemplation of a possibility so awful that it banished
sleep. And she lay awake all night, companioned by
fear. Towards dawn she got up, went to the drawing-
room, took down the volume of the dictionary which
contained the article on typhoid fever, and, returning to
bed, studied it minutely till the murky daylight of London filtered into the room. She even committed a great
part of it to memory, learning with a feverish intensity

of concentration which she had never been able to summon up when studying for an examination in the days of
her youth. And all the time that she was learning the
silent voice kept repeating: "You hypocrite! You
hypocrite!" The words ticked in her brain as a clock
ticks in a lonely room. But she defied them. A great
life, perhaps, was at stake, and the whole of her happiness. One sentence which she read—she knew she could
never forget it, even if she lived to be very old—was as
follows:

> "No drug is known to cure the disease; and in
> many cases none is required."

She clung to that sentence; she cherished it in her
mind. As she dressed, while she breakfasted—she forced
herself to eat as usual—she repeated it over and over;
to her it meant this: "A doctor would be of no use to
him; I can do all that a doctor could do." She thanked
God for that sentence.

After breakfast she walked to Cadogan Square. She
had sent a message to the Bureau to say she could not
go there either in the morning or afternoon. She had
resolved to give all her strength, all her powers, to Sir
Hector. She knew she had nothing to give to anyone
else.

The day was brilliantly clear, but intensely cold. She
welcomed the sharpness of the air as a tonic. Although
she had had no sleep, she felt violently alive. As she
walked, by way of the Park, and then down Sloan Street,
she strove to gather her forces together. She had resolved what to do. She meant to remain in the house
all day, to spend the night there if necessary, to take
charge of the case like a doctor as well as like a healer.
She would fill Miss Burnington with confidence in her.
She was bracing herself for the fight of her life. There
was no longer any question in her mind of giving in,
of acknowledging that she was doubtful, of yielding her

place to Sir Mervyn or anyone else. A change in her had come with the sleepless night. The fibre of her nature seemed to have hardened under the stress of the agony she had gone through. There are crises in which the human being either breaks down or becomes fierce and almost brutally defiant. Olivia had not broken down. But something tender and beautiful in her, something sincere and very delicate, seemed to have snapped like a string drawn too tight. Fernol's visit had made her for the moment unscrupulous. He had put fear in her, and in fighting down fear she had caught something of the brutality of the soldier in battle.

When she reached the house in Cadogan Square, and was waiting for the door to be opened, she said to herself:

"He has slept well. He is better to-day. The illness is leaving him." And when the footman came she was smiling.

She wished him "good morning," and went upstairs. Miss Burnington met her on the first landing.

"He's better, isn't he?" said Olivia.

"Please come in here before you go up to him," said Miss Burnington in a low voice.

She shut the drawing-room door carefully. Then she said:

"Miss Traill, why did you tell Mr. West my brother was ill?"

"But I haven't told him."

"Haven't you seen him since you were here yesterday?"

"Yes. I saw him last night."

"He called early this morning to ask how my brother was. I didn't see him. The footman said as far as he knew there was nothing the matter but a slight cold. You must have said something."

Olivia explained how she was startled by hearing the telephone, and what she had said exactly before she knew Fernol was speaking.

"I am very sorry," she said. "But I never mentioned your brother's name."

"But he guessed who it was. Why was that?" asked Miss Burnington.

As she spoke she looked at Olivia with suspicion in her eyes. There was something of half-veiled hostility in her look and manner.

"How can I tell? I never even hinted to Fernol that there was anything wrong with your brother."

"Then it's very strange."

Miss Burnington paused.

"I don't like Mr. West," she said, after a moment of silence. "I know he's your friend, but there's something in him I shrink from. I think he's abnormal in some way. If people like him find out that Hector is ill, I can't answer for what I might do."

"I don't understand you."

"Hector is worse this morning. He's had a very bad night. I shan't be able to allow this sort of thing to go on much longer."

Olivia knew now she was speaking to an enemy.

"You visit my brother," continued Miss Burnington. "You keep the doctors out by doing so. But have you any idea what is the matter with him?"

"Yes," said Olivia firmly.

"Then, what is it?"

"I shall be more certain to-day. You must not think that because I am only a healer I know nothing about illness."

"Have you ever studied either medicine or surgery?"

"Not as doctors do, but——"

"Exactly!" interrupted Miss Burnington. "You haven't. You know nothing of the science. And yet you dare to take chances with such a life as my brother's! I speak strongly, but I can't help it. I feel strongly. I must tell you this, Miss Traill: if anything should happen to Hector you will be held responsible by public opinion—and by me."

"I will take the risk. He trusts me. That is enough for me."

"I suppose you realise that, if Hector doesn't get better, it will soon be impossible to keep his illness from the public. It will get into the papers. It will go all over the world. And the fact of your presence by his bedside——"

"Isn't he up?" Olivia interrupted sharply.

"No—not to-day. . . . The fact of your presence by his bedside will be a public scandal. It will make my brother ridiculous in the eyes of the world, and I'm afraid it will make you—odious."

"You are trying to frighten me, but I am not to be frightened. I have too much faith in myself."

"Do you really believe in yourself?" said Miss Burnington. And she looked at Olivia as if she would probe into the depths of her, would drag into the light her sincerity or insincerity.

"I have always believed in myself. And your brother must believe in me or he would call in the doctors."

"He has always hated doctors. And he's tremendously obstinate. But you can bring him to reason. Refuse to treat him. Tell him you think it is very serious and he ought to call in a doctor, and I'm sure he will do it."

"Yes, and put me down as the humbug I am not! No, Miss Burnington, I will not do that."

"Well, if it all becomes known the whole world will laugh at my brother. I know what people are. A great soldier, a great public man in the hands of the faith healers! It would ruin Hector. No man's reputation can survive that sort of thing. If you are ready to gamble with his life at least pause and think before you gamble with his reputation."

"I am sorry," said Olivia, with a sort of cold obstinacy which concealed a turmoil of emotion. "I understand your anxiety. It makes you rather cruel to me, but I suppose that is natural. So I won't resent it. No one can care more for your brother's safety, for his future, for his honour and fame than I do——"

"Are you of his blood, then?" interrupted Miss Burnington, with uncontrollable bitterness.

"No, but I——" Olivia broke off, startled by the wildness of her own imprudence.

"Yes, Miss Traill?"

"I have his interests and his safety at heart. Indeed—indeed I have."

"Well, I will say no more. But I warn you that, in certain eventualities, I shall act on my own responsibility. I shall defy my brother's wishes, even his orders. Although I am only a woman, I have something of his obstinacy, and I shall not let him die without showing it."

"Die!" said Olivia, struck by the word as by a blow in the heart.

"Yes—die."

The two women gazed at each other for a moment, and in that moment Miss Burnington read Olivia's secret.

"He is going to recover," said Olivia, with a strong effort to control herself. "I know it. I am not afraid either for him or myself."

"Very well!" said Miss Burnington, with icy coldness. "Please go to him. Shall I take you up?"

"No, don't trouble. Is it the door next to the sitting-room?"

"Yes."

"Then I know it."

And she left the room.

As she ascended the stairs she felt as if the devil went with her. Never before had she been conscious in this sharp way of the evil within her. Perhaps, blinded by self-conceit, she had thought that she was one of the exceptional people who are naturally good. But now—she could not help it, she thought—she was deliberately giving herself to evil. The strange thing was that her love drove her down the broad path. It was her love which had waked in her defiance, insincerity, fear, selfishness, even hardness. It was her love which had changed her into a humbug. She felt at that moment that she would do anything, risk anything, rather than acknowledge that she had no more real faith in herself. She knew that she ought to say to Sir Hector, "I thought I had cured Fernol West, but I was wrong. I know that now, and it has shaken my belief in my healing power. Your health is more precious than his. I have no right to try to do for you what I have failed to do for him." When she reached the door of his bedroom she stood outside for a moment. For a moment there was a struggle between the good and evil within her. For a moment she was uncertain what she would do when she entered the room. But her hesitation was short lived. She remembered Sir Hector's quiet remark: "No consideration should be shown to failures." And when she opened the door she had made up her mind to go on, even to the edge of the precipice, even perhaps into the gulf.

Sir Hector was stretched on a narrow, very long bed in a plainly furnished room. His face was turned towards her as she came in. She had set her face in an expression of calm self-confidence. And as she looked at him this expression did not change, though she saw at once that he was much worse. His colour was ghastly; his features had sharpened; the torches of fever were alight in his eyes. But he was apparently normal in mind. The first thing he said to her was:

"It hasn't acted yet."

"The power? You must give it time. Miracles are not worked in a moment."

She sat down by the bedside.

"In a case like yours, we must make use of every means that can help."

"Means?" he said, moving restlessly on the pillow.

"Yes. You mustn't suppose that because I heal people without medicine or surgery I neglect elementary precautions. That would be foolish, even wicked. Don't you think so?"

"I can't think clearly," he said. "My head's too infernally bad."

"Don't bother about anything."

She laid her hand on his broad forehead.

"Just give yourself up to me and all will be well with you."

"It seems deucedly odd to come to this," he murmured through a sigh.

"Shut your eyes. I am going to try to get you to sleep."

He shut his eyes obediently. When he did that she was conscious of the child in him and knew her love better. And the obedience of this man whom so many had obeyed revived for a moment her belief in her power. Surely such a man could not yield himself to her if she were really impotent. He was a judge of men. Could he be utterly deceived in a woman? She was suddenly strengthened. Still keeping one hand on his forehead she tried to pour all her soothing strength and her love into it. And presently sh saw he was sleeping.

Meanwhile Miss Burnington was in her bedroom putting on a hat and a warm fur coat. She had not intended to go out that morning while she waited for the faith healer, but the scene with Olivia had driven her to a resolve. She was, like her brother, decisive. Hesitation, prolonged mental debate, were foreign to her nature. Before she came up to her bedroom she had ordered her car to come round as soon as possible. Within a very few minutes she was on her way to Harley Street. Sir Mervyn Butler had never done her any real good; Olivia, it seemed, had cured her. Yet now she was hurrying to Sir Mervyn to ask his advice. Such a proceeding might be unreasonable. Perhaps it was. She did not trouble about that. For years she had been accustomed to consult Sir Mervyn. He looked strong. She liked him and she knew he liked her. And, besides, he was a doctor and celebrated. After the painful scene with Olivia, she felt she must see him. She knew that the fact of her brother's illness must shortly get out. Such a thing could not be kept secret for long. Sir Mervyn was the model of professional discretion. She knew of no one else to whom she could entrust her anxieties.

When she arrived at the doctor's house his waiting-room was thronged with visitors. Of course, she had no appointment, but the man-servant was certain that Sir Mervyn would see her, although he was, as always, "very much taken up." While she sat in the large handsomely furnished room among the silent, or softly whispering, strangers, Miss Burnington felt a little less miserable. Sir Mervyn hadn't cured her, but he must have cured multitudes of others, or else why should he be so famous? The sight of the crowd renewed her natural woman's faith in doctors. There was something substantial to rest upon. Olivia Traill—what status had she? And she dared to love Hector! Miss Burnington was jealous of her brother. His long indifference to women had given her a delicious sense of security. Often and often she had thought to herself, "Hector only cares for me." The knowledge that now another woman was in possession of him made her heart burn with something that was very like hatred. And yet, through it all, she could not help being grateful to Olivia. That day she held in her many emotions.

Twice the man-servant appeared and mysteriously summoned an anxious being to the august medical presence. A third time he opened the door, swept Miss Burnington with a sympathetic glance, raised his blonde eyebrows, and formed some cabalistic words with his large and respectable lips. A moment later she was in Sir Mervyn's sanctum.

He welcomed her cordially, yet with a definite touch of friendly sarcasm.

"In spite of the descendant of the Apostles!" he said.

Miss Burnington blushed slightly.

"It's very good of you," she said, rather nervously. "You might very well have refused to receive me, especially without an appointment. But——"

"I knew the headaches would come back," he interrupted, with a sort of bland pity.

"But they haven't," she acknowledged, almost like one ashamed.

He looked largely taken aback, but quickly recovered himself.

"That's well! That's well! Then what is it? The nervous affliction has reappeared in some other part of the organism?"

"Well—no."

"Dear me!"

He cleverly hid his disapprobation and drowned his appearance in intelligent inquiry.

"It's Hector."

"Sir Hector! But he's never ill," said Sir Mervyn, with a touch of not wholly ungenerous regret.

"He is very ill."

The great doctor leaned back in his chair with an expression of almost fatalistic resignation, as one who bows to the inscrutable decree of a doubtless benign Providence.

And Miss Burnington developed her story.

He listened in silence till the end.

"And what do you wish me to do?" he then said, in a very detached voice.

"How can we let this go on? It is madness."

"Of course it is. But you must remember you set the example."

"I know and I blame myself bitterly."

"Don't distress yourself. The young woman has colossal determination and push, like all these successful frauds. Their stock in trade is small but effective; complete ignorance, unbounded self-confidence, a plausible tongue, and a hide of brass. I'm afraid I can't consent to meet her in consultation."

"You surely can't suppose——"

She stopped, as if unable to make mention of such an outrage.

"No," she went on. "But couldn't you come to the house this evening—she's sure to be there still—and see her, and try to bring her to a sense of the danger of the position? Do, Sir Mervyn, if you still have any friendship for me. She might listen to you. She might be afraid of you."

Sir Mervyn pursed his full lips meditatively.

"If she went on attending Hector and he were to die, what would happen?"

"It would be a serious business for the young woman."

"Make her understand it. Frighten her."

"The matter requires thinking over."

"If you will only come, I will make Hector see you. His illness is sure to get out in a day or two, and if it gets into the papers that he's called in a faith healer, what will people say?"

"I fear they might say—mind you, I don't pledge myself that they will—they might say that your brother was not the most suitable choice that could be made for the Viceroyalty of India."

"Exactly! We can't risk that. If you have any friendship for me you will come."

"Very well!" said Sir Mervyn, after a suitable pause.

She took his large soft hand impulsively.

"That's good of you. But I knew you would. I knew your generous nature. And, of course, you won't say a word."

"Good Heavens, Miss Burnington!"

She left him feeling thoroughly rebuked but burning with gratitude.

That afternoon, just after four, he arrived at Sir Hector's house.

His mouth was set in a grim expression as he mounted

the stairs to the drawing-room. He had a profound
veneration for science, and an active hatred of quacks.
He genuinely believed that Olivia was a conscious im-
postor, and that Fernol West was a neurotic young millionaire, whom she had probably hypnotised into the
delusion that she had cured him of some nervous disease, and who doubtless supplied her with money. He
had come there that day determined to give her no quarter. He had already struck hard at her in the Press.
Now he had the chance of finishing her off in a personal
encounter. It was a great opportunity and it should not
find him wanting.

Miss Burnington joined him almost immediately, looking nervous, but determined.

"It is good of you!" she said. "You are a true friend
in need."

"I have the highest regard for you both. Is she still
here?"

"Oh, yes. Do sit down for a moment. Take this
chair. I want to tell you something."

"What is it?"

"You know that young man, Mr. West?"

"The neurotic boy she claims as a cure. I saw him
that once."

"Well, it's most extraordinary; he's been here again."

"Again?"

"Oh, I don't think I told you! He called early this
morning to ask how Hector was."

"Then he knows of this illness?"

"Evidently. Yet Miss Traill swears she never mentioned my brother's name to him in connection with illness."

Sir Mervyn smiled.

"You don't believe her?"

He smiled again, as if he considered that was quite a
sufficient answer.

"If she hasn't he must have guessed it somehow."

"That would be rather remarkable, wouldn't it?"

"It's all inexplicable to me. Anyhow he called again just now and made the most minute inquiries of the footman. He wanted to know what was the matter and whether any doctor had been called in."

"And what was he told?"

"The footman said, according to his own account of the interview, that he only knew that my brother was keeping his room and that Miss Traill had been in the house all day. Then, he said, the young gentleman seemed quite satisfied and gave him a sovereign."

"Most extraordinary!"

"Isn't it? John has been with us since he was a boy and would tell me everything. What do you think of it all?"

"What can one think except that Miss Traill and this neurotic young man are acting together? She must have told him something. I shall be very much surprised if it isn't all in the papers to-morrow morning."

"Oh, Sir Mervyn! I must tell you one thing more. Just before Hector was taken ill, Mr. West dined alone with me and my brother. At dinner there was a discussion about Miss Traill. Mr. West got very excited because I said I couldn't be sure she had really cured me of my headaches. (He had wanted me to acknowledge publicly that she had cured me.) Finally he asked my brother whether if *he* were ill and Miss Traill seemed to cure him—Mr. West didn't say seemed—Hector would let the world know it."

"And what did Sir Hector say?"

"My brother said he would, and let them laugh at him as much as they liked."

"Was your brother quite well at the time?"

"Perfectly well."

"And you say he became ill—when?"

"I thought he didn't look quite himself the very next day. And from then on he grew gradually worse."

Sir Mervyn looked very grave. He sat in silence for moment while Miss Burnington watched him.

At last he said:

"Had your brother ever said, or implied, that he might possibly trust himself to Miss Traill if he ever were ill?"

"He never said so to me, not in so many words. But I think he believed Miss Traill had cured me, and when he felt ill he told me he would have Miss Traill, and that he had a debt to pay and was determined to pay it."

"He might have told her before he was ill that if he ever were ill he would send for her," said Sir Mervyn.

"I suppose so."

"And that young man——"

He paused.

"It's all very strange, isn't it?" said Miss Burnington.

"Yes."

"What do you think?"

The doctor, who seemed sunk in deep thought, shifted slowly in his armchair.

"When Mr. West dined with you, were you in the room all the time?"

"Naturally—that is, till I left him with my brother to finish their wine."

"And then, of course, Sir Hector was with him."

"Hector came upstairs with me and went to the telephone for a minute."

"While Mr. West remained alone in the dining-room?"

"Yes."

There was a silence.

"Why do you ask me all this, Sir Mervyn?" Miss Burnington said at last.

"Oh—well! Put it down to professional curiosity."

"Professional!"

"Ah! And now, can I see the young woman?"

"I'll make her come down to you."

She got up.

"One moment! Suppose she refuses?"

"Surely she can't!"

"She might."

"Then what do you advise?"

"If you'll allow me I'll write her a note."

He got up, went to the writing table, sat down, took pen and paper, and wrote a few lines, which he enclosed in an envelope.

"If she refuses you might give her that."

Miss Burnington took the note.

"I'll do everything you tell me. Oh, I'm so thankful you are here!"

And she hurried out of the room, while the doctor left the writing table and went to stand by the fire. The expression of grim sarcasm had left his powerful face. As he gazed into the flames he looked profoundly thoughtful and stern.

IV

It seemed a long time to Sir Mervyn before the door opened and Olivia came in. She held his note in her left hand and her face was white. When he turned from the fire and saw her, he bowed grimly.

"I see you've read my note, Miss Traill," he said.

"Yes."

"So much the better. I'm here at the urgent request, I might say on the insistence, of Miss Burnington."

"I know. She told me."

"Hadn't we better sit down? We've got to come to an understanding."

"Yes."

Olivia sat down, and the doctor followed her example.

"What does this note mean?" she asked. "You say in it, 'If you do not see me I shall be compelled to seek information as to Sir Hector's condition elsewhere. I shall be compelled to seek out your friend, Mr. Fernol West.' What has Fernol West to do with Sir Hector's illness? Sir Hector sent for me and I came. I have a right to be here as he wishes it. I have never told Fernol West about his illness."

"And yet he knows. He has just been here for the second time to inquire about Sir Hector."

Olivia looked startled.

"Didn't Miss Burnington tell you about it?" said Sir Mervyn.

"No."

"Then—let me do so."

He repeated Miss Burnington's account of the interview with the footman and the giving of the tip. While he was speaking he kept his eyes fixed on Olivia, and it seemed to him that beneath her rigid expression he detected the shadow of a great fear. She sat without moving till he had finished. Then she said:

"I can only repeat, I never told Mr. West that Sir Hector was ill."

"Who did, do you think?"

"I don't know."

"Perhaps it was unnecessary that anyone should tell him," said Sir Mervyn, significantly.

After a moment of hesitation she said, slowly, and with a sort of dull heaviness,

"How could that be? Please tell me what you mean."

But he did not answer her question.

"Miss Traill," he said, with stern coldness, "don't you think it would be wise to turn over this case to me? It is all very well to play about with neurotics. Nerve cases may possibly be susceptible sometimes to suggestion. Wild, inconsequent boys may be influenced, for a time, by a determined woman. But what can you hope to achieve with a man of iron like Sir Hector? You may perhaps kill him . . ."

"Oh, how dare you—how dare you?" she interrupted, with sudden passion.

". . . by not treating him properly," pursued Sir Mervyn inflexibly. "And even if you don't do that, you may easily destroy his reputation as a man of common sense, a man with a great brain, in the eyes of the world. For once a man is laughed at he is diminished to the size of the ordinary fool in the sight of all those who laugh at him. But cure Sir Hector of a dangerous illness you can't. And you know that as well as I do. All this faith healing bluff is perfectly useless. You have nothing to gain in this house, and everything to lose. For your own sake I advise you to go. If you do this and if, when I examine the patient, I find no reason to take any other course, I promise to let you alone."

"No reason!" she said, in a low voice. "How could there be a——"

Her voice died away. She was looking at him, and now he saw distinctly fear in her eyes.

"You think . . . you imagine that——"

Again her voice failed, as if smothered by emotion. A deep flush spread over her face and even down to her neck. She bent her head like one moved almost beyond endurance, clasped her hands tightly together, and remained still for two or three minutes. And there was something so terribly sincere in her look and attitude that Sir Mervyn was taken aback in spite of himself, and was conscious of pity mingled with a sudden perplexity. As Olivia said nothing more, and the silence at last became intolerable to him, he broke it by saying, in a voice which he tried to make as hard and unemotional as possible,

"Now you have my promise, will you leave Sir Hector in my hands?"

Then Olivia looked up.

"Tell me why you think I am here," she said, in a low voice.

"To carry on your faith healing imposture, I suppose," returned the doctor, trying to fight against the sudden change which—he scarcely knew why—had taken place in his feeling towards her within the last few minutes.

"I have not been a humbug in my life," she said, with intense earnestness. "I have believed in my power to heal. I have believed that it was a gift made to me by God."

"In that case you have been self-deceived. But that doesn't make you any the less a public danger."

"I—I will never bring danger to him," she said. Tears stood in her eyes.

"You don't understand me at all," she added.

"Indeed?"

"No; not at all. But how should you? Why should I expect——"

She got up.

"Please go up to him. You can tell him I asked you to because I was afraid, perhaps, I wasn't capable of——"

She stopped. Sir Mervyn looked away from her.

"Very well," he said. "You have done the right thing at last, Miss Traill."

He made a movement to go but she stopped him.

"I'll stay here. But you must come back and tell me exactly what you think. I must know. I have a special reason. I've got to know what is the matter with Sir Hector."

"Wait here then. I will come back presently."

He saw a sort of agony of inquiry in her eyes

"You promise to tell me—whatever it is?"

The doctor hesitated. But something in her eyes overcame any reluctance which he felt.

"I will tell you," he said.

"Very well."

He left the room. As he went upstairs he wondered at himself. This woman had made an impression of sincerity even upon him. He found himself pitying her; he even found himself liking her.

When he had gone Olivia walked about the room for a few minutes, then stood at the window and looked out into the square.

The twilight was falling over London. The darkness of night was at hand. To-day, for the first time in her life, she realised imaginatively the horror of darkness, and she knew that she did this because there was darkness in her own soul. As she gazed out of the window, she understood that the human being carries everything within those mysterious recesses which can never be fully explored—heaven and hell, light and darkness.

"What a mystery I am!" she thought. "And I used to think I understood, even that I knew. I understand nothing. I know nothing."

How incalculable are the human impulses! She had entered that room a few minutes ago with the intention of fighting Sir Mervyn, in spite of the words he had written, words which conveyed a scarcely veiled threat. And now she had capitulated. And Sir Hector would know it, would know that she had no faith in herself, that she could not carry out her job, that she acknowledged herself to be a fraud. And yet she was not a fraud, but a sincere and deeply loving woman.

There seemed to be no continuity in her any more. Her purposes were divided, antagonistic. A hideous uncertainty replaced her old firmness and strength. She had become the dwelling-place of warring emotions. Fear had entered into her, the malady which carries disease through every part of the soul.

Sir Mervyn's revelation of Fernol's second visit to the house had changed a horrible suspicion into something more definite, into a tremendous apprehension. Very soon no doubt she would know the truth. Sir Mervyn would tell her. She knew that an abominable thought about her had entered his mind; she knew, or believed she knew, when it had died there. He was no longer the enemy he had been. But if he discovered something terrible, what would he do? Would his foul suspicion revive? It might. And then——

She saw herself plunged in the mud of a hideous scandal.

At last she came away from the window and sat down near the fire. And there she remained for over an hour. No one came to her. The house was silent, save for an occasional footstep overhead. She had time and opportunity for what seemed a lifetime of thought and feeling. And all the time, through it all, she was waiting strung up like one accused of a crime for the verdict. She knew herself innocent, and yet she was weighed down by a sensation of acute apprehension, almost of guilt. At that moment she realised as never before the responsibility she had assumed when she undertook to heal others. She had become answerable for Fernol.

Would Sir Mervyn never come down? What could be happening upstairs? What could he be doing? She thought of Sir Hector sleeping with her hand on his forehead. He had only slept for a very short time, but he had yielded to her influence. A painful jealousy invaded her as the time went on, tingled all through her. She began almost to regret that she had abdicated. Perhaps all her fear and suspicion were ridiculous. Suddenly it occurred to her that Sir Mervyn might have come to the house that day with a deliberate policy. He might have made up his mind to frighten her in order to get her away from the patient. The medical profession was notoriously prejudiced, and Sir Mervyn had shown a special animosity against her ever since her arrival in England, and even before he knew her. Besides, she had perhaps cured the patient whom he had been unable to cure. That fact alone was enough to make him hate her. And as he had failed with Miss Burnington, he might fail with Sir Hector.

She got up, threw his note into the fire, and went towards the door. She felt at that moment driven, and capable almost of an act of violence. This prolonged delay was insupportable to her. She wished to put an end to it. She would go up to the sick man's room and find out for herself what was happening. But as she opened the door she saw Sir Mervyn coming down the stairs with Miss Burnington. At that moment she hated them both. Her jealousy made her hate them.

She stopped. Miss Burnington came up to her.

"Thank you, Miss Traill," she said. "You have done the right thing and I am grateful to you."

Olivia said nothing. She did not dare to speak lest she should say something violent or horrible, something unforgivable, which would oblige her to leave that house and render her return to it impossible. Miss Burnington looked at her in surprise, as if expecting some words from her, and then added,

"I am going downstairs to give some directions. I believe Sir Mervyn wishes to speak to you."

"Very well," Olivia forced herself to say.

Still looking surprised, Miss Burnington went on down the stairs and Olivia returned to the drawing-room, followed by Sir Mervyn, who shut the door carefully behind him.

"What is it?" asked Olivia, as he came towards her.

"I am not certain yet, but I think he is probably in the first stage of typhoid fever."

Olivia was conscious of a strange sense of deep relief, as if a burden fell from her. But there mingled with it a feeling of outrage.

"I thought it might be typhoid," she said.

"You didn't say so."

"What would have been the good? What am I to say anything to a doctor? But now, haven't you anything to say to me?"

The sense of outrage was growing in her. She felt it burning her.

"To say! Well, I suppose you realise now what would have happened if a doctor had not been called in?"

"I didn't mean that at all."

"Please tell me what you did mean."

"Did you come here intending to frighten me?"

"I came here because I was asked—begged to come."

"I daresay you did. But wasn't it your policy to frighten me?"

"What makes you think so?"

"That note of yours for one thing."

"Why should my note have frightened you?"

"What did you intend to convey by it?"

"Exactly what I wrote. If you had not come down to see me, I should certainly have gone to see Mr. West."

"Why? What did you——"

She paused. She felt like one on the edge of danger. Yet something drove her to take the onward step.

"What did you suspect?"

The doctor hesitated. At last he said,

"Under the present circumstances I don't think it is necessary to say."

"That means that you acknowledge how erroneous, how—how monstrous your suspicion was."

"You can interpret my meaning as you like," he replied coldly.

"Is that your idea of honesty? Is that the English idea?" she said bitterly.

"I am not in the least ashamed of anything I have done," he said, inflexibly.

"But that wasn't all. When I came down to see you you hinted . . . you implied that . . . that . . . I can't say it!"

"Miss Traill, as you have brought up this very painful subject, I am willing to say to you that I believe I have made a mistake about you, though I consider it a not wholly unnatural one. Since I have seen you to-day I do believe in your *bona fides*. I thought you a conscious charlatan. Now I think you merely a self-deceived woman."

"I made him sleep only this very day when the fever was on him."

"Indeed! For how long?"

"Not for long. But doesn't that show——"

"It really is useless for us to argue about it. I consider all faith healing an absolute imposture."

"And Miss Burnington's cure?"

He replied to her question by another.

"And Mr. Fernol West's cure?" he retorted.

Olivia winced. Sir Mervyn saw it and mercilessly pressed his advantage.

"What of that?" he said. "I have just told you that I have come—I scarcely know how or why—to believe in your honesty. Tell me—do you honestly believe you have made that young fellow sound?"

"I—I thought I had. His parents, his friends, every-one thought I had."

"And do you think so still?"

"I don't know."

"That is honest," he said, almost with heartiness.

"You only met Fernol once. How can you——"

"Miss Traill," he said. "I will match your honesty with mine. To see a man like Mr. West once is enough for anyone trained as I am, fortified as I am by a long medical experience. Shall I tell you exactly what I think about him?"

"Tell me."

"I think he's acutely neurotic. I'll go further. I shouldn't be surprised if he has the seeds of madness in him."

"Madness!—Fernol!" she whispered.

He had put her fear into words, and by doing so had given it a vehement life such as it had not had before.

"Why—what has he done to make you think he is mad?"

"I don't say he has done anything. I have no actual proof of his madness. But have you never had the same suspicion as I have?"

Olivia tried to say "no," but her lips made no sound.

"Such an accident as I understand he had, might easily have an effect on the brain from which it could never recover," said Sir Mervyn.

"Then do you still think—but you say you believe it is typhoid?"

"I think it probably is."

"Then——" she paused, looking at him.

At this moment the drawing-room door opened and

Miss Burnington came in hurriedly, with a newspaper in her hand. She looked greatly agitated.

"I've telephoned as you told me to," she said to Sir Mervyn. "But oh, the worst that I feared has happened."

"What is it?"

"Look at this! In the evening paper! And I hear they telephoned from the office some time ago to have it confirmed before putting it in. Sidney answered and told them it was nonsense, that my brother only had a slight cold, but they have put it in all the same."

"Our Yellow Press!" said Sir Mervyn, taking the paper from her. "Where is it?" he asked.

Miss Burnington pointed to a paragraph. He read it.

"This must be contradicted at once—to-night," he exclaimed. "Miss Traill—read it. I shall want you to authorise a contradiction."

As he spoke he handed the paper to Olivia, and she read the following words:

SIR HECTOR BURNINGTON AND THE FAITH HEALER.

As we go to press we learn that the famous general, Sir Hector Burnington, who has been mentioned as the probable future Viceroy of India, has been seized with sudden and severe illness. We are informed that he has refused to call in a doctor and has placed himself unreservedly in the hands of the American faith healer, Miss Olivia Traill, whose name has been so much before the public of late, and whose methods have brought forth such severe condemnation from the medical profession. This will be a hard blow for the doctors. It will also probably come as a surprise to the public, who, hitherto, have been under the impression that Sir Hector Burnington did not estimate the capacity of women too highly. In our late edition we hope to be able to state the exact nature of the great general's illness. Our informant was unable to satisfy our curiosity on this point. But that Miss Olivia Traill is in charge of the case there is no doubt whatever.

As Olivia looked up from the paper she met Miss Burnington's eyes.

"If this isn't contradicted at once it will ruin Hector!" said Miss Burnington bitterly. "What can we do?"

Before either Sir Mervyn or Olivia could answer the footman opened the door. Miss Burnington turned with nervous abruptness.

"What is it, John?"

"A gentleman has called, Ma'am. He says he is a representative of the *Evening Dispatch* and begs to see you for a moment. He also asked for Miss Traill, Ma'am."

"For Miss Traill? Did you tell him Miss Traill was in the house?"

"He knew it, Ma'am. He said: 'I know Miss Olivia Traill is in the house. Please ask her to give me a moment. I shall only keep her a moment.'"

"Oh, Sir Mervyn! What shall we——"

"May I settle the matter?" said the doctor.

"Oh, yes. Please do what you think best."

"Very well."

He turned to the footman.

"Please show the gentleman into the library, and say that Sir Mervyn Butler, of Harley Street, will be down to see him in a moment."

"Yes, sir."

The footman went out.

"This visit is providential," said Sir Mervyn. "We shall be able to get a *démenti* out at once and knock this rumour on the head before the papers have time to turn it into a sensation. But you must help us, Miss Traill."

"What do you wish me to do?" asked Olivia.

"I shall ask you to give me a written statement to take to that man downstairs. Of course you realise who the informant mentioned here"—he struck the paper with his forefinger—"must be?"

"I? How should I know? I have nothing to do with it. When Sir Hector called me in I told him that if I was able to cure him I should like him to promise me never to tell anyone either that he was ill or that I had been able to help him. If you don't believe me ask him."

Sir Mervyn and Miss Burnington exchanged glances.

"You really told him that!" said the doctor.

"Yes."

"That was, I must say, very fine of you," he said. "Very disinterested indeed."

"I only wanted to cure him, nothing but that."

"Thank you, my dear," said Miss Burnington. "I'm afraid I——"

"Oh, please—never mind!" said Olivia. "You have both of you misunderstood me utterly."

There was an awkward silence, which the doctor broke by saying,

"Surely you realise that the informant who gave this information to the Press must have been Mr. West."

"Perhaps it was."

"Of course it was."

"How could I help it?"

"You couldn't. But only you can kill this rumour."

"But it was true."

"It isn't true now," said Miss Burnington.

"We must give out a statement which must go into the paper to-night if possible," said Sir Mervyn, going over to the writing table. "The only question is how to word it."

He sat down, took a pen and drew a sheet of note-paper towards him.

"If you will allow me, Miss Traill, I'll write down what I think will do, read it out to you and then ask you to copy and sign it."

"Very well," she said, in a dull voice.

Suddenly she felt tired. She longed to lie down, shut

her eyes and forget everything; forget her old enthu-
siasms, forget her lost faith, forget Fernol West and the
devotion to her which had brought about this horrible
situation, forget even Sir Hector and her great love for
him. She knew that Sir Mervyn was right. She knew
that it must be Fernol who was responsible for the dreadful paragraph which, perhaps, hundreds of people were
reading, and repeating to other hundreds at that very
moment. And she was scarcely able to doubt any longer
that Fernol was also responsible for something else—
for something so terrible that the mere thought of it
would surely make her life hideous to her for ever. For
the first time she felt the burden of existence as a loathsome load which she longed to cast away from her. For
the first time she thoroughly understood the temptation
of suicide.

"Let me see!" said a meditative voice.

She looked across the room. Sir Mervyn had drawn
out a pair of spectacles rimmed with tortoise-shell and
perched them on his broad nose. Miss Burnington had
gone to stand near him and was looking over his shoulder.
She stared at them both, and they both seemed remote
from her. It was difficult for her to believe that this man
and this woman had anything to do with her. Sir Mervyn moved his lips, as if silently forming some words,
and frowned, wrinkling his ample forehead. Then he
bent over the paper and wrote, slowly, occasionally stop-
ping for a moment to consider. Presently he paused and
turned towards Miss Burnington.

"Do you think that will do?" he said, in a low voice.

Miss Burnington bent nearer to the paper.

"Admirable!" she said, after a moment. "The very
thing."

"I think so. . . . I think so!"

He looked across to Olivia over his spectacles.

"Miss Traill!"

Olivia heard a voice say "Yes."

"I'll just read out what I have written."

He paused.

"You are listening, Miss Traill?"

Again the voice said, "Yes."

"This is it."

He cleared his throat, and leaning back in his chair read in a loud and important voice:

"A paragraph in the 'Evening Dispatch' has just been brought to my notice containing the statement that, seized with sudden illness, General Sir Hector Burnington has refused to call in a doctor, and has placed himself unreservedly in my hands. I wish to deny emphatically that there is any truth in this statement. I am not attending Sir Hector Burnington, who is being treated by Sir Mervyn Butler, of 21B, Harley Street. I must ask you to give this denial publicity. The fact that I have been to Sir Hector Burnington's house merely as a friend to inquire after his health has doubtless given rise to this ridiculous rumour."

Sir Mervyn looked across again at Olivia.

"And then your signature," he said.

"You want me to sign that?" said Olivia.

"If you kindly will. And I shall ask you to copy it out first. . . . It must be in your own handwriting."

Olivia crossed the room slowly. Sir Mervyn got up from the table.

"Here is the pen."

"Thank you."

She took it and sat down. For a moment the written words swam before her eyes. Then they grew clear. She began to copy them slowly and carefully. Sir Mervyn and Miss Burnington, who at first had stood behind her, left her and went softly over to the fireplace. She heard them whispering together as she wrote. And she felt as if she were writing her own condemnation. Presently she came to the last sentence, to the final words: "this ridiculous rumour." There she stopped. She still kept the pen in her hand; she still leaned over the paper. Her eyes stared at the word "ridiculous." That was what she had become—ridiculous; ridiculous in her own eyes, and in the eyes of the man she loved. How had he taken that confession of hers? She did not know that yet. She looked across the room to those two figures by the fire. They were no longer whispering together. They were silent now, watching her.

"Is anything the matter, Miss Traill?" said Sir Mervyn's voice. "Is there anything in the wording you object to?"

"Oh—no! I have no right—none—to object to anything now. It is not true, of course, but how can I object?"

"I don't understand. What is it then?"

And he came towards the writing table, looking curiously at her.

"What did he say when you told him?" she asked.

"He?"

"What did Sir Hector say?"

"He was too ill to say much."

"But what did he say?"

"As far as I remember, he said, 'very well—if she can't manage it, do the best you can.' "

"That was all?"

"He added, 'I was willing to pay my debt.' I think his mind was beginning to wander."

"Thank you."

She leaned down over the paper, copied out the last sentence, and signed her name at the bottom.

"Here it is!" she said, getting up.

Sir Mervyn took the paper and read it carefully.

"That's quite right. Thank you, Miss Traill. Now I'll go down."

He turned to Miss Burnington.

"I shall only be a few minutes."

And he left the two women together.

"Won't you come to the fire?" said Miss Burnington, after a silence.

The voice was gentle, almost pleading.

"I am not cold, thank you."

"But do come and sit down. You must wait and just hear the result of Sir Mervyn's interview with this man."

"Yes."

Olivia went over to the fire and sat down.

"I'm very sorry about all this—very," said Miss Burnington in a quick, anxious voice. "I know you must think me a most ungrateful woman. I am really distressed. But—but I love my brother very much. And he is of such inestimable value to his country that I felt obliged to do what I did. Can you understand? Can you try to forgive me?"

"I understand," said Olivia.

"Anything I can do to show you how I feel about you I will gladly do. If you think—if it would be any good —I will say that I—that I owe my own cure to you."

"You don't!" said Olivia.

"But surely——"

"You don't. I can't heal anyone. I have no faith in myself."

"But you don't mean to say——"

"I say that I have deceived myself. I thought I possessed a power which I didn't possess. You were quite right not to believe in me. You saw what I didn't see, what Fernol and the others didn't see. You needn't reproach yourself. I didn't cure you. I didn't cure Fernol. And I could never have cured your brother. I shall never again attempt to heal anyone."

"I—I am sorry!" said Miss Burnington, almost helplessly.

Again the silence fell between them. It lasted a long time. Olivia broke it at length by saying:

"Is he very ill?"

"I'm afraid he is. We've sent for a trained nurse. Meanwhile, Sidney, his valet, a most devoted man, is with him. I shall go up directly Sir Mervyn comes back."

"Many people recover from typhoid, don't they?"

"Yes. We—we hope for the best."

Again the silence fell. And this time it lasted till Sir Mervyn came back.

"It's all right," he said. "I found the young man quite amenable. Your denial will appear in the late edition to-night, Miss Traill."

"I am glad."

"And I've written and signed a bulletin which will be affixed to the front door. That is necessary. There have been several inquiries since I went down-stairs. Mr. West has been again."

"Mr. West!" said Miss Burnington. "Did you see him?"

"No. John told me. He came just as I was about to go into the library. I forbade John to let him in, or to trouble you about it."

"Does he know you are here?"

"Yes. I understand John had some difficulty in getting rid of him. But he's gone now."

Sir Mervyn looked at Olivia, who had sat in silence during this short conversation with her eyes fixed upon him.

"I think," he said, addressing Miss Burnington, "that it would be well if you returned to your brother."

"Yes, yes, I'll go!" she said, getting up quickly.

"I'll follow you almost directly. I expect Nurse Swann will be here in a moment."

Miss Burnington turned to Olivia.

"If I don't see you again to-night——" she said.

She held out her hand.

Olivia took it.

"Thank you for all you have done."

And she left the room. Then Sir Mervyn turned very gravely to Olivia.

"I didn't wish to say anything about it to Miss Burnington. She has enough to trouble her already. And I'm afraid undue excitement might make her ill again. But I must tell you. John informed me that Mr. West was in a very excited state when he called just now."

"Excited!" said Olivia. "How—how did he show it?"

"When he heard I was in attendance on Sir Hector he became violent and wished to force his way into the house. He demanded to see you. John was obliged to get rid of him by telling him a lie."

"What lie?"

"John said you weren't here, that you had gone home."

"And then——"

"He went away muttering angrily to himself. I'm afraid we shall have trouble with him. There's no doubt in my mind that a doctor ought to see him."

"Poor Fernol!" she said. "Poor Fernol!"

"It's a grievous business. Is he living quite alone?"

"Yes."

"Where?"

"At the Savoy Hotel."

"It's difficult to know what to do. It would be worse than useless for me to come into contact with him. He has conceived a violent hatred against me no doubt. He said as much to the footman. And I saw it that evening I met him here. I think the best thing I can do is to give you the address of a first-rate man in such cases."

He took out a card and wrote on it a name and address in pencil.

"You might communicate with him. He will advise you better than I can."

"Who is he?" said Olivia.

"The best specialist we have for—for mental cases. And now I must go to Sir Hector!"

"Good night," said Olivia.

She took the card.

He stretched out his hand and grasped hers, almost with cordiality.

"One word more!"

"Yes?"

"I must warn you against seeing Mr. West alone for the present. Don't communicate with him. Don't let him in. Have you any servants?"

"No; I'm quite alone."

"On no account let him in."

"Thank you."

The footman opened the door.

"Nurse Swann has just come, sir."

"Good! Send her up to Miss Burnington."

"Yes, sir."

The footman went out. Sir Mervyn hesitated, although there was surely nothing more to be said between him and Olivia.

"I don't quite like your going away alone," he said.

"I am accustomed to being alone."

"Yes—but to-night!"

Suddenly he went to the door, opened it, and called down the staircase.

"John! John!"

"Yes, sir?" came the footman's voice from below.

"Please call a cab for Miss Traill."

"Yes, sir."

The doctor came back.

"Drive home. I would rather you didn't walk."

"Very well."

"Do you live in a flat?"

"Yes."

"There's a hall porter?"

"Yes."

"Will you promise me to take him up with you as far as your flat door?"

"I'm not afraid of anything."

"No, no; of course not. But will you do as I say?"

"If you wish it."

"And on no account allow Mr. West to be shown up if he should call. He probably won't. But he might. Good night again."

Again he took her hand and pressed it. Then they parted. Olivia went downstairs and he went up to his patient.

Olivia had to wait a few minutes in the hall while the footman stood on the pavement with his whistle at his lips. She looked into the darkness, searching for the figure of a man. She saw no one. At last a cab glided up.

As she drove away in the darkness she knew what it was to feel lonely. Everything that had meant life to her seemed to have fallen away from her suddenly. She had failed in her job; or, rather, she had thrown it up because she feared failure. The main purpose of her existence had been withdrawn out of her reach. For with the abrupt fading of her faith had vanished for ever any power of healing she—perhaps—had once possessed. She knew quite well that she would never dare to try to heal anyone again. She could never be such a humbug as to attempt without faith that which she believed could only be accomplished with faith. Her career, therefore, was at an end. The man whom she loved might die. If he lived it could surely be only to despise her. Her chief friend in London had become to her a reason for apprehension, almost for horror. To think of him was to feel a cold breath from the abyss, to know the shuddering of nightmare.

Yes, she knew loneliness that night.

Sir Mervyn's reiterated warnings had not brought to the birth in her any physical fear. The fear that companioned her was wholly of the imagination and of— she fancied—the most intimate region of the heart.

"Poor Fernol!" she thought. "Poor Fernol!"

So the tragic grip had taken hold of him. The sharp fangs of an evil fate had fastened themselves in him. And all her energy, her will, her faith, her long effort had been wholly in vain. She thought of his mother and father far away in America, and the tears rose in her eyes. It was almost incredibly sad.

When the cab drew up before Buckingham Palace Mansions she looked quickly out through the window. There was no one waiting before the entrance. She got out, paid the fare, and went in. The porter in uniform stood by the lift.

"Has anyone been here for me?" she asked.

"Yes, Ma'am."

"Mr. West?"

"No, Ma'am. Lord Sandring."

And he gave her a card with Lord Sandring's name on it and some words pencilled on the back. Without reading them, she stepped into the lift and was taken up to her floor.

"You might just open the door for me," she said to the porter.

"Certainly, Ma'am."

He inserted his key and opened the door. She went into the little hall. As he was about to close the door she said:

"Just a moment!"

"Ma'am?"

Sir Mervyn's last warning was present in her mind: "On no account allow Mr. West to be shown up if he should call." She had made no promise to obey it, but now, as she recalled the look in the doctor's face, the sound of his voice, she resolved that she would.

"If Mr. Fernol West should call to-night, please don't show him up," she said.

"Very well, Ma'am. I'm to say you are out?"

"Yes, please. Wait! You are sure to be in the hall?"

"Oh, yes, Ma'am. I shall be there."

"Thank you."

He left her and shut the door, leaving her to her immense loneliness. She went into the bedroom, took off her jacket and hat, then walked to the little drawing-room and turned on the electric light. Lord Sandring's card was still in her hand, with the card given to her by Sir Mervyn. She turned the former over and read:

"Just seen the 'Evening Dispatch.' This is grand. That HE *should be among the believers! Ecco un trionfo!—S."*

Ecco un trionfo! Poor Lord Sandring! His joy would soon be turned into bitterness. She laid down the two cards, and looked round the familiar little room, which she had actually been able to think of as home since she had been in London. Now it was the cage of her loneliness. She was confined in it with the hours. The night lay before her, and then—all the future. She thought of beasts in captivity, going to and fro behind the bars with their wild eyes fixed on the other side of the world. What had she to look to?

The two armchairs by the fire, with their suggestion of repose, of meditation, or of happy talks, made her shiver when she looked at them. She glanced again at Lord Sandring's card. She would write to him. It would be something to do and it was absolutely necessary that he should know the exact position of affairs in regard to herself. She owed him an immediate explanation. She tore up his card, sat down, and began to write to him her confession of impotence. As she wrote a sort of brutal desire to hurt herself woke up in her. In the strongest words at her command she described her complete disbelief in her own powers, her absolute determination never again to attempt to heal any living creature.

"You will never see me again at the Bureau. I know I shall cause you great pain by this letter, but anything is better than pretence. I cannot play the humbug with you, or with anyone. I know my own impotence, and I wish everyone who has heard of me to know it too. I am not more than others; I am less, because I have made

claims which have no basis of fact. I can do no good to anyone. I may have even done harm to many. I don't know. But I do know that, from to-night, I will never set myself up as the superior of others. As to Sir Hector Burnington, I am not attending him. He knows I consider myself quite incapable of curing him of his illness. Sir Mervyn Butler is with him. Forgive me the disappointment and pain this letter will cause you, and, with gratitude for all your kindness,

"Believe me,

"Your sincere friend,

"OLIVIA TRAILL."

She put this letter into an envelope, addressed it, stamped it, and laid it on the table. It could go by the morning's post. She did not want to go outside the flat door, or to ring and call the porter up to her. Yet, perhaps, it would be best if Lord Sandring got it by the first post on the morrow with the newspapers containing her statement. (She had little doubt that many of the papers would copy the announcement in the late edition of the *Evening Dispatch.*) Perhaps she ought to send away the letter that night. After some hesitation—she seemed to be made up of hesitation now—she rang the bell for the porter. In a few minutes he came up, let himself in with his key, and opened the door.

"You rang for me, Ma'am?"

"Yes."

She took up the letter.

"Could you put this in the post for me?"

"Certainly, Ma'am."

She gave him the letter and he turned to go. But when he was just going out of the room she called him back.

"One moment!"

"Ma'am?"

"If Mr. West should call I—I think I will see him."

"Very well, Ma'am."

She saw a faint look of surprise on his stolid face.
"I am to show him up then, Ma'am?"

"Well—yes. Yes, show him up. But perhaps he won't call."

"I couldn't say, Ma'am."

The expression of surprise grew more definite. He stood for a moment, then walked heavily out.

Had she really summoned him, not because of the letter, but on account of Fernol? She was not sure. She was sure of nothing to-night. But she now felt that to follow the advice of Sir Mervyn would be the act of a moral coward. Fernol had come to England only because of her. He had implicitly trusted her; had given himself to her in a peculiar, a touching way. His father and mother had an almost childlike confidence in her, admiration for her. Could she fail their boy in what was, perhaps, the supreme hour of his fate? That would be an act of almost loathsome weakness on her part. Her natural unselfishness rose up again in her, asserted itself almost violently. After all, did it matter now what happened to her? She had still a duty to carry out, at whatever cost to herself. If she deserted Fernol now, because of the horror which had attacked her imagination, no shred of self-respect would be left to her. She knew that she would have to condemn herself utterly.

Suddenly the battle was over. She felt a slight sense of relief. Whatever Fernol was, whatever he had done, she would recognise her responsibility towards him, would try to fulfil it to the uttermost.

"I don't matter any more," she said to herself. "But I won't be afraid. I won't be afraid. If I am afraid I am the most contemptible of all creatures."

Usually she went out at about half-past seven to have her dinner at a small Italian restaurant close to Victoria Station. But to-night she had resolved not to go. She went into the kitchen of the flat, made herself some strong tea on the gas stove, drank it, and ate some bread and butter. Then she sat down to wait for Fernol. She now felt quite certain that he would come.

Soon after nine she heard the clang of the door-bell. He had come. Again that horror of the imagination seized her and shook her. But she strove to overcome it, to summon up all her courage. Nevertheless as she got up and went down the passage she was trembling. She opened the door and saw Fernol.

"So you're here!" he said.

His angry eyes searched her face. He looked excited, hostile. His face was as the face of a stranger.

"Of course I am here," she said, in a level voice. "Come along in."

He frowned as he came in.

"Leave your coat."

He said nothing more, but quickly pulled off his coat and threw it down on the floor of the hall.

"Please pick up your coat and hang it up properly," she said.

He shot a glance at her sideways, hesitated, then obeyed her.

"And now come right in."

Her instinct was to make him go in front of her, but she did not give way to it. She walked on and heard his step close behind her. She was glad when they were in the drawing-room, and she could face him again.

"Sit down, Fernol."

"No, thank you."

"Anyhow, I will."

And she sat down, retaining an air of calm self-possession. He stood on the hearthrug and put his hands in his pockets. Then he took his right hand out and fidgetted with his watch-chain. His eyes roved all over the room avoiding hers.

"What's that?" he exclaimed in a loud voice.

"What? Where?"

"There! On the table!"

She looked and saw the card Sir Mervyn had given her

with the name of the specialist in mental diseases written upon it.

"That! Oh, it's only——"

Before she could prevent it he had gone to the table and picked up the card.

"Sir Mervyn Butler!" he exclaimed. "Do you mean to tell me——"

He turned the card over and read what was written on the back.

"What's this?" he demanded, still in a loud voice. "What's the meaning of this doctor's name?"

He came back to the fire with the card in his hand.

"What do you want with these cursed doctors? Why aren't you with Burnington?"

"Try to behave properly and I will tell you."

"You'd better!" he retorted.

"Put that card down."

"Why should I?"

"Because it's mine and I tell you to do so."

He dropped it on the floor.

"I've made a nice mistake," he said, with intense bitterness. "I believed in you and you're as treacherous as all the rest of them. What have you done? Why aren't you with Burnington? What's Mervyn Butler doing there? Why is he there, I say?"

"I'm going to tell you if you'll only listen and be quiet."

"Go on!"

"Fernol, did you go to the *Evening Dispatch?*"

"Of course I did."

"How did you know Sir Hector was ill?"

"Never mind. That's my business."

"How could you have known?"

"Didn't he swear he would send for you? Didn't he? Or did you tell me a damned lie?"

"Hush! He did send for me."

"Then—then you're going back to-morrow? You're going to throw that old humbug into the street?"

"Sir Mervyn is not a humbug, Fernol."

"He is. He pretends to cure disease and he can't. He takes money for what he can't do. All the doctors do that. And you, who can cure, don't take a farthing. And the world howls against you and sticks to the humbugs. But now they'll know. All London will know. I'll take care of that. But you must back me up. I'll bring it off. I'll work it all. That's why I'm here. You need a man to run you, one that knows the ropes. See how I worked the *Evening Dispatch?*"

He broke into a laugh.

"That was a surprise for the doctors, wasn't it? That was one from the shoulder, eh? When are you going back to throw old Butler out? I'll go with you. I want to see the fun. You owe that to me, Olivia, for if it wasn't for me——"

He stopped short and put his hand to his mouth, and a crafty look came into his face.

"Fernol, what have you done?"

"Never mind. When are you going back?"

"I am not going back."

"Not——"

He bent down and stared into her eyes.

"I'm not going back. Sir Hector is dangerously ill."

"Why not? All the better for you! Now's your chance to show what you can do."

"I am not going back."

The boy's face, which had been flushed, went suddenly white.

"You're going to let me down! After all I've done for you!"

After a moment of painful hesitation Olivia said, in a gentle voice, which sickened her as she heard it, because it sounded so false:

"Dear Fernol, if you don't tell me what you have done, how can I know what I owe you? You leave me in the dark. Is that friendship? How can two friends work together when one of them is left in ignorance of what the other is doing? Put me wise and then——"

"Yes—then?" he said eagerly.

"Then I shall be able to understand thoroughly what it is my part to do."

"That's horse sense, Olivia! Now you're talking!"

Again one hand went to his watch-chain.

"You will do your part if I tell you?"

"Fernol, have I ever let you down?"

She felt like a traitor to friendship as she spoke. But the time for sincerity was past. At all costs she had to know.

"No, never. But, if I tell you, will you go back to-morrow?"

"I'll go to Cadogan Square to-morrow."

"You swear that?"

"I promise you."

His face was transfigured.

"Olivia, old girl, I've done the wonderful thing I've always wanted to do for you. I've given you the great chance of your life."

"How, Fernol?"

"It was I who made Sir Hector get ill."

Somehow—she never knew how—Olivia forced herself to meet the triumph in his eyes with a look of gratitude. She even held out her hand to him. He grasped it.

"How did you do it?"

"Don't tell! . . . I've got a friend in Guy's Hospital. I made up to him for you, though I hate all the doctors. I managed to get hold of a culture of typhoid bacillus one day, when I was with him in the laboratory. (He was injecting typhoid into a rat.) That night I dined with Sir Hector I put some of it into his wine."

"Thank you, Fernol," she said, by a fierce effort concealing her horror.

"I gave you your chance."

"Yes, you gave me my chance."

"And you won't let it slip?"

His eyes were on her; his hand was always at his watch-chain, twisting it to and fro.

"You'll put that old humbug into the street? You'll go there to-morrow and stay there till you've cured Burnington?"

After a moment of silence Olivia said slowly:

"What if I went to-night?"

The boy's face shone with enthusiasm.

"That's the way! Tackle old Butler to-night! But you've never told me how he got in?"

"Miss Burnington went and fetched him."

"Just like her! But why did you let him go near Sir Hector? Why did you leave the house and let him stay in it?"

"I didn't know what to do. Miss Burnington insisted."

"Isn't Burnington master in that house?"

"Yes, of course. But he's ill. And that makes it all difficult. I was there all day."

"Go back now and throw Butler out. I've done my part as a friend. Go and do yours now I've told you."

"Yes, I'll go and do mine," she said, faintly, in spite of the effort she made.

She got up.

"I'll come with you!" he cried excitedly.

"No; I want you to stay here."

"Here? Why?"

"I'll just go and get things quite clear, and then I'll come back and tell you. If you come, there'll be trouble with Miss Burnington. She doesn't like you. Nor does Sir Mervyn."

"I'll wring his neck if I get at him!" he said savagely.

"Let me go alone. Promise me to stay here—promise me!"

"Very well. I don't so much mind now you know."

His air of triumph returned.

"You know me now, Olivia," he said. "And you know whether I care or not."

"Yes, I know now."

As she left him to go to her bedroom, she bent quickly and picked up the card from the floor. Instantly a suspicious look came into his face.

"What do you want with that?" he said, fiercely.

"Only to throw it into the fire," she replied.

As she turned to the flames she managed to read the specialist's name and address. She dropped the card into the fire. Less than five minutes later she was out of the flat. In the hall she found the porter.

"Mr. West is staying on in the flat," she said. "I have to go out, but I shall soon be back."

"Very well, Ma'am."

She looked hard at the man. He was an old soldier, sturdy and strong, with a powerful, unemotional face.

"Look here!" she said. "I am going to say something to you which I beg you not to repeat."

"Honour bright, Ma'am."

"My friend, Mr. West, isn't quite himself to-night."

The porter looked much more intelligent.

"I'm going to fetch someone to see him. He's promised to wait for me. But, if I'm delayed, he might try to go. If he does, will you do your very best to detain him?"

"I will, Ma'am."

"Persuade him—don't let him go."

"I'll see to it, Ma'am."

"I shan't forget you."

He smiled slightly, and she hurried away. She found a cab and drove to the specialist's house. Luckily he was at home. He received her in his consulting room. He was a big, burly man, with enormous shoulders, a kind, strong face, and fearless and honest brown eyes. Olivia took a fancy to him at once. As briefly as she could, she laid the case of Fernol before him, after telling him that Sir Mervyn had given her his address. She did not tell him Fernol's terrible secret. She was resolved, if possible, to keep that hidden for ever. But she told him quickly the history of the boy's accident, his condition afterwards, his apparent cure by her, his coming to London, her increasing anxiety about his state of health while in London, shown by his fanatical devotion to her interests, and his fanatical hatred of those whom he deemed her enemies. When she came to the Burningtons she found her task difficult. But she told as much as she dared, not sparing herself.

"My poor friend longed for Sir Hector to fall ill, so that I might cure him," she said. "And by an evil chance he fell ill."

Then she described Fernol's visits to the house in Cadogan Square, his tipping of the footman, and the scene he had made when he discovered Sir Mervyn's presence in the house. She also told about the newspaper paragraph.

"Sir Mervyn urged me not to see Mr. West to-night," she said. "But I did. I felt it my duty to see him. I—I can't tell you quite all that happened, but I'm absolutely sure the poor boy is mad. I know it. I have reason to know it. I dare not let him go. He is quite alone in London. To-morrow—even late to-night—the papers will publish a statement from me saying that I am not attending Sir Hector and that Sir Mervyn Butler is. If Mr. West sees it I am sure something terrible will happen. He is not sane. He might do anything. He is waiting in my flat now. He thinks I have gone to Sir Hector to turn Sir Mervyn out. Think of it! Can you help me?"

"Not a doubt of it!" said the doctor, after a moment of thought. "I suppose," he added, "you have told me everything of importance bearing on your friend's mental condition?"

As he said this the honest brown eyes looked remarkably penetrating.

"I have told you all I can tell," she answered. "He is fanatical about me, because, poor boy, he thinks I have cured him. It's—it's very tragic for me."

"Yes; I can understand that. Well, the first thing to be done is for me to see him. I'll go at once. If, when I have seen him, I find clear indications of mental trouble, I can arrange for him to be under proper supervision."

"You won't . . . I couldn't bear for him to be put in a madhouse," said Olivia. "His father is a millionaire. I can cable to him. I'm sure he will come over."

"I have a home of my own at Hampstead for mental cases. I could take him there and watch him."

"Yes—yes. Oh, that would be the best thing possible for him."

"But I must tell you that, if I don't satisfy myself that his mind is astray, I can do nothing."

"I'm sure you will see that I am right about him."

"Very well."

The doctor got up.

"One moment! I must go to the telephone," he said.

He left the room and was away for nearly ten minutes. When he came back he had an overcoat on and his hat and gloves in his hand.

"Shall we go?" he said.

"I'm ready. You wish me to take you into the flat?"

"I wish you to drive me there. On the way I'll tell you what I propose to do."

They went out and got into the waiting taxicab.

When they arrived at Buckingham Palace Mansions, a big motor-car was standing before the entrance.

"Now," said the doctor, "you'll remain in the cab as I suggested. Have you your key?"

"Yes. Here it is."

She gave it to him. He got out, walked to the motor and stood by it for a moment, evidently speaking to someone inside. Then the door of it was opened, and a short, strongly built man emerged and joined the doctor on the pavement. After a short colloquy the doctor returned to Olivia.

"I'm going to tell your man to go a little further on," he said. "It may be better, in certain eventualities, for you not to be just here, in front of the entrance. I may be some time. Try not to be anxious. I will return to you as soon as I can."

"I'll wait," said Olivia. "But hadn't I better just speak to the porter?"

"To be sure. I'll find him."

He went into the building and came out almost immediately with the porter.

"Is Mr. West still here?" asked Olivia.

"Yes, Ma'am."

"He hasn't tried to leave?"

"I haven't seen him, Ma'am. I've been here all the time. He must be still upstairs."

"Then please take this gentleman up."

"Yes, Ma'am."

The doctor spoke to the taxi-driver. As he turned to go into the house, followed by the porter and the man who had got out of the motor, Olivia's cabman drove on for, perhaps, a hundred yards, and then stopped. Olivia looked at her watch. It was half-past ten. She sat back in the cab and waited. For a few minutes she sat perfectly still, and then abruptly something within her, some barrier, seemed to break, and she was shaken by a passion of tears. She had controlled herself for too long, and now Nature took revenge upon her. The effort she had made when she took Fernol's hand after his hideous revelation, the hand of one who would perhaps prove to be the murderer of the man whom she loved, was the cause of this sudden and tremendous reaction! She felt now a sort of rage against Fernol. She hated him as she wept. Her pity for him was swept away. Whatever his fate he deserved it. Let him pay for what he had done; pay to the uttermost farthing! He had attacked the man whom she loved. And Sir Hector would die. All hope of his conquering the disease which was beginning to ravage him failed in Olivia at that moment.

She saw nothing but blackness. She was drowned in blackness; submerged with the Furies. Her body trembled from head to foot. She clenched her hands. And she hated with her whole soul; hated the boy who had done this deed for her sake.

"Let him pay!" her brain kept crying out. "Let him pay!"

The cabman stirred on his seat. Presently he half turned. Then he slowly got down. The window of the cab was drawn up. He approached it. Then he laid his hand on the door. Olivia saw him and instinctively shrank into the corner farthest from the door. The man turned the handle and looked in.

"Did you call out, lady?" he said. "Did you want somethin'?"

Olivia managed to say "No."

The man muttered some words, and shut the door. Then he lit a pipe and walked up and down on the pavement. His interruption, the sight of his homely and moving figure, recalled Olivia to a cold sense of the present realities. She heard a clock strike eleven. The tears still streamed over her face, but now she began to wipe them away; and presently she was able to stop crying. But she kept on shivering like a child and her teeth chattered convulsively.

Half an hour passed. A sort of numb calm enfolded her. She felt frigid, detached and hard. The cabman reopened the door.

"How long are you goin' to be, lady?" he said, in a hoarse voice.

"I don't know."

"Because I don't want to be out all night. We aren't made of brick nor of stone neither, whatever some people think. There's some——" he broke off, and stared down the road in the direction of the Mansions.

"What is it?" said Olivia.

"There's someone comin' out, lady. I'm sure I do 'ope it's them, that I do."

He still stared into the night.

"There's that car——" he paused. "I do b'lieve it's the gentleman comin' at last. Yes, it is!"

A couple of minutes later Dr. Soames appeared at the window. He looked very grave. His face was slightly flushed and there was a glint of something like excitement, or unusual energy, in his eyes. His coat was buttoned up to the chin, and the collar was turned up to his ears.

"You can drive back to the Mansions," he said to the driver.

Then he opened the door.

"Shall we walk there?" he said to Olivia. "It's only a step."

"I'll get out," she said.

When she was out the driver turned the taxicab and drove off.

They followed on foot.

"He's gone," said the doctor.

"Gone! Where?"

"I had two men there with the car. He'll be all right with them, poor fellow. They've taken him away."

"Then——?"

"You were quite right. He's not fit to be at large."

"Was he violent?" she asked, without interest.

"Yes, at the end. But I know how to deal with such cases. He's being taken to the home I told you of at Hampstead. He'll have every care."

"Oh!"

"You mustn't see him for some time."

His tone was decisive. They were now in front of the Mansions.

"Will you come in?" she said, indifferently.

"I'll come in for five minutes. Then I should advise you to get to bed."

"I shan't sleep."

"Yes, you will. I'll take care of that. I'll only be a minute," he added to the taxi-driver.

The man began to grumble, but the doctor silenced him
with some money.

When they were upstairs Olivia led the way mechanically to the drawing-room.   But she paused at the door.
The room was in great disorder.   An armchair was overturned, a small table had been broken, and the books
which had been on it were strewn about the floor.

"What has happened?" she said.

She turned to the doctor.   "What did he do?"

"Never mind."

Quietly and swiftly he put the room to rights.

"Now sit down."

She obeyed.

"Won't you take off your coat?" she said.

"No, thank you."

She noticed that he still kept the collar up.   He saw
her eyes on it, and said very simply,

"I'm not quite presentable."

"He attacked you?"

She spoke without any real interest, mechanically.

"He isn't himself.   But we'll get him better in time, no
doubt.   I should cable to his father to-morrow."

"Very well."

"You didn't tell me that he suffers from hallucina-
tions," said the doctor, looking her straight in the face.

"I didn't know it."

"Well, he does," said the doctor firmly.   "He thought
I was Mervyn Butler."

She was silent.

"No doubt he hasn't shown that side of his malady to
you.   He has also acute ego-mania.   He imagines that
he's done something very great, very wonderful.   He
has no conception whatever of right and wrong.   He's
in the condition when he might commit a crime and
boast of it to anybody."

"It's just as well I fetched you," she said.

"Yes.   Now we won't talk any more to-night.   I'll
see you some time to-morrow.   By the way, the reason

you mustn't see him is a painful one, but I'd better tell you it. He has conceived a violent hatred for you."

"Has he?"

"Yes. He realises that you fetched me, a doctor, to him. That has turned him against you. He thinks you his greatest enemy."

"Perhaps I am," she said, coldly.

The doctor glanced at her, then took a small box from his overcoat pocket.

"Can you get me a glass of water?"

"Why?"

"I'm going to give you a couple of these and see you take them before I go. You've got to have a night's sleep."

She got up heavily, went out and came back with a glass of water.

When she had taken the pills he grasped her hand.

"Go straight to bed. You promise me?"

"Yes, I promise. But I know I shan't sleep."

He smiled.

"And I know you will. Good night."

He shook her hand and went to the door.

"Give a kind thought to the doctors," he said, and went out.

"Does he know?" Olivia thought vaguely. "Has Fernol told him? Does he know?"

Then she obeyed his direction, went to her room, undressed, and got into bed.

She felt tremendously tired, even exhausted. Her brain became dull and sluggish. It seemed to her that her body was heavy like a mass of lead.

"If only I could sleep!" she thought. "But I know I shan't."

That was her last thought before she slept. . . .

A month had passed, and Olivia was still in London living in the little flat which had seen Fernol's tragedy. Her life, which had been so active, so full of that putting forth by which, as she had once said to Fernol, she drew in strength, had become lonely and monotonous. She saw very few people, went out very seldom. Her name, once the subject of discussion and of polemics in the Press, was now never mentioned in print, and seldom in any conversation. There had been a brief outburst when her statement had appeared in the papers denying that she was in attendance by the bedside of Sir Hector, but it had soon died down. Lord Sandring was bitterly disappointed in her. Her defection had given the final blow to his ambitions. After a painful interview, in which he had brought all his vitality to bear in an effort to persuade her to reconsider the decision so almost brutally put forth in her letter to him, he had acknowledged himself beaten by closing his Bureau of Psychic Healing. He had played his trump card, and fate had out-trumped him. There was nothing more to be done. The most remarkable woman in America had laid him out. He retired to his estates, and began to breed Herefordshire cattle and to go in for Müller's exercises. Why Miss Traill—she was no longer Olivia to him—remained in England he could not imagine, unless it were on account of that poor chap, Fernol West, who was still in the doctors' hands, and who, of course, in such a situation must not be expected to get better.

But it was not on Fernol's account that Olivia stayed on, laughed at and despised when she was remembered, a practically self-confessed failure. She could do nothing more for Fernol. She dared not even go to see him. His mother and father had arrived from New York, and therefore her responsibility was ended. And Fernol's maniacal hatred for her persisted. It was a fixed idea with him that she was his enemy and had deliberately ruined his life by giving him into the hands of the doctors. He had fought the doctors for her, and this was her reward to him.

Mr. and Mrs. West, in their misery, had shown the greatest delicacy, the greatest kindness to Olivia. They knew that she had done her very best for their son, and they were still generous in their gratitude. Nevertheless, it was not possible for them to feel towards her as they had formerly felt. They had regarded her as the saviour of their adored son. Now they could only look upon her as a well-meaning and warm-hearted woman who had done her utmost, and who had failed in her endeavour. She felt pity concealed in their gentle courtesy to her, and she could scarcely bear to be with them. The look in their eyes reminded her of the belief in herself which was gone for ever; the pressure of their hands intensified her regret for the faith which was lost.

And Fernol, their son, hated her. She had become part of his madness.

She stayed on in London because of Sir Hector.

He was still dangerously ill with typhoid fever, hovering between life and death. She could not leave England till she knew whether he would live or die. She never went to the house in Cadogan Square. Although Miss Burnington and Sir Mervyn Butler had never said a word on the matter, she knew that, after the statement which had appeared in the *Evening Dispatch,* any visit from her might revive the rumour that she had gone there as a faith healer, anxious to interfere with the doctors, or summoned as a last hope because they could do nothing more.

She had made up her mind to complete self-sacrifice. And she was not a woman who believed in half measures. But she was kept informed of the state of the man whom she loved by Sir Mervyn Butler. The almost impossible had come about; her former antagonist and she were now staunch friends. Sir Mervyn had recognised the stark sincerity of the woman whom he had despised and done his best to ruin when she first came to London, and he had told her so in words which had kindled in her generous nature a warm response. Strangely, she now looked upon him as perhaps her best friend in England. Sir Hector was too ill to be the friend or the enemy of anyone. And Miss Burnington, who had called on Olivia more than once, and tried to show her the greatest kindness, was obviously never quite at ease when with her. Between the two women lay dividing memories, and also the knowledge of a shared secret, which had never been spoken of by them, and so set them apart from each other.

The fifth week of the illness was nearly over when one evening Sir Mervyn Butler called on Olivia, just before she was about to leave the house for the Italian restaurant where she dined modestly alone every day. He came in with his usual rather ponderous dignity, but there was an unusually kind look in his eyes.

"He's better!" he said, immediately, without even greeting her. "The crisis is past."

"You think—will he recover?"

"I don't see why he shouldn't now. But, of course, it will be a long business, and I don't know whether he will ever be the man he was. In fact, at his age I doubt it."

Olivia said nothing. At that moment she did not dare to speak. She was rejoicing, and yet she felt stricken. For if that man had no great future, what would his life be worth to him?

"I have two things I must tell you," continued Sir Mervyn, knitting his brows and looking straight before him. "Another man has got the Viceroyalty of India."

"Oh!" said Olivia.

It was a little cry, and all the pity of woman was in it.

"My dear, he couldn't be fit for such a post for a long time, if ever. I should be against his returning to a strenuous life in the East."

"But his great ambition wrecked! Oh, what will he do when he knows?"

"He's a strong character. He'll take the blow standing."

She was silent, trying to control her emotion.

"The other thing I must tell you is this. He has asked for you."

"For me!" she said. "Oh, no!"

"He wants you."

"He doesn't know! He doesn't know!"

"Doesn't know what? I don't understand you."

"How can I—after all that has happened—Miss Burnington would be afraid to have me in the house."

"I consider it necessary for you to go there. His mind must not be troubled. He is insistent to see you."

"But is he quite himself?"

"Yes. He's terribly weak, of course, like a child almost. But his mind is quite clear. Surely you won't refuse to go to him?"

He was beginning to look surprised.

"I thought you had a strong regard for him."

"I have."

"Then what holds you back? Miss Burnington perhaps? But she wishes you to come."

"She asked you to tell me?"

"No. I should have done that in any case. My duty is towards my patient. But, of course, I spoke to her about it."

"What did she say?"

"She said, 'Beg Miss Traill to come. Tell her from me that I hope she will let bygones be bygones.' I don't think it would be like you to——"

"Oh, no, no! It isn't that!"

Her intense agitation was obvious. She seemed to be torn by some interior conflict.

"What will you do?" he asked.

"I'll go. If he wants me I must go. But to-morrow— I can't go to-night. Don't ask me to—please."

"Very well. But I have your promise for to-morrow?"

"Yes, yes. But if the newspapers——"

"They won't, I dare say. But even if they do, it doesn't much matter now."

"No; it doesn't much matter now," she said.

"She loves him!" Sir Mervyn said to himself as he descended the stairs. "What an old fool I have been not to see it before."

And during his drive back to Cadogan Square he pondered over women, and came to the remarkable conclusion that possibly Miss Burnington had known for some time what had just come within the grasp of his admirable intelligence.

"Women are quick," he said to himself. "They're very unreasonable, but they're damned quick."

He knew something about them after all!

Three weeks later Sir Hector was treading slowly and feebly on the road to recovery. His natural strength was beginning at last to assert itself, and though he was still very weak he was gaining every day. Olivia was often at the house, sitting by him, talking to him, reading aloud to him, generally books of travel or memoirs of military men. One day he asked for Omar Khayyam, and she read to him for an hour.

When she had just read the lines:

"One moment in annihilation's waste,
One moment, of the well of Life to taste—
The stars are setting, and the Caravan
Draws to the Dawn of Nothing—oh make haste!"

he stopped her.

"That's enough," he said, in the voice that was growing stronger every day.

Olivia shut up the book.

"The old chap thought pretty much what I've been thinking—when I could think at all—as I lay here," he said. "One moment of the well of Life to taste. It isn't very much, is it?"

"No," she said.

"I've sometimes wondered whether I've made the most of the part of the moment I've had till now."

"I'm sure you have," she said, wondering.

"I'm not."

"But think of the work you've done!"

"Work isn't everything after all. What about yours?"

"Mine is over," she said.

She and he had never yet spoken of her abdication. He had never alluded to it in any way since they had met again.

"I heard that," he said. "And I reckon mine is over too."

"Oh, no!" she said earnestly.

"Perhaps you think I don't know about the Viceroyalty?"

"I—I—I had no idea. Your sister thinks——"

"I don't! Yes, and so does the doctor. They've kept the newspapers from me."

He smiled grimly.

"No doubt they meant to . . . what is called 'break it to me' when I got better. But Sidney told me over a week ago."

She felt shaken with pity for him.

"I'm sorry," she said. "I'm sorry."

There was nothing else she could say just then.

"It's all right. I shouldn't be fit for the job now," he said, calmly.

She was silent.

"I've always lived to do jobs," he went on, without any emotion. "Perhaps I've made a mistake. How old are you?"

"Nearly twenty-nine," she answered.

"And I'm hard on the way to sixty. Do you think of me as an old man?"

"No!" she said, with a sudden gust of passion.

He looked at her hard from his pillow.

"Could you bring yourself to marry me?" he asked.

All the blood in her body—so it seemed to Olivia—rushed to her face, then retreated from it.

"I!" she said. "You—you don't know what you owe to me."

"Yes, I do."

"You don't! You don't! I never meant to tell you or anyone. But now I must. It is owing to me that you will never be Viceroy of India."

"How do you figure that out?" he asked, with a look of keen astonishment.

Then, in plain, simple words she told him all about Fernol.

"Poor boy!" she said. "He did it for me, because he thought I had healed him. I have been wicked enough to hate him for doing it. But he thought he was working for me."

Sir Hector lay for a while in silence. Then he said: "Does anyone else know?"

"I don't think so; unless in his madness he told the doctor. And the doctor would probably not believe it."

"Wasn't West mad when he told you?"

"I know it is true. I know he did it."

Sir Hector stretched out his thin hand.

"You've done the right thing by me," he said, "but you're a woman of courage. I knew that directly I clapped eyes on you. When I get well shall you and I keep West's secret together?"

*   *   *   *   *   *

Fernol West has been taken back to New York by his parents. A great surgeon out there, who has recently examined him, thinks it possible that a certain operation on the brain may eventually cure him. That lies in the future.

Sir Hector Burnington and Olivia were married not long ago.

To the great astonishment of Lord Sandring and of London, Sir Mervyn Butler gave her away.

THREE: THE HINDU

I HAVE a friend whom I will call Sir William Turnbull, although that isn't his name. He is a famous specialist in nervous diseases, lives in Cavendish Square, London, and leads, I should think, a very interesting, though certainly an arduous, life. He is a white-haired man, with a long white moustache, a rather beaky nose, blue eyes, and an inexpressive face. His voice is quiet; his manner is always tranquil, seldom animated and scarcely ever vivid. In general conversation he says but little. But when I am alone with him at night, as I am perhaps once a month, he tells me interesting and sometimes fascinating stories of the people who consult him. Of course, he never reveals their real names. I have noted down some of these "cases" in a book. Two or three days ago I was looking over it and came upon a strange narrative. It concerns a newspaper proprietor, and I call it "The Hindu."

"John Latimer came to consult me about a year ago" (said the doctor, in his quiet, rather colourless voice). "He owns several big papers, and is an extremely successful man. In person he is a large, rather burly, individual, just over forty, with brown eyes, short brown hair, a firm mouth and chin, and a straightforward but unaffected manner. But when I first saw him he looked very ill. He had a furtive demeanour which was at odds with his dominating appearance; his large hands were terribly restless, and by various other signs I was able to judge of his condition. It was very bad.

217

When we had had a little talk I realised that behind
Latimer's nervous state there was some prompting tragedy, some haunting fear or misery, and that until I could
find out what it was I could do very little for him. I
told him this.

"But it will take a long time," he said. "If I'm to go
thoroughly into it——"

"Nothing else would be of much use," I interrupted.
"But I can only give you half an hour this morning.
Could you come again"—I consulted my engagement
book—"say, on Thursday afternoon?"

"What!" said he, with a deplorable accent. "Three
days ahead?"

"That seems to be my first free hour," I replied.

"Oh, but——" Latimer paused. Then he thrust forward his powerful head and exclaimed:

"I don't want to wait so long. Will you waive eti-
quette and dine with me at my house, say, to-night?"

"That's very good of you."

"Good!"

His lips twisted, and his big hands shifted on his
knees. He clasped them tightly together.

"Good!" said he. "Why, doctor, I'm hanging on to
you as my only hope. I've heard that you succeed where
everyone else fails. Can you come and will you?"

I said I would, and I went.

The Latimers live—let us say—at 4A, Portman Square.
I was there by half-past eight the same evening, and
found Latimer waiting for me in a very eccentric drawing-room, which, I have reason to believe, was a replica
with slight variations of an interior Mrs. Latimer had
seen when witnessing the Russian ballet. She came in
almost directly, one of the thinnest women I had ever
set eyes on, perhaps thirty-eight, tall, good-looking in a
wasted sort of way, with brown hair which framed a
low forehead, white cheeks, and pale observant eyes. She
wore jade ear-rings in her rather large white ears and
jade bracelets on her sticks of arms. She greeted me

quickly in a voice which sounded thoroughly over-worked. Almost immediately we went down to dinner.

The dinner was quite super-excellent. During it Mrs. Latimer talked with a sort of anxious pertinacity. Latimer said little. I did my best, which is pretty bad as you know. When dinner was over Mrs. Latimer got up and held out her hand.

"Good night," she said, in her tired voice. "I am going to bed."

"To sleep?" I asked.

"No, to read. I'm not much of a sleeper. Good night, Johnny."

Her pale eyes travelled quickly over her husband's face and figure. Then she turned and went out of the room, her long ear-rings swinging gently beneath her white ears, one thin hand holding the jade bracelet on her left arm.

"Will you smoke, doctor?" asked Latimer.

"No, thank you, I never smoke," said I.

"And you don't take coffee. Nor do I—now. Then let us go to my room where we shan't be interrupted."

"With pleasure."

Latimer led the way to a large library on the ground floor behind the dining-room. There were no Russian ballet touches in it. All was plain, comfortable, and practical. Books were ranged round the walls. Deep armchairs were set near the fire. Dark green curtains hid the windows. A telephone was handy on a big flat writing table. And the silence in this sanctum seemed of a special brand, heavier, deeper than the silence of the dining-room.

Latimer shut the door.

"No one will disturb us here," he said. "Do sit down by the fire."

"Thank you," said I. "Now you can be as long as you like. You'd better tell me everything as far as you can remember, until I interrupt you."

"Oh, as to that, I have an excellent memory."

"Good."

I leaned back in my chair calmly, laid one hand over the other, and gazed into the fire. I took care not to look at all observant. Latimer was glad of that.

"I'll smoke my pipe, if you'll allow me," he said, and he filled and lighted his pipe with deliberation. Then he sat down rather heavily, and began to speak in his steady baritone voice.

"As you know, doctor, I'm a newspaper proprietor, and control *The Daily Echo, The Week, The Evening Journal,* and *The Sunday News.* Lately my control has really been nominal. I've been travelling. I have no children. My papers bring me in a great deal of money. I'm a very successful man."

He sighed deeply, puckered his brows, and let his firm chin drop for a moment, as he looked down on the floor.

"My wife is clever and artistic, and, like many clever women, imaginative and apt to be carried away by whims. I, on the other hand, have always been looked upon as a hard-headed, practical man, good at organisation, the last sort of type, I suppose, likely to be the prey of the imagination. In fact, many of my friends say I haven't got one."

He smiled bitterly.

"If I had, some of them have said—I should be a bigger man than I am. I tell you this lest you should presently be inclined to fancy that my appearance belies me. For I know I look stolid enough. Well, now——"

He drew his armchair a little nearer to mine. "It began in this way. Do you remember, about fifteen months ago, there was a great pother about psychical research?"

"Do you mean when Professor Elton launched a violent attack in one of the papers?"

"In my paper, *The Daily Echo.*"

"Was it? On one of the principal investigators for the Psychical Research Society?"

"Yes. Till then I hadn't bothered myself about such

matters. I hadn't had time. But the row attracted my attention, and the multitude of letters which poured into the office proved to me how deep was the interest taken in occult matters by men and women in nearly all walks of life. I showed some of these letters to my wife, who, of course, had long ago attended *séances,* played about with planchette, had her fortune read in her hand, and so forth. She is a Christian Scientist and was a Buddhist, or *vice versa;* I'm not quite sure. She likes plenty of variety in her life. Anyhow, all these psychic matters were an old tale to her. To me, however, they were not, although, of course, like everyone else, I had heard a good deal about them casually.

"Well, I thought I'd look into them in my off moments, see for myself what I could make of them. First, I put up one of my cleverest young men to make investigations for me—to prepare the ground as it were; and then I came in. I went with this young man, not in my own name, of course, to a sitting with a so-called 'psychic' whom he considered to be not the ordinary humbug. I went a second time, a third time. My wife didn't know about it. Unless my young journalist blabbed—and I think I was too valuable to him for him to be such a fool—nobody except himself and the psychic knew about it. And the psychic didn't know who I was. The result of these investigations, although I was thoroughly incredulous when I started them, was that I felt there was, in the common phrase, 'something in it.' We had a lot of messages which seemed to be sheer bunkum. But we had one which was really remarkable. It referred to my wife."

Latimer had by now finished his pipe. He knocked the ashes out of it, and laid it down with a slow and careful gesture.

"This came at the last sitting I attended with my newspaper man. After it I decided not to sit again with him present. It informed me—I tell you this because I've decided to tell you everything—that my wife ceased to love me in a certain month of a certain year. It, moreover, stated that the reason for her change of heart—I believe she had been sincerely attached to me—was the fact that she had come under the influence of an Indian, a Hindu, at the time mentioned. All this was conveyed to us by the medium, who was a man, but when in a trance was apparently controlled by the spirit of a woman called Minnie Harfield. This Minnie Harfield in real life, so the spirit stated, was a woman of but humble class whom the Hindu had taken to be his mistress and had discarded on meeting my wife. Owing to her despair at this desertion, Minnie Harfield had committed suicide. No doubt"—here Latimer shot a self-conscious glance at the doctor—"all this seems to you a farrago of absurdity. So it did to me. But the medium gave the Hindu's name—Nischaya Varman—and certain details of his appearance, position and acquirements. These things, of course, had hitherto been unknown by me."

"And were these statements given fluently by the supposed spirit?" I asked.

"No, with some apparent difficulty, and as it were under cross-examination."

"By you?"

"By me. Yes. I—I became interested."

"Naturally. Go on."

"When the sitting was over I walked away with my journalist. He's an extremely clever and shrewd young man, or he wouldn't be on my staff. Nevertheless, I played a part with him. There seemed nothing else to do. I told him that I was totally unable to verify what the medium had said, and that I absolutely disbelieved in the medium's *bona fides*. The Minnie Harfield spirit I jeered at. I added that I was resolved never to visit the medium again, and that I relied on him—the journalist—never to speak of what had just happened to anybody. He replied that, of course, he would do as I wished, and that no doubt we had both been listening to a series of foolish lies, deliberate inventions of the medium. And there ended my association with him in occult matters."

"Can you tell me his name?"

Latimer looked surprised.

"His name is Maurice Isaacs. Needless to say he's a Jew."

"Thank you. Well?"

"Well, now, doctor, I had told Isaacs that I absolutely disbelieved what the medium had said about my wife and the Hindu. Nevertheless, I determined to find out, if possible, whether there was anything at all in it. You see, I was by way of investigating—eh?"

"Precisely!" I said.

"I knew that my wife was a great admirer of Mrs. Sidon, the Theosophist and lecturer. I also knew, as of course you do, that Mrs. Sidon, who usually lives in India, has a very wide acquaintance among the natives. Certain women of society occasionally gave evening parties to meet Mrs. Sidon when she was in London. My wife had been to these parties. It was quite probable that she had met Easterns in that circle, though I could not remember that she had ever spoken to me of having done so. Had she ever met a Hindu called Nischaya Varman? That was what I wanted to know. Chance favoured my curiosity. The London season was just beginning, and one evening my wife mentioned that Mrs. Sidon had returned from India and was to give a lecture on 'The Mysteries' at Queen's Hall on the following Sunday.

" 'Are you going?' I asked.

" 'Yes,' she answered.

" 'I should like to go with you,' I said.

" 'Of course—come. You've never heard her, have you?'

" 'Never.'

" 'She speaks better than any man I ever listened to.'

"On the Sunday we went. We sat not far from the

platform. On it there were several Indians. I saw my wife looking at them directly we had taken our places.

" 'Do you know any of those dark fellows?' I asked her.

" 'Yes. That'—she indicated a slim boy—'is the boy whom many people in India expect to develop into a world teacher.'

"I knew his name and said it.

" 'And who are the others?'

"But at this moment Mrs. Sidon came on to the platform dressed in white, and looking like a Pope, and for the next hour and twenty minutes no voice was heard but hers.

"When the lecture was over I told my wife I wished she would take me behind and introduce me to Mrs. Sidon, by whose speaking powers I had really been impressed. She seemed rather surprised by my request.

" 'She must be well worth knowing,' I said.

" 'Yes; but she doesn't want to know everybody,' said my wife rather doubtfully.

" 'Do you think she'd mind if you took me?'

" 'It's nothing to do with the newspapers?'

" 'On my word of honour—not.'

" 'Then I'll find out if we can see her.'

"She did, and I met Mrs. Sidon. I also met two or three of her Indian adherents, which was what I had intended to do. And with one of these, a Hindu called Satyavan, I managed to become so friendly in a few minutes that it ended by my arranging to meet him again at dinner during the following week. I did not tell my wife about the dinner. She was talking to Mrs. Sidon at the moment and did not hear us fixing up the appointment.

"Satyavan and I did dine together at the Indian Restaurant. Have you ever heard of it?"

"No, never," I answered.

"Well, it's not a hundred miles from Piccadilly Circus, a quiet, unpretending little place on a first floor, where you get native cooking that's quite good. We had an excellent meal. We had to send out for wine, which I drank but which was refused by my new friend. I dare say you will have guessed my reason for cultivating the acquaintance of Satyavan. As he was a Hindu, living in London and frequenting the circle of Mrs. Sidon, I thought it probable that he might know Nischaya, if, indeed, such a person really existed. Towards the end of dinner I drew a bow at a venture.

" 'By the way,' I said, 'you seem to know most of Mrs. Sidon's followers. What has become of Nischaya Varman?'

" 'Did you know him?' said Satyavan, fixing his deep eyes upon me.

" 'No; but I have heard of him.'

" 'He passed over to the other side three months ago.'

" 'Ah! He was rather a remarkable man, wasn't he?'

" 'Very. He had great powers, a strong, very strong personality. Mrs. Sidon had a high opinion of him and often consulted him when she was writing. He was in communication with the masters.'

" 'But he had a—a rather strong earthly side, too, hadn't he?' I asked.

"Satyavan, who was lighting a cigarette, gazed at me for what seemed a full minute before he said:

" 'He was a man like other men in certain ways.'

" 'Ah! Poor Minnie Harfield!' I ejaculated.

"Satyavan's face did not change, but his unfathomable and very sad eyes seemed to challenge me.

" 'You knew her then?' he said.

" 'No; but I know all about her. She killed herself on Nischaya's account.'

" 'Well, if she chose to!' said Satyavan. 'A man cannot stay in one place for ever. We are travellers. We pass on from one place to another, from one soul to another.'

" 'From one body to another?' I hazarded.

" 'The body is very little. No doubt Minnie Harfield had to expiate some fault committed in a former existence. She gave Nischaya much trouble, as did other women. A man must not be the prey of women.'

" 'No, indeed. There is so much in life besides love. The activities of the brain——'

"I branched off to other topics, doctor. Satyavan's confirmation of the medium's statements about Nischaya and Minnie Harfield made a great impression upon me. Do you wonder?"

"Not altogether," said I, non-committally.

"But I had yet to confirm the most important statement of all, the one which concerned my wife. I—I care for my wife."

There was a moment of complete silence. Then Latimer resumed:

"I resolved to return to the medium. I resolved to try to get into communication through him, not with Minnie Harfield again, but with someone else. By this time I had come to believe in the medium's powers. I made an appointment with him by telephone without giving my name, and went to Fulham—he lived there— alone at night. On this occasion I told the medium I had come with a special purpose, but said nothing as to what it was. The medium, who was a very weak-looking young man, with thin, primrose-coloured hair, flabby white hands, a bending body, and a very genteel Cockney accent, seemed pleased and heartened. I remember he said I was very sympathetic. We sat down in a small, vulgar room on the first floor, with a portrait of H. P. Blavatsky on the wall, and a rep-covered sofa near the window. Before we began the actual sitting, however, I inquired of the medium whether there was any means of summoning a particular spirit through him. He had, he had already informed me, two 'controls,' but was sometimes taken possession of by spirits whom he rather irreverently spoke of as 'outsiders.' I made him understand that I was there that night to communicate with an outsider. How was I to do it?

"My young gentility—he was very ineffective when he was not entranced—seemed puzzled by the question. He advised me, however, as soon as he fell into the trance condition to 'put my mind on' the spirit I wished to communicate with.

" 'Do spirits come at call, then?' I asked. 'I have been told you ought never to fix your mind at a sitting, but ought always to try not to force anything.'

" 'There are no rules as I know of,' he said weakly. 'They may come or they mayn't. It's just as it happens.'

"He was not illuminating, and I let him alone. Obviously he knew little more about such matters than I did. He was, perhaps, merely an instrument. Indeed, I must say for him that he claimed to be nothing else.

"We sat. He fell presently into a trance. I followed his suggestion. I 'put my mind on' the Hindu. Indeed, that night I could have done nothing else. With all the mental force, the power of will, at my disposal I summoned him to come and to communicate with me. Presently the medium's usual controls, Katey and Johannes, came in turn, or purported to come. They talked a good deal about matters uninteresting to me, and I became very irritated and almost despairing. Then the medium came out of his trance. I was—I confess it— by now in a high state of nervous tension. It may seem ridiculous to you, doctor, but sitting there in that vulgar little room in a Fulham slum, with that ignorant genteel young man, I was companioned by the feeling that there, and only there, could I arrive at a knowledge of the truth about my wife. It seemed to me—of course I was strung up—that already I felt some influence, which I believed to be the Hindu's, not far from me; that it had been attracted towards me by my mental demand; that, perhaps, only a very slight obstacle stood between me and it. And there, meanwhile, was the medium weakly patting his white forehead with his flabby hands, and murmuring that he must refresh himself with a glass of sherry and water. Sherry and water!

"Well, I controlled myself. I believe I showed no sign of the intense nervous irritation I was feeling. I let him swallow his disgusting refreshment, and then I urged him to try again.

"'Oh, but I'm gone quite flabby with it,' he protested. 'They take it out of me, I do assure you.'

"I said I would double the fee.

"'It isn't only the money,' he said. 'A man must know when to stop.'

"I aimed a blow at his vanity then. Without mentioning my name I told him I had great influence with the newspapers, that already I was much struck by his powers, that I sought a complete proof of them.

"'I feel you can give it to-night,' I said. 'We were on the very verge of something remarkable when you came out of the trance.'

"'How do you know that?' he asked, sipping at the sherry glass with his too flexible lips.

"'I felt it. I feel it now. There is something that wants to communicate, and can't unless you are entranced.'

"He seemed impressed by my earnestness, and glanced round the dingy room with his pale eyes.

"'Well, I'll see what I can do,' he said, with the air of one making a concession. 'But, my word, shan't I be poor-spirited after!'

"To cut further detail, doctor, for I don't want to weary you—no, really—the medium did eventually fall once more into a trance, and that night, for the first time, the spirit of Nischaya, the Hindu, purported to control him, to come into connection with mine."

"You say purported!" I observed. "Then you are still not thoroughly convinced?"

As I spoke I turned slightly in my armchair and looked rather sharply at him.

"I want—I want to be unprejudiced. I want to put fancies at a distance."

Latimer suddenly sprang up from his chair, with a movement almost startingly swift in so heavy a man, and, standing by the fire, he continued:

"You shall be the judge. That's why I am telling you the whole business."

"Give me the material necessary to form a judgment on," I said.

"After the medium had been entranced for a few minutes, perhaps five, a very peculiar voice spoke out of him. Have you ever heard a Hindu speaking?"

"I don't think I have."

"In my opinion it was the voice of a Hindu. The voice stated that it was Nischaya Varman who was speaking. It seemed very reluctant to communicate. In fact, the whole impression produced on me upon that occasion was one of deep and almost violent reluctance. You know how it is when you, as it is called, force something out of a person."

"Yes."

"The Hindu spoke like one forced to speak and almost malignant under the obligation. I didn't care. I went straight to the point. I spoke at once of the Minnie Harfield communication, and asked for the truth of the matter. There followed a long silence, during which the medium seemed strangely agitated. The impression on me was of a human being rent. It was almost a convulsion, and alarmed me. Nevertheless my curiosity prevented me from interfering. I continued to sit. I continued almost fiercely to demand the truth from the Hindu. I seemed to feel opposed to me in the room a tremendously strong influence which nevertheless my force of will had compelled to draw near to me in despite of its own desire. I believe I have a strong will. I don't like anything to get the better of me. And just then the thought of my wife stiffened my will, doctor. Had she been overcome by this influence when it was in life to my horrible detriment? Then it was surely my part to compel it to my will now. I was resolved. I was hard as steel. All dread, if I had had any, of things occult utterly left me. The convulsions of the medium did not deter me. I insisted. I said, 'You shall not go. I forbid you to go. I brought you here. I forced you to come and I'll force you to remain.' I felt the thing, whatever it was, struggling against me."

"How?" I interjected.

"I can't tell you. These occult things can't always be told of, even when they are known. I say to you that I felt the thing struggling, like moving water all about me."

"Yes?"

"Until it broke away, as an enemy might tear himself out of your hands. It was gone. The medium awoke. Poor chap! He was very exhausted that night. He asked me what had happened. He seemed frightened. I did my best to reassure him, for I was resolved to make of him my instrument, at whatever cost to myself or him, until I had got through him the information I wanted. By this time I was convinced that I really was in communication with some other plane, or world, call it whatever you like. I know little of spiritist jargon. I had momentary doubts, of course. But I know my inner conviction must have been as I say because of my intense preoccupation with the medium, my resolute determination to use him. If I had not secretly believed, I could not have been so ruthless. If I had known that the weak young man in Fulham would suffer in health, even would eventually die, because of the efforts to which I urged him, I should not have desisted from them.

"As I said, he was very exhausted that night. When he seemed a little better I paid him double his fee and said I was coming again on the following evening. He said that really he couldn't risk it. I replied I should come. He drank some more sherry and almost piteously protested. I asked him if he had any idea of what was happening when he was entranced. He said that as a rule he was quite unconscious, but that during the last sitting he had been faintly aware of something which had seemed to be tormenting him, doing him harm.

" 'And look how it's left me!' he concluded. 'I'm all to pieces, really I am. You've brought something you oughtn't to 'a' brought, something bad, something with too much power. I dunno!'

"His words added to my determination. The end of it was, doctor, that I overcame all the objections of the poor thing by sheer bribery. He found I was rich. He realised that I was influential, and he became my creature. It did him much harm. It practically wrecked his health for a time. I didn't care.

"I won't describe my sittings with him in detail. It isn't necessary. I'll merely give you my general impression of the sum of them.

"During them, so it seemed to me, there began and persisted a relentless struggle between two wills, mine on this plane, and another—the Hindu's, as I supposed—on some other plane. It was almost as if two men were striving on either side of a doorway, one to drag the other through it into the room where he was, the other not to be dragged through. The wretched medium was, as it were, the doorway. The door was opened only by his falling into trance. At other times it was fast shut. My whole being was bent upon overcoming the intense resistance of the Hindu to my desire that he should answer to my summons and hold communication with me.

"In the first sittings—three or four—he came, or purported to come, and spoke a few words. But just as I was beginning to feel that perhaps my power was going to prevail over his, he was gone. It was as if he died out of the medium. I had the impression of a receding wave. My irritation at these escapes was intense, but my will was not weakened by frustration. I am accustomed to carry through things that I undertake. I was resolved to carry this thing through."

"You had come to be absolutely certain, then, that it was really the spirit of the Hindu?" I dropped out.

Strong man though he was Latimer looked shame-faced.

"I suppose I had. Yes, I had."

"Go on!" said I.

"I took to timing the visits of the Hindu to that vulgar room in Fulham, and I found that with each sitting the period during which I was in communication with him grew slightly longer. This encouraged my persistence. But the creature was horribly alert, was wary as a snake. His communications were fragmentary, and often almost meaningless. By degrees, however, I arrived at a very definite conception of him, a conception of sinuous power, of brooding imaginative thoughtfulness, varied by outbreaks of slippery cunning. And I detected in him fascination."

"In what did the fascination lie?"

"I could scarcely tell you. But—well, now and then there came from the lips of the medium, speaking in the Hindu's voice, a phrase that pierced, or in which there was poetry. And at those moments I knew that a woman might be moved by such phrases spoken in such a way, moved to the trembling that is like the trembling of a violin string. Words catch at women when the voice that speaks them in strange. Women love a strange voice even when it's ugly. Haven't you noticed that in regard to actors?"

He did not wait for me to answer, but continued:

"At last one night I attained my object; I forced the Hindu to come directly the medium was entranced, although till then he had always been preceded by the medium's usual 'controls.' Not only did I force him to come immediately, but I forced him to speak of my wife. Hitherto, when I had mentioned my wife, either I had received evasive or unmeaning replies, or the

Hindu had died out of the medium who had abruptly returned to consciousness. On this occasion, however— why, I don't know—I felt a power as of iron within me, a merciless faculty which seemed to enable me to use my power as never before. The impression I had was of pinning something down, something that struggled to escape but could not. I—sometimes I wish now that it had succeeded in escaping."

Latimer paused. There was a dawning of horror in his eyes.

"Why do you wish that?" said I.

"Do you think it possible—or, let me say, can you imagine it to be possible, for one here on earth, on this plane, so to exercise power over a being on another plane that the being is in some strange way dislodged from his natural sphere, and cannot regain it? Could such a thing be?"

"I have had no experience in such matters," I replied.

"Or another thing might happen," continued Latimer, staring hard at me with eyes that now had an inward look. "If a man forced something to come to him, when it was wholly bent on not responding to his summons, it might afterwards refuse to go when he wanted to get rid of it. It might revenge itself in some such way as that."

"Do I understand then that you made the Hindu come, and that he did not go as on former occasions? Is that what you mean?"

"He came—yes, and he seemed to go. But that may have been his cunning. Anyhow he came, and I asked him about my wife. Briefly, he said he had known her, had subdued her to his power. About physical things nothing was said. I gathered that her mind and nature had undergone the impress of his, that she had been willing to do anything he told her to do, that she had looked to him as her master. That was enough for me."

"You believed it then?" I said.

"That night I did. And I was seized by a sort of mad

rage such as I had never thought to experience. I believe
I was almost frenzied. I longed to get at the Hindu. I
was physically moved. I wanted him, this seducer of
women, there before me in the body. It drove me almost
mad to think that, having done his vile work, he had
tranquilly passed away into some other sphere while I
was unconscious even of his existence. Keep this in
your mind, doctor; I wanted the Hindu in the body that
night that I might punish him in the body. I remember
clenching my fists; I remember the perspiration breaking
out upon me. I am a very ordinary man, doctor, with
plenty of the unregenerate brute in me, and there was
something in my peculiar situation calculated to madden
such a man. At such moments men go to the animal
within them. I did that. I sent up to the Hindu a silent
cry—'Come back from the place where you are that I
may punish you as you deserve! Come back!' This
silent cry persisted in me till I felt absolutely exhausted.
I fell back in my chair. My eyes—I remember—closed.
My whole body became cold and almost numb."

Latimer had been speaking with unusual intensity,
but now his manner changed, turned to an almost frigid
dryness. He paused, lit a cigar with slow deliberation,
sat down near to me, crossed his legs, leaned forward,
and said:

"Now we come to the matter which altered my life,
sent me travelling, and at last brought me to your door.

"As on former occasions, the Hindu seemed to die
out from the medium, who emerged from his trance.
I paid a big fee and got up to go. Looking down on
the trembling and white-faced young man, I said:

" 'I may not need to come to you again.'

"He stared at me with his pale eyes. He seemed unable to understand what I said.

" 'If you are ever in difficulties,' I continued, 'you can
always write to this address.'

"And I gave him the name and address of a confiden-
tial secretary of mine, and went out."

"And has he ever written to the address?" I asked.

"He has, a good many times," answered Latimer, with a hint of impatience.

"And received help?"

"Of course; liberal help."

"Go on."

"That night, as it happened, I found my wife sitting alone in the drawing-room when I got home. She was reading the last pamphlet by Mrs. Sidon. Raising her eyes from it as I came into the room, she said:

" 'How ill you look, Johnnie!'

" 'I feel just as usual,' I answered.

"I glanced down at what she was reading.

" 'More of Mrs. Sidon!' I said. 'Do you think that sort of thing does you much good?'

"She looked at the pamphlet.

"It's deeply interesting."

" 'Is it? And where does it lead you—into light, or into darkness?'

" 'Certainly not into darkness,' she answered.

"She looked at me again with, I thought, a flickering of curiosity.

" 'Have you got anything against Mrs. Sidon?' she asked. 'I thought you admired her. You were anxious to know her.'

"I sat down rather deliberately. I was trying hard to control myself, not to show the excitement, the—the— it was almost rage that was boiling up in me.

" 'She's a remarkable woman,' I said. 'But don't you think she might easily upset very sensitive people, throw them off their balance?'

" 'Sensitive!' she said. 'Do you mean by that weak?'

" 'Why should you think so?' I replied.

"At that moment, doctor, I was on the very edge of telling her all I had learnt from the medium. I wanted to tell her. I longed to disturb her equanimity, to attack her ferociously for the silence she had kept. But beneath my anger, my acute sense of wrong, there was something else, something cautious—it's a part of my very nature, I suppose, and I have cultivated it, for I know its value. And this caution lifted his voice. I got up abruptly, and, before she could answer my question, I had left the room.

"It was just ten o'clock. I was gnawed by a horrible restlessness. I took my hat and went out, thinking I would go down to the big building where my papers are produced. I started to walk. It was a damp and foggy winter's night. The fog was not dense, but it added to the mystery and the dreariness of the darkness. I crossed Oxford Street, and when I came to the farther side of it decided—I don't know exactly why—that I would not go to the office. I think I felt then a necessity to be quite alone. Anyhow, I walked on and soon found myself in Grosvenor Square. It seemed entirely deserted, but I crossed over to the pavement that runs by the railings of the square garden, and there, feeling safe in my loneliness, sheltered by the softly trailing fog, I walked slowly and, I think, very quietly, brooding over the misery that was mine. I had walked round the square more than once, always keeping to the pavement on the garden side, when a man slipped by me in the fog and immediately was gone. I hadn't time to see his face, or even to notice how he was dressed, though it was not so densely dark but that I could have got an impression of him had I known he was coming upon me. His passing disturbed me, indeed it distressed me strangely."

Latimer paused.

"Strangely!" I said. "What do you mean by that?"

"Well, it made me feel uneasy," Latimer answered, with an air of discomfort which almost suggested shame. "I—I found myself suddenly aware of the dark loneliness of the garden on my left, disliking it—imaginatively, I think. And—this will seem very contemptible to you, doctor——"

"Certainly not!" said I.

"Well, I went over at once to the other side of the

square, where I had the houses close on my right. This done, I walked on again slowly.

"I was just about to cross the road by the house at the corner of Duke Street opposite to the Japanese Embassy, when I realised that someone was approaching me. I did not hear him—I knew it was not a woman—but I felt him coming; I felt, too, that he was the man who had already once passed me when I was on the opposite pavement. I stopped short. I had a mind to turn sharply to my right down Duke Street, and to get away from the approaching stranger. But the cessation from movement seemed to recall me to my normal self, and I understood at once that—I think for the first time—I was the prey of something very like unreasoning fear. The knowledge came to me like a hard blow. I tingled with shame. And instantly I walked on to meet the man who was approaching me. We met under a lamp. He was an Indian."

"Ah!" I ejaculated.

Latimer looked at me sharply.

"Had you expected that he would prove to be an Indian?" he said.

"Please go on. Don't question me," I replied.

After a rather long silence Latimer resumed:

"This Indian wore a soft black hat and a brown coat, almost buff-coloured, with the collar turned up. He slipped by me, without looking at me, and immediately disappeared into the fog. His height was much less than mine. He seemed to be very thin. I guess that he had very small bones. I could, I suppose, have picked him up and thrown him into the road without turning a hair. Yet I felt afraid of him."

Almost furtively Latimer glanced at me, and a dull flush of red showed on his powerful face.

"I can honestly say that I had never felt afraid of a man till that moment," he added.

"Why did you feel afraid of this man?" I asked.

"Well, I was startled when I saw he was an Indian. That seemed to me very strange."

"Because at the moment you happened to be thinking deeply about an Indian."

"Yes."

"An odd coincidence—but nothing more."

"That's what I told myself. I battled with myself, with a strong, almost overpowering desire to get away from the square at once. And almost immediately—I had stopped for a moment on the pavement—I went forward. As I did so I knew that in a few minutes I should meet the Indian again. It was inevitable. He had chosen Grosvenor Square for a nocturnal prowl as I had. Perhaps, indeed, he lived, or was staying, in the square. When I met him again I was quite decided not to be disturbed. Well, doctor, not long after I had passed the Italian Embassy and was at the end of the square nearest to Hyde Park, I was aware that the Indian was again drawing near to me. I heard no footfall. He was a silent mover. But I knew that he was close to me. And this time my fear of him increased. Indeed it was only by a strong effort that I checked myself from—well, call it bolting if you like. We met again under a lamp. This time I forced myself to stare hard at the man. He was certainly a Hindu."

"What makes you think that? Did you see him plainly?"

"Fairly well. He was a Hindu. He slipped by me noiselessly without looking at me, and immediately disappeared into the fog. I turned. I gazed after him. I listened. And, doctor, I sweated. My whole body ran with sweat. After standing for two or three minutes I left the square by the nearest turning. It was Upper Grosvenor Street. I reached Park Lane, met a taxi, hailed it and drove straight home. My wife had gone to bed, but I saw her light. (We slept in communicating rooms.) I did not disturb her. I took a cold bath——"

"Very injudicious!" I said.

"Was it? And went to bed. I won't describe the night. It was a bad one. During the following day I attended to business as usual. I had an engagement for the evening, to dine out with my wife at a house in Eaton Square. About four I telephoned to her to say I couldn't go with her, as I should have business to attend to late. I also telephoned to my prospective hostess. I felt in no fit state for society. Besides, I wanted to dine elsewhere. Soon after eight I started on foot for the Indian Restaurant."

"Can you tell me exactly what led you there?"

"I felt a sort of horror of darkness, of what is sometimes called 'colour.' Therefore I went where I knew I should meet colour. That was an act of defiance. But in addition I was driven by an intense, probably morbid, curiosity. I wanted to see the Hindu again, to see him in full light."

"Why should he be at the Indian Restaurant?"

"I thought he might be there. It is a place frequented by Indians."

"I understand."

"I walked rapidly from my house, crossed Piccadilly Circus, and was soon at the restaurant. Mounting the stairs, I entered the first room. I must tell you that the restaurant consists of two rooms, or rather, perhaps, I should say of one large room divided into two compartments by a screen of wood and glass. In the first compartment there are several small tables. In the second there is one long table. I don't know, but I conclude that those who dine in the second compartment pay a regular pension, come to the place habitually. When I got in I found a party of seven people dining at a table close to the window in the first compartment—three Indian men, an Englishman, and three Englishwomen. Four more Indians were dining, each one alone, at separate small tables. In the compartment beyond I saw three or four heads as I stood for a moment. Then one of the three young women who served gave me a smile and indicated a table. I hung up my coat and hat and sat down facing the room and the screen.

"The man I had met in the square was not among the diners."

"But you could not see the faces of those in the farther compartment, could you?" I interposed.

"No; but he wasn't in the farther room. I felt it."

"Go on."

"I ordered my dinner. When it came I began to eat very slowly. On my right hand was the party of seven. They had a couple of bottles of champagne on the table, were half through their dinner, and were talking and laughing in lively fashion. Solemnly the dark men at the little tables ate, and smoked cigarettes while waiting for food. I watched the English girls chattering to their strangely expressive companions and thought about my wife and the dead Hindu. Had she ever dined here with him? I imagined them sitting together at one of the little tables eating dishes of the East, deep in converse, and the blood went to my head, doctor. I had no appetite, but I forced myself to eat. When I had finished one thing I ordered another. I wished to prolong my stay. Presently I asked for a bottle of wine. It had to be sent out for. While I was waiting for it two or three people, all coloured, dropped in and passed into the farther room beyond the screen. At last the wine arrived, and the girl who waited on me came with it to my table smiling. She stood in front of me to uncork it, and I spoke to her. She replied. We talked for a moment, and my mind was taken away from its brooding and expectation. We were both laughing, I remember, and I was looking at her while she drew the cork, when I was aware that a man came in softly and quickly and passed into the room beyond the screen. I saw him, as it were, with the tail of my eye. He had on a soft black hat, a brown, almost buff-coloured coat. I did not see his face. But I knew it was the Hindu of Grosvenor Square.

" 'Who is that?' I asked the attendant.

"She put the bottle down on my table.

" 'Who d'you mean?' she asked, looking round.

" 'The man who has just gone into the other room,' I said. 'In a black hat and brown coat.'

" 'One of our regular people, I s'pose,' she said. 'I didn't catch sight of him. Is your wine all right?'

"I sipped it and made some answer. She went away.

"I stared towards the screen. Through the opening in it I saw two or three people sitting at dinner, but not the man who had just passed in. Half an hour went by. My seven neighbours left their table hilariously, gathered together their coats and wraps, and went laughing down the stairs. Other diners finished their meals, paid their bills and departed. Some came from the inner compartment, but not the Hindu. I sat over my wine, pretending to drink, smoking and waiting. Now and then I saw the girls, when they were not attending to customers, glancing at me and whispering among themselves. Evidently they were surprised that I sat so long. I was now the only customer on my side of the screen and I could see no one at the long table in the second compartment; nor did I hear any sound of voices coming to me from the hidden part of the room. Nevertheless I knew that the Hindu was still there. He had gone in and he had never returned. He must be there. I was resolved to wait where I was till he came out. I should then have a full sight of him, a full and definite impression of him. Presently I ordered coffee. The young woman, when she brought it, remarked:

" 'You're the last. We're closing in ten minutes from now.'

" 'You're glad when closing time comes?'

" 'Rather.'

" 'But I'm not the last,' I said. 'There's still someone in the farther room.'

"She looked surprised and raised her fair eyebrows.

" 'No, there isn't,' she said. 'Everyone's gone.'

" 'Not the man with the black hat and the brown coat whose name I asked you.'

" 'Well, you are a funny one!' she said archly. 'If you don't believe me come and see for yourself.'

"I took her at her word and went with her to the opening in the screen. The long table was cleared. The compartment was empty. And, doctor, there was no way of leaving it except through the compartment in which I had been sitting.

" 'What d'you say now?' said the girl.

" 'That I made a mistake,' I answered.

"I gave her a tip, took my hat, and went off down the stairs. But I had not made a mistake. The Hindu had gone into the compartment beyond the screen but he had never come out of it."

"Are you absolutely certain he didn't come out when your attention happened to be distracted from watching for him?"

"It never was distracted. I feel sure of that."

"Well, what did you make of it?"

"I think you know," said Latimer.

"I wish you to tell me," I said firmly.

"Very well."

Latimer paused, then sat forward and closed his hands into fists like a man making a strong effort.

"When I met the Hindu in Grosvenor Square I felt at once that there was something dreadful, something wholly unnatural about him, something which made me want to get away from him. The same feeling came to me in the Indian Restaurant when he passed through the compartment in which I was sitting; it was with me till I looked and found him gone. Then suddenly I knew why his nearness had horrified me. As I made my way down into the humming street I felt like a man condemned. For I was certain that I had seen Nischaya Varman, the man who had taken my wife from me and who was what we call dead. In a wild moment of anger, I had striven to summon him to me that I might punish him. He had obeyed my summons that he might punish me."

"So you considered yourself haunted by the Hindu?" I said calmly.

"Since that night I have seldom known what it is to feel safe."

"Give me the facts. You have seen the Hindu—I mean by that had the impression of seeing him—many times?"

"Many times. But do you believe the whole thing is a delusion on my part?"

"Haven't you come to me in the hope that it is so, and that I may be able to prove that it is by getting rid of it?"

"In my situation one hopes mad things and catches at every straw," said Latimer morosely.

"Now what happened after that night at the Indian Restaurant?"

"I was badly shaken but I made a fight of it. All that night I fought what seemed to be my own knowledge. I told myself that I was ill. If I pulled myself together, if I ceased henceforth to traffic with mediums, if I drove the whole matter out of my mind and gave myself up to the daily work then, I told myself, all would be well."

"A very good programme, though it didn't cover quite everything."

"You mean—my wife?"

"Did you proceed to put it into execution?" I asked, ignoring Latimer's question.

"I tried to. I put my back into it, doctor. I gave myself more than ever to my newspapers, the children I had created—the only children—and I saw scarcely anything of my wife. I did not visit the medium again, of course. By then I had a horror of him, and of all his brethren. Several days passed without any special incident occurring. But I was never free from apprehension; I never even for a moment had the impression that the menace I was so conscious of had been removed from me. I'll go further and tell you the exact truth. I knew it had not been removed.

"One night my wife said:

" 'I've got a box to-morrow for the first night at the St. James's Theatre. I've asked'—she mentioned some friends. 'Will you come?'

"I was on the point of refusing when I noticed in her eyes an expression of—I thought—suspicious and intent inquiry. Immediately I decided to go. And I went. You know what a St. James's first night is; a crowd of people one has seen everywhere. The boxes are very large. We had three people with us, and were all able to sit in line. I was in the corner next the stage and could see practically the whole of the stalls. During the first act I happened to notice that one stall, rather far back and well in the middle of the house, was empty. Doctor, directly I saw this empty stall I knew who was presently coming to fill it. I was seized with a sort of horrible panic which made me know, and I did not take my eyes from the little gap in the crowd till the woman next me said:

" 'Do you hate the drama, Mr. Latimer?'

" 'No,' I answered. 'On the contrary, I'm fond of the theatre. Why d'you ask me?'

" 'Well, you never look at the stage.'

"She was gazing at me with an expression of definite surprise which put me at once on my guard. I devoted, or seemed to devote, all my attention to the stage from that moment, but, doctor, I knew—I'll swear it—the exact instant when that empty stall was filled. I felt the arrival of the Hindu."

"You didn't see him come in?" I asked.

"No, because I wouldn't look. But directly the curtain went down I turned. And he was there looking straight at me. For the first time I saw him fully, saw his whole face and his head uncovered. He was in evening dress, doctor."

"Just so," I said casually.

"There was something intense and, I thought, unrelentingly malignant in the gaze of his profound and lambent eyes. They said to me, 'I am here to punish you.' I got up. My wife was lifting an opera glass. She put it to her eyes and looked down upon the stalls. I saw her examining the long rows of seated figures, beginning with those nearest to the stage. What would happen when she saw the Hindu? I was painfully excited. I longed to draw her attention to him, to say to her, 'Look at that man. Do you remember him?' But I pretended carelessness. I talked to our friends. I discussed the play, the people in the house. And all the time furtively I was watching my wife. Presently it seemed to me that she was staring through her glasses straight at the Hindu. Yet her hand did not tremble, her face did not change. I heard her say:

" 'What an odd gown Mrs. Lester has on!'

" 'Where is she?' I asked, bending to her.

" 'Over there, a little to the left, near Sir Charles Digby.'

"She made a gesture towards the stalls. I looked and saw Mrs. Lester, an acquaintance of ours, sitting in the row behind the Hindu, and perhaps three feet to his left. There was a discussion between my wife and one of the women in our box about Mrs. Lester's gown, which I interrupted—I couldn't help it—by saying:

" 'What a remarkable-looking Indian that is.'

" 'An Indian! Where is there an Indian?' said my wife.

" 'Close to Mrs. Lester, the row in front of her to the right.'

" 'I don't see him,' said my wife.

" 'Nor I,' said the woman next to her.

" 'There!' I said, pointing, and leaning forward in my excitement. 'Surely you must see him—a Hindu.'

" 'But I don't see him!' said my wife, also leaning forward, and gazing apparently straight at the Hindu.

" 'You're looking right at him now!' I exclaimed.

"As I spoke the lights went down and the curtain rose on the last act.

"When the play was over and the actors were being called for, I searched once more for the Hindu. But he had vanished."

"And nobody saw him but yourself, so far as you know?" I observed.

"So far as I know—nobody."

"Now before you go on I want to ask you a few questions," I said.

"Very well," said Latimer, more calmly.

"You've been travelling, I understand?"

"Yes."

"How many times did you see the Hindu before you left England?"

"About eight or nine times in all, I should think."

"Did you ever see him in the daytime?"

"No."

"Did you ever try to speak to him?"

"No. I intended to, but—when the moment came something always held me back."

"Have you ever spoken to your wife about him, except that night at the theatre?"

"No."

"I gather that you suffered so much from these appearances that you decided to leave England?"

"I did."

"In the faint hope, I suppose, of leaving the Hindu behind you in England?"

"It was very ridiculous of me, no doubt," said Latimer painfully.

"It was a very natural thing to do. Change of scene you know! Where did you go, and did you go alone?"

"You don't want to hear any more about my English experiences?"

"We needn't go into them just now, I think. Well?"

"I took my man, Cradon, with me. We went first to Marseilles and stayed at the Hôtel du Louvre."

"I know it. Now go on. Resume your narrative."

"Oh!"

Latimer hesitated, then refilled his pipe, lit it, and said nervously:

"Let's see—where was I?"

"At Marseilles, the Hôtel du Louvre."

"To be sure. Yes, Marseilles."

He puffed two or three times at his pipe, staring before him. Evidently he was trying to fix his mind which had wandered away.

"When I had crossed the Channel, had left Paris behind me, and was running down South," he said at length, "I had a sense of relief. A burden seemed to have fallen from my shoulders. The sun shone at Marseilles. The city was full of almost boisterous animation. As I stepped out of the train I remember I felt more optimistic than I had felt for many weeks. This happy sensation persisted during the day. I intended passing a couple of nights at Marseilles to—well, to test a certain matter. If things were satisfactory I thought of going on to the Riviera. I slept well the first night, and the second day was without any unpleasant incident. I began to hope. I looked back on the dreadful persecution—it was most dreadful, doctor—I had suffered in England from the Hindu, and I was able to think that my tortured nerves had conjured up that dark apparition. It was due, perhaps, merely to a morbid condition of mind produced by ill-health; and that ill-health—I now told myself—had been brought about by the shock of the medium's revelation about my wife. In the bright sunshine of Marseilles the blackness of the past began to fade. I was even able to say to myself that out of the mouth of the medium lies had come to me. I could not, of course, doubt the Minnie Harfield statement about the Hindu's existence and her suicide. But I tried to doubt, and almost succeeded in doubting, the statement about my wife. There was, I acknowledge, little reason in such a differentiation between the two statements. Nevertheless, I think I made it. That day I was almost light-hearted. But in the evening all my misery was brought back by a hideous incident. You know the hall of the Hôtel du Louvre which fronts the covered courtyard into which carriages can drive?"

"Yes."

"After dinner in the restaurant I was sitting there, smoking and reading a newspaper, when the hotel omnibus drove up from the station with some newly arrived travellers. I realised this, as one may realise a thing when reading, without really attending to it. Travellers got out—I know—went to the bureau, took their rooms, received the tickets with their room numbers, and so forth, and passed by me on the way to the lift which, you'll remember, is in the centre at the bottom of the staircase. I went on with my reading, knowing all this and not attending to it. But suddenly a horrible sensation came upon me. It was the sensation I had had that night in Grosvenor Square, when for the first time I set eyes on the Hindu. I felt that he was coming into the hall, that he was passing me. I did not look up. I tried to deny the assertion of my mind and body—for I felt him with both. With my eyes glued to my paper I said to myself, 'You are a morbid fool. He is not here. Some casual traveller is passing you.' And I strove to read on. But something overcame my resolution. It was like a sort of terrible curiosity, insistent, stronger than my will to defy it. I swung round abruptly in my chair and looked towards the staircase. Doctor, I saw the Hindu with his back to me on the point of entering the lift which had just descended from an upper floor. He wore the black hat, the almost buff-coloured coat. He went into the lift. The lift man, with a click, shut the gate. The Hindu turned and looked full at me. Then the lift shot up, carrying him out of my sight."

Latimer's face was tormented. It was easy to see how

even the mere recollection of this incident made him suffer.

"I had almost dared to think myself free," he said with a hoarse note in his voice. "And now I—the—the thing had followed me. I was conscious at that moment of its horrible persistence, of the malignity by which it was driven. At that moment something that was like sheer desperation seized me. I threw down my newspaper and got up from my chair. I saw the manager in the bureau, and I went up to him.

" 'Those travellers,' I said, 'who have just arrived. What train did they come by?'

" 'The *rapide* from Paris, monsieur.'

" 'A traveller from London would be likely to come by that train?'

" 'If he had stayed the night in Paris, monsieur, he would.'

" 'Have you the names of those who have just come in the omnibus?'

" 'Yes, monsieur. They are all in the visitors' book.'

" 'May I see it?'

" 'Certainly, monsieur.'

"He pushed it towards me. I looked. I scarcely know, but I think I had a wild hope of seeing some Indian name unknown by me, of finding that my fears had betrayed me, and that the Hindu who had just mounted in the lift was some ordinary traveller on his way to the East. There was no Indian name in the book. I saw surprise dawning in the manager's face.

" 'I thought I might find the name of—of a friend,' I muttered, turning away.

" 'Quite so, monsieur,' said the manager, with detached courtesy.

"As I left the bureau I saw the lift standing empty with the attendant beside it. I went to it and got in. The man followed.

" 'Which floor, monsieur?'

"I told him. Directly the lift had started I pressed ten francs into his hand.

" 'Who was that Indian gentleman you took up just now?' I said.

" 'An Indian gentleman, monsieur?'

" 'Yes.'

" 'But I took no Indian gentleman.'

" 'Do you deny that a moment ago you took the lift up?'

" 'Certainly not, monsieur.'

" 'Very well. An Indian was with you in the lift.'

" 'Pardon, monsieur, but monsieur is mistaken.'

" 'But I saw you go up.'

" 'There was no one in the lift with me, monsieur, I assure you! I took the lift up because the bell on the fourth floor rang. I have just brought a lady down.'

" 'Do you deny that there was an Indian with you when you went up, a man wearing a soft black hat and a light brown coat?'

" 'Monsieur is mistaken. I was quite alone in the lift.'

"For over a minute the lift had been stationary at my floor. The expression on the man's face warned me that I was wasting my time and arousing strong suspicions concerning my own sanity. Without another word I got out of the lift and went to my room. Next morning after a sleepless night I left the hotel. I might almost say I fled from it."

"And you went to the Riviera?"

"No. I crossed the sea. I heard there was a ship starting for Philippeville in Algeria. I went on board. I suppose I had a mad idea of escaping from that traveller who had pursued me from England. Of course it was a crazy notion. One may escape from a living man. The sea may be an effectual barrier between you and him. But I was pursued by one who could overpass any barrier at will. I knew this, and yet, when we were out at sea, when Marseilles had disappeared on the horizon, I felt some sense of relief. After a voyage of about thirty-six hours, I landed at Philippeville. I stayed there one night, then took the train and went on to a little place called Hammam Meskoutine, where there are hot water springs impregnated with sulphur."

"What took you there?" said I.

"Hitherto I had always seen the Hindu in the midst of men, either in London or in Marseilles. Hammam Meskoutine I knew to be a tiny place buried in the African solitude, though far from the desert. I thought, 'Perhaps he will not follow me into the solitudes.'

"The hotel at the baths stands quite alone, surrounded by a delicious flowering country, smiling and intimate. The sulphur springs boil up out of the earth at a little distance away. There is a small, but well-arranged, bath establishment just below the hotel, which is of the bungalow type, with all the rooms on the ground floor. Mine opened by a French window on to a paved walk. Beyond was an open space with trees bounded by outbuildings. On the right, and at right angles, was a terrace backed by the public room of the hotel. Few people were staying there, only some four or five Colonial French people. The landlord was cordial; the servants were friendly, cheerful and attentive. And the whole atmosphere of the place was serene and remote, yet eminently happy. Even my man, Cradon, was struck by the sweet tranquillity of this African retreat.

"'I've always liked towns, sir,' he observed, on the evening of our arrival just before dinner. 'But I think a man could forget all about them here.'

"Something in the commonplace words cheered and almost reassured me. Suddenly it occurred to me that perhaps I, for years a colossal worker, untiring in energy and always living in the midst of crowds—for I never took a real holiday—had, without being aware of it, become thoroughly overworked."

"Why not?" I said. "What more likely?"

"You think"—a gleam of hope shone in Latimer's eyes—"you think overwork might——" He stopped.

"But madness would be worse than all!" he muttered, as if to himself.

"Madness! Rubbish!" I said. "You're no more mad than I am."

"You are sure?" said Latimer, whose eyes at that moment had an almost imploring expression.

"Positive," said I. "If I thought otherwise I should take you to-morrow to Vernon Mansfield, the specialist in lunacy—if you'd come."

A faint smile flitted over Latimer's face.

"But if I'm not mad then I am really haunted, I am really the victim of a diabolic persecution. There's no other alternative."

"I'm not at all sure of that," I said. "No, no; don't ask me questions. Go on—till I stop you. Did anything happen at Hammam Meskoutine?"

"Yes."

"What was it?"

"Nothing happened the first night. But I felt very uneasy on account of my room being on the ground floor, and opening by the French window on to the paved walk. There were Persiennes of wood outside the window, and before going to bed I shut them securely, but, nevertheless, I disliked the idea that anyone could walk, or pause, outside within a few feet of me as I lay in bed."

"But if you were haunted what was to prevent the Hindu from appearing in your room, even with doors and windows locked?" I asked.

"I know, I know," returned Latimer. "But that had never happened, and, as a matter of fact, it never did happen. I always saw him in circumstances which seemed to make it possible that he was an ordinary man. He never appeared and disappeared as so-called ghosts are said to do, though on one or two occasions, as at the Indian Restaurant, it was impossible for me to imagine the means of his exit from the place to which I had seen him go."

"So you were not afraid of seeing him with you when you had locked the door and shut the window?"

"Somehow I was not. But I dreaded his coming along the pavement, and, perhaps, lingering in the night outside my window. Therefore I lay awake. But nothing occurred on that first night, and the dawn broke heralding a day of celestial clearness, such as we never see in England. Insects were humming, I remember, as I came out into the sunshine that morning. Two or three Arabs were dreaming under the eucalyptus trees. There was a marvellous peace, a clear serenity in the atmosphere, which affected my spirits happily. I felt drowsy after my almost sleepless night, but there was nothing to do, and it occurred to me that it would be pleasant to seek some shady place, to lie down among the wild flowers which abound in that region, and, like an Arab, to dream away the shining hours. After breakfast on the terrace and a pipe, I, therefore, wandered away from the hotel into the smiling and empty country, which was peopled chiefly, it seemed, by butterflies. First I took my way to the sulphur springs; then I made a détour, and presently came upon a most delicious stream, bordered thickly with aromatic shrubs and bushes. Besides the windings of this stream I strolled on for some time till I came to a place where it made a loop and widened out into a sort of pool. Here there were shade and silence, and I lay down on the bank, pulled my hat down over my eyes, and, presently, fell deliciously into a light sleep. I don't really know how long I slept, but when I woke—I did not open my eyes immediately—I knew at once that I was no longer alone beside the stream. I heard no sound except the wide hum of the insects, and the very faint and sucking murmur of moving water against earth and weeds, but I felt men near me, silent men. And in a moment the faint scent of tobacco was in my nostrils. Then I opened my eyes, and saw not far from me a group of meditative Arabs. Three were squatting on the bank at the edge of the stream, shrouded in burnouses, calmly contemplating me, and smoking. A fourth was lying stretched upon the ground entirely muffled up in voluminous clothing. The whole of his head and face was hidden from me. I supposed him to be in a very profound sleep.

"I gazed at the Arabs and the Arabs gazed at me tranquilly. Their presence was really soothing. They were picturesque and immobile. Nevertheless, as soon, I think, as I was absolutely wide awake, I was aware of a feeling of distress. I looked from one to the other. Then my eyes fell on the sleeper and remained fixed on him. He looked just like a long bundle which had been flung down by the waterside. But I divined a body beneath the muddle of garments. And while I looked the bundle stirred and a bare leg was thrust into view. The leg was dark brown and abnormally thin, as thin as a stick.

"Doctor, as soon as I saw it I thought of the Hindu. I stared at the leg, noting the fineness of the ankle, and a sick shudder went through me. I got up. I wanted to get away, and yet I felt I must see the face of that sleeping man. I stood for a moment, trying to collect myself, to consider what to do. Then I forced myself to approach the group. I took out some money and offered it to the Arabs. They held out their hands gravely. As I was giving them the money the bundle stirred. A thin arm came out of the clothes. Then a face and a pair of glittering eyes showed themselves. Again I looked on the Hindu."

Latimer ceased speaking for a moment. He seemed to be profoundly moved.

"Now you had your opportunity," I said. "Of course you took it. Of course you made sure that this man was a comrade of the Arabs, that they were aware of his presence among them. Of course you gave him money, too. Didn't you?"

Latimer shook his head.

"I thought of that as I stood there. I meant to do it.

I tried mentally to force myself to do it. But I couldn't, doctor. Horror had seized me. I left them. I plunged into the thick undergrowth. My only idea was to get away."

"While you were there did any of the Arabs appear to take any notice of the huddled figure?"

"No. They were looking at me."

"And when the figure moved?"

"None of them looked at it. Their eyes were always on me."

"If only you could have plucked up courage on that occasion," I said, with intentional brusqueness, "you would have found that you had to deal with some wandering Oriental. You missed your chance."

"Possibly—on that one occasion," said Latimer.

"You told me," I continued, still brusquely, "that during your last sitting with the medium you longed for the Hindu's bodily presence that you might punish him. You told me that you made an intense effort of the will to force him to return to earth. According to your account your effort was successful. Did you never attempt to take advantage of your success?"

"I have thought of that too," said Latimer, with a sort of morose shame. "I thought of that many times. But the Hindu seemed to lay upon me a prohibition. I cannot exactly explain its nature to you. His will seemed to come upon me and to prohibit me from playing the man. That fact was, and is, perhaps the most distressing part of my whole experience. The Hindu's will bound me fast in cowardice. Nevertheless I did make one attempt to break the spell. It was while we were at Tunis."

"Tell me about it," said I. "And then, perhaps, I will not trouble you to give me the whole of the remainder of your adventures."

"Do you—have you formed any opinion?" exclaimed Latimer, with sudden excitement.

"Perhaps I have. But I shall not tell it to you to-night," I answered. "Some time will be needed to confirm or upset it."

"But can't you say at least——"

"Not now," I interrupted. "Tell me what happened at Tunis. Did you go there soon?"

"I left Hammam Meskoutine the day after I saw the Hindu beside the stream, and I went straight to Tunis, where I arrived very late at night. For some reason—I think the Foreign Minister had just disembarked there from Paris to assist at some French national demonstration—the European hotels were crowded. I tried three of them and could not get a room. The last I went to was the Grand. There they recommended me to try what they called a native hotel. It was now the dead of night. The manager sent with me a Maltese man, a sort of tout, I supposed, to show me the way. He carried my hand luggage with the help of my man, Cradon, who was by this time in a somewhat depressed, not to say, surly, humour. We walked for about ten minutes, or perhaps more, and came into the native quarter, close to the bazaars. We turned into an alley, which had a sufficiently evil look, and presently arrived at a door above which was a light showing the words, 'Hôtel Taxim.' The guide pushed the door which opened showing a tiled stairway, up which we went and arrived at a sort of large landing where, to my surprise, we found three enormous women, with artificial flowers in their greasy black hair, sitting solemnly on a yellow settee near a cottage piano. The guide spoke in Arabic to one of them, in a low voice and at considerable length. The creature arose heavily, went to a bureau, found some keys, and then, moving lethargically, showed me to a door which she unlocked and opened carefully. Within was a clean bare bedroom, fairly large, with a tiled floor. The luggage was put down, and in a few minutes I was alone with the door locked. Cradon, whose face had been a study in respectable consternation during these proceedings, was, I understood, to be lodged in some other part of the house. I undressed at once and went to bed.

"In the morning rather early I rang the bell, intending to ask for coffee. After a long pause I heard a shuffling sound outside as of someone moving over the tiles in loose slippers. The shuffling ceased at my door, and then there came a light, I might almost say a fragile knock. I—I felt that a very thin hand had struck that blow, and I hesitated to open the door."

"Did you open it?" I asked, as Latimer was silent.

"No," he said very painfully. "I couldn't. I—I was afraid."

"What did you do?"

"I called out in French that I wanted coffee and a roll. There was no answer, but I heard the footsteps shuffle away."

"A servant of the house, of course; probably a woman."

"I don't know. While I waited for the coffee I tried to pull myself together. I was horribly ashamed of my panic. I realised that my nerves were going absolutely to pieces. It's very unpleasant for a man when he—he's obliged to realise that, doctor."

"Nerves can be put right," said I firmly. "And it's my job to see to that."

A sort of momentary relief came into his face, but it faded away immediately.

"Nerves couldn't play such tricks," he said, in a low voice.

"If you knew as much about them as I do," I said, "you mightn't be so free with your negatives. Did the coffee and roll come?"

He started.

"The coffee? Oh—yes, presently it did. I heard a quite different footstep from the shuffling tread, and there came a bang on my door. I opened, and there stood my Maltese guide of the night before with a breakfast tray. He gave me a rough *'Bon jour,'* came into the

room and set the tray down. He was about to go away
when I stopped him.

" 'Who told you I wanted coffee?' I asked.

" 'The bell rang,' he replied.

" 'You didn't answer it.'

" 'But I have answered it, m'sieu!' he said, pointing
to the coffee tray.

" 'You didn't come to take my order?'

" 'No, m'sieu.'

" 'Someone did. Someone came and knocked, and I
called out. Who was it?'

" 'I don't know. There are often people about in this
house.' He smiled in a rather peculiar way.

" 'Could it have been a native servant? Do they wear
loose slippers?'

" 'I don't know who it was,' said he brusquely. 'You
should have opened the door.'

He smiled again, with a peculiarly knowing look. Then
he added:

" 'I heard the bell and I knew it was for coffee. And
there it is!'

"He pointed again with a dark brown hand, gave me
a monkey-like smirk, and hurried away. I noticed that
he wore strong boots which made a squeaking noise on
the tiles.

"That morning Cradon gave me certain information
about the reputation of the house we were in, and I
resolved to sally forth and see if I could bribe the
management of the Tunisia Palace Hotel to give me
rooms there.

"As I was about to descend the tiled staircase of the
'Taxim,' which led out to the alley through a Moorish
archway, I saw in the archway, leaning against the wall,
the thin figure of a native wearing a turban. When I
put my foot on the first stair he turned and looked up
at me. Doctor, it was the Hindu. I stood still for a
moment. That prohibition came upon me from him,
and I was afraid to go down. While I paused he moved

into the alley, crossed slowly a patch of sunlight and disappeared. It was then that I made a determined effort to break the spell which bound me to cowardice. Something rose up in me which defied the will of the Hindu. It was, I think, a sort of panic courage such as comes at moments to the most timid of God's creatures; such courage makes men run upon danger, go out to meet pain. I hurried down the stairs and into the alley. I took the way the Hindu had taken. Before me I saw several native figures strolling along with that sort of indolent nonchalance which is so characteristic of the East. They all looked much alike, and I could not identify one as the Hindu. I followed, came up with them one after the other, and looked narrowly into their faces. But I did not see my man. I hurried on and found myself almost immediately in the slipper bazaar. Here there was already a crowd, and I despaired of coming upon the Hindu, though I seemed to feel all this time that he was near to me."

"What did you intend to do if you came upon him?" I said.

"Lay hands on him," said Latimer. "Find out at once and for ever what he was. I mingled with the crowd. Flies were buzzing and men were buzzing like flies. There was a tumult of voices and a silent tumult of gestures. But through the tumult glided many who were silent and who seemed detached. And among these silent ones I sought for the Hindu. But I sought for him in vain, and I grew tired.

"Presently, from a tiny hole where he sat cross-legged in the midst of his wares behind a little counter, a perfume-seller leaned out and called to me. I then stopped, sat down on a wooden bench, and tested his perfumes as he rubbed them delicately on my outstretched hand and wrist. And while this happened my sense of the Hindu's nearness left me. The perfumes—amber, lilac, attar of roses, geranium—affected me, seemed to steal upon my will and to lull the fever of my intention. The Hindu had escaped from me. Let him go! However, I felt neither courage nor cowardice. For a brief space I dropped into rest.

"I was buying a diapered bottle of geranium when I realised that a man had stopped close behind me. I looked round and saw an enormous Tunisian, with gigantic moustaches, and black eyes which shone with cunning, who stared steadily at me.

" 'Monsieur is rich!' said he, in French. 'Monsieur wishes to buy beautiful things. I will take him to Babouchi Brothers. There he will see carpets that are worth millions.'

" 'Very well,' said I.

"And I paid for the perfume and followed the tout, who looked and moved like the Emperor of some glittering fairy tale. When we reached his patron's bazaar I found that it was really one of the finest in Tunis, if not the finest. On the ground floor there was a large hall lined with splendid carpets, full of embroideries, weapons, ancient lamps, incense burners, screens of exquisite woodwork. Rows and rows of shelves were piled with stuffs of multi-coloured hues. A fountain played in a corner, throwing up scented water. From this hall a staircase led up to a balcony which ran all round a courtyard open to the sky, and from this balcony opened a veritable network of narrow and shadowy rooms, a maze crammed with all sorts of things—furniture, carpets, prayer rugs, bronzes, ivories, tiles, and I know not what. Looking here and there into the shadowy recesses of this maze, I saw figures of dark-hued men moving, squatting, or standing in watchful attitudes, waiting, no doubt, for opportunities to display the treasures by which they were surrounded.

"Doctor, when I mounted to this balcony and stood in the midst of this maze, I was suddenly again aware of the presence of the Hindu. I did not see him, but I felt him; and I was absolutely certain that the figure I had seen leaning against the archway of the Taxim

Hotel had escaped from me into this warren full of
hiding-places, and was somewhere quite near to me.
Again I felt fear, but I remembered that I had set forth
in pursuit of the Hindu, and I resolved to face the thing
out this time. I had suffered so much through yielding
to fear that I was driven at last into action. The most
intimate part of me tried to rush down the staircase, to
be lost in the crowds of Tunis. I defied that part, which
seemed me. I had just then the impression of being
two persons, and the weaker rose up to do battle with
the stronger of the two, and for the moment got the
better in the contest.

" 'I'll look at all your best things,' I said to the enormous tout, who was always with me. 'But first let me
wander about by myself.'

" 'I will show monsieur.'

" 'No,' I said, 'I wish to go round by myself. I don't
mean to steal things.'

"He protested volubly, but showed no inclination to
leave me.

" 'Very well,' I said. 'Then I won't buy anything.'
And I made as though to be off. This brought him
promptly to obedience.

" 'Go anywhere, monsieur!' he cried. 'You are English. All the English are honest.'

"He paused.

" 'And so generous!' he added, showing an upturned
palm.

"I crossed it with silver and left him.

"Doctor, then began a hunt through that Oriental
maze. I entered the chamber nearest to me and went
slowly through it, pretending to examine the treasures
it contained, now and then handling a weapon, or holding a fold of silk to the light. The native attendants,
I must tell you, left me alone. The tout had somehow
managed to convey to them a hint that I was a mad
Englishman, whose mania was to be allowed free scope
for a time. Later, of course, I was to pay for it.

"From room to room of the maze I went, always conscious of the presence of the Hindu in some remote recess of it. Sometimes he seemed almost close to me, at other times he receded. I had the sensation that he was playing with me, was luring me on like a malignant will-o'-the-wisp. But my resolve did not falter. I had braced myself to the encounter. I was on his track, and I was resolved to come up with him.

"After threading several windings of the maze, I was aware of a strong and drowsy smell of incense. When it first reached my nostrils I was standing in a small room full of prayer rugs. They lay heaped upon shelves, strewn upon the floor, and in piles upon the divans. Seated in the midst of them was a thin black man with mournful eyes, who was twisting a necklace of bright yellow beads through his fingers. As I smelt the incense, which came to me from a dark chamber on my right, not yet visited by me, I knew that the Hindu was close by. It may seem very absurd, but—but the incense seemed to tell me so. I felt as if his personality, his will, floated to me as smoke wreathes and floats from an incense burner—almost as if they were mingled with that scented smoke of the East which perfumed the maze. I remember I thought of the malignant genius who came out of his prison in smoke.

"Making a great effort to conquer my repulsion and fear, I approached the threshold of the chamber beyond and, without entering it, looked stealthily in. It was very dark. (Afterwards I knew that thin Indian hangings obscured the light from the balcony.) In the gloom I perceived many grotesque idols arranged upon pedestals, and small tables of inlaid work in which fine ivory, ebony, mother-of-pearl and cedar-wood were blended. They looked down, peered down fatuously or maliciously, too, from tall cabinets. Lamps of dingy metal and dark-coloured glass hung from the ceiling, across which carpets were stretched. The scent of the incense here was very strong, almost overpowering. After a pause

I ventured into the room. It was long and much larger than I had expected, running back in an almost black vista peopled with curiosities. I could see no one in it. Nor could I see the brazier from which the smoke of the incense came. As I stood there I began to feel like one coming under the influence of a drug, slightly intoxicated, faintly light-headed. There was a divan near me covered with embroideries. I sat down on it and leaned back."

"Did you still feel the nearness of the Hindu?" I asked.

"Yes. I felt that he was almost close to me. As I did not move for several minutes the black man in the room I had quitted stole in, I suppose to see what I was doing. He only remained for an instant, but soon returned bringing me Turkish coffee and cigarettes. He set them down on a low table by the divan and vanished without making a sound. I drank two cups of coffee. It had a stimulating effect upon me. The queer lightheaded sensation diminished. I stood up and looked all round me.

"On every side I saw the dim faces of the idols smiling or rigid in the gloom. They seemed to me at that moment to be an audience assembled there to witness the encounter between me and the Hindu. I knew now that he was somewhere in that room with me. We were enclosed together at last, and I was resolved to face him.

"All the back part of the room was indistinct from where I stood. He must be hidden there among the rummage of cabinets, carpets, and ornaments. Walking very slowly and warily, and calling all my will power to fight down the unnatural fear which always overtook me when the Hindu was near me, I went towards the back of the room. I walked on till I saw the wall at the end, which was hung with carpets. Rolls of carpet were stacked against it. Some of them, standing on end, looked like dwarfish forms in the twilight. The scent of the incense was here much stronger, and as I

stared about me I presently saw a faint spiral of scarcely
defined smoke curving quite near me. I stood still by a
tall cabinet. On the wall, close to my hand, there was
a sword with a Damascene blade. My hand went up
to it instinctively, took it down and gripped it. Then
I did what I had done in the medium's rooms at Fulham. I sent out to the Hindu the silent cry, 'Come to
me from the place where you are that I may punish you!'
I exerted the whole strength of all my being. In a moment among the rolls of carpet I saw something stirring
low down. It seemed to uncurl, doctor, to stretch itself,
to extend itself towards me. I saw thin arms held out
for an instant; then a thoroughly defined human body
in a long native robe rising from the place where it had
been crouched near the incense brazier. Beneath the
snow-white folds of a turban I saw a man's dark face
and attentive eyes. It was the Hindu. I said something
—I don't know what, but I addressed him. There was
no reply. He simply stood there looking at me. Then
I—I attacked him."

"You laid hands upon him?" I interjected.

"No, I couldn't do that. I struck at him with the
blade of the sword. I scarcely know what happened.
The light was very dim. But he must have moved with
abnormal quickness. For there was a crash. The sword
flew out of my hand, and when the black man glided in
from the adjoining room a—it's horribly absurd, doctor!"

"Never mind. Tell me."

"A bronze statue of Buddha lay at my feet. The
sword was splintered and the Hindu was gone."

"The attendant of the room of the idols, you mean?"

Latimer said nothing, but his face was grimly obstinate, the face of the man under the obsession of the
fixed idea.

"And when the black man came?" I asked.

"I paid for the statue and for the sword, and got away
quickly."

"And since then?"

"I have seen the Hindu on several occasions, but I have never attempted to speak to, or confront him. On the contrary, I have got away from him. And—and the persecution has increased. I know he follows me. I am certain he is always seeking me."

"That will do for the moment," I said. "Now will you do what I tell you?"

"Yes."

"Very well. To-morrow you will go into a rest cure which will last six weeks. I have an establishment at Hampstead arranged for nervous sufferers, with nurses of my own selection. You will have a first-rate male nurse. For six weeks you will be isolated from the world. You will have no letters, no newspapers, no visitors except myself. The Hindu will not be able to come near you. Do you understand?"

I got up and laid my hand on his forehead.

"You will not see the Hindu for six weeks," I repeated in a firm voice several times.

Latimer looked at me in silence. I took away my hand.

"You will call at my house to-morrow at ten with any luggage you require. The male attendant who will look after you and give you massage will be there to go with you to Hampstead. You will be at my house punctually at ten."

"I will," replied Latimer in a low voice.

"And now," said I, in a brisk and practical tone, "I'll ask you to give me a couple of addresses."

"A couple of addresses?" said Latimer in a surprised voice.

"Yes; the address of the medium you visited at Fulham, and the address of the Jewish journalist who accompanied you on your first visit there."

"But why do you want them? What can——"

"Mr. Latimer," I said, "I am accustomed to have my own way when I take up a nervous case. I have my own

methods of working. Nobody need fall in with them.
On the other hand, I am perfectly free to refuse to treat
you. And I shall refuse unless all my instructions are
carried out."

"But what can my giving you those addresses have
to do with my cure?"

"Possibly everything," I replied.

Latimer looked at me for a minute in silence. Then
he went to his writing-table, wrote out a couple of addresses and handed them to me.

"Thank you," said I. "And now I'll wish you good
night. Don't sit up. Go straight to bed, look steadily
at some shining object—half a crown will do—and say
aloud, 'When I have counted ten my eyes will close and
I shall fall into a refreshing sleep.' Say this several
times, and try to believe it while you're saying it. I tell
you now that your eyes will close and that you will
sleep. Good night."

He seized my hand and held it fast.

"But do you really believe that—that you can bring
this persecution to an end?"

"I have very little doubt of it. I fully expect to get
rid of the Hindu."

His grip tightened on my hand.

"I shall do exactly what you tell me to do," he
said.

And from that moment I knew that he would.

Next morning punctually at ten Latimer arrived with
his luggage, and I handed him over to the nurse I had
spoken of. He disappeared from the world for six
weeks. Before he left my consulting-room he told me
that he had followed my directions and had slept well
the night before. My last words to him were:

"Remember you will not see the Hindu for six weeks."

"Thank God!" he replied.

He then went away looking almost cheerful.

I had now three things to do in connection with his
affairs. I had to see the medium, the journalist, and

Mrs. Latimer. I decided first to visit the medium. That same evening I looked his name out in the telephone book. His name, let us say, was Algernon Wigston. I found it and called him up. A very soft and genteel voice answered, and said:

"Yes? Beg pardon! Yes?"

"Mr. Algernon Wigston?" said I.

"Yes, indeed!" said the genteel voice. "I am Mr. Wigston."

"I have heard of your marvellous powers," I said. "Could you give me a sitting? It is very important."

"Oh, reely!" said Algernon.

"Money is no object," I breathed into the telephone.

"Who is it, please?" said Algernon.

"I prefer not to give my name. It's rather well known. But I will pay any reasonable fee you care to name."

After a slight pause the voice said:

"I'm very much sought after. What would you say to three guineas?"

"That it's extremely moderate considering your reputation," said I.

A very pleased voice made an appointment with me for the following evening at nine. I kept it.

When I arrived at 2, Amelia Villas, Fulham, a small maid, wearing her cap very much on one side, showed me into the room Latimer had described to me, and in a few minutes I was joined there by Algernon Wigston. At first sight he looked a weak, well-intentioned and rather foolish young man, but I had only been with him for two or three minutes when I noticed that his pale and wandering eyes could look very sly on occasion, and that he was by no means devoid of shrewdness. I paid him a few compliments, which he received with gusto, but avoided answering his questions, which were directed to finding out who had told me about him and his wonderful powers. Finally, when I had made up my mind as to his character, I asked for the promised "sitting." He complied with my request. We sat down at a table, placed our hands upon it, and very soon he seemed to go into a trance.   Something of this sort followed.

His "control," Katey, took possession of him and babbled foolishly till I made up my mind to get to business. Then I said:

"I wish to speak with Minnie Harfield."

The medium jumped, and there was a dead silence.

"I am here to-night to speak to Minnie Harfield," I continued.   "The woman who committed suicide on account of the Hindu, Nischaya Varman."

Silence prevailed.

"I ask for Minnie Harfield," I said in a sterner, more insistent voice.

The medium writhed in his chair, breathed hard, and then slowly opened his eyes showing the whites.

"They've left me," he said in a weak voice.

"Who has left you?" said I.

"The controls."

"Let us try again," I said.

"I don't feel well," he murmured.

"Take some sherry and water," I said.

Again Algernon jumped.

"Sherry! How did you know——" He stopped.

I could see by his expression that he was debating what line to take with me, whether to "stand up to me" or to try at once to get rid of me. He chose the latter course.

"I'm afraid it's no good to-night," he said. "I don't feel well. There's something wrong. I'm afraid I must ask you to come another evening. As to the fee——"

"There'll be no difficulty about that," I interrupted, "if you answer a few questions which, possibly, the spirits might not understand."

"Questions!" he said. "I'm not here to answer questions."

"But I'm here to get them answered," I said. "And I don't mean to go till you've satisfied my curiosity on certain points."

"Who are you?" he cried.

"I'm acting for Mr. Latimer," I replied.

His natural pallor was accentuated. There seemed to be a touch of green in it at that moment.

"Mr. Latimer!" he said, getting up and pressing his flabby white hands on the table. "Are you a—a lawyer?"

"Never mind what I am. I'm here on Mr. Latimer's behalf. You've had a good deal of money from him recently."

"He told me——"

"I know. And you took him at his word."

"I—I've only had——"

"Half of the money sent by his secretary," I interposed. "Or perhaps less than half. The rest went to Mr. Maurice Isaacs, the journalist who brought him to you."

Algernon sat down.

"Has—has Isaacs blabbed?" he stammered.

"You'd better make a clean breast of it," I said. "Otherwise I'm afraid you'll find yourself in very serious trouble. Mr. Latimer isn't a man who can be tricked, or even defied, with impunity."

"Has Isaacs——"

"Look here, Mr. Wigston," said I. "How could I know about this affair if Isaacs hadn't talked?"

That seemed to decide him. Suddenly he became shrill with anger against Maurice Isaacs.

"He put me up to it!" he exclaimed. "I've never done such a thing before. I'm an honest medium, I am. The spirits use me. I've always lived honest. The greatest people in London have been to me. I've had Royal people in this very room."

"But Isaacs led you astray. You're more sinned against than sinning, eh?"

"That's it!" he cried. "You've got it. Isaacs tempted me. That man's the devil and a Jew rolled in one. He come to me"—Algernon's grammar got shaky at times under the influence of excitement—"and he led me on;

said how very wonderful I was with miraculous powers, and how it troubled him to see me living so humble. 'You might be rolling,' he said, 'and here you live poor in the midst of plenty. Look here,' he said, 'I'll do you a good turn if you like.' And then he goes and tells me one of the greatest and richest men in London, the biggest newspaper owner of the day, was coming with him to test me. 'Convince him of your powers!' says he, 'and your fortune's made. But fail to and he'll ruin you, get his knife into you in every paper in England.' I fell in a sweat. I did indeed. And then he played upon me. 'Suppose when I bring him,' he says, 'the spirits let you down? What then?' I sat and just sweated. 'Don't they ever let you down?' he says. I couldn't but answer they did. 'And then you're ruined,' he says. 'You're down and out.' 'I won't see him,' I says. 'If you don't he'll go for you,' he says. 'Be a man. Take him on and make your fortune out of him.' 'Put me in the way, for God's sake,' I says. And, to cut it short, he put me in the way. He pitched me a tale about Mr. Latimer's wife and a Hindu, and how a woman called Minnie Harfield had killed herself from love of the dark fellow, and a lot more. 'It's all true and he don't know it,' says he. 'Dribble it out to him by degrees. Start in your own way and presently get to Minnie. Act according to how he acts. We'll stand in together with regard to the cash.' Well, I did as he said. I presently got to Minnie, and when he was on the string I dribbled it out to him. Isaacs taught me things to say, made me take things out of a book by some Indian feller, called Tagory."

"Exactly. And you were never in a trance at all."

"Not with him I wasn't, but——"

"I know. And the cash? How much has Isaacs taken?"

Algernon grew scarlet with rage.

"Three-quarters of everything I've had, if you'll believe me!" he almost screamed, lifting his puny little arms. "Day in and day out he's been here. 'Write again to the seketery,' he says. 'You can get what you like. Put it across!' he says. And——"

As I had learnt enough at this point I brought our pleasant little interview to a close. I must confess to an act of weakness. I gave Algernon three guineas. It was quite wrong of me, but—— Well, I was pleased with myself that night, and it was my egoism which gave him his fee. He took it with an air of self-respect which did credit to his ingenuity, and I left him to the refreshment of his sherry bottle.

On the following day, again in the evening, I paid a visit to Mr. Isaacs. I had taken the precaution of telephoning to him beforehand, asking for an appointment, giving my name simply as Turnbull, and stating that I wished to see him for a very important reason. I ventured to add that I was a friend of his employer, Mr. Latimer, who had spoken very favourably of his abilities to me. Apparently Isaacs had no suspicion of a trap, for a suave voice replied through the telephone suggesting an appointment at a club. I answered that I would prefer to call at his private address in the Bloomsbury district, if it would not put him to inconvenience. After a perceptible pause Isaacs agreed to the suggestion and appointed the hour of nine for our meeting. I was there to the minute, and rang the bell of a flat on a third floor. The bell was answered almost instantaneously by a quite well-dressed young Jew, with dark, crinkly, and very thick hair, clever dark eyes, good features and an air of unshakable self-possession. I noticed at once that he was the sort of man likely to prove attractive to unrefined women, and to be attracted by them. He was smart, and in a way handsome; he looked sensual; and he knew not the meaning of shyness, a quality which is anathema to the modern young woman.

"Are you Mr. Turnbull?" said Isaacs, looking me over swiftly.

"My name is Turnbull," I said.

He held out a welcoming hand.

"Glad to see you. Do come in."

"This is only a bachelor flat," he remarked, taking my hat and umbrella. "I live here alone."

As he spoke I noticed his forehead wrinkle in a momentary frown, as his eyes noted something in the comfortable sitting-room beyond me. I walked in, he followed me closely, and immediately, in a swift but casual way, got rid of a woman's long white glove which was lying on the back of a sofa. At the same time he shot a searching glance at me, but I was looking at some caricatures of public men which hung on the wall, and I don't think my expression at the moment was intelligent.

"Do sit down," he said. "Will you have a drink?"

"Thanks. No; I've just dined."

We sat down, and Isaacs said:

"Very sad about Mr. Latimer, isn't it? We never see him at the office now. He seems gone all to pieces. And he's such a marvellous man."

"He seems to think very well of you," I said.

A gratified smile curved Isaacs's rather thick lips.

"Glad to hear you say so. You're a friend of his?"

"I hope at any rate to prove myself so," I answered.

Isaacs looked at me narrowly.

"But I thought you said through the telephone——" he began.

"I'm attending him as a doctor."

"Oh, you're a doctor! I hope you don't think badly of his condition?"

"I expect to see him all right soon."

"That's good hearing. And now—I think you said there was an important matter you wished to discuss with me?" He looked sharply inquisitive.

"There is. You're a very intelligent man, Mr. Isaacs. Mr. Latimer told me so, and I can see it now for myself. Why d'you allow women to ruin you?"

The change in his face was startling. It grew instantly harder, more common and much more animal. The cheek-

bones looked more prominent, and the lips stretched showing the large white teeth.

"Women!" he said. "What d'you mean? What d'you
know about me and women?"

"I know you've been playing a very dirty game on
Mr. Latimer to get money, and you spend that money
with women. Come, come now, Mr. Isaacs, you didn't
hide that white glove quite quickly enough."

"What's it to you if I choose to have women friends?"
he said fiercely. "And I haven't ever played dirty with
Lat—Mr. Latimer. I work hard for him, and he pays
me a good screw for it. What d'you mean by coming
here to interfere with my private affairs?"

He got up.

"I'll ask you to go at once!"

"If I do, I think you'll be sorry for it," I said quietly.
"Do you want to be indicted for conspiracy and obtain-
ing money by false pretences?"

"I haven't. What do you mean?"

His eyes pierced me.

"Simply that Algernon Wigston's given you away,"
I said.

His jaw dropped.

"Wigston—you—Latimer has——"

He stopped.

"Mr. Latimer has told me of your visits with him to
Fulham, and Wigston has informed me of the fraud you
suggested and he carried out, and also of the money
transactions between you."

"But—but Latimer—does he know that—that——?"

"I am going to tell him to-morrow."

Isaacs dropped down into a chair.

"For God's sake, don't. I shall be ruined."

"No doubt."

"It wasn't my fault. It's the women."

"They are an expensive luxury, I know, especially
nowadays when they all wear silk stockings."

"They bleed a man white. Don't tell Latimer."

"I shall," I said. "But on one condition I'll undertake, before I tell him, to get from him a promise not to proceed against you and ruin you publicly."

"But he wouldn't do that," said Isaacs, sharply and swiftly.

"Why not? Because of his wife?"

"Well, he wouldn't."

"He will. I'll take care he does, unless you make a clean breast of the whole story of Minnie Harfield and the Hindu. And be careful to stick to the truth. I am going to check your story. Tell me the whole truth and I'll undertake that Mr. Latimer shall let you alone. Of course you'll have to leave his employment. You'll have to resign from his staff."

Isaacs looked very blank.

"If you don't he'll kick you out, of course," I said; "I can't undertake to prevent that. You can choose. Either——"

"Who are you?" he interrupted. "What right have you, a mere ordinary doctor——?"

"I'm Sir William Turnbull of Cavendish Square," I interrupted.

"What, the great nerve man!" he was good enough to exclaim.

"Yes. Mr. Latimer has put himself entirely in my hands. He will do exactly what I tell him to do in this matter. That I can promise you. Your future lies with me, Mr. Isaacs, whether you like it or not. I advise you to tell me the truth."

Well, he told it to me. It seems that Minnie Harfield was at one time a friend of his, that he introduced to her Nischaya, the Hindu, whom he had met at one of Mrs. Sidon's lectures, and that she did eventually commit suicide on the Hindu's account. So far the medium had related facts.

"And as to Mrs. Latimer's connection with the story?"

I had to press Isaacs on that point. He was suspicious, and wanted to know whether Mrs. Latimer had been approached by me, whether she knew of her husband's visits to the medium. I declined to satisfy his curiosity, but left him with the impression that possibly I had taken her into my confidence.

"She did know Nischaya," he said.

"I'm aware of that," I said blandly.

"Why d'you ask me then?"

I didn't think it necessary to inform him that I was aware of it because he had just told it to me.

"Mrs. Latimer knew Nischaya, but why did you put such shameful lies about her into the medium's mouth?"

"How d'you know they're lies?"

"Never mind. But I do know."

At that moment I was merely guessing, but my guess, it seemed, was right. For, after a pause, Isaacs answered:

"She tried to do me a bad turn."

"But she didn't know you."

"No; but she knew my work. And she hated it. She thought it beastly vulgar. And she said so more than once."

"To whom?"

"To Latimer. She wanted him to get rid of me. He didn't tell me, but I got to know of it through one of the editors to whom he repeated it."

"That was a very poor reason for trying to ruin her reputation."

"Oh," he said coarsely, "it wasn't so much that. I knew the way to get him on the string was to bring in her name."

That same evening I drove straight to Portman Square, sent in my card, and asked to see Mrs. Latimer. She was at home, and I was shown into the drawing-room, where she was reading by a shaded electric lamp. She got up quickly when I entered, and came towards me.

"Sir William Turnbull!" she said. "He isn't worse?"

As the footman went out and shut the door she added:

"He—he's not going mad?"

I took her thin hand.

"Of course not," I said cheerily.

"But what is the matter with him? Sometimes he frightens me."

"His nerves have broken down through long over-work. But I shall get him right. And you can help me!"

"How?" she said eagerly.

"May I sit down?"

"Oh—please do."

I was with her for more than an hour, and I laid the whole matter before her. Latimer hadn't given me leave to do so, but that didn't bother me. I was out to cure him, and knew the best way to do it. She was very indignant at one point of the story, and was evidently deeply hurt by her husband's injurious suspicions.

"How could he believe such a thing, and about a Hindu, a man whom I scarcely knew?" she said. "A man whom I only met two or three times, and always in public?"

She got up. She was naturally a highly strung woman, and she was quivering with nervous excitement.

"Let me tell you a little about the nervous system and about the power of suggestion," I said.

And I gave her a short lecture, which I needn't repeat to you, on the tricks nerves can play on a man, and on the cruel powers of neurasthenia. When I left her that night I think she had almost forgiven her husband. Certainly she loved him very much.

When the six weeks of Latimer's rest cure were just up—it was, in fact, his last night in the house at Hampstead—I sat down beside his bed, and I told him all that had happened while he had been secluded. I never saw a man by turns so indignant, so ashamed, and so relieved. He was furious at having been taken in, bitterly ashamed at having suspected his wife and at having been duped by a couple of rogues, and immensely relieved at realising that he had certainly never been in communication with the denizen of another world. As we talked I saw his fear of the Hindu die away. But presently anxiety again shone in his eyes, and he exclaimed:

"But, doctor, surely I must have been mad. I saw the Hindu again and again. How do you account for that?"

"I believe that in Grosvenor Square you really met an Indian who was out for a stroll like yourself. The encounter was entirely fortuitous. It only made such a deep impression upon you because of what had just happened at the medium's. At the Indian Restaurant I believe you saw the same man, and that he left the place at a moment when your attention was distracted, although you thought that your watchfulness never ceased. No doubt you saw a living Indian, though perhaps not the same one, at the St. James's Theatre."

"But my wife didn't see him!"

"Merely because she had not really turned her glasses upon him, though you fancied she had."

"But at Marseilles!"

"On that occasion I think you were the victim of your nervous system and of auto-suggestion. It is possible that a dark man passed you and went up in the lift."

"But the attendant denied it!"

"Probably he had made two journeys up and down while you were at the bureau, instead of one, as you believed, and on the second of these journeys he had really gone up alone."

"That's possible!" said Latimer.

"At Hammam Meskoutine you saw a native whom you mistook for the Hindu. At Tunis the same thing occurred. But—mind—I do not exclude the possibility of your having sometimes imagined that you saw a figure, an appearance, before you when in fact there was nothing. You have overworked for years. There are heavy penalties attached to such folly."

"But you really don't think I'm mad?"

I smiled.

"I may possibly come to think you are if, when you

go out again into the world, you continue to meet with the Hindu," I answered. "But I don't think you will."

As a matter of fact, from that night to this Latimer has never set eyes on the Hindu.

*   *   *   *   *   *

Sir William Turnbull paused.

"What about Isaacs?" I said.

"He cleared out without waiting for Latimer's appearance at the office."

"And—Mrs. Latimer?" I hazarded.

"She and her husband seem quite happy together again. She still reads Mrs. Sidon's pamphlets. Some people say that Latimer is completely dominated by her now, that she rules him in everything."

"And—you? What do you say?"

"Well," said the doctor, smiling. "It's generally very dangèrous for a man to be forgiven by a woman. Women forgive and—remember."

FOUR: THE LIGHTED CANDLES

I AM very fond of moving about and seeing fresh places, but I hate the tedium of railway travelling. On a misty night, therefore, when I stepped into the Paris express to go to Rome, I anticipated a long and weary journey, and was in no very cheerful mood. I had engaged a berth in the sleeping-car, and had stipulated that it must be in a compartment that held only two, and I had some hopes of having the compartment to myself. But when I came into it these hopes were at once dispelled. The beds had not yet been made, and on the long plush-covered seat a traveller was already established, calmly smoking a big cigar. As I came in he bowed slightly and cast an inquiring glance upon me. I returned his salutation and his glance, arranged my things as conveniently as possible in the small space allotted to us, replaced my hat by a cap, and sat down beside him.

In a few minutes the train glided out of the Gare de Lyon, and the attendant came to ask if he should make our beds. I glanced at my companion and he at me.

"You wish——" he began.

"No!" I said; "I'm in no hurry. I couldn't sleep so early."

"Nor I. Shall we say in another hour, then?"

"Certainly."

I told the attendant, and we were left alone.

Then I lit a cigar and looked for something to read. I had with me a book which I had bought at Victoria, called "Real Ghost Stories," and some papers. The book I lifted up, then laid down again between me and my companion. I thought I would glance through the French papers before I attacked anything else. The papers were full of news of an upheaval in Russia—sad, even horrible, reading. Presently I had had enough, and, turning to get my book, I met my companion's eyes.

"Terrible, this Russian business, isn't it?" I said.

"Frightful. I wonder how it will end."

We fell into a desultory conversation. My companion, a man of about forty, English, but an Englishman of the cosmopolitan species, was agreeable and interesting. Now and then he showed a gleam of imagination which attracted me. I began to be glad that I was not going to be alone on the journey. After some talk about Russia, he said:

"I see you've got a book about ghosts with you."

"Yes," I said. "I haven't read much of it yet. Stead brought it out. Perhaps such a book would bore you."

"Not necessarily."

"In it, I see, he says something to the effect that it is almost impossible to be in a company of people not one of whom has seen a ghost, or had some ghostly experience. I wonder if that is so."

"I don't know. It may be. It would be if I were one of the company—at least, I believe so."

"Then you have had such experience?"

"Well, I think so. And, oddly enough, it had—or so I must believe—some connection with Russia."

"I wish you would tell it to me."

"I will with pleasure. But, if it is to be interesting, my narrative must be rather detailed and long."

"Capital. I must tell you I'm a writer, so perhaps I shall be the better able to appreciate your story."

"Use it, if you think it's worth using. By the way, are you bound for Rome?"

"Yes."

"So am I. And it was in Rome that these circumstances took place."

"So much the better!"

He smiled. Then, as the train rushed on through the night towards the frontier, he told me very quietly this tale of the lighted candles.

"Although I do not claim to be unusually brave," he said, "I have a peculiar dislike, I may almost call it a peculiar dread, of a coward. If I may say so, it amounts to this—I fear fear. Nothing irritates and distresses my nerves so much as the sight of an exhibition of terror. Nothing makes me so uneasy as the proximity of a fearful being.

"Well, three years ago I went to Rome in the autumn with the intention of settling down there for the winter. I wished to be quiet and my own master, so I resolved to take an apartment instead of going to a hotel, and as soon as I arrived I intended to visit an agent and to make inquiries as to where I could find a suitable one.

"I arrived in Rome early in the morning, and scarcely had I got out of the train before a porter came up and asked me if I were going to a hotel or if I wanted an apartment.

"Perhaps you know that a good many of the porters in Rome act as touts for flat-owners, and get a commission upon any business done through their means.

"I told the man that I did want a furnished apartment, and he begged me to come at once with him and see the one he had mentioned. He described it as *bellissimo* and *stupendo,* and was so persuasive that I got into a cab with him and went to look at it.

"Before I arrived in Rome I had had some idea of settling in one of the old quarters, of trying to find something in the Via Giulia, perhaps, or the Via delle Botteghe Oscure, something with a touch of romance about it, or a hint of mystery. But when I saw the porter's flat it suited me in many respects so well that I decided to go into it at once.

"It was a modern apartment on the third floor of a good-sized house, looking out upon an open space which was rented by a man who gave lessons in bicycling. As it had no houses opposite to it, and faced south, it got plenty of sun, and was extremely cheerful. It was also well furnished, and contained as many rooms as I required. The rent was remarkably reasonable, and before the morning was over I had taken the flat for three months from its owner, an Italian woman, who kept a tobacconist's shop.

"That very night I was installed in it. Now I must just describe it to you.

"When you entered the flat you found yourself in a hall with chairs and an oaken settle. On the right of this hall were three rooms—my bedroom and dressing-room and the dining-room. These rooms looked out on to the open space I have already alluded to. Opposite to the dining-room, on the other side of the hall, was the drawing-room, which was rather dark, and had a window looking on to a small garden surrounded by the backs of houses. Parallel with this drawing-room was a narrow passage which led to a kitchen on the left, and which ended in a servant's bedroom. Both of these looked out on to the backs of the houses surrounding the little garden, and from their windows one could see the windows of the staircase of the house in which my flat was. This section of my flat, in fact, jutted out at right angles to that part of the house which contained the staircase, and was commanded by the staircase windows. I hope I make myself clear?"

"Quite," I answered.

"There was also a bathroom at the end of the hall between the drawing-room and the dining-room.

"I intended to engage a woman to act as my cook and housekeeper and a man to open the door and valet me. But on the first evening I was alone. The Padrona came in to make my bed and see that I had candles, matches, and the few things absolutely necessary. Then she withdrew with a *buona sera,* and a hope that I should be comfortable. She was a large and oily Neapolitan, and as she uttered her final remark I thought her bulging black eyes rested upon me with a rather peculiar expression, half-searching, half-defiant.

"When she was gone I went again over the flat. In the servant's room, upon a table under the window, stood a candle and a box of matches. The candle was new and had never been lighted. Why I did it I don't know, but I remember putting a match to it idly, holding it up, glancing round the room, then setting it down again upon the table, and—I believe—extinguishing it.

"Night had closed in, and I presently went out, dined at a restaurant, looked in at a theatre, and returned home. It was late when I reached the front door of the house and let myself in with one of my two latchkeys. I was at once confronted by the blackness of the stone staircase. All the lights were out, and I had not taken the precaution of providing myself with a candle end to illuminate my progress to the third storey.

"I struck a match and began to go up as quickly as I could. Before I got to the first floor the match had gone out, and I made some groping steps in the darkness. Then I struck a second match, which lighted me to the second floor. There it sputtered and died down, and I stood still for a moment fumbling for a third match. But there was not one. I had been smoking a good deal during the evening and had exhausted my supply.

"*Diavolo!*" I thought.

"Then I remembered that there was a box full on the little table in the hall, and I moved on cautiously, feeling my way, until I reached the staircase window, which looked out upon the windows of my kitchen and the unoccupied servant's bedroom. In the latter there shone a light.

"I stood still. I was greatly astonished.

"Over the window a thin white blind hung down, through which the light was visible. For some short time—two or three minutes I suppose—I stood on the staircase watching it. Who could be there, in my flat, at this time of the night? Had the Padrona returned to seek something? Or had some malefactor—I drew out my revolver, cocked it, crept up the stairs, and very quietly inserted my key in the door, after some groping, as I was without a light. The door opened, I stepped into the hall and felt for the matches, all the time straining my ears to catch the smallest sound. I found a match, struck it, and set it to the candle. Then, leaving the front door open, I went on tiptoe to the entrance of the passage, at the end of which was the door of the servant's bedroom. It stood open, and I saw the bed and the wall illuminated by the light within. I waited, listening intently. I heard nothing. Then I walked swiftly into the room. It was empty. On the table under the window stood a lighted candle burned down almost to the socket. I took it up and went from room to room. The flat was empty. Nothing had been disturbed.

"When I had finished searching I shut the front door, barred it for the night, and went to bed.

"The explanation of the candle being lighted must be a simple one. That was what I was telling myself. I must have forgotten to extinguish it. I remembered lighting the candle. I remembered extinguishing it. So my mind told me. But my mind must have been playing me false. I must have left the candle burning. And yet I could have sworn—but then we often could, couldn't we?"

I nodded.

"Telling myself this, giving my own memory the lie, as it were, I turned over and soon fell asleep.

"In the morning I went forth early to an agency and engaged a cook, a charming woman called Lucia, a native of Albano. She agreed to begin her duties with me that very day. This done, I paid a visit to my *Padrona di casa*. I had a question to ask her.

" 'I suppose there is no other latchkey to my flat besides mine?' I said to her. 'You haven't one you could lend me for my servant?'

" 'No, signore, I have only the one.'

" 'I'll have another made,' I said carelessly.

"I had been thinking of the lighted candle of the preceding night, and had wished to find out whether the Padrona had means of access to my flat. It seemed not. Evidently, therefore, my memory had been at fault.

"I went to get another latchkey made for my cook, and dismissed the matter of the lighted candle from my mind—for the time.

"Lucia was married, and lived with her husband not far from me, so till I engaged a man-servant I was alone in my flat at night.

"I dined at home that evening, and stayed in till Lucia had gone away for the night. When the front door had closed upon her, I went down the passage to the servant's room. The candlestick had been moved, no doubt by Lucia, and placed on a little stand beside the bed, with a fresh candle in it and the box of matches laid near by. Wooden shutters had been fastened over the windows. I had not noticed them before. I glanced round the room. Then I went out.

"I spent the evening at the Salone Margherita, reading the *Tribuna,* and listening to a variety entertainment. When I got home it was about ten minutes to twelve. This time I had provided myself with a candle-end to light me up the staircase, and I reached my door without difficulty, let myself in, lit my candle, barred the door and went at once into my bedroom. There I began to undress.

"Now, I must tell you that I am not at all a nervous or suspicious man. I have been about the world and slept soundly in many strange places. Yet that night, when I was about to get into bed, I felt an odd uneasiness come over me, as if I had left something undone, something that imperatively ought to be done. I stood for a moment in my pyjamas by the dressing-table. What was it that I had forgotten to do?

"After a moment's hesitation I opened my bedroom

door and looked out into the hall towards the place where the passage began. A faint light issued from it. Leaving my candle in the bedroom, I went on my stockinged feet to the passage and stared down it. Beside the empty bed the candle was burning, the candle which, to-night, I had left unlighted.

"Again I went into the room and found no one. Again I went over the flat and found everything in its place, no sign of any intruder.

"This time I felt really uncomfortable. It was now obvious to me that someone, some stranger hidden I knew not where in Rome, possessed a key of my door, and, for some reason which I could not divine, visited my flat at night when I was out of the way. What could be this person's purpose? And why should so furtive a creature be so careless as to leave a lighted candle to tell me of his, or her, nocturnal entry? I now felt quite certain that it was not I who had left the candle lit on the previous night. My memory had not betrayed me. For a long time I stood wondering uneasily, and when I at length got into bed I could not sleep.

"I thought again of the Padrona, that Neapolitan woman with the searching eyes. But she denied having a key of my door. And if she had one, why should she come at night? I wondered who had been my predecessor in the flat. Whoever it was might have carried away a latchkey on leaving, might have it still, or might have lost it. It might have passed into other hands. All my sense of comfort, of being at home in the flat, was rapidly departing.

"Only towards morning did I fall asleep.

"The next day I again called on the Padrona on some pretext, and in the course of my conversation carelessly asked to whom the flat had been let before I took it. The woman suddenly looked glum.

" 'To a Russian,' she answered, after a pause.

" 'A man?'

" 'No, signore. The Princess Andrakov.'

" 'And she has left Rome?'

" 'The Princess is dead, signore.'

"She shut her loose-lipped mouth with a snap. Somebody came into the shop, and I went away.

" 'The Princess Andrakov.' As I went out into the sunshine I was mentally repeating that name and wondering—idly, I thought—what the princess had been like.

"It was a glorious day, and I strolled on till I reached the church of the Sacred Heart, at the top of the steps that lead from the Piazza di Spagna to the Trinita de' Monte. There I paused for a moment and glanced down.

"A peculiar-looking man, young, perhaps twenty-five years old, was coming up from the Piazza. He was tall, fair, with a broad face, a flat nose, very prominent cheekbones, and long frizzly light hair. He was dressed in frayed trousers, an old green overcoat, and a soft and dusty black hat. I thought he looked like a Russian student. When he reached the top of the steps he stopped for an instant beside me, then walked on towards the Pincio. I followed—I don't know why. Simply, I had to go somewhere, and on a fine morning what can one do better than walk towards the Pincio? Just in front of the Villa Medici the young man stopped to look at the view over Rome. I stopped, too, drawn to stillness by the splendour of the city lying beneath the splendour of the clear sky.

"And then—I don't know how—we were talking. I and this young man, talking in French, and soon with a freedom that was almost like intimacy.

"He was, I found, a Russian, and an art student. We spoke of art, of Rome and its wonders, of—I have really forgotten what else. But I know that presently, when we were going to part, the young man handed me his card, in foreign fashion, and I gave him mine, with my Roman address written on it. He glanced at it, then started, and stared at me rather oddly.

" 'Have I given you—what is it?' I asked.

" 'Nothing, only—you are living in a house in which I had once an—an acquaintance.'

" 'The Princess Andrakov?' I asked.

" 'Yes. Did you know her, monsieur?'

" 'No; but I have the flat she formerly occupied.'

"The young man looked at me, I thought, with great attention.

" 'She is dead, I understand,' I continued.

" 'Oh, yes, she is dead.'

" 'Did she die in Rome?'

" 'Yes, monsieur.'

" 'Did she die in the flat?'

" 'Yes, monsieur.'

" 'I wonder'—I was thinking now of the lighted candles—'I wonder whether she was a careless person,' I said, trying to speak carelessly.

" 'Careless, monsieur?'

" 'Yes.'

" 'Have you any particular reason for asking me that question, monsieur?'

"I hesitated. This young man was an absolute stranger to me, and I am not, as a rule, accustomed to take strangers into my confidence. But there was something in the look of his large, light eyes which told me I might go on. And I did. I related to him what I have related to you—the episode of the lighted candles.

"When I had finished, I said:

" 'What I am wondering is this: whether my predecessor in the flat lost her latchkey, or gave it to one of the servants.'

" 'The Princess had no servants,' he said.

" 'No servants?'

" 'No, she was a very peculiar person.'

" 'Indeed?'

" 'Yes, a very suspicious nature. She was afraid to have servants in Rome.'

" 'Why?'

" 'She was afraid they might be got at.'

"He used a French expression equivalent to that phrase of ours.

" 'By thieves?' I asked.

" 'Well—no. It is a disagreeable story, but the princess is dead, and——'

"He hesitated.

" 'I knew her in Russia,' he said at last. 'Her husband was an important man, a general, at one time a Governor of a province in Southern Russia. There had been some trouble there, and he was sent to stamp it out. His methods of stamping out trouble were not appreciated either by the peasants or by the revolutionaries. He was hated, but the princess was more than hated; she was execrated.'

" 'Why?'

" 'She was an aristocrat of the hardest, most reactionary type. She egged her husband on to excesses. There is no doubt of that. She openly boasted of it. He would not have done half of what he did if it had not been for her. He was the Governor of a province, but she was his governor. Everybody knew it. The end of it was that one day at a railway station he was assassinated by a young girl.'

" 'Horrible.'

" 'The girl disappeared, perhaps to Siberia. The princess disappeared—to Rome.'

" 'Was she afraid?'

" 'Terrified. I must tell you that she was an old woman, a skinny, coquettish old woman, years older than her husband. And, as I believe sometimes happens with people of advanced age, her nerves, which had seemed to be of iron, suddenly snapped. In one day she was changed from a cruel tyrant into a cringing, terror-stricken coward. That day was the day of her husband's murder. For she, too, had been condemned, and she knew it.'

" 'That was why she left Russia?'

" 'Yes, she fled. She came to Rome and took your

flat under an assumed name. For though she was a princess, her real name was not Andrakov. In Rome her fear grew upon her. She believed she had been dogged. She ceased to go out. She kept no servants for fear they might be bribed by those who had vowed to destroy her. The porter's wife brought up her food, and she received it at the front door. She lived in a room at the back of the house, for fear she might be seen and recognised from the street if she went near to the front windows. And finally she died of sheer terror in that back room. A warning had been thrust into her letter-box telling her that her place of retreat was known.'

" 'Then she died in the room where the candles are lighted?' I asked.

" 'A back bedroom, the only one.'

" 'Yes; but, excuse me, monsieur, how do you know all this?'

" 'Oddly enough, the Princess had shown me and my family kindness, monsieur. She was fond of my mother, who had been a reader to her. (She was a very intellectual woman.) And she partly paid for my studies in Rome. I ought to be grateful to her, and so I am. But even my gratitude could never make me feel any affection for her. Three or four times I was admitted to see her in the flat. But towards the end she became afraid even of me. She was found dead in that back bedroom, with an expression of abject terror on her face and a guttering candle beside her. They broke into the flat as she did not answer the door when the porter's wife brought her food. It seems she had only just died. But for more than twenty-four hours she had not answered the door.'

"Such was the young Russian's story of my predecessor in the flat.

"I must confess that it scarcely made my new home seem more home-like to me. When I was back again in it my imagination set to work. I called up mentally the 'skinny, coquettish old woman,' barred in alone there, a prey to perpetual terror, living in solitude in the little room that looked out upon the garden, finally finding her sentence of death in the letter-box and succumbing to an access of senile fear, with a guttering candle to light her into eternity.

"A guttering candle beside her. The young Russian was not without an appreciation of detail. Why had he happened to mention that one? Probably because I had told him of the lighted candles. The mind goes back sometimes without being aware of it. Do we not know this from our dreams?

"My friend of the morning had not offered any suggestion for the elucidation of my mystery. I remembered that only after I had left him. His narrative of the princess had drawn him away, and me with him, into another channel of thought. But, if it had not been so, what explanation could he have suggested? Somebody had means of access to my flat, and had used these means two nights running. That was all I knew. What more could this young man know? My having thus entered into conversation with the only person admitted to the flat while the princess occupied it was one of those strange coincidences which occur continually in life.

"All that day my mind dwelt upon the Russian's narrative and the lighted candles, trying, I think now, to find a link between this dead old woman of an evil nature and the person who came to the flat from which her corpse had been carried out. Those Russians who had plotted her death, could they——? But at this point I had the sense to realise that I was allowing myself to be carried away into absurdity. The person, whoever it was, who visited my rooms, must, of course, know that they were no longer occupied by the princess.

"That night I dined at home, and when Lucia left me and I had been over the flat I settled down in the drawing-room with a cigar and a book. I had extinguished the gas in the hall and left the door of the drawing-room open, for, to tell the truth, I had little inclination for reading. I knew that I was going to listen for the sound of a key inserted in my front door, for a step in the hall. If the visitor of the two previous nights came a third time—well, he or she would find the host who had been lacking before. I said to myself that, of course, no one would come since I was at home. My going out must have been seen. To-night the fact that I did not go out would doubtless be known. No one would come.

"Nevertheless, I waited and listened with the door open into the dark hall.

"In the distance I heard the muffled roar of Rome. Somewhere out there was the person who came to my flat by night, unless, indeed, the intruder dwelt within this building full of apartments. The time wore on. I read some pages of my book, but scarcely knew what I read, so attentive was my ear to catch the smallest near sound.

"If anyone came he should not enter without my knowledge.

"But at last the distant sounds began to die down. It was deep in the night and weariness overtook me. I resolved to go to bed, and got up to do so, at the same time looking at my watch. A quarter to one. I had had no idea that the hour was so late, and realised for the first time how intently I had been listening, with what anxiety I had been waiting.

"Having lit my bedroom candle, which was on the writing table, I turned out the gas and stepped into the hall. Owing to the situation of the drawing-room I was at once opposite to the passage. It was dark, and the door of the servant's bedroom was shut. Had I shut it? I could not remember. I waited a moment, looking at the door. Instantly I was aware of a pale, small ray of light issuing from the darkness directly before me. It came through the key-hole of the door. Within the room the candle was lighted.

"By whom?

"This time I held my breath. I was conscious of a feeling of extraordinary disquietude, almost of fear, of

a strong repugnance against going into the chamber of
the lighted candle.

"It seemed to me that, if I did so, I should find within
a skinny, coquettish old woman; that as I opened the
door all the coquetry would die out of her; that my entrance would be greeted with a harsh, strangled cry of
fear.

"At that moment, for the first time, I seemed to be
conscious of the nearness to me of terror. And the
thought of this terror near me made my hair bristle up
on my head.

"What I really wanted to do just then was to go
straight out of the flat, down the stairs, and into the open
street, to find myself under the stars, to see the lights in
the cafés, to hear the hum of happy people. What I did,
after a pause, was to relight my candle, walk quickly,
with a firm step, down the passage, and brusquely fling
open the door of the bedroom.

"Silence, emptiness, and beside the bed, burning
steadily, the lighted candle.

"I stood looking round.

"It was a small, uninteresting room, containing a bed,
a chair, a table, a washhand-stand, a stand for a candle
by the bed. The wooden shutters were closed. From
the wall an oleograph of the Madonna and Child regarded me with lack-lustre eyes. In that bed the old
princess had died of terror. Upon that stand had been
the guttering candle, lighted as a protection against the
trooping terrors of the night.

"And now—who lighted the candles in this room?

"I sat down on the only chair the room contained, sat
down resolutely—for I did it against my will—and tried
to reason the matter out. On the previous two nights I
had supposed, I had felt quite sure, that someone who
possessed a key of the door had come in for some purpose I could not divine, had lighted the candle in order
to see to accomplish that purpose, and had gone away,
carelessly forgetting to extinguish the candle. But to-

night no one had entered the flat. I had been alone in
it. And yet the candle had been lighted. By what?
And why?

"By what? I had got to this point in my thinking.
Was it extraordinary? There are certain things one
can say one knows. That night I knew that no one could
have come into the flat without my knowledge. It was
impossible to open the front door without noise with a
key. Without a key the front door could not be opened
at all. I knew that the door had not been opened. The
windows of the kitchen and the back bedroom were
securely closed and were shuttered. No one could have
got in by them. Nevertheless the candle had been
lighted.

"Therefore, I asked myself the question: by what had
it been lighted?

"In the passage, when I first saw the ray of light, I
had felt as if the old Princess were secluded within the
room; as if I caught the infection of her fear. But now
my terror—for I suppose it must have been the touch
of terror that made my hair rise—was abated. I felt
calmer, and I tried deliberately to be receptive; to make
myself, as it were, an empty vessel into which might be
poured the truth of that room.

"I should tell you that, at the time of which I speak,
I was neither a believer nor an unbeliever in another
world, in spirit agencies. I kept an open mind, capable,
I trust, of conviction. Nevertheless, I was not prepared,
at a moment's notice, to swallow marvels without investigation. I cannot, however, deny that since my meeting
with the Russian student I looked upon this dull little
room with altered eyes. And now as I sat in it, I felt
about it strangely.

"As I told you, I was now calm; at least, I believe so.
I let my mind alone. I sat, if I may use the expression,
with all my mental muscles relaxed. The vessel was
empty. It seemed to me that something flowed into it
and filled it like a fluid; some influence, some personality

that was inhabiting the room. It seemed to me that I was conscious of the shivering touch of fear; that I heard far, far off, faint and yet horrible, the shuddering cry of fear; that I knew—because somehow I was told —why that candle had been lighted; and that it had been lighted by something that dwelt in that room and was abjectly afraid of being killed in the dark.

"Ridiculous, you will say. The story of the Russian student peopling an excited mind with imaginations. I tried to say the same thing to myself. I left the room presently (carrying the candle that had been so mysteriously lighted with me, and shutting and locking the door behind me), saying the same thing to myself. I lay awake saying it.

"You must not think I yielded feebly to crazy ideas unworthy of a full-grown man. I did not. I combated them as you would. And when the morning came I resolved that if I had peopled the back bedroom with figments of the imagination, I would people it now with something very different.

"By lunch-time I had engaged a man-servant. He was not a Roman, but a Sicilian, who had only just come to Rome in the hope of earning some money. He was about twenty-four, pleasant, and active-looking, and had excellent references from a well-known Sicilian family in Palermo. Like the cook, he was ready to come to me at once, and as I was in a hurry to have him, the bargain was promptly made.

"That afternoon he entered my service.

"Now, at about four the same day I was again at the Pincio, strolling near the parapet of the terrace, and listening to the music, when I encountered the Russian student. He took off his hat and looked inclined to join me. And I was nothing loth. We presently sat down together on two chairs in the sunshine, and I told him of the episode of the previous night. When I had finished I added that I had now engaged a Sicilian man-servant, who would sleep in the back bedroom, and that he entered my service that day.

"The young Russian, who had listened to me with deep attention, shook his shoulders with a movement that looked like a shiver.

" 'I would not be your servant, monsieur,' he said. 'I would not sleep in the bed where the old Princess—ooh.'

" 'But this man knows nothing and will feel nothing.'

" 'What if the candle is lighted?'

" 'Then you——?'

"I paused.

" 'Monsieur,' he said, 'in Russia we are superstitious. I am glad you have engaged this young man. You say he is of the people of Sicily. The Sicilians are bold, but they are sensitive. This man knows nothing about your flat, about the little room, about the lighted candles. Let him be a touchstone. Can I say that? If he feels nothing, if he sees nothing—very well, there is nothing, and there is some simple explanation of the lighted candles. If not—if he is affected, if he fears, then there is something.'

"He added, after a moment of thought:

" 'They say, those who are superstitious, that three lighted candles are a sign of death.'

" 'Many English people think that too.'

" 'Do you, monsieur?'

" 'I have never bothered about such things. The strange—by that I mean the abnormal, using the word in the sense in which it is generally used—has been a stranger to me until now.'

"Giovanni, the Sicilian servant, settled in very comfortably, and seemed pleased with his room. He was a gay-looking youth, and that evening, when I heard him laughing and talking with Lucia in the kitchen, I felt as if a cloud which had been lowering over me were lifting.

"I did not go out that night, and went to bed early, and slept well."

My travelling companion stopped speaking at this point.

"What is it?" I asked. "Is anything the matter?"

"Well," he answered, "I never can recall the next day without a feeling of horror."

"Why? What happened?"

"Simply this. In the morning when Lucia arrived, Giovanni did not come out of his room. When I got up and asked for him, she said that he had not opened his door. I thought he had overslept himself, went to his room, and found the poor fellow dead."

"Good heaven! Why? What had he died of?"

"There was an expression of terror on his face. I went at once for a doctor, who examined him, and said that his death was caused by heart failure. Although he had looked strong, he had had a very weak heart. The same day Lucia gave me warning. She said that the Evil Eye had looked upon my flat."

"And you?"

"I removed to a hotel. Do you wonder?"

"Not at all."

"Unfortunately I had taken the flat for three months, and was obliged to pay the rent. I did so, and, of course, it continued to be my flat, although I did not live in it. Giovanni was buried and the flat remained empty, I keeping the keys and able to go in and out whenever I liked."

"And did you ever go there?"

"I did with the Russian student. I must tell you that my acquaintance with him developed into a sort of intimacy. His knowledge of the old Princess, I think, attracted me to him. For I must confess that I could never think of the lighted candles and of Giovanni's death without thinking of her. But I soon grew to like him for his own sake. There was something unconventional, enthusiastic about him that pleased me. But I also had other reasons for seeking him. He puzzled me. Despite his enthusiasm, his frankness, even his apparent

carelessness, he was reserved. I was always conscious
that there were depths in this young man which I had not
sounded, that there were mysteries in his character which
I had not explored.

"It was as if one always saw a door wide open, yet
could never go into the room beyond, a room that was
dimly lit.

"I had told him about the fate of my servant and my
departure from the flat. He said, 'You did wisely.
Death is there.'

"One day, perhaps three weeks after Giovanni's death,
we were dining together at the Café Berardi, near the
Piazza di Spagna, when—I scarcely know why—I was
moved to tell the Russian that, though I had left the
flat, I was often tormented by an itching desire to go
back to it, if only for an hour now and then; that something seemed to draw me to the door, yet that, when I
was there, I felt a reluctance to enter.

" 'Have you ever gone in again?' he inquired.

" 'Not since the day I left. Can you understand my
sensation?'

" 'Yes. Where mystery or fear abide there is always
fascination. Why, they say that even murderers find it
difficult to keep away from the places where their crimes
have been committed.'

" 'I suppose——' I hesitated.

" 'Yes, monsieur?'

" 'I suppose you wouldn't come into the flat with me
one night—say to-night—and spend an hour and smoke
a cigar?'

"He darted at me a swift look that, I fancied, was
suspicious.

" 'I?' he said. 'Why should I go there?'

"I was surprised by his emphasis.

" 'Merely to keep me company.'

" 'Oh, I see.' His voice was changed. 'Well, why
not?'

" 'Perhaps you dislike the idea?'

"With a sort of sudden gush of frankness, eminently characteristic of him, he said:

" 'I both dislike and am attracted by it. Why shouldn't I speak the truth, monsieur? I connect your apartment with horror—the death from fear of the Princess, my patroness—therefore I am drawn to it. I have long wanted to go there. Yet in all Rome there is no place I dread so much. That is the truth. Make of it what you can.'

" 'Let us go,' I said with sudden decision, getting up from my chair.

"He seemed startled by my abruptness, but after an instant's hesitation he got up too.

" 'Very well,' he said.

"And again he cast at me a glance that seemed a glance of suspicion. I wondered what it meant. We went out, got into an open cab, and drove to the house in which my deserted apartment was.

" 'You've got the key, then, monsieur?' said the Russian, when I gave the cabman the address.

" 'Yes.'

"He said nothing more during the drive. When we reached the house it was not yet ten; the porter was still up and the lamps were still burning on the staircase. The porter looked much surprised to see me.

" 'You have come back, signore!' he exclaimed.

" 'Only for a little while. I'm not going to stay.'

" 'Better not,' the old man muttered. 'Better not.'

"He glanced at my companion.

" 'But perhaps the signore is thinking of taking the apartment. I have seen him here before, when the——'

" 'Basta,' said the Russian rather roughly.

"And he began to mount the stairs.

" 'This signore is a friend of mine,' I said to the porter. 'He has not come after the apartment.'

"And I followed the Russian to the third floor, leaving the old man mumbling to himself.

"I found my friend—I will call him Drovinsky—

standing on the third landing, with his hand on the balustrade of the staircase. As I came up he said in a low voice:

" 'Now, what are we here for?'

" 'Why, to——'

" 'No, but what are we going to do? Doesn't it seem rather absurd for two grown men——?'

" 'You want to cry off,' I said, rather bluntly, I fear.

"Again that glance of suspicion.

" 'No, monsieur. Only let us know why we are doing this.'

" 'Inside I'll tell you.'

"I inserted the key in the door and we stepped into the hall. In a moment I had lit the gas.

" 'There is gas in the drawing-room, too,' I said. 'Let us sit there.'

"Drovinsky was standing by the hall door, which he had shut.

" 'Very well,' he said.

"He followed me closely as I went to the drawing-room.

" 'How deserted it looks already,' I said, lighting the gas.

" 'Yes. Now, are we to sit down and smoke?'

" 'I wonder if I can find a candle. I left some candles.'

" 'Why do you want a candle?'

" 'Merely to look into the rooms. Wait a moment.'

"I found a candle in the kitchen, lit it and went over the flat. Meanwhile Drovinsky remained in the drawing-room. When I came back I said:

" 'It is just as I left it.'

" 'Naturally.'

" 'Yes. Well, shall we light our cigars?'

" 'And you will tell me why we are doing this?'

" 'But you know already,' I said, taking out my cigar case. 'You yourself have told me. Where mystery and fear abide——'

"And I lit my cigar and sat down. He laughed and followed my example.

" 'But, after all, do they, can they, abide here?'

"He glanced round at the very small modern furniture of the small modern room, and laughed again. And his own laugh seemed to answer 'Yes' to his question.

" 'I think they can abide wherever tragedy has been. And tragedy has been here.'

" 'You mean that poor fellow?'

" 'And the Princess Andrakov.'

" 'Oh, the Princess——'

" 'Could anything be more tragic than to die in terror alone, at night?'

" 'She had brought terror to others.'

"His voice was suddenly hard. He had sat down near me and had begun to smoke. I confess that, knowing the Princess had been kind to him, I was sometimes rather surprised by the way in which Drovinsky spoke of her. I was surprised now.

" 'But you were a friend of hers,' I said.

" 'Scarcely that. Because she had liked my mother the Princess certainly did something for me. Still, I cannot be blind to her character.'

"He looked at me searchingly.

" 'What is it?' I said.

" 'I wonder—I wonder what your view of me would be if I were to tell you something. It is very strange that here, in this place where she died, I feel a strong, an almost overpowering inclination to speak.'

"He stopped, still looking at me with deeply inquiring eyes.

" 'Speak then,' I said.

" 'Do you remember my saying at Berardi's that I believed murderers often were compelled to come back to the places of their crimes?'

" 'Yes.'

" 'Well—I have done that.'

" 'You!' I cried, startled.

" 'I killed the Princess Andrakov.'

"I sprang from my seat in horror.

" 'Wait, monsieur,' said the Russian. 'My weapon was a letter.' "

" 'What do you mean?'

" 'It was I who put into her letter-box the paper which told the Princess that her place of concealment was known, and it was the terror caused by that communication that killed her.'

"I sat down again.

" 'You meant to warn the Princess so that she might escape?'

" 'Monsieur, I wished her to die.'

" 'Why?'

" 'If she had not died, I should have killed her.'

" 'Your patroness? The woman who had been kind to you?'

"I was not a free agent. I belonged to a secret society whose orders I had to obey. The assassination of the Princess fell to my lot.'

" 'And you would have——?'

" 'If she had not died—yes.'

"He spoke calmly, fatalistically, but, as he finished, he glanced towards the door almost as if he expected someone to come in.

" 'You were in Rome for that?' I asked.

" 'No, monsieur. It was advisable for me to get out of Russia, so I came here. Because I was here I was chosen to kill the Princess when it was known that she was in Rome.'

" 'And you——?'

" 'No,' he interrupted. 'I did not tell them. What do you think of me?'

" 'I think you have a great deal of nerve.'

" 'Why?'

" 'To come into this apartment after what I have told you.'

" 'But I am not alone.'

"The devil prompted me to say:

" 'Would you pass a night here alone?'

" 'Why should I?'

" 'Would you for a bet?'

"I knew the man was very poor. The devil certainly was at my elbow.

" 'I will bet you a thousand lire to one,' I said, 'that you won't do it.'

" 'You are joking?'

" 'No, a thousand lire to one. *Parola d'onore.*'

"I saw that he was tempted.

" 'To-morrow morning I will come here. We will breakfast together, and you shall have a thousand lire.'

" 'If I do it,' he said, with obvious hesitation, 'I make one proviso.'

" 'What is it?'

" 'I will not go into the back bedroom.'

" 'You need not.'

" 'Very well, then, monsieur, I accept your wager.'

"Oddly enough, directly my proposition was accepted I began to regret having made it.

" 'But if you feel——' I began.

" 'Monsieur, I accept your wager. *Parola d'onore!*'

" 'Certainly,' I replied hastily, seeing that he thought I was jibbing at the idea of losing my money. *'Parola d'onore.'*

"There was a short uneasy silence between us, during which neither looked at the other. Then I said:

" 'Well, I think I'll be off now. What time shall I come to-morrow morning?'

" 'When you please, monsieur.'

" 'Shall we say eight o'clock?'

" 'Certainly—eight o'clock.'

" 'All right. There's the candle if you want to use the front bedroom. There isn't any gas there.'

" 'Thank you, monsieur.'

"A constraint had certainly come between us since the Russian's confession and my suggestion of the wager.

"I went out into the hall. He followed me.

" 'You know the front rooms?' I asked.

" 'No, monsieur.'

" 'This is the dining-room.'

"We went into it. The shutters were not closed, and I went to the window to close them. Before doing so I felt the window to see if it was fastened. It flew open, and, by a faint moonlight, I saw the open space opposite, used by bicyclists for their lessons. A dark figure was standing there motionless as if looking up at the house. I stared at it for a minute. Then I shut the window and closed the shutters. We went together through the two remaining rooms and came to the hall door.

" 'Good-night,' I said.

" 'Good-night, monsieur.'

"Again reluctance overtook me—reluctance to leave him there alone.

" 'You are really going to stay?'

" 'Really.'

" 'You don't think——'

" 'I am going to stay.'

" 'His voice was strange as he said those last words. I began to believe that, apart from the money, he now wished to remain, that he had a more personal reason for his desire. And I thought of his words about the fascination of fear.

" 'Good-night, then,' I said.

"I held out my hand. He took it for a moment. His hand was very cold.

" 'Good-night, monsieur.'

"His high cheek-bones, light eyes, frizzly hair, disappeared as he softly closed the door.

"I walked home to my hotel which was at some short distance off, asking myself almost angrily what had prompted me to make the suggestion of the bet. Why should I wish the Russian to spend the night alone in the flat? There could only be one reason and that condemned me. I thought there was some danger there.

This bet had forced me to fa   fact. I knew now that
I believed the flat to be still occupied by all that was
left of the old Princess—all that was left above ground.
The body was hidden in the grave, but the essence of
that formerly terrible and latterly terrified human being
had been released from the body and remained where
the body had died."

At this moment the attendant put in his head.

"It is twelve o'clock, messieurs. Shall I make the
beds?"

"I've just finished," said my companion.

"Another five minutes," I said, putting five francs into
his hand.

He disappeared yawning into the rocking corridor.

"There really is little more to tell," said my companion. "In the morning, at eight o'clock, I was at the
flat door. I let myself in with my key and before I
had shut the door, called out in a voice which was
deliberately cheery and commonplace:

" 'Monsieur Drovinsky!'

"There was no reply. I opened the bedroom door on
the right. It was unoccupied.

" 'Monsieur Drovinsky! Drovinsky!' I called again.

"Silence.

"With an effort I shut the front door, and, walking
softly, went to the dressing-room, then to the dining-
room. Both were empty. So was the drawing-room, into
which I next looked. I began to think that I had won
my bet, that Drovinsky had not remained in the flat for
the night. But there were still three rooms to be examined, the bathroom, the kitchen, and—but I knew
Drovinsky would not have entered the back bedroom.
When taking my bet he had made it a proviso that he
need not go into it.

"No one in the bathroom. No one in the kitchen.

"The door of the back bedroom was shut. I confess
I hesitated to open it. Of course, Drovinsky had gone
away. It was useless to look into this room. He had

told me that he would not enter it. My task was over.
I turned away from the door. I even walked a few
steps down the passage. Then I stopped. I knew I was
playing the coward. I was afraid to go into that room.
I remembered Giovanni's death, and—I threw open the
door.

"Drovinsky lay on the bed, his face turned towards the
door, the light, frizzly hair falling across his cheeks.
His eyes were open. The flickering flame of a candle,
burned down to the socket, wavered across them, the
semblance of the inner flame of life.

"But they were dead eyes in a dead man's face."

My companion stopped.

"But," I said, "that's not all?"

"Remember," he answered, "this is a true story. Life
is not an adroit novelist who gathers up all the threads."

"Why should the Russian have gone into that room?"

"I imagine—I feel sure—that the fascination of fear
led him there."

"And you think he—he was visited?"

"As Giovanni was? What else can I think?"

"To me," I said, "the strangest part of the whole
story is the lighted candles."

"The corpse candles. And to me. The first, it is true,
I may possibly have lighted myself. My memory may
have betrayed me. It is just conceivable. The second
may have been lighted by someone who gained access
to the flat while I was out."

"But the third?"

"To me the third is entirely inexplicable. I once told
this story to a man, however, who explained it in this
way. He said that Lucia, my cook, must have lighted it
and left it lighted by accident when she went home. I
told him that after her departure I had looked into the
room and found it in darkness. He asked me if I had
looked in with a lighted candle in my hand. I acknowledged that I had. Then, he said he was not convinced.
I myself had carried light into the room and might not

have observed a light already burning in it. This irritated me, and I said, 'Then my eyes can absolutely deceive me?' 'All eyes deceive at times,' he replied. And then he told me of an odd fact bearing upon his statement. It was this:

"He was in perfect health, and was staying in a country house. He went in the middle of the day into a small room to write a letter. This room had only one door, from which you saw at once the whole of the room. There was no dazzling sunshine, just ordinary diffused daylight. He opened the door and saw that the room was empty. This pleased him, as he did not wish to be disturbed while writing. He shut the door, and, walking quickly forward to the writing-table, encountered a solid body. There was a man in the room, a fellow-guest standing directly before him. For some reason, quite inexplicable, he had looked hard at this person and had not seen him—had not seen that anyone was there. He told me that when he came up against this invisible man his blood ran cold with surprise, and his bones seemed to turn to wax.

"So the eyes can trick. Well, it may be so with me. How can I, how dare I, swear it was not so?"

"And the Russian's death?"

"Heart failure, like Giovanni's. Since then I have not entered that flat, and I believe it has not been let. Before I took it, it had got a bad name. That must have been why the Padrona looked at me so strangely. She was wondering if I had heard anything, wondering whether I was brave or merely ignorant."

"No doubt. And one thing more. That dark figure you saw apparently watching the house from the bicycling ground?"

"Ah! I have sometimes wondered whether that dark figure held any key to the mystery. Could Drovinsky have earned the wrath of any of his brothers in crime? Could any enemy have known he was in the flat that night—have gained entrance? Could there have been a

scene and could Drovinsky have died in a fit of passion?
Non lo so, as the Italians say. Perhaps the whole thing
has a natural explanation."

"But you believe the contrary?"

"And possibly I am a fool."

He threw his cigar end out of the window into the
darkness. As he did so the attendant came in once
more to make the beds.

And this time we let him make them.

FIVE: THE NOMAD

I

THE fate of Madame Lemaire had certainly not been an ordinary one. She was French, of Marseilles, as you could tell by her accent, especially when she said *"C'est bien!"* and had been an extremely coquettish and lively girl, with a strong will of her own and a passionate love of pleasure and of town life. From her talk when she was seventeen, you would have gathered that if she ever moved from Marseilles it would be to go to Paris. Nothing else would be good enough for her. She felt herself born to play a part in some great city.

And yet, at the age of forty, here she was in the desert of Sahara, keeping an *auberge* at El-Kelf under the salt mountain! She sometimes wondered how it had ever come about, when she crossed the court of the inn, round which the mules of customers were tethered in open sheds, or when she served the rough Algerian wine to farmers from the Tell, or to some dusty commercial traveller from Batna, in the arbour trellised with vines that fronted the desert.

Marie Lemaire, who had been Marie Bretelle, at El-Kelf! Marie Lemaire in the desert of Sahara attending upon God knows whom: Algerians, Spahis, camel-drivers, gazelle-hunters! No; it was too much!

But if you have a "kink" in you, to what may you not come? Marie Bretelle's "kink" had been an idiotic softness for handsome faces.

She wanted to shine in the world, to cut a dash, to go to Paris; or, if that were impossible, to stay in Marseilles married to some rich city man, and to give parties, and to get gowns from Madame Vannier, of the Rue de Cliche, and hats from Trebichot, of the Rue des Colonies, and to attend the theatres, and to be stared at and pointed out on the race-course, and—and, in fact, to be the belle of Marseilles. And here she was at El-Kelf, and all because of that "kink" in her nature!

Lemaire had had a handsome face and been a fine man, stalwart, bold, muscular, determined. He did not belong to Marseilles, but had come there to give an acrobatic show in a music-hall; and there Marie Bretelle had seen him, dressed in silver-spangled tights, and doing marvellous feats on three parallel-bars. His bare arms had lumps on them like balls of iron, his fair moustaches were trained into points, his bold eyes were lit with a fire to fascinate women; and—well, Marie Bretelle ran away with him and became Madame Lemaire. And so she came to Algiers, where Lemaire had an accident while giving his performance. And that was the beginning of the Odyssey which had ended at El-Kelf.

"Fool—fool—fool!"

Often she said that to herself, as she went about the inn doing her duties with grains of sand in her hair.

"Fool—fool—fool!"

The word was taken by the wind of the waste and carried away into the desert.

After his accident Lemaire lost his engagements. Then he lost his looks. He put on flesh. He ceased to train his moustaches into points. The great muscles got soft, were covered with flabby fat. Finally he took to drink. And so they drifted.

To earn some money he became many things—guide, *concierge,* tout for "La belle Fatima." He had impossible professions in Algiers. And Marie? Well, it were best not to scrutinise her life too closely under the burning sun of Africa. Whatever it was, it was not very successful; and they drifted from Algiers. Where did they go? Where had they not been in this fiery land? Oran on the Moroccan border had seen them, and the mosques of Kairouan, windy Tunis, and rockbound Constantine, laughing Bougie in its wall by the water, Fort National in the Grande Kabylie. They had been everywhere. And at last some wind of the desert had blown them, like poor grains of desert sand, from the bending palms of Biskra to the mud walls of El-Kelf.

And here—God help them!—for ten years they had been keeping the inn, "Au Retour du Désert."

For ten long, hot, dry years, and such an inn! Why, at Marseilles they would have called it—well, one cannot tell what they would have called it on the Cannebière! But they would have found a name for it, that is certain.

It stood alone, this inn, quite alone in the desert, which at El-Kelf circles a small oasis in which there is hidden among fair-sized palms a meagre Arab village. Why the inn should have been built outside of the oasis away from the village I cannot tell you. But so it is. It seems to be disdainful of the earth houses of the Arabs, to be determined to have nothing to do with them. And yet there is little reason in its disdain.

For it, too, is built of sun-dried earth for the most part, and has only the ground floor possessed by most of them. It stands facing flat but not illimitable desert. The road that passes before it winds away to land where there is water; and from the trellised arbour, but far off, one can see in the sunshine the sharp, shrill green of crops, grown by the Spahis whose tented camp lies to the right of the caravan track that leads over the Col de Sfa to Biskra.

Far, far along that road one can see from the inn, till its whiteness is as the whiteness of a thread, and any figures travelling upon it are less than little dolls, and even a caravan is but a moving dimness shrouded in a dimness of dust. But towards evening, when the strange clearness of Africa becomes almost terribly acute, every speck upon the thread has a meaning to attract the eye, and set the mind at work asking:

"What is this that is coming upon the road? Who is this that travels? Is it a mounted man on his thin horse, with his matchlock pointing to the sky? Or is it a woman hunched upon a trotting donkey? Or a Nomad on his camel? Or is it only some poor desert man, half naked in his rags, who tramps on his bare brown feet along the sun-baked track, his hood drawn above his eyes, his knotted club in his hand?"

After ten years Marie Lemaire still asked herself such questions in the arbour of the inn, when business was slack, when her husband was away, or was lying half drunk upon the bed after an extra dose of absinthe, and the one-eyed Arab servant, Hadj, was squatting on his haunches in a corner smoking keef.

Not that the answer mattered. She expected nothing of the road that led from the desert to her. But simply her mind, stagnant though it had become in the solitude of Africa, had to do something to occupy itself somehow. And so she often stared across the plain, with an aimless *"Je me demande"* trembling upon her lips, and a hard expression of inquiry in her dark brown eyes, whose lids were seamed with tiny wrinkles. Perhaps you will wonder why Madame Lemaire, having once had a passionate love for pleasure and a strong will of her own, had consented to remain for ten years in the solitude of El-Kelf, drudging in a miserable *auberge,* to which few people, and those but poor ones, ever came.

Circumstances and Robert Lemaire had been too much for her. Both had been cruel. She was something of a slave to both. Lemaire was an utter failure, but there lurked within him still, under the waves of absinthe, traces of the dominating power which had long ago made him a success.

Madame Lemaire had worshipped him once, and adored his strength and beauty. They were gone now. He was a wreck. But he was a wreck with fierceness in

it. And command with him had become a habit. And
Africa bids one accept. And so Madame Lemaire had
stayed for ten long years drudging at the inn beside the
salt mountain, and staring down the long white road for
the something strange and interesting from the desert
that never, never came.

And still Lemaire drank absinthe, and cursed, and
drowsed. For ten long years! And still Hadj squatted
upon his haunches and drugged himself with keef. And
still Madame Lemaire stood under the trellised vine,
with the sand-grains in her hair, and gazed and gazed
over the plain.

And when a black speck appeared far off upon the
whiteness of the track, she watched it till her hard eyes
ached, demanding who, or what, it was—whether a
Spahi on horseback, a woman on her donkey, a Nomad
on his camel, or some dark and half-naked pedestrian
of the sands, that travelled through the sunset glory towards the lonely inn.

II

Although Robert Lemaire was a wreck he was not
an old man in years, only forty-five, and the fine and
tonic air of the Sahara preserved him from complete
destruction. Shaggy and unkempt he was, with a heavy
bulk of chest and shoulders, a large, pale face, and the
angry and distressed eyes of the absinthe slave. His
hands trembled habitually, and on his bad days fluttered
like leaves. But there was still some force in his prematurely aged body, still some will in his mind. He
was a wreck, but he was the wreck of one who had been
really a man and accustomed to dominate women. And
this he did not forget.

One evening—it was in May, and the long heats of
the desert had already set in—Lemaire was away from
the *auberge,* shooting near the salt mountain with an
acquaintance, a colonist who had a small farm not far
from Biskra, and who had come to spend the night at El-

Kelf. This man had a history. He had once been a
hotel-keeper, and had reason to suspect a guest in his
hotel of having guilty intercourse with his wife.

One night, having discovered beyond possibility of
doubt that his suspicions were well founded, he waited
till the hotel was closed, then made his way to his
guest's room, and put three bullets into him as he lay
asleep in his bed. For this murder, or act of justice,
he got only ten months' imprisonment. But his business
as a hotel-keeper was ruined. So now he was a small
farmer. He was also, perhaps, the only real friend Lemaire had in Africa, and he came occasionally to spend
a night at the Retour du Désert.

Upon this evening of May, Madame Lemaire was
alone in the inn with the one-eyed servant Hadj, preparing supper for the two sportsmen. The flies buzzed
about under the dusty leaves of the vine, which were
unstirred by any breeze. The crystals upon the flanks
of the salt mountain glittered in the sun that was still
fiery, though not far from its declining.

Upon the dry, earthern walls of the inn and over the
stones of the court round which it was built, the lizards
crept, or rested with eager, glancing patience, as if alert
for further movement, but waiting for a signal. A mule
or two stamped in the long stable that was open to the
court, and a skeleton of a white Kabyle dog slunk to and
fro searching for scraps with his lips curled back from
his pointed teeth.

And Madame Lemaire went slowly about her work
with the sand-grains in her hair, and the flies buzzing
around her.

Nothing had happened. Nothing ever did happen at
El-Kelf. But for some mysterious reason Madame Lemaire suddenly felt to-day that her existence in the desert
had become really insupportable. It may have been that
Africa, gradually draining away the Frenchwoman's
vitality, had on this day removed the last little drop of

the force that had, till now, enabled her to face her life, however dully, however wearily.

It may have been that there was some peculiar and unusual heaviness in the air that was generally of a feathery lightness. Or the reason may have been mental, and Africa may have drawn from this victim's nature, on this particular day, a grain, small as a grain of the sand, of will-power that was absolutely necessary for the keeping of the woman's stamina upon its feet.

However it was, she felt that she collapsed. She did not cry. She did not curse. She did not faint, or lie down and stare with desperate eyes at the vacant dying day. She did not neglect her domestic duties, and was even now tearing, with a flat key, the cover from some tinned veal and ham for the evening's supper. But something within her had abruptly raised its voice. She seemed to hear it saying: "I can't bear any more!" and to know that it spoke the truth. No longer could she bear it: the African sun on the brown-earth walls, the settling of the sand-grains in her hair, the movement of the flies about her face, wrinkled prematurely by the perpetual dry heat and by the desert winds; the brazen sky above her, the iron land beneath, the silence—like the silence that was before creation, or the monotonous sounds that broke it; the mule's stamp on the stones, the barking of the guard-dogs upon the palm roofs of the distant houses in the village, the sneering laugh of the jackals by night, that whining song of Hadj, as he wagged his shaven head over the pipe-bowl into which he pressed the keef that was bringing him to madness.

She could not bear it any more.

The look in her face scarcely altered. The corners of her mouth, long since grown grim, did not droop any more than was usual. Her thin, hard hands were steady as they did their dreary work. But the woman who had resisted somehow during ten terrible years of incompatable monotony suddenly died within Marie Lemaire, and the girl of Marseilles, Marie Bretelle, shrieked out in the middle-aged, haggard body. "This fate was not meant for me. I cannot bear it any more."

Presently the tin which had held the veal and ham was empty, save for some bits of opaque jelly that still clung round its edges; and Madame Lemaire went over to the dimly burning charcoal with a dirty old fan in her hand.

Marie Bretelle was still shrieking out, but Madame Lemaire must get ready the supper for her absinthe-soaked husband and his friend the murderer from Alfa.

The sportsmen were late in returning, and Madame Lemaire's task was finished before they came. She had nothing more to do, and she came out to the arbour that looked upon the road. Here there was an old table stained with the lees of wine. About it stood three or four rickety chairs. Madame Lemaire sat down—dropped down, rather—on one of these, laid her arms upon the table, and gazed down the empty road.

"*Mon Dieu!*" she said to herself. "*Mon Dieu!*"

She beat one hand on the table and said it aloud.

"*Mon Dieu! Mon Dieu!*"

She stared up at the vine. The leaves were sandy, and she saw insects running over them. She watched them. What were they doing? What purpose could they have? What purpose could anything have?

Always the hand tapped, tapped upon the table.

And Marseilles! It was still there by the sea, crowded, gay with life. This was the time when the life began to grow turbulent. The cascades were roaring under the lifted gardens where the beasts roamed in their cages. The awnings were out over the cafés in that city of cafés. She could almost see the coloured edges of stuff fluttering in the wind that came up from the harbour and from the Château d'If. There was a sound of hammering along the sea. They were putting up the bathing sheds for the season. It would be good to go into the sea. It would cool one.

A beetle dropped from the vine on to the table close

to the beating hand. Madame Lemaire started violently. She got up, and went to stand in the entrance of the arbour. Marseilles was gone now. Africa was there.

For ten years she had been looking down the road. She looked down it once more.

It was the wonderful evening hour when Africa seems to lift itself toward the light, reluctant to be given to the darkness. Very far one could see, and with an almost supernatural distinctness. Yet Madame Lemaire strained her eyes, as people do at dusk when they strive to pierce a veil of gathering darkness.

What was coming along the road?

Her gaze travelled onwards over the hard and barren plain till it reached the green crops, on and on past the tents of the Spahis' encampment, near which rose a trail of smoke into the lucent air; farther still, farther and farther, until the whiteness narrowed towards the mountains, and at last was lost to sight.

And this evening, perhaps because she longed so much for something, for anything, there was nothing on the road. It was a white emptiness under the setting sun.

Then the woman felt frantic, and she beat her hands together, and she cried aloud:

"If the Devil himself would only come along the road and ask me to go from this cursed hole of a place, I'd go with him! I'd go! I'd go!"

She repeated it shrilly, making wild gestures with her hands towards the desert. Her face was twisted awry. She looked just then like a desperate hag of a woman.

But it was the girl of Marseilles who was crying out in her. It was Marie Bretelle who was demanding the joys she had flung away in her youth for the sake of a handsome face.

"I'd go! I'd go!"

The shrill cry went up to the setting sun. But no one answered, and nothing darkened the arid whiteness of the road that wound across the plain and passed before the inn-door.

Night had fallen when the two sportsmen rode in on
mules, tired and hungry. Hadj came from his keef to
take the beasts, Madame Lemaire from her kitchen to ask
if there were any birds for her to cook. Her husband
gave her a string of them, and she turned away from
him without a word, and went back into the house.

There was nothing odd in this, but something in his
wife's face, seen only for a moment in the darkness of
the court, had startled Lemaire, and he looked after her
as if he were inclined to call her back; then said to his
companion, Jacques Bouvier:

"Did you see Marie?"

"Yes. She looks as if she had just stumbled over a
jackal," and he laughed.

Lemaire stood for a minute where he was. Then he
shouted to Hadj:

"Hadj! A—Hadj!"

The one-eyed keef-smoker came.

"Who has been here to-day?"

"No one. A few have passed the door, but no one
has entered."

"Good business!" said Bouvier, shrugging his shoulders.

"Business!" exclaimed Lemaire, with an oath. "It's
a fine business we do here. Another ten years, and we
shan't have put by ten sous."

"Perhaps that is why madame has such a face to-
night!"

"We'll see at supper. Now for an absinthe!"

The two men walked stiffly into the inn, put their guns
in a corner, went into the arbour that fronted the desert,
and sat down by the table.

"Marie!" bawled Lemaire.

He struck his flabby fist down upon the wood.

"Marie, the absinthe!"

Madame Lemaire heard the hoarse shout in the kitchen, and her face went awry again.

"I'd go! I'd go!"

She hissed it under her breath.

"Sacré nom de Dieu! Marie!"

"V'là!"

"The devil! What a voice!" said Bouvier in the arbour.

Lemaire was half turned in his chair. His hands were slightly shaking, and his large white face, with its angry and distressed eyes, looked startled.

"Who was that?" he said, moving in his chair as if he were going to get up.

"Who? Your wife!"

"No, it wasn't!"

"Well, then——"

At this moment there was a clink and a rattle, and Madame Lemaire came slowly out from the inn, carrying a tray with an absinthe bottle, a bottle of water, and two thick glasses on china saucers upon it. She set it down between the two men. Her husband stared at her like one who stares suspiciously at a stranger.

"Was that you who called out?" he asked.

"Of course! Who else should it be? Who ever comes here?"

"Madame is a bit sick of El-Kelf," said Bouvier. "That's what is the matter."

Madame Lemaire compressed her lips tightly and said nothing.

Her husband looked more suspicious.

"Why should she be sick of it? She's done very well with it for ten years," he said roughly.

Madame Lemaire turned away and left the arbour. She was wearing slippers without heels, and went softly.

The two men sat in silence, looking at each other. A breath of wind, the first that had come that day, stole from the desert and rustled the leaves of the vine above

their heads. Lemaire stretched out his trembling hand
to the absinthe bottle.

"For God's sake let's have a drink!" he said. "There's
something about my wife that's given my blood a turn."

"Beat her!" said Bouvier, pushing forward his glass.
"If you don't beat them be sure they'll betray you."

His wife's treachery had set him against all women.
Lemaire growled something inarticulate. He was thinking of the days in Algiers, of their strange and often
disgraceful existence there. Bouvier knew nothing of
that.

"Come on!" he said.

And he lifted his glass of absinthe to his lips.

At supper that night Lemaire perpetually watched his
wife. She seemed to be just as usual. For years there
had been a sort of sickly weariness upon her face. It
was there now. For years there had been a dull sound
in her voice. He heard it to-night. For years she had
had a poor appetite. She ate little at supper, had her
habitual manner of swallowing almost with difficulty.
Surely she was just as usual.

And yet she was not—she was not!

After supper the two men returned to the arbour to
smoke and drink, and Madame Lemaire remained in the
kitchen to clear away and wash-up.

"Isn't there something the matter with my wife?"
asked Lemaire, lighting a thin, black cigar, and settling
his loose, bulky body in the small chair, with his fat
legs stretched out, and one foot crossed over the other.
"Or is it that I'm out of sorts to-night? It seems to me
as if she were strange."

Bouvier was a small, pinched man, with a narrow face,
evenly red in colour, large ears that stood out from his
closely shaven head, and hot-looking, prominent brown
eyes.

"Perhaps she's taken with some Arab," he said.

"P'f! She's dropped all that nonsense. The devil!
A woman of forty's an old woman in Africa."

Bouvier spat.

"Isn't she?"

"Oh, don't ask me about women! Young or old, they're always calling the Devil to their elbow."

"What for?"

"To put them up to wickedness. Perhaps your wife's been calling him to-night. You look behind her presently, and you may catch a sight of him. He's always about where women are."

"Ha, ha, ha!"

Lemaire laughed mirthlessly.

"D'you think he'd show himself to me?"

He emptied his glass. Bouvier suddenly looked terrible—looked like the man who had put three bullets into his sleeping guest.

"How did I know?" he said.

He leaned across the table towards Lemaire.

"How did I know?" he repeated in a low voice.

"What—when your wife——"

"Yes. They didn't let me see anything. They were too sharp. No; it was one night I saw *him* with his mouth at her ear, coming in behind her through the door like a shadow. There!"

He sat back with his hands on his knees. Lemaire stared at him again.

Again the wind rustled furtively through the diseased vine-leaves of the arbour.

"It was then that I got out my revolver and charged it," continued Bouvier, in a less mysterious voice, as of one returned to practical life. "For I knew she'd been up to some villainy. Pass the bottle!" . . .

"Pass the bottle! . . . Why don't you pass the bottle?"

"Pardon!"

Lemaire pushed the bottle over to his friend.

"What's the matter with you to-night?"

"Nothing. You mean to say . . . why d'you talk

such nonsense? D'you think I'm a fool to be taken in by rubbish like that?"

"Well, then, why did you sit just as if you'd seen him?"

"I'm a bit tired to-night; that's what it is. We went a long way. The wine'll pull me together."

He poured out another glass.

"You don't mean to say," he continued, "you believe in the Devil?"

"Don't you?"

"No."

"Why not?"

"Why not! Why should I? Nobody does—men, I mean. That sort of thing is all very well for women."

Bouvier said nothing, but sat with his arms on the table, staring out towards the desert. He looked at the empty road just in front of them, let his eyes travel along until it disappeared into the night.

"I say, that sort of thing is all very well for women," repeated Lemaire.

"I hear you."

"But I want to know whether you don't think the same."

"As you?"

"Yes; to be sure."

"I might have done once."

"But you don't now?"

"There's a devil in the desert; that's certain."

"Why?"

"Because I tell you he came out of the desert to turn my wife wrong."

"Then you weren't joking?"

"Not I. It's as true as that I went and charged my revolver, because I saw what I told you. Here's madame coming out to join us."

Lemaire shifted heavily and abruptly in his chair.

"Hallo!" he said, in a brutal tone of voice. "What's up with you to-night?"

As he spoke he stared hard at his wife's shoulder, just by her ear.

"Nothing.   What   are   you   looking   at?   There isn't——"

She put up her hand quickly to her shoulder and felt over her dress.

"Ugh!" She shook herself. "I thought you'd seen a scorpion on me."

Bouvier, whose red face seemed to be deepening in colour under the influence of the red Algerian wine, burst out laughing.

"It wasn't a scorpion he was looking for," he exclaimed. His thin body shook with mirth till his chair creaked under him.

"It wasn't a scorpion," he repeated.

"What was it, then?" said Madame Lemaire.

She looked from one man to the other—from the one who was strange in his laughter, to the other who was even stranger in his gravity.

"What have you been saying about me?" she said, with a flare-up of suspicion.

"Well," said Bouvier, recovering himself a little, "if you must know, we were talking about the Devil."

The woman started and gave the table a shake. Some of her husband's wine was spilled over it.

"The Devil take you!" he bawled, with sudden fury.

"I only wish he would!"

The two men jumped back as if a viper of the sands had suddenly reared up its thin head between them.

"I only wish he would!"

It was Marie Bretelle who had spoken, the girl of Marseilles, who still lived in the body of Marie Lemaire. But it was Marie Lemaire from whom the two men shrank away—Marie Lemaire changed, startling, terrible, her haggard face furious with expression, her thin hands clutching at the edge of the table, from which the wine-bottle had fallen, to be smashed at their feet.

For a moment there was a dead silence succeeding

that second shrill cry. Then Lemaire scrambled up heavily from his chair.

"What do you mean?" he stammered. "What do you mean?"

And then she told him, like a fury, and with the words which had surely been accumulating in her mind, like water behind a dam, for ten years. She told him what she had wanted, and what she had had. And when at last she had finished telling him, she stood for a minute, making mouths at him in silence, as if she still had something to say, some final word of summing up.

"Stop that!"

It was Lemaire who spoke; and as he spoke he thrust out one of his white, shaking hands to cover that nightmare mouth. But she beat his hand down, and screamed, with the gesture.

"And if the Devil himself would come along the road to fetch me from this cursed place, I'd go with him! D'you hear? I'd go with him! I'd go with him!"

IV

When the scream died away, one-eyed Hadj was standing at the entrance to the arbour. Madame Lemaire felt that he was there, turned round, and saw him.

"I'd go with him if he was an Arab," she said, but almost muttering now, for her voice had suddenly failed her, though her passion was still red-hot. "Even the Arabs—they're better than you, than absinthe-soaked, do-nothing Roumis, who sit and drink, drink——"

Her voice cracked, went into a whisper, disappeared. She thrust out her hand, swept the glasses off the table to follow the bottle, turned, and went out of the arbour softly on her slippered feet.

And one-eyed Hadj stood there laughing, for he understood French very well, although he was half-mad with keef.

"She'd go with an Arab!" he repeated. "She'd go

with an Arab!" And then he saw his master's face, and
slipped back to his keef-pipe.

The two Frenchmen sat staring at one another across
the empty table under the shivering vine-leaves, which,
were now stirred continually by the wind of night. Lemaire's large face had gone a dusky grey. About his
eyes there was a tinge of something that was almost lead
colour. His loose mouth had dropped, and the lower lip
disclosed his decayed teeth. His hands, laid upon the
table as if for support, shook and jumped, were never
still even for a second.

Bouvier was almost purple. Veins stood out about
his forehead. The blood had gone to his ears and to his
eyes. Now he leaned across to Lemaire.

"Beat her!" he said. "Beat her for that! Hadj heard
her. If you don't beat her, the Arabs——"

But before he had finished the sentence Lemaire had
got up, with a wild gesture of his shaking hand, and
gone unsteadily into the house.

That night Madame Lemaire suffered at the hands of
her husband, while Bouvier and Hadj listened in the
darkness of the court.

V

It was drawing towards evening on the following day,
and Madame Lemaire was quite alone in the inn. Hadj
had gone to the village for some more keef, and Lemaire and Bouvier had set out together in the morning
for Batna.

So she was quite alone. Her face was bruised and discoloured near the right eye. Her head ached. She felt
immensely listless. To-day there was no activity in her
misery. It seemed a slow-witted, lethargic thing, un-
deserving even of respect.

There were no customers. There was nothing to do,
absolutely nothing. She went heavily into the arbour,
and sank down upon a chair. At first she sat upright.
But presently she spread her arms out upon the table,

and laid her discoloured face on them, and remained so for a long time.

Any traveller, passing by on the road from the desert, would have thought that she was asleep. But she was not asleep. Nor had she slept all night. It is not easy to sleep after such punishment as she had received.

And no traveller passed by.

The flies, finding that the woman kept quite still, settled upon her face, her hair, her hands, cleaned themselves, stretched their legs and wings, went to and fro busily upon her. She never moved to drive them away.

She was not thinking just then. She was only feeling —feeling how she was alone, feeling that this enormous sun-dried land was about her, stretching away to right and to left of her, behind her and before, feeling that in all this enormous, sun-dried land there was nobody who wanted her, nobody thinking of her, nobody coming towards her to take her away into a different life, into a life that she could bear.

All this she was dully feeling.

Perfectly still were the diseased vine-leaves above her head, motionless as she was. On them the insects went to and fro, actively leading their mysterious lives, as the flies went to and fro on her.

For a long time she remained thus. All the white road was empty before her as far as eye could see. No trail of smoke went up by the growing crops beside the distant tents of the Spahis. It seemed as if man had abandoned Africa, leaving only one of God's creatures there, this woman who leaned across the discoloured table with her bruised face hidden on her arms.

The hour before sunset approached, the miraculous hour of the day, when Africa seems to lift itself towards the light that will soon desert it, as if it could not bear to let the glory go, as if it would not consent to be hidden in the night. Upon the salt mountain the crystals glittered.

The details of the land began to live as they had not

lived all day. The wonderful clearness came, in which all things seem filled with a supernatural meaning. And, even in the dulness of her misery, habit took hold of Madame Lemaire.

She lifted her head from her arms, and she stared down the long white road. Her gaze travelled. It started from the patch of glaring white before the arbour, and it went away like one who goes to a tryst. It went down the road, and on, and on. It reached the green of the crops. It passed the Spahis' tents. It moved towards the distant mountains that hid the plains and the palms of Biskra.

The flies buzzed into the air.

Madame Lemaire had got up from her seat. With her hands laid flat upon the table she stared at the thread of white that was the limit of her vision. Then she lifted her hands and curved them, and put them above her eyes to form a shade. And then she moved and came out to the entrance of the arbour.

She had seen a black speck upon the road.

There was dust around it. As so often before she asked herself the question: "Who is it coming towards the inn from the desert?" But to-day she asked herself the question as she had never asked it before, with a sort of violence, with a passionate eagerness, with a leaping expectation. And she stepped right out into the road, as if she would go and meet the traveller, would hasten with stretched-out hands as to some welcome friend.

The sun dropped its burning rays upon her hair, and she realised her folly, and took her hands from her eyes and laughed to herself. Then she went back to the arbour and stood by the table waiting. Slowly—very slowly it seemed to Madame Lemaire—the black speck grew larger on the white. But there was very much dust to-day, and always the misty cloud was round it, stirred up by—was it a camel's padding feet, or the hoofs of a horse, or——? She could not tell yet, but soon she would be able to tell.

Now it was approaching the watered land, was not far from the Spahis' tents. And a great fear came upon her that it might turn aside to them, that it might be perhaps a Spahi riding home from his patrol of the desert. She felt that she could not bear to be alone any longer; that if she could not see and speak to someone before sunset she must go mad.

The traveller passed before the Spahis' camp without turning aside; and now the dust was less, and Madame Lemaire could see that it was a Nomad mounted on a camel.

With a smothered exclamation she hurried into the inn. A sudden resolve possessed her. She would prepare a couscous. And then, if the Nomad desired to pass on without entering the inn, she would detain him.

She would offer him a couscous for nothing, only she must have company. Whoever the stranger was, however poor, however filthy, ragged, hideous, or even terrible, he must stay a while at the inn, distract her thoughts for an instant.

Without that she would go mad.

Quickly she began her preparations. There was time. He could not be here for twenty minutes yet, and the meal for a couscous was all ready. She had only to——

She moved frantically about the kitchen.

Twenty minutes later she heard the peevish roar of a camel from the road, and ran out to meet the Nomad, carrying the couscous. As she came into the arbour she noticed that it was already dark outside.

The night had fallen suddenly.

VI

That night, as Lemaire and Bouvier were nearing the inn, riding slowly upon their mules, they heard before them in the darkness the angry snarling of a camel.

Almost immediately it died away.

"Madame has company," said Bouvier. "There's a customer at the Retour du Désert."

"Some damned Arab!" said Lemaire. "Come for a coffee or a couscous. Much good that'll do us!"

They rode on in silence. When they reached the inn, the road before it was empty.

"*Ma foi,*" said Bouvier. "Nobody here! The camel was getting up, then, and Madame is alone again."

"Marie!" called Lemaire. "Marie! The absinthe!"

There was no reply.

"Marie! *Nom d'un chien!* Marie! The absinthe! Marie!"

He let his heavy body down from the mule.

"Where the devil is she? Marie! Marie!"

He went into the arbour, stumbled over something, and uttered a curse.

In reply to it there was a shrill and prolonged howl from the court.

"What is it? What's the dog up to?" said Bouvier, whipping out his revolver and following Lemaire. "The table knocked over! What's up? D'you think there's anything wrong?"

The Kabyle dog howled again, slunk into the arbour from the court, and pressed itself against Lemaire's legs. He gave it a kick in the ribs that sent it yelping into the night.

"Marie! Marie!"

There was the anger of alarm in his voice now; but no one answered his call.

Walking furtively, the two men passed through the doorway into the kitchen. Lemaire struck a match, lit a candle, took it in his hand, and they searched the inn, and the court, then returned to the arbour. In the arbour, close to the overturned table, they found a broken bowl, with a couscous scattered over the earth beside it. Several vine-leaves were trodden into the ground near by.

"Someone's been here," said Lemaire, staring at Bouvier in the candlelight, which flickered in his angry and distressed eyes. "Someone's been. She was bringing him a couscous. See here!"

He pointed with his foot.

Bouvier laughed uneasily.

"Perhaps," he said—"perhaps it was the Devil come for her. You remember! She said last night, if he came, she'd go with him."

The candle dropped from Lemaire's shaking hand.

"Damn you! Why d'you talk like that?" he exclaimed furiously. "She must be somewhere about. Let's have an absinthe. Perhaps she's gone to the village."

They had an absinthe, and searched once more.

Presently Hadj, who was half mad with keef, joined them. The rumour of what was going forward got about in the village; and other Arabs glided noiselessly through the night to share in the absinthe and the quest, for that night Lemaire forgot to lock up the bottle.

*   *   *   *   *   *

Bu the hostess of the inn at El-Kelf has not been seen again.

SIX: THE TWO FEARS

I

MRS. ALLINGTON was afraid. She had always been what is called a nervous sort of woman. Constitutionally delicate, thin, small and pale, with large, anxious, brown eyes, her whole appearance suggested sensitiveness and an almost shrinking timidity. A widow now, she had been married young to a man who did everything "in his own way."

He had loved her, but in his own way. He had been kind to her, but in his own way. He had eaten and drunk, taken his pleasures and undergone his misfortunes, worshipped himself and paid homage to his Creator in his own way. And some had thought that his way was a trying one. Most of his friends and acquaintances had called him at one time or another a trying man. Several had gone so far as to say of him that he had a way with him that would have tried a saint.

Mrs. Allington may, or may not, have been a saint; anyhow, she never said, and never showed, that her husband tried her. She fell in with all his wishes while he was alive, and appeared to mourn him with deep sincerity when he was dead. She had looked very anxious while he was with her, largely presiding over her life; she continued to look very anxious after he was—as Miss Allington, her knitting, charitable sister-in-law, put it—"gathered in."

It seemed as if she couldn't look anything else.

A fixed expression may with time become almost as

deceptive as a mask. If a woman always looks anxious, nobody bothers about her anxieties; perhaps, indeed, nobody believes in them. By displaying she may actually conceal.

So it was with Mrs. Allington.

When the European war broke out she was living in a small house in Kensington with her only child, Ivo, who was just twenty-five, and who was doing well as a journalist.

Mrs. Allington had just enough for her necessities; but for her comforts, for those innumerable small things which draw some of the austere harshness out of life, which paint in a little warm colour on the grey, she was dependent upon Ivo.

But for Ivo she must have lived in a cheap boarding-house instead of in that cherished possession—247, Lenorva Road, West Kensington. But for Ivo really nice dresses—not many, and never expensive, but in a modest way satisfactory—would have been "beyond her." But for Ivo she could not have indulged in occasional visits to the theatre and occasional pleasant afternoons at the Ballad Concerts, followed by tea in Bond Street. Ivo was clever and had the artistic temperament—which implies startling irritabilities and occasional exhibitions of nerves upon the tight-rope—but he was very good to his mother in his own way, which was not inherited from his father.

And now Mrs. Allington was full of fear connected with Ivo. Two fears, in fact, possessed her soul. She was afraid that Ivo would enlist in the army Kitchener had begun to form for active service against the Huns. That was fear number one. And she was afraid that he would not enlist. And that was fear number two.

She felt that she simply couldn't bear it if Ivo enlisted, and she knew that she couldn't endure it if he didn't. As she said absolutely nothing about either of her two fears, and merely went on looking extremely anxious, nobody had the least suspicion that she was not "just as usual."

Even Ivo, who was supposed to be so intuitive, and to whom human nature was said to be an open book, even Ivo had no notion that his mother was in any way worried. To tell the truth, he thought he was doing all the worrying that was being done at 247, Lenorva Road.

When the war broke out he had had tremendous visions of "finding himself" as the ideal war correspondent. But Kitchener—everything was put upon Kitchener by everybody—had other views. Or so it was rumoured. There were not to be any war correspondents. And so for a time Ivo went on in the old way of a successful young free-lance. He wrote about war in West Kensington, and khaki began to appear in the streets. It became more and more mysteriously prevalent. One saw it in the Tube; one jostled against it in the Underground; one sat beside it upon the tops of 'buses; one met it unexpectedly in great abundance on coming round corners; it tramped about the parks, and did remarkable manœuvres in sunlit public gardens, and sang along the Mall, and whistled its way along the Embankment beside the old brown river.

And Ivo began to worry.

He was a clever boy and a good sort of boy, but he was of the intellectual rather than of the muscular type. He was decidedly an individualist, and, though he was a journalist, he was much concerned about art. He knew all the ways of the Cubists, the Futurists, the Vorticists; he was very keen on the Russian ballet; he was deeply interested in what Mr. George Moore was going to do next, and swore almost passionately by Granville Barker.

In music his taste ran rather to Scriabine than to the composer of "Tipperary."

And so he worried quite a good deal.

And in Mrs. Allington fear number two began to grow and to attain conspicuous proportions.

How perfectly terrible it would be if Ivo didn't enlist!

The sons of neighbours and even of friends began to

change colour; from the blue serge, or the dull green of Harris tweed, or the black of that cloth which is made up into "morning coats," they faded—or was it bloomed? —into khaki.

And the young men who hadn't changed colour became louder in their assertion that it would be a short war, "all over long before these fellows in a hurry get their rifles."

Mrs. Allington lay awake night after night, and fear number two crouched beside her pillow.

What would she do if Ivo didn't enlist?

II

She and her son did not talk very much about the war. Ivo honestly thought that she "didn't take much stock of it," and she thought—well, who knows what little women think about the great things, and the men who are in them? But she noticed the khaki. She noticed it so much that she saw the world clad in it. For her there were no more trousers, there were only puttees.

One day, when fear number two impended over her like a Colossus, Ivo said to her in a very casual way:

"I suppose you could get along on a good deal less than you do, mother—at a pinch, eh?"

Fear number two shrivelled and was gone, and fear number one lifted itself suddenly to the height of Mrs. Allington's heart; but she went on looking anxious, and said in her usual voice—a very light and rather faded soprano:

"Yes, dear, I suppose I could, at a pinch."

"That's what I thought. It's generally possible to knock off a few things. Most of us wade through super-fluities."

"Dear?"

"My way of saying we complicate our needs."

"Oh, I see."

But he felt perfectly certain she didn't. Ivo was apt

to think that his mother didn't see things.   He loved her more than he knew and more than she knew, but he didn't consider her at all clever.   You see, he was clever himself, and that fact shut certain doors against him.

During the next few days Mrs. Allington was never alone.   Always day and night fear number one was with her.

How terrible, how almost unbearable it would be if Ivo were to enlist!   She looked very anxious and exactly as usual.

Ivo, meanwhile, was going through a mental struggle which actually made him lose weight.   He wanted to enlist and he hated the idea of enlisting; he longed to be a patriot and to prove his patriotism, and he loathed the thought of giving up his career, and still more the thought of being a private in the midst of a crowd of privates, of having to live always, day and night, in public, hopelessly and everlastingly mixed up with all sorts and conditions of men with whom probably he would not have an "idea in common."

At moments he longed to be sixteen, at other moments he pined to be forty-one, and look it.   He thought of Mr. Roger Fry and the Post-Impressionists, of Mr. George Moore and "The Apostle," of the Russian ballet and "Thamar," of the strange and realistic novel he meant to write, the novel which would take him out of journalism.

He also thought of his mother.

Had he the "right" to sacrifice his mother on the altar of his patriotism?   He was a free lance in journalism. No one would continue a salary to him if he joined the colours.   It would mean pinching by his mother; it might even mean the giving up of 247, Lenorva Road.   Could he, ought he to require this of his mother?   It would be beastly sleeping in a tent in the damp—perhaps on Salisbury Plain—with a hugger-mugger of fellows who had never even heard of half the things which meant so much to him. Surely an only son oughtn't to do that when swarms of brothers were showing their sleek heads and fancy socks all over the country without a thought of joining the Army.

But the khaki—the khaki! Everywhere it met him like a summons; and at last he said to his mother abruptly:

"They seem to want a lot of men for this war, mother—eh?"

"Yes, dear," said Mrs. Allington, in the faded soprano.

"Kitchener seems very keen on increasing the numbers."

"Does he?"

"Well, you see the appeals on all the walls. That can only mean one thing."

He spoke rather irritably.

"I don't look at the walls very much, dear," said Mrs. Allington vaguely.

Ivo was silent for a moment. He got up, went to the window of the little sitting-room, and looked out upon Lenorva Road, that stretching paradise of stucco. His lips were pursed and his brown eyes stared. They saw a black cat, which moved between the expressionless houses like a creature whose nature belonged to the jungle.

"And my nature?" he thought. "Does it belong to Lenorva Road or to England?"

He turned round.

"Would you advise me to join, mother?" he asked.

Then, on either side of her stood the two fears, tall, stiff, forbidding, like sentinels with fixed bayonets. She waited a moment, not looking at them; then she said:

"Well, dear, as you say, they seem to want a lot of men for this war. And if Lord Kitchener is really very keen on increasing the numbers, perhaps——"

But at this point the faded soprano faded quite away.

"I'll join, mother. It may mean leaving Lenorva Road."

"Whatever it means——" said Mrs. Allington.

And there she stopped, perhaps because of surprise. For a strange thing had happened—the two sentinels with the fixed bayonets had vanished.

She never saw them again.

    *   *   *   *   *   *

Ivo joined—never mind what regiment. Presently he fell at the Dardanelles.

His mother received the telegram announcing his death in a cheap boarding-house where she is living now in Rova Crescent, Shepherd's Bush.

I saw her walking alone down the road not very long ago. She was dressed in a very ordinary black gown, not such a good gown as she used to wear in the days when she lived at No. 247. But what struck me was her expression.

She no longer looked anxious. If it hadn't been Mrs. Allington I should have thought she looked proud, proud in a beautiful way.

As I took off my hat to her I thought:

"So the widow still gives her mite."